"Douglas has penned a delightful romp in this Victorian adventure novel about the only woman Sherlock Holmes ever admired, and indeed she lives up to the honor." —*Publishers Weekly*

"A hundred years from now, readers will still be raving about the world's greatest detective, but for many the name on their lips may very well be Adler instead of Holmes." —*Romantic Times BookReviews (4 stars)*

"Holmes and Irene do their most charming (if in Holmes's case, unwitting) work together." —*Kirkus Reviews*

"Douglas has made Adler a superb detective and invented a perfectly delightful—and perfectly puzzling—series of cases for her." —*The Fort Worth Press*

W9-CFQ-772

By Carole Nelson Douglas from Tom Doherty Associates

*These are revised editions
†Also mystery

# FOREWORD

**My previous** works collated the nineteenth-century diaries
of Penelope Huxleigh, a parson's daughter, and recently discovered fragments from the supposedly fictional accounts of
John H. Watson, M.D., regarding the activities of Sherlock
Holmes, the world's first consulting detective. Readers of
these works will know that it violates the scholar-editor's
code to intrude into the material at hand.

In previous volumes, I confined myself to the discreet after-
word. There I merely smoothed out apparent inconsistencies
between the Watson-related accounts of Sherlock Holmes so
far published and new revelations from the Huxleigh diaries
about the only woman admitted to have outwitted Sherlock
Holmes, Irene Adler.

Readers will also know that I have insisted from the first
that Sherlock Holmes was no fictional construct, but a historic personage. Additionally, I argued that the Huxleigh diaries—with the details of Irene Adler's life both previous and
subsequent to her allegedly fictional meeting with Holmes in
the story titled *A Scandal in Bohemia*—support my theory:
Holmes was real; Irene Adler was real. Indeed, to my mind
the only suspect personage in the Holmes canon is Watson.
This may have been a convenient pseudonym for the actual

biographer, who has successfully hidden behind the "author-ship" of Sir Arthur Conan Doyle for a century.

Now I have uncovered evidence of such a startling nature, an "adventure" of Sherlock Holmes (although it is actually a lost adventure of Irene Adler) that is so linked to documenta-ble historic events that I believe no rational person can read it without admitting that Holmes is far from a figment of anyone's imagination. In addition, this new material sheds fascinating light on a personage later to become a key figure in the Holmes saga.

Because this evidence stems from incontestable historic events in the complex region known as "Afghanistan" only for the past century, I find it imperative to insert a modern section to preface the Huxleigh diaries and Watson fragments and to provide the needed narrative continuity. Rest assured that I have not abandoned the scholar's code. To convey an authentically compelling tone, I have commissioned an unem-ployed historical novelist and former schoolmate of mine from Forth Worth, who steeped herself in the proper disci-plines in order to portray the flavor of the times and the events themselves. Even the Holmes biographer (who may or may not have been Sir Arthur) on occasion used the omni-scient third-person voice to depict events that none of the principals had witnessed.

So I follow in established footsteps, but beg the reader's pardon and patience nevertheless. Chronology is paramount to the narrative that is about to unfold, which has sinister application to the conflict in Afghanistan in our day, as well as that in the twilight of the nineteenth century.

Fiona Witherspoon, Ph.D., F.I.A.*
November 5, 1991

*Friends of Irene Adler

Oh, Gods! From the venom of the Cobra, the teeth of the Tiger, and the vengeance of the Afghan—deliver us.

—Hindu Saying

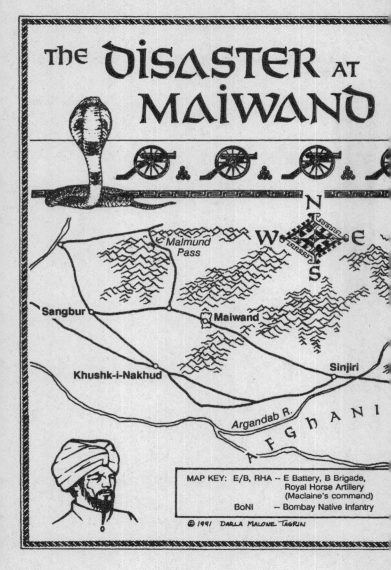

# THE DISASTER AT MAIWAND

Malmund Pass

Sangbur

Maiwand

Khushk-i-Nakhud

Sinjiri

Argandab R.

AFGHANI

MAP KEY: E/B, RHA -- E Battery, B Brigade,
Royal Horse Artillery
(Maclaine's command)

BoNI -- Bombay Native Infantry

© 1991 DARLA MALONE TAGRIN

Afghans

Maclaine
initially

1ST
BoNI

2 cos
30TH BoNI

Ghazi
attack

E/B, RHA

2 Guns

Subsidiary Ravine

30TH BoNI

66TH Berkshires

3RD Light
Cavalry

Retreat

Cavalry retreat

Main Ravine

Khig

KANDAHAR

STAN

Baggage

Last stand
of 66TH

Mandabad

Baggage

# BATTLE OF MAIWAND
## 27 July 1880

# A
# Soul
# of
# Steel

# Chapter One

# WHEN TWO STRONG MEN...

**Near Sangbur, Afghanistan:** *July 25, 1880*

In the very lap of Asia lies a land so fierce and desolate—if not undefended—that were the demons of every faith to collaborate in creating a Hell that would prostrate Christian, Hebrew and Moslem alike in united terror, its name would remain . . . Afghanistan.

Stretching horizontally across the neck of the Indian subcontinent like a hangman's noose, Afghanistan bridges Persia on the west and Tibet and China on the east; British India on the south; and to the north—the great outstretched Russian bearclaw.

Searing in summer and frigid in winter, this unholy landscape huddles behind the scimitar curves of two great mountain ranges—the Himalayas and Karakorum on the east, and on the west the six hundred ridged miles of the Hindu Kush.

Wherever men of adventure and a martial bent gather, the Hindu Kush is spoken of in awed tones. To the timid homebound soul, it is enough to say that the phrase translates as "dead Hindu."

No wonder is it that neither India nor Russia has extended its borders to meet across this dread wasteland. Nor is it any wonder that in the closing decades of the nineteenth century the two great nations of Russia and Britain should nervously dart closer to armed conflict there, like two dogs fighting over the same hideous bone. Possession and advantageous position are the only prizes of what has been called the Great Game between two strong empires. The bone itself is worthless, and bitter gnawing at that.

This is Tartary, ancient road of merchants and conquerors, the no-man's-land separating the northern frontiers of India—Kashmir and the Kush—and the southern fringes of Russia—Tashkent and fabled Samarkand. A lonely wasteland to the unobservant eye, the arid vastness of Afghanistan supports dozens of warring tribes, united only in their devotion to freedom from foreign meddling and their willingness to wreak havoc on interlopers. The traveler, and woe to anyone foolish enough to go solitary into these bleak acres, is never as alone as he may think—or as he may be allowed to think, for a time.

Thus, should a wheeling vulture spy a human form cast lengthwise in a notch atop a bleak ridge, he will not swoop closer to investigate unless he is especially hungry. Such culinary booty is common after the bandits have made their usual forays. Every abandoned traveler is assured of a final, grisly welcome somewhere.

But the lone man visible only to the airborne vulture on this particular summer's day was not lost, or mad, or abandoned. He was present for a purpose, and so was the telescopic spyglass pressed to one eye, its brass carefully darkened so no unnatural twinkle should alert any lurking marauders.

Even a spyglass could barely penetrate the jagged profiles of distance-blued mountain ranges and the tiny camel caravan trickling down a steep incline like a broken string of amber beads. Both men and the tough, two-humped beasts native to these forbidding steppes seemed cloaked in the sere shades of the desolate region, hardly more animate than the darker patches of thornbushes and other scrubby vegetation that punctuate the frozen waves of sand and rock.

The caravan was too immeasurably distant to alarm the watcher, but he rolled over suddenly, aware of the vulture's scant shadow, and turned a dark face to the blazing blue sky. Summer spread its searing, fawn-colored tent over Afghanistan and the heat was horrific, even under the billowing shade of a burnoose.

In an instant, the man collapsed his instrument and tucked it into the leather kit bag belted at his waist beneath the flowing robes. From the bag he pulled something that glinted in the hollow of his hand, a pocket watch, which he consulted. Then he snapped shut the engraved lid and quickly put it away.

The vulture shadow fattened without warning. The man scrambled to his haunches, stretching an arm for the Enfield rifle that lay alongside him, but caution came too late. Another robed man stood motionless below him on the ridge back, a Snider breech-loading rifle slung over one shoulder carelessly enough to be instantly available.

"You are late," the first man said in a language shocking amid that arid wasteland—English.

"I forgo carrying a Burlington Arcade timepiece in Afghanistan," the other said sardonically, moving closer. "One day all of your native dialects will not suffice to talk you out of some tight corner, Cobra."

"Nor will your fabled trick of padding up behind a fellow unheard always save your skin, Tiger," the first man replied with an unamused grin that revealed disarmingly blackened teeth.

Tiger sat on a rock, baggy Turkish trousers ballooning around his knees. He doffed his burnoose's hood, revealing a turban. Under those native wrappings lay a broad, intelligent brow and strong, pugnacious features that indeed boasted the ferocious jaws of a tiger—and unblinking eyes of bright, lapis blue.

"I need that tracker's skill," Tiger said with harsh pride. "I lack your facility for passing among these mountain bandits as one of them. But stealth serves me as well as boldness has served you. We are both yet alive.''

Cobra grunted. Unlike the other man, his skin had been toasted to the nut-brown color of a native, and his eyes, if a trifle hazel, seemed almost black in their swarthy setting. Yet beneath it all, and especially in conference with one of his own kind, lurked the aspect of a young English gentleman, no matter how dangerously he played at native tribesman.

"There will be battle," Cobra said, weary of their usual jousting. He did not like Tiger, did not trust the man, though he was an old India hand; Cobra could not say why.

The turban nodded. "Battle, blood and dust. We will have a rare round of it in a day or two. The command underestimates the Amir's forces, as usual. Burrows is a fool."

"He has not seen much action," Cobra admitted with the unease of a young officer discussing the commander. "And Ayub has some crackerjack artillery: two elephant-drawn heavy batteries, twenty-two horse artillery batteries and eighteen mule-drawn mountain batteries, not to mention seven bullock-drawn field batteries."

"The lad can count!" the older man sneered in a way meant to pass as humor-at-arms. "You will soon be heading behind-lines to report all this?"

Cobra nodded. "Not that the command much listens to me."

"The sash-and-sword set never puts much store in the advice of London lads gone native like yourself. You should have stayed in the regiment and clung to your spit-and-polish."

"After the war it is the political chaps who advance," Cobra put in. "And do they heed your reports any more than mine? So is your scouting done?"

"Oh, aye, I have sashayed up the ridges and down the gullies 'til the vultures are sick of the sight of me."

"Better to be seen by them than by the Ghazi fanatics or the Afghan tribesmen."

"Or the women!" Tiger gave a mock shudder. "The Ghazis may kill everything that moves for Allah, but I would rather face one any day. At all costs, do not get wounded and let the village women have at you, boy. They have a real taste for torture, even more than the men. Better to shoot yourself."

"War stories."

Tiger smiled. His teeth were strong and yellow, like a big cat's, leaving no question of why he had earned his *nom de guerre*. "War stories tend to be war truths. Remember that, and remember who told you."

"But you have scouted no surprises for our troops?" Cobra asked.

"No hidden caches of elephant-drawn artillery, no. I have spent two weeks crawling around this bloody dust-laden kiln, and I should know."

"Odd." Cobra got out his spyglass and swept it over the parched landscape below. "Hyena said he had seen you up north recently, in Balkh, near the Russian border."

"Hyena *said*, did he? Like all of his breed, he is much for slinking around after the danger—saying, and little for doing. But he is right, although it was a bit longer ago than that." Tiger leaned inward, his voice so compelling that Cobra lowered his glass to meet the bright blue gaze so ripe with conviction. "That is what I have come to pass to you today. The immediate area is clean as a camel's tooth, but a Russian agent has been doing a mazurka hereabouts to no good. 'Sable' is the code name—vicious, surreptitious beasts they are, too. That is all I've discovered: except for the fact that an officer in our command has been compromised."

"An officer? Will betray us? Why?"

Tiger shrugged. "Could be for gold, or for the rubies in the far Afghan hills—now there is a bribe to make a man's heart clench, a ruby mine! Could be a woman in Simla, with eyes brighter than the Koh-i-noor diamond, but another officer's wife, and blackmail. Oh, my poor lad, the world is rotten with fat fruit, ripe for teasing another's will to one's own. You are such a babe at espionage."

Cobra stiffened in irritation, which no doubt further amused Tiger. "Still, I am the one to report back. What does it matter if the terrain favors us when one of our own may turn? Do you have a name?"

"A name." For the first time, Tiger seemed uncertain.

"Well?" After having his competence challenged, Cobra counterattacked with a vengeance. "What good is it to know the foul deed in advance if you do not know the doer? If you are right, and I happen to think you are, we will engage the Afghans within a day or two. Do you mean to say that all your slinking around on soft cat feet has only turned up a rumor?"

Tiger's mustache bristled like brutal whiskers. "I hesitate to name the man on a matter of such dishonor. But it is . . . Maclaine."

"Maclaine of the Royal Horse Artillery? We need all the artillery we have against the Amir." Cobra stirred, concealing his spyglass. "I had best be making for the plain. This is dire news."

"Wait!" Tiger pulled the burnoose hood over his head, putting his betraying blue eyes into deep shadow. "Let an old game hunter sniff out the trail before you start back. That vulture is still circling. It may spy only carrion, but—"

Cobra nodded. No scout superior to Tiger inhabited all of India. The older man scrabbled sideways across the rocks scorpion-swift, the rifle in his hand cocked like a stinger, until he was out of sight.

Tiger's bag lay on the rocks. Cobra hesitated, as if fearing a sting, but then rapidly unbuckled the straps and studied the contents—quinine pills, a compass and water flask like his own, ammunition, a mustache comb—more likely catch an Afghan with a pocket watch than with one of these! Cobra frowned. He knew not for what he searched, only that he did not trust the bearer.

And then he felt a welt within the leather. His sun-stained fingers probed, working a secret flap loose. A folded document lay in his hand, written on heavy soft paper, so it should not crackle. Odd words. Afghan words. And Russian. Some sort of drawing, a cryptogram.

It took Cobra a moment's work to stuff the paper into his own kit, to replace Tiger's bag in the searing sun as if it had never been touched. He was not as green as Tiger thought. Something in the man's manner today had fanned Cobra's usual dislike into embers of outright suspicion. A British force and the fate of India were at stake. If he were wrong, he would take the consequences. And right or wrong, he would have Tiger to answer to.

He never heard the espionage agent return, but a swelling shadow swooped down suddenly, like a vulture, and squatted near him.

"All clear," said Tiger, smiling . . . smiling like a well-fed big Bengal cat.

## Khushk-i-Nakhud, *Evening, July 26, 1880*

On occasion the orchards surrounding Kandahar scented the night air with perfumes that infiltrated even the city's narrow, filthy streets. Here, however, in the British camp midway across the waste that lay between Kandahar and the river Helmond, the only certain fragrance wafted from the plentiful droppings of the beasts of burden needed to transport the baggage and equipment of twenty-five hundred fighting men.

Cobra, now in uniform, slipped unnoticed among the soldiers in the pungent darkness. Horses neighed in answer to ill-tempered bagpipelike brays from the camels. All beasts, native or not, led a brutal life in these parts, and often a short one.

By the muted lantern light of an army soon to go head-to-head with the forces of Ayub Khan, Cobra dodged the shoulder-high wooden wheels of E Battery, B Brigade of the Royal Horse Artillery. The commander of two of these big guns was Lieutenant Hector Maclaine.

Cobra found his man propped against one of the stone enclosures that bracketed the camp, staring into the impenetrable night. Stars sparkled like bright brass buttons above, but no enemy campfires mirrored these hot points of light below. The two men could have been alone in a coal mine with fool's gold salting the ceiling, save for the faint rustles of restless men and animals.

"Stan!" Maclaine greeted the newcomer in surprise. "I doubted you would return before we broke camp."

"Had to report," Cobra said shortly.

"And are we dragging pack and packhorse to greet Ayub Khan tonight, as rumor has it?"

"Perhaps. I merely report to St. John. He carries the news to Slade and the brigadier. Then news becomes rumor."

"Insane that a frontline scout never reports directly. Damn clumsy system."

"Perhaps." Cobra was silent for several moments, as if, used to hurried clandestine meetings, he had forgotten how to converse in other than staccato fashion. "I have uneasy news, Maclaine, and from the look of it, the command will not listen."

"Command lives to order others to listen, not to heed its own scouts' words." The smile in Lieutenant Maclaine's voice was evident even in the dark.

"That is what I fear!" Cobra burst out. "They will not listen, not about Ayub Khan's superior artillery, not about Tiger . . . not about anything."

"What is wrong, old man? Too much time spent in solitary on the boiling sands?"

"Burrows is getting spoiled spy-work, and I know it. I am going out again to scout Maiwand. The previous report sounds too perfect: a long ravine for an attack base and no flaws in the terrain."

"That does not sound like the Afghanistan that has scrubbed our boots raw," Maclaine agreed.

"Just what I thought. I have scoured the ground like a dust devil, and found a secondary ravine to the east no one has reported. If we see action at Maiwand tomorrow, the RHA will be in the vanguard. Keep your eyes and ears open, full-bore," Cobra cautioned him. "You have nothing . . . troubling you?"

"Nothing save dust and heat, a gulletful of quinine pills and a noseful of horse manure. Have I ever struck you as a nerve-ridden man?"

"No, you have not," Cobra answered soberly. "That is what troubles me. Someone who has no notion that I know you has accused you of having a guilty conscience."

"I?" Maclaine leaped up. "Who is this liar? I'll call him out in midbattle, though six dozen Ghazi fanatics charge us."

"This is serious spy-work," Cobra said. "Leave it to me. But for God's sake, Mac, keep a sharp eye about yourself from now on."

"Can you say no more?"

"Nothing until I learn more. God guard you all tonight."

"And you, Stan," Lieutenant Maclaine said. "I vouchsafe we will next meet on a battlefield—or in heaven."

"Just so long as it is not in an undeserved hell," Cobra answered, edging silently into the darkness.

After he had gone, Lieutenant Maclaine stamped a booted foot like a restless horse. Officers of the Royal Horse Artillery were used to chaos, danger, dust and gunpowder. Innuendo and behind-hand dealing, or sinking into the native culture, as Cobra did, was more foreign territory than Afghanistan.

"Odd fellow," Maclaine muttered to the apparently empty and unheeding night.

Cobra was gone by then, eeling through the dark as if it were a silent, immobile sea. He slithered past a wooden wheel and the stolid forms of resting horses, through thinning tents, into the open waste.

Beyond the camp and beside a last solitary stone, Cobra stooped to disinter his native robes, his mind on a jumble of oddities, not the least of which was his friend Maclaine's role in the coming events.

He never heard a sound. All at once the night's opaque ebony curtain dropped upon his head with a tremendous thud. Warm red velvet oozed over his eyes, into his surprised mouth, as he felt his skull split from side to side, a chasm opening into an utter darkness blacker than even the Afghan night.

## Chapter Two

# ... EAST MEETS WEST

### The Battle of Maiwand, *July 27, 1880*

Heat haze and dust perform a whirling dervish dance in the distance. But a few thousand yards away, unseen masses of milling men and horses churn as the Ayub Khan's forces move into battle positions.

The hour is early, only nine-fifteen in the morning. Between the two forces lies a flat, merciless Afghanistan plain, already seeming to quiver under the blast-furnace heat, as if viewed in a wavy mirror. A village or two hump carcass-fashion ahead. The only other shelter on the pitiless plain is the ravine previously scouted, fifteen to twenty-five feet deep and fifty to a hundred feet wide, running like a wound toward the northeast.

Brigadier General Burrows rides forward with the general of the cavalry, Nuttall.

"Blackwood!" he orders. "Take Fowell's and Maclaine's sections forward across the ravine under the escort of a troop of the Third Light Cavalry." He watches the sections grind forward into the dusty no-man's-land between the British position at the ravine and the unseen—but not unreported—Afghan hordes arranged into a scimitarlike arc twenty-five hundred yards beyond.

Thus does battle fall upon the British like an afterthought. By ten-thirty A.M. Fowell's two guns open fire from a position five hundred yards northwest of the ravine. Even as the two generals watch with some complacency, for generals expect their orders to be carried out, a sudden spurt, a geyser-burst of dust, erupts on Ayub's front lines.

"What—?" begins Burrows, certain that the Afghan artillery has not yet been drawn into position.

"Must be . . . Maclaine!" Nuttall rises in his stirrups. "Damn fool, he's galloping his guns directly to the front gate of the Afghan position. Why on earth—?"

"Disobeying orders," Burrows roars. "That is why."

The two generals keep a sudden silence, each calculating the advantages and disadvantages of having an artillery section a mile in advance of the regular troops. Soon a mounted messenger, with orders for Maclaine's guns to pull back, is racing into the dust toward his position. Messages from Blackwood are sent as well, telling Fowell's artillery section to move forward where it has a chance of hitting the enemy positions.

In time, by a process of seesawing, Maclaine's position pulls back and Fowell's pushes forward to two thousand yards in advance of the ravine. They form a united front, backed by a half-company of the Sappers and Miners and the infantry, with the Sixty-sixth Berkshires on the far left.

For half an hour only the British artillery pounds the parched Afghan earth. Then Ayub's guns begin heaving, spitting heavy shells into the British lines from breech-loading Armstrongs.

"Ayub has more guns than a battleship," Nuttall shouts into the dusty din as he watches the artillery sections and his cavalry take repeated poundings.

"So Cobra's report said," the brigadier grumbles. "Why are the Sixty-sixth Berkshires so sluggish about holding the line?"

A scout charges up at that moment with the reason: "A shallow ravine joins at right angles to this, sir! Along it the Afghan rifles are harrying our rear baggage section. The men and animals are in disarray, and the Sixty-sixth is forced to deform the line to defend themselves."

"Another ravine? No spy or scout reported this! Then we are in danger of being surrounded, and Ayub has ten to fifteen thousand men to our nineteen hundred field soldiers!" The brigadier grows suddenly quiet. Not until now has it occurred to him that the sun may not set on a British victory.

"Guns!" bawls another officer, riding up. "In the subsidiary ravine. Two artillery guns, pounding the Sixty-sixth."

Dire news comes charging at Brigadier General Burrows after that: the left wing formed by the ambushed Sixty-sixth is steadily being cut down; E Battery, B Brigade of Royal Horse Artillery is ordered to fire one more round, but, ahead of the infantry, is almost surrounded. Maclaine at their forefront fails to retrieve his guns, leaving them to the enemy and retreating under shots fired at a range of only fifteen to twenty yards.

"We need those guns back," Brigadier General Burrows barks.

"Let me order Nuttall to lead a cavalry charge at the captured guns," Leach urges.

Moments later the general watches a saber of dust plough toward the Afghan-surrounded guns, but the charge quickly sputters and retreats.

Nuttall, his face gritty with sand, rides up.

"Charge again," the general orders.

"Impossible, sir," Nuttall replies.

The general eyes the dust storm that is the battlefield. "If another charge is impossible, then so is victory."

Nuttall meets his eyes but says nothing.

By one-thirty P.M. the smoothbore batteries have exhausted their ammunition and withdrawn to the main ravine for restocking. Blackwood, severely wounded, is retiring to the rear also, a gravely wounded Fowell with him. Enemy irregulars harass the coattails of the valiant Sixty-sixth.

An hour and half later, the battle is over; a vast column of

British soldiers and sepoys, native Indian forces, flee south toward Kandahar, mounted Afghans harrying its flanks.

Bodies litter the landscape, thousands of robed Afghans, hundreds of uniformed British troops. The severely wounded fall to the Afghan enemy and die before they can be rescued. Retreat is graceless as well as bitter, punctuated by the bullets of Afghan snipers and the knives of local peasants. Men and animals mill in chaos.

Among them wanders Lieutenant Hector Maclaine, dazed and disillusioned. By now the men have fought for hours without rest or food or water. At dusk, Maclaine ventures into a village in search of the one essential, water. Villagers converge upon him and five Indian soldiers, taking them prisoner. No one notices.

Also among these cheerless, fleeing men is the spy known as Cobra. The cavalry retreat, plunging back through camp, has awakened him from the violent blow to the head. He staggers onward, in the direction the British go: south to Kandahar, sixty miles over the hills and through the mountain passes.

Cobra doubts that he can make such a trek in his present condition, but he must. He must tell the command of Tiger's perfidy. He must reach Kandahar. He must move one foot before the other one more time. . . .

He falls, his face in the familiar dust. He is breathing sand now rather than air, and can feel the earth's hot tremors as running men and hard-hooved beasts bound over this contested ground. Through the seven veils of dust thickening in the setting sun's scarlet train, Cobra sees a figure from a fever dream lurching toward him: a man in uniform carrying a leather satchel.

It is too late, Cobra wants to say, but his dry, heat-blistered lips barely move. The man with the leather bag comes on.

# Chapter Three

# AFGHANISTAN PERCEIVED

**London:** *June 1889*

"Well, Watson, you are thinking of Afghanistan again, I perceive."

"I beg your pardon, Holmes?"

"Surely I need not apologize for being observant, Watson?"

"Indeed you should, when you go stealing into a man's thoughts like this."

"Then you admit it?"

"Admit what?"

"Afghanistan, of course."

"I was not aware of dwelling on that unkindly land, but my thoughts may have drifted in that direction. No doubt you soon will tell me how you read them."

Holmes leaned back in the velvet armchair with an expression of satisfaction. "Perhaps *you* would care to tell *me*."

"I do not know why, when you will pull the rug out from under my poor speculations, as you usually do."

"Pshaw, Watson. You underestimate your own capacities. Think, man! It is *your* mind that I have presumed to read. Either refute my conclusion or explain it."

I looked around our too-familiar rooms in Baker Street,

trying to reconstruct the thoughts that had idly streamed through my mind while I had gazed out the bow window on the drizzle of a sullen summer day.

"I suppose," I began, "that I was looking at something incriminating." Yet no souvenirs of my Army surgeon days in Afghanistan decorated the walls. Holmes was the sentimentalist, if I may be so bold as to call him that. At least he was the pack rat, for the domestic landscape teemed with memorabilia of his vocation as a consulting detective, not the least of which was the pointillist pattern of bullet holes punctuating the farther wall with the admirable initials *V.R.*, for Victoria Regina.

"There is much incriminating to observe in these rooms," Holmes said with a smile as he watched me. "Fortunately most of it has incriminated others, not ourselves. Go on."

"Humph." Where exactly had I been staring when Holmes had interrupted my reverie? Out of the window? Not really. Ah. "The photograph of General Gordon has led you in the direction of Afghanistan, has it not, Holmes?"

"How could it? 'Chinese' Gordon campaigned in China and died in Egypt, both sufficiently far from Afghanistan to have no obvious connection."

"Still, I vaguely recall gazing at the old fellow's gilt-embroidered uniform. At least he represents the rough quarter of the globe that Afghanistan shares."

"Very well, Watson, very well! I confess. You were indeed musing on the late general, and a fine-looking subject for contemplation he makes in his fez, with his stars of rank festooning his Oriental tunic. But *you* were my ultimate clue on the direction of your thoughts."

"I said nothing."

"No, but you absently massaged your left shoulder, the site of the wound you took at Maiwand, which caused you to be cashiered out of the Army. Does the damp trouble you?"

"Not so much as the dryness of your deductions," I mumbled, shifting on my chair and only realizing then that the shoulder did indeed ache a bit, as did my leg.

Holmes's quick eyes followed my own to the leg. "A secondary wound, Watson?"

I stirred uneasily, pricked by an annoyance I seldom felt with Holmes, for all his amazing and eternal prescience. "Merely the combined inroads of a damp day and a certain age," said I, "common to inhabitants of our great but fogbound city. I am stiff from sitting."

"Ah." Holmes commented with the bland skepticism of a physician on hearing a symptom reported by its bearer. "No doubt. Although I have seen you favor the leg before."

"The wound was in my shoulder, Holmes. You know that! The surgeons who treated me in Afghanistan know that! This nonsense of the leg is some sham you have manufactured to explain your deduction. I know what I am thinking and I do not require translations from nearby observers, no matter how brilliant."

"Of course not, dear fellow," Holmes murmured contritely. "I merely wondered why you might be thinking of Afghanistan at this late date. Obviously," he finished insincerely, "I was mistaken."

I said no more. Seldom did my friendship with Holmes tread near the shoals of irritation, but this was one of those rare times. It was ridiculous to suppose that I should care to dwell on Afghanistan after the severe wound and the tedious, long recovery I endured in that unhappy landscape.

The jezail bullet that shattered my shoulder bone and sheared the subclavian artery would have been fatal if my orderly, Murray, had not flung me over a packhorse and rushed me to the British lines. When I was recovering at Peshawar in India, enteric fever hammered me down. For months I lingered on the borderline of death itself. A mere shadow of myself shipped home for England on the troopship *Orontes* in 1881. That was the shade who had met Sherlock Holmes. When we two decided to share rooms, I little guessed what an unforeseen tack my life would take as I became a witness to my friend's astonishing deductive abilities. But I did not always welcome his keen and tireless mind presuming to read mine.

Afghanistan, indeed. For once my detective friend was on a false trail. I had virtually forgotten Afghanistan. Even if I had not been inclined to do so, my months of fever-ridden illness had wiped most details of my wounding and recovery from my memory, thoroughly enough even to baffle the mind-reading abilities of Mr. Sherlock Holmes.

# Chapter Four

# PEARLS BEFORE PARROTS

"**Araggk. Pieces** of eight. Pieces of eight." Casanova peered over my shoulder and cocked his gaudy head.

"You may be able to intone flawless French," I said severely, "but you cannot count in any language. There are only five pieces here."

The gleam of rubies, diamonds and pearls matched the appetite in Casanova's beady eye. It was fortunate that he was caged, for I suspected that he would have snatched up one of my prizes in a thrice otherwise.

The parrot ambled down his scabrous perch, chortling to himself, while I returned to my self-appointed duty of tending the family fortune.

For a peerless beauty of her era, my American friend Irene Adler Norton had precious few jewels to show for it. She who had introduced Tiffany's spectacular shoulder-to-hip corsage of diamonds to the Milan opera audiences, and who had worn Queen Marie Antoinette's lost Zone of Diamonds around her waist at her wedding (albeit discreetly under her overskirt) had not retained these fabulous treasures, being too poor or too indifferent.

The array that sparkled in her tapestry-covered jewel box was modest, yet each item told a story. On rainy days it amused me to polish my memories along with Irene's jewels, for she herself could never be bothered to fuss over her possessions, no matter how rare or valuable.

So I shined true treasure along with mere souvenir. The outstanding single piece was a twenty-five-carat diamond, the only one Irene had kept from the French queen's long-lost, floor-length girdle of jewels. The next most valuable piece was undoubtedly the diamond choker mounted on velvet. This was a gesture of thanks from Charles Lewis Tiffany, the world-famous jeweler to whom Irene sold the queen's Zone once she had whisked it from under the rather prominent nose of the Baker Street consulting detective Sherlock Holmes.

The most precious article glittered on my palm like a giant dewdrop—a Tiffany piece modest in cost and execution, but the first gift from Irene's husband-to-be, barrister Godfrey Norton. Godfrey, who displayed a legal precision even when under the influence of a romantic impulse, had chosen the perfect insignia for my friend: a diamond-studded musical clef intersecting an equally resplendent key at an angle reminiscent of crossed swords.

"Music and mystery," I can still hear Godfrey saying with that tone of light seriousness that so becomes him. "They are the keynotes of your life, my dear Irene."

Music, I fear, had become a background motif once Irene was forced to leave the Prague opera and to live in virtual anonymity in Paris after the affair of the King of Bohemia's photograph, not to mention the possible pursuit of Sherlock Holmes. Mystery, however, was proving to be a less fragile pastime.

I centered the clef and key on the moss-green velvet within the jewel box and considered the next item. As in a wax museum, the more gruesome exhibits had the more enduring fascination. I picked up the blood-bright ruby brooch shaped like a five-pointed star. It lay on my palm, a glorious stigma, the only gift that Irene had accepted from Wilhelm Gottsreich Sigismond von Ormstein, King of Bohemia. He had meant it to be a consolation prize for relegating Irene from

**A Soul Of Steel** 21

potential royal bride to certain royal mistress after his succession to the throne on the death of his father. Irene, who had refused all jewels during their courtship, accepted this last poisonous symbol of the King's personal betrayal, and fled—with myself—across most of Europe.

To recover the photograph of the two together that Irene took with her as a safeguard, King Willie pursued her to London. When his thugs failed to dent Irene's armor of cool wit, he engaged Sherlock Holmes to recover the photograph, but even that did not help him. The ruby brooch shone like limpid drops of blood under the brisk buffing of my cloth, and I dropped it to the velvet with sudden distaste.

On the Valencia-lace dresser scarf awaiting my attentions lay another loathsome object—not by its associations but by design. This was the work of Charles Tiffany's son Louis—a tortured representation of an anonymous sea slug decked with pearls. Irene insisted that the work was unique, would even one day be valuable, but she was ever an optimist on all fronts. I was sorely tempted to "lose" the ugly thing during one of my cleaning ventures. Certainly the world would not miss a single sinuous and bilious enameled brooch.

Perhaps the most shuddersome of Irene's souvenirs, however, was the plain gold wedding band, which dated from the day she and I met in 1881. She had received it from the hand of a man I shall never forget, Jefferson Hope, an American who drove our first shared cab ride together. When he became gravely ill en route to Irene's humble Saffron Hill lodgings, he confessed a strange tale of perfidy in the American Great Salt Desert involving a woman betrayed and revenge unto the second decade. He was a murderer, that man, though his victims were villains, and he gave Irene the ring of his tragically lost love Lucy.

Only days after that dramatic encounter we read of his capture in the rooms of Mr. Sherlock Holmes, the amateur detective. We were to see Mr. Jefferson Hope no more. He died in police custody shortly after. Mr. Sherlock Holmes proved to be quite another matter indeed.

How Irene had foiled the supposedly peerless detective and the King of Bohemia in the matter of the photograph—and the unsuspected Zone of Diamonds! She had wed, then fled with, a worthier man, Godfrey, with the Zone and the photograph, and most important, with her virtue and integrity intact.

Now the French village of Neuilly near Paris became the newlyweds' home. And now I, Penelope Huxleigh—once Irene's chambermate and Godfrey's typewriter-girl—had joined them. Now, of course, Godfrey required a secretary to manage his correspondence in international law. Since arriving in France the previous summer, I had mastered the language in its written form, though I still stumbled over its spoken cadences.

As an orphaned, unmarried parson's daughter past thirty, it seemed fitting that I should amuse myself by polishing Godfrey's punctuation and Irene's jewelry. One in my social position cannot expect much glamour from life, although my association with Irene first, and now both the Nortons, unfortunately involved me from time to time in a mysterious doing or other. Indeed, had it not been for my sensible counsel on many occasions, my good friends might not be here to enjoy the proceeds of the queen's diamonds. They remained an impetuous pair abroad, even the usually stable Godfrey, when it came to some puzzle in the neighborhood.

Fortunately, all had been quiet after the Montpensier affair, which had begun with a drowned man on Bram Stoker's Chelsea dining-room table in London years before and ended recently in perfidy and lost treasure in Monaco. Yet that resolution had been last fall, and 1889 was now half over, happily with no sign of some new, outré investigation on the horizon. So like any idle sailor polishing brass, I brightened the souvenirs of previous escapades and secretly hoped that they would be the last of their kind. A respectable married couple has far better things to do than to meddle in the affairs of others, especially when those affairs involve theft, murder,

"that you have found some puzzle for me to unravel amongst your exceedingly dull legal documents?"

"I fear my cupboard is bare," he said, hastily sipping the black coffee he had learned to prefer since meeting Irene.

Godfrey, too, looked most debonair, as the French say, attired in a shiny top hat and walking suit and carrying a malacca cane. One sometimes forgot that Godfrey was such a fine-looking gentleman, so royally did Irene's beauty and style command public attention. She always radiated the air of the opera diva she had been—a confidence and intelligence of manner that was most striking in a woman.

No wonder all eyes in the little sidewalk café under the ponderous shadow of Notre Dame fixed on Irene's charming pantomime of feeding the little brown wren, which had flitted back to her shoulder to beg for more.

Speaking of little brown wrens, I suppose that I should mention my disposition and attire that late June day of 1889. My habit of making complete notes in my diary had not failed me that day, and by evening it would prove to be a most astounding date, to say the least. That morning, however, I was innocent of pending revelations, and wore a brown plaid walking suit trimmed in suede velvet cuffs, reveres and collar. My bonnet was suede felt topped by a panache of ostrich tips and wings shaded, like foul coffee soothed by variations of cream, from soft suede to darkest brown. The bonnet had been purchased in Paris at Irene's order, despite my fear that it was frivolous. I need not have worried. I could have worn scarlet satin bloomers and she sackcloth, and I would have gone unnoticed in Irene's company.

Fortunately, I have never been afflicted with the female fault of welcoming personal attention, and Irene's beauty was all the more effective for being unaffected, so we made an ideal pair. I had long since grown resigned, even relieved, to escape public notice when with such a stunning companion.

Some must not only serve by standing and waiting, but by sitting and taking copious notes, and such had been my reluctant role in our previous adventures, such as the Escape from the King of Bohemia, the Distasteful Matter of the Drowned Sailor, the Incident of the Tattooed Heiress, and other intrusive puzzles that flocked to Irene's vicinity like . . . the wrens of Paris.

"You are pensive, my dear Nell." Godfrey leaned toward me with twinkling eyes as gray as the Paris skies. "No doubt you contemplate the likelihood of Irene finding another mysterious matter to investigate. Surely you are safe from such scandals in the saintly shadow of Notre Dame."

"Saintly, indeed," I admitted, "but too tricked-out for my Protestant tastes." I looked up at the gargoyles grinning from the bristling parapets crowning the great cathedral's mass across the street. I had no doubt that these ancient stone guardians were more successful in warding off fiends than I would be at shielding Irene from the temptation of a puzzle.

As my eyes dropped back to earth and half the population of Paris out for a stroll in its Sunday best, they lit upon a disreputable figure—a robed and turbaned man of bearded, dark mien who might have materialized like Beelzebub in Faust's study. I do not like to stare at the less fortunate, or the possibly more predatory, but it was clear that this . . . apparition was gazing toward our threesome.

"Godfrey—"

"Yes?" His eyes left Irene and the greedy little bird.

"There is a man—"

"There usually is on the streets of Paris, and usually several."

"He is watching us."

Godfrey smiled ruefully. "Your use of the plural is kind, but not accurate. He is watching Irene. Most men do."

"You take this sort of thing extremely well, Godfrey. No doubt it is the cool temper required by the courtroom. This man—and I did not look long, I did not wish him to receive any illusions as to my interest—is most savage looking! He does not look a Christian gentleman at all!"

Godfrey looked around with that admirable discretion that Irene is always urging upon myself, to no avail. "Ah. I see.

The bearded Oriental man who looks half beggar and half brigand, and no doubt all infidel to you. But Paris is the crossroads of Europe; men of all races convene here freely."

"But not to look at us! Even at one of us. I find it most disturbing."

"He will likely move on. As we can do ourselves." Godfrey took up his cane and leaned toward Irene, who had been lost in feeding the inordinately tame wren. "We should take our leave," he suggested quietly.

She started, then began to don her dashing, though unconventional black gloves, suitable only for mourning. "Was I ignoring you? Dreadfully sorry. I was wondering if Casanova might not like this precious little one for a companion— although Lucifer would like it too well, I fear!"

Lucifer was the black Persian cat Irene had "given" me on my arrival in Paris the previous August. He was large and lazy and, despite my distaste for cats, often lay across my diary as I wrote or lounged in my lap when I attempted some domestic duty, such as the crochet work that his wicked claws would snarl.

"I agree," said I, gathering up my reticule. "That is the trouble with these so-called 'romantic' sidewalk cafés of Paris; they provide a fishbowl for the sharks that prowl the streets to prey upon. Godfrey, that scoundrel is not moving on. If anything, he is coming closer. Hurry!"

"Oh?" Irene came out of her trance and began to look around in the manner she recommends to me: missing nothing but appearing to overlook everything.

"Do hurry, Irene! Once again you have attracted the attention of some unsavory individual. I will not have our Sunday ruined by an unseemly incident. I knew coming into Paris would be a mistake."

Irene instantly singled out the very man whose demeanor so agitated me. "He is only some poor foreign beggar, Nell."

"Some foreign *rogue* who would see *us* poorer, no doubt. Please, Irene! For once could you refrain from involving us in a public scene? We need only step along to the Left Bank and our coachman will collect us, and we will have had a totally enjoyable outing with not one thing to mar the day."

"Oh, very well." Irene took Godfrey's arm with an indulgent smile at me, but she moved so languidly I feared the rude watcher would have time to bolt toward us and do whatever he so clearly had in mind: beg, beseech, or berate us with some insanity.

Godfrey extended his other arm, which I took, and we threaded through the tables to the street. Most of the passersby were respectable to the point of being fashionable. Top hats bobbled past the blue turban that never left my view, and a tall, blonde woman with golden sable fur burnishing her hem and shoulders brushed past the watching man, oblivious to his unsavory nature. Paris accepts anything. We swung right to escape his view and began crossing the street, forced to pause as a fruit vendor pulled his fragrant cart past us.

I heard no footsteps behind us, but felt such an imperative sense of haste that I crimped my fingers into Godfrey's arm.

"Why, Nell," said he with a reassuring smile. "You are actually worried."

"Indeed. Please, you must whisk Irene away before—"

A presence loomed at our backs. I glimpsed the red-gold pelt of a sable and inhaled a heady foreign perfume—only the fashionable lady but unaccompanied, how odd . . . and then another figure hove to behind me—the mysterious foreigner about to bump into us! We three turned at once, for different reasons: Irene sensing the unknown and rushing to meet it; Godfrey determined to inspect and confront the object of my alarm; I knowing that Fate in bizarre guise was about to enmesh Irene—and Godfrey and me—in another dangerous puzzle.

There he stood, the man who had so unnerved me. And an unnerving figure he was, his skin chestnut-brown, his face and form gaunt beneath garments that were a patchwork of European and Oriental castoffs.

*You see!* I almost shouted triumphantly in front of all the

Sunday strollers. You *see?* Here it begins again; Irene drawing mystery and skulduggery as a magnet attracts metal.

The fellow, having reached us, fixed us with disbelieving eyes that were—oddly—a shade lighter than his swarthy foreign face. He swayed upon his feet, his pale hazel eyes narrowing, as he stared stupidly at me and intoned in perfect Sloane Square English, "Why, it *is* Miss Huxleigh, indeed."

Then he collapsed to the cobblestones like a sack of potatoes. Irene regarded me inquiringly, even accusingly.

"I do not know!" Staring down at the unconscious man, I could only repeat the obvious. "I cannot speculate how he knew my name, but I most certainly do not know—have never known, never seen—"

"He saw you," she interrupted. "He saw you and could not believe that he knew you."

"The f-feeling is mutual," I stuttered, aware of onlookers gathering around us. "I tell you I have never seen this man before, nor do I hope to again."

Godfrey had bent to examine the creature at the same moment that a waiter from the café rushed over with a glass of red wine. The French belief in the curative value of wine rivals only their conviction in their own cultural superiority. More of that gruesome liquid fell upon the man's barbarously embroidered shirt than on his lips, but he stirred at this bloody baptism, his eyelids fluttering.

"Miss Huxleigh," he murmured as if dreaming.

I stepped back, appalled, my hands clasped at my throat, which was dry. "I have never met the fellow, I swear."

Irene regarded the fallen man from the lofty pinnacle of consideration for a moment; though she was the softest-hearted of women when moved, she was not one to be deceived by false weakness. Then she addressed me dryly.

"Although you pride yourself on strictly abiding by the Holy Writ, Nell, it is not necessary to follow the New Testament example and deny any association yet a third time. Whatever your memory of a connection, this, er, gentleman clearly knows you and your name. Since he has been taken ill—"

"A ruse!" I interrupted, my cheeks hot with anger at the attention the bounder had drawn in my innocent direction.

"A ruse by another name may be a true illness." Irene waited for Godfrey to report on the fellow's condition.

"I am no medical man," he said, glancing up with a sober face, "but it looks like a legitimate illness to me."

Irene nodded briskly, her ostrich plumes bowing faintly to the gesture. "We will take him back with us to Neuilly, then. Our carriage will accommodate him if you ride up with André," she told Godfrey. She gave me a wicked smile. "Or perhaps Nell would prefer to ride with the coachman rather than with our mysterious charge."

My throat felt stuffed with cotton, but I managed to speak. "If you wish to play Good Samaritan to this *stranger*, far be it from me to interfere. But I would never agree to anything so improper as riding with the coachman."

"Good," Irene returned. "I knew I could rely upon you, Nell, to do the proper thing. Godfrey, you must tend the poor man while Nell and I fetch the carriage. Guard him well." With that cryptic instruction, Irene took my elbow and steered me into the crowd milling before the great stone cathedral.

"Paris is unlucky for us," I commented morosely when Godfrey came down the narrow stairs of our cottage at Neuilly after helping the coachman install our mysterious invalid in an upstairs bedchamber.

Godfrey frowned at the chamomile tea our maid, Sophie, had prepared for me, and went to the sherry decanter instead. He returned with a half-full glass and presented it with a bow. "For thy stomach's sake. It has had a turn."

I seldom partake of alcoholic beverages, but my throat was still dry so I sipped the potion, which struck me as no more unappealing than drinking from the perfume flagon Irene kept on her dressing table. "He may have contracted some virulent Oriental disease," I muttered.

"He may have," Godfrey admitted. "We are taking him on faith, given his acquaintance with you."

"You must not! As I told Irene, I do not know——" Footsteps descended the stairs. I paused, loath to subject myself to another reminder from Irene that the wretched man knew me even if I did not know him. Our buxom maid appeared in the hallway.

"You need help?" Godfrey asked in rapid French that I had only lately begun to follow well. "André has gone for Dr. Mersenné in the village."

"*Non, Monsieur,*" Sophie replied, adding—if I understood her correctly—that Madame Norton was having no difficulty disrobing the man!

I turned on Godfrey like an angry goose, so furious I could only hiss my disbelief.

"No, no, Nell. André and I disrobed him for bed. Irene is merely searching his clothing for clues."

"Worse! They might be disease-ridden, vermin-infested——"

"Decently clean, if a bit worn," came Irene's cheery overriding tones from the foot of the stairs. She entered the parlor, her eyes belladonna-bright, though curiosity was her only cosmetic. "Such a puzzle," she added happily, perching on the arm of Godfrey's chintz-upholstered easy chair. "His Eastern outer clothing hides European underwear and his body is sun-browned to the waist, yet his legs are as white as a fish belly."

"Irene!" I remonstrated faintly.

"I am sorry, Nell." Irene sounded genuinely contrite for once. "I should not have said anything so forward as 'fish belly.' "

"You are having fun with me. At least until now your interest in the condition of strange gentlemen's bodies confined itself to corpses."

"We may have one on our hands yet," Godfrey put in a trifle grimly.

"This man may . . . die?"

"But you must not worry, Nell," Irene said. "You do not know him."

"That does not mean I wish him to die, disreputable as he is. He may have had a tragic life . . . have been cast out while a child. He may have contracted a dreadful malady in far-off China while ministering to the heathens."

"Nell is right in one thing," Godfrey told Irene. "It has the look of a foreign fever. Dr. Mersenné may know what, I hope."

Irene nodded, equally grave. "I also hope Dr. Mersenné can diagnose the large puncture wound in his upper right arm."

"The bite of some huge, exotic spider," I suggested.

"More like the injection of some huge, exotic needle," she returned.

"A needle? You mean a syringe? Then he has already seen a doctor."

Irene leaned over and lifted my barely touched glass of sherry from the marquetry table upon which it sat. "I do not think so." She sipped consideringly. "I believe we may have a mortally ill man upon our hands, and one so recently stricken that he did not yet know it himself."

"How recently?" I asked, puzzled.

"Even as he paused to observe us outside the café. In fact, I believe that he has 'fallen ill' because he recognized someone."

"Some . . . one?"

Irene toasted me with my own glass. "You, my dear Nell. I must congratulate you: you have led a most delicious and likely dangerous mystery straight to my doorstep." She eyed Godfrey with rather ferocious jubilation. "To *our* doorstep, my dears. Now we must keep our guest alive so we can learn who is trying to kill him, and why. And we must discover why our formidable documenter Nell does not recall a man who remembers *her* so vividly that the passage of years and a major dislocation in place does not deceive him even on the brink of physical collapse."

"He is not in the least respectable," I protested in explanation of why I should not be expected to recognize such a man.

"That," said Irene severely, "is no excuse."

## Chapter Six

# A POISONOUS PAST

**The cottage** at Neuilly was becoming a routine rest-stop for wayfaring strangers. I watched from the front parlor that afternoon as Dr. Mersenné arrived in an officious hush and was rapidly ushered upstairs. I was reminded of Louise Montpensier's arrival on the premises just last autumn: disheveled, wet, hysterical and freshly tattooed.

In Louise's case, there was the evidence of good jewelry upon her person to recommend her. All the turbaned stranger bore in the way of mitigating accoutrements was European underwear, according to Irene, hardly a recommendation in conventional circles!

Still, I shared the anxiety that attends a crisis. My worry was increased by the troubling fact that the man had indeed seemed to know me—or to recognize me, rather. Irene's assertion that the fellow had been attacked in some invisible way right before our eyes—or behind our backs, to put it more accurately—was even more disturbing. It promised that this inconvenient person would not simply vanish from our lives as swiftly as he had appeared, at least not until Irene had satisfied herself as to his identity and discovered the reason for the apparent attack.

I should inject here an architectural note. Although our residence at Neuilly was commonly referred to as a "cottage," this was not the humble, squat dwelling to be found dotting the English countryside. This cottage was two-storied and rambling, like all buildings that date to an assortment of centuries past. It offered narrow stairs, low doorways, and floors paved in slate, stone or broad wooden planks. The place thronged with dormers and unexpected window seats, and the kitchens were a flagstone-floored horror reminiscent of Torquemada's torture chambers, replete with wrought-iron hooks and a massive, man-high hearth perfect for spitting a pig. Numerous bedchambers nestled under the lead-tiled eaves above. The entire arrangement demonstrated that French facility for combining the grand and the cozy. I must admit that I found it amenable.

So we had room aplenty for any unclaimed wretch lucky enough to fall into the path of Irene's curiosity. I kept my own curiosity, which Irene has often accused of being more sluggish than Lucifer after a culinary expedition to the surrounding fields, well reined, despite the hustle and bustle overhead.

At last patience was rewarded. A parade of footfalls on the ancient stairs brought the doctor down first, then my friends. I was reading the *London Illustrated News* with great concentration.

"A most bizarre case," Dr. Mersenné was declaring. "You are correct about the puncture wound, Madame Norton, but no ordinary medical needle made it. A hypodermic needle, no matter how fine, is hollow. Whatever pierced our friend's arm was not. Furthermore, it has taken a rather crude bite of his flesh. Most clumsy. Mademoiselle."

Dr. Mersenné nodded at me as Godfrey gestured him to the chintz armchair and offered him a glass of brandy. I have never known a physician to refuse spirits, and the French especially are no exception.

"Furthermore," he continued as Irene and Godfrey seated themselves before him like attentive pupils, "what is the point of skewering a fellow with a narrow point if one is not injecting some foreign substance? To get his attention?"

"His attention had already been deeply engaged by one of

our party," Irene answered. "You are certain that our guest has not received a recent dose of poison, then?"

"How can I be certain, unless the miserable fellow dies?" The doctor laughed long and easily. "Your own English doctors," he said, like everyone else wrongly assuming that because Irene was married to an Englishman and was friend to an Englishwoman she must be English and not American, "would perhaps nail down the diagnosis with a harder hammer, but my guess is that the man suffers from a chronic fever contracted on the Indian subcontinent."

"India." Godfrey narrowed his eyes and tented his fingers in his best barrister manner. "His dress, of course, comes from that part of the globe."

"I did not see him dressed." The doctor drained his glass and rose, his scuffed black bag again in hand. "But his complexion bespeaks many years in a foreign clime, if he is indeed an Englishman, as you surmise."

"He addressed us in English," Irene put in, "or, at least, he addressed Mademoiselle Huxleigh in that language. His accent was perfect."

"So is your French accent, Madame," Dr. Mersenné said with a bow that was a little too low and a little too long.

"That is true." Godfrey led the doctor to the passage. "Appearances can be deceiving and so can aural impressions." The two men ambled toward the front door.

"Well," I asked Irene, "is it poison or fever, and will he live or die? Like most physicians, Dr. Mersenné was indefinite."

She regarded me closely. Lucifer chose that moment to stalk into the parlor and brush against my skirts. Irene rummaged in a Sèvres box on the marquetry table until she had found a cigarette and one of Lucifer's namesake matches. I found her habit of prefacing the answers to momentous questions with such stage business most annoying.

Irene smiled at me through her veils of smoke, looking like a snake charmer working with a ghostly subject. "He may suffer from both: fever and poison. Doctors are so unimaginative. From my observation, the puncture wound would accommodate any one of a dozen hatpins I have on hand. Or that you have."

"A hatpin?"

"Do not sound so skeptical, dear Nell. I have put a hatpin to good use in my own defense on numerous occasions. Seven to ten inches of sharpened steel is nothing to underestimate, particularly if it is dipped in a toxic substance. Hatpins are miniature rapiers, and often a woman's best defense. Why could they not be a man's downfall?"

"I have never regarded a hatpin as lethal," I admitted, "but then I see the world with the innocent eyes of a parson's daughter." At this announcement, Lucifer narrowed his emerald eyes and leaped onto my lap, there to switch his tail most commandingly. "Why must this creature cast himself upon my skirts?"

"Apparently innocent parson's daughters are as attractive to cats as they are to mysterious strangers."

"Oh, I see I will never live it down," I retorted. "And you still have not said whether the man would live or die."

"I do not know, Nell, any more than Dr. Mersenné does." Irene snuffed her cigarette, then rose and smiled down at me. "All I know is that the swarthy gentleman upstairs requires constant tending. We shall have to take turns nursing him, you, Sophie and I."

"I can stand guard as well," said Godfrey as he returned from seeing the doctor out. "Who will take first watch?"

They stood there, shoulder to shoulder, my handsome friends, and eyed me blandly.

"Perhaps Nell should," Irene suggested at last. "After all, the man is asking for her."

I stood so abruptly—and unthinkingly—that Lucifer thudded to the floor with a furious hiss. The sound was echoed by the parrot Casanova in his cage, but no noise was louder than the oceanic roar of my inner disbelief.

A sickroom always reminds me of a wake to which no one has yet come. My melancholy in the presence of illness is no doubt due to my lot as a parson's daughter. From an early age I made myself useful to my father and his flock, and running sickroom errands was one thing a child could do.

Simply closing the shutters in daylight and putting a dormant form in the bed linens had transformed our cheery upstairs bedroom into a slightly sinister place. A paraffin lamp glowed softly on the bureau, casting enough light to reveal the figure in the bed.

"He looks quite different," I exclaimed, keeping my distance nevertheless.

"A fascinating man," Irene said, her voice vibrant with its most dramatic timbre.

"How can you say that? You know nothing about him."

Her amber-brown eyes fairly scintillated. "Ah, that is what makes him fascinating. Speculation, darling Nell, is always much more exciting than information. What do you think of him now?"

"He will not—"

"Awaken? I cannot say. At the moment he is quiet. You may study him safely."

"I wish Godfrey were—"

"We are better off without Godfrey now."

"Why?"

Irene flashed me a probing look. "You might prefer privacy when you discover who he is."

"You are here, are you not? And I do not require privacy, I require belief. You really think that I know this man?"

"Not . . . yet."

I sighed pointedly and examined this most inconvenient person. Against the pallid bed linens, his profile was etched as sharply as charcoal on canvas. Not even illness could bring pallor to that tea-stained face. Yet his gaunt features were well modeled, and the absence of the turban revealed hair of a lighter brown than his beard, grizzled at the temples.

Drawing nearer, I found myself unable to guess his age. Perhaps the extreme thinness made him seem older. Certainly the sun had tanned his skin until it cracked at the outer eyes into a fan of fine lines.

He moaned and I leaped back, my skirts brushing against my shoes like a swiftly drawn theatrical curtain swaying over the boards. My heart beat in the same breathless rhythm.

"He will not bite, Nell. Quite the contrary. Sophie was unable to get even a leek gruel down him."

"Leek gruel! I can hardly blame the man. An invalid should have barley soup and custards, not some foreign fluid made from disgusting bulbs."

My indignation must have stirred the sick man. I heard another moan from the bed, and then—to my chagrin—my own name was intoned, or slurred, rather.

"Miss . . . Huxleigh."

I leaped backward like a scalded cat, despite Irene's promise that he would not bite. Who was this man? How dare he know me when I did not know him? Was it some kind of dreadful trick?

Irene's warm hand took my icy one in a firm grip, the only grip she ever used. "He cannot hurt you, Nell, but obviously you have inspired some powerful memory. Think! If he has been poisoned and should die, you may be the clue to his past, and to the poisoner. Is there anyone you have not seen in some years?"

"M-my late father."

"Someone alive, or presumed dead, perhaps. Someone from Shropshire?"

I had not thought of the county of my upbringing for many years. "No one from Shropshire would come to such a condition as this."

Irene's grip loosened in disappointment. "Oh, come now. As I remember, you yourself had come to a sorry state in London when I met you, but—what?—three years from Shropshire's genteel safety. You had been wrongly dismissed from your position, had no lodgings, no food . . . indeed, had I not intervened you might have become as hungry and ill as this man."

Her words prodded me closer to the bed. Was there truly someone I knew beyond this intimidating appearance? Someone from Shropshire? Or who had left Shropshire before I did?

My heart stopped. At least my hand, which had come to rest over that organ, could feel no flutter in the general vicinity.

"Yes, Nell?" Irene urged, her voice the intense hiss of a demonic barrister conducting a cross-examination. "What have you remembered?"

"Not . . . what. Who." I whispered, as she did, not because it was a sickroom, but because I hardly dared credit the notion that invaded my mind.

I leaned nearer the semiconscious man. Could this be what had become of my once-attentive curate, the sole man ever to have courted me in any manner, however tentative? Could this be Jaspar Higgenbottom, returned from converting the heathens of Africa, himself converted to sun and turbans and the scent of alien spices?

"Nell?" Irene shook my hand, which she still clutched.

"Er, no. This is no one I remember. The ears are wrong."

She leaned over me to inspect these organs.

"What is wrong with them?"

"N-nothing. These are quite well shaped and discreet. The person of whom I was thinking had far more prominent—and unfortunate—ears."

"Oh. A shame. And did this large-eared person of your acquaintance abandon Shropshire for a foreign land?"

"Yes."

"And why have you never mentioned this interesting globe-trotter from your past?"

"Because he was not! Interesting. I am sorry, Irene, but he was my father's curate for a time, and rather tedious, I fear. I am certain that he is still being tedious in Africa. But he is not here."

The patient reached up a hand of bronze. "Miss Huxleigh," he murmured.

I blushed.

"Most intriguing." Irene sat on the edge of the bed, her brow furrowed in concentration. "Whenever you go on one of your governess tirades he calls your name. Obviously, the sound of your voice as well as your appearance rings a bell with him. Could it be the schoolroom bell? Could this be a former charge?"

"Irene! I may be past thirty, and some of my erstwhile charges may be twenty or so, but I assure you that this man is not one of them."

"No." She regarded him cold-bloodedly. "It is hard to tell, of course, but I would guess him to be our age." She quirked a brow in my direction.

"Perhaps."

The sick man lashed his head from side to side, as fever victims do when trying to elude the heat and pain of their malady. I unthinkingly picked up the damp cloth Sophie had left in a Sèvres basin and dabbed at his forehead.

"Mary," he said suddenly.

I gave Irene a triumphant look and wrung the cloth out over the basin. "You see. Huxleigh is not a unique name. It is Mary Huxley, poor woman, who chafes his mind."

"Hmm." Irene looked unconvinced. She rose with a sigh. "Since you are doing nurse duty, you might as well tend him until dinner. Godfrey can stand watch then, and I shall take the first part of the night."

"You have given yourself the bitterest hours. He will be most restless then."

Irene grinned demoniacally. "He will also be most talkative. Call me if his condition should worsen."

She was gone, leaving me with a cloth dripping onto my sleeve cuff and a delirious stranger on my hands.

"I see her game, of course," I told my indifferent charge as I swabbed his face again. I was getting quite used to the sun-darkened skin, despite the man's obvious English origin. No wonder Irene was curious; this man must have quite a tale to tell should he live to murmur more than a few ambiguous names. "She hopes that I will meditate upon your features and recognize you from mere proximity. But I shan't."

I sat back in the straight chair by the bedside to watch and wait. His face had turned toward my voice, although his eyes had remained shut, an arrangement I much preferred. "Mary," he murmured again. A name infinitely more common than Penelope, I reflected smugly. For once Irene the Female Pinkerton was utterly on the wrong track. "Little Mary," he repeated, stirring my sympathy, for the man obviously spoke of a child. "And Allegra."

This name caused me to sit up straighter. Allegra Turnpenny had been one of my charges during my last position of governess a decade before, at the end of the 'Seventies . . . and a Mary Forsythe was one of her little friends who had come to the house on Berkeley Square!

"And Miss Huxleigh," he went on in a mumble that I was thankful Irene was not present to hear. "Berkeley Square."

And suddenly I knew! I leaned forward, studying these altered features for any trace of their original expansive merriment. There was none. Yet, oh, I was grateful for Irene's pragmatic "privacy."

For somewhere beneath this weather-worn mask lay the face of my charges' young uncle, Mr. Emerson Stanhope, who had gone so gaily off to war in a dazzling red uniform. Who had once played a surprise game of blindman's buff with me in the schoolroom and touched my naive heart with a deathless and most inappropriate hope for one who was far above my station.

The door to the chamber swung slightly ajar. I started as if caught filching handkerchiefs. A shadow tumbled in from the passage. Lucifer swaggered over to the sickbed, then bounded onto my lap. For once I felt no urge to instantly unseat the beast, but let him curl into my skirts and proceed to purr and rhythmically dig his claws against the grain of my plaid wool skirt. I drove my fingers into his long hair as into a muff and finally felt warmth tinge my fingertips as shock eased into a kind of stupor.

And so I was when Godfrey entered the chamber an hour and a half later.

"All well?" asked he.

"He has not stirred," said I, picking up the sleeping cat and slipping from the room.

If Godfrey noticed anything odd in my manner and gazed after me, I did not look back to see.

## Chapter Seven

# DELIBERATE DEATH

"**How did** your vigil go last night?" Godfrey asked in his most persuasive baritone at breakfast the next morning. He lifted a small crystal jar. "Would you care for some marmalade?"

"Quite peacefully," I replied, taking the marmalade jar. "And how are the sausages this morning?"

"Excellent," said he. "So there was no disturbance to your patient?"

"None at all. Slept like a lamb. Would you care for some ham?"

"No, thank you."

"And did the patient have an episode during your watch?" Godfrey shook his dark, handsome head almost regretfully. "Nothing. He did not even call out your name."

"How disappointing. Is there any honey? Ah, thank you. And, Irene . . . did she mention anything significant occurring when she returned from her time on duty?"

Godfrey paused in dosing a croissant with a dollop of pale, sweet country butter. "Ah . . . it was rather late. We had other matters than your mysterious gentleman to, er, discuss."

"Truly? I cannot imagine Irene being distracted from a mystery so near at hand for anything."

Godfrey shrugged with masculine modesty. "She was fatigued, no doubt, from her late hours sitting up with the sick man."

"And she did not report any delirious revelations?"

"She reported delirium, but no revelations," Godfrey said at last with the hesitant air of a man conveying the exact truth in an utterly different context from the one under discussion.

"Then it has been a most unproductive night," I summed up, biting as daintily as possible into my condiment-laden roll. I dislike the taste of French baking, which is much over-rated by the easily led, and have been forced to resort to disguising the dough with sweets.

"I would not say that the night was unproductive." Irene swept into the small breakfast chamber in a blonde lace comb-ing mantle, her russet hair rippling over her shoulders.

It occurs to me that during the years I have recorded Irene's adventures, or rather, recorded my adventures while living with Irene, that my descriptions of her coloring have varied. For some annoying reason, the exact shade of Irene's hair, even her eye color, shifts with the hour of the day, the hues of her clothing and the range of her moods. Beyond being a gifted actress, she is a human chameleon upon whom the light plays tricks, sometimes painting her hair auburn, at other times brunette. Her eyes have that fascinating tiger's-eye qual-ity of mellowing to orbs of honeyed amber and darkening to coffee-dark brown when her pupils swell with agitation.

That gay, green June morning in Neuilly Irene was never-theless a walking palette of autumnal hues, as warming as well-steeped tea.

She accepted the coffee cup that Sophie instantly brought her and poured several dollops of clotted cream into it, care-lessly stirring the mess with the nearest utensil, a fork. Could the Beauties of Europe watch Irene eat whatever pleased her, there would be more than ground glass in her rouge pot, as happened once in the dressing rooms of La Scala.

"Well, my dears." Irene looked brightly from Godfrey to me, unaware of the current day's aura. "And have you been comparing notes on our patient's progress? What do you think?"

"That you hardly look as if you had sat up half the night," I answered tartly. I had slept barely at all after the strain of fleeing the sickroom and then toying with the dinner that had followed under Irene's formidable scrutiny.

Irene smiled. "Oh, I was up more than half the night at that, Nell, but *I* have not worried about confessions I must make in the morning, as you have."

"What confessions?"

"You might start," she suggested, sipping the scalding coffee with true American bravado, "by telling us the identity of the sunburnt hero upstairs."

"What makes you think that Nell knows?" Godfrey asked.

"Why do you call him a hero?" I demanded simultaneously.

She blinked and stared from one of us to the other. "My, but we are testy this lovely morning. To answer your questions: Nell has always known the man, Godfrey; she simply did not recognize him until last evening." Irene addressed me next. "As for his being a hero, I found a medal concealed in his shoe. What do you say to that?"

I sipped my tea, which had cooled to tepid peppermint consommé. "That I am relieved to learn that the fellow actually *wore* shoes."

Irene laughed delightedly. "You are doing a splendid job of pretending ignorance, but I could tell from your manner last evening that something troubled you. Surely only knowing the identity of the sick man could deaden your palette to Veal Malmaison."

"I suppose he revealed that while you were sequestered with him later?"

"Alas, no. He was as irritatingly mum on the subject then as you are now."

"Perhaps it is a conspiracy," Godfrey suggested, "between our Nell and the mysterious stranger from the East."

"You are a cold-blooded pair," I put in, "to show such

curiosity about a man who may be dying from some subtly administered poison."

"A hatpin is hardly subtle, Nell," Irene corrected me. "And I think that the poison it bore is not fatal to this particular victim. Besides," she added blithely, shaking her napkin free of pastry flakes, "his fever broke in the night. I expect him to be perfectly intelligible this morning."

I could not keep from jumping in my chair. "Why did you not say so the first thing? We must let the poor man know where he is, so he does not panic."

Irene's warm hand covered my icy fist like a tea cozy. "He will not panic. He knows he is among friends."

I was about to ask how this could be, but feared I would not like the answer. So we finished breakfast—or my friends did. I had suddenly lost my appetite, as I had last night at dinner. "I do believe I know him," I admitted at last, "but he has changed so much . . ."

"Perhaps you have as well," Irene said almost consolingly.

"I? Not in the least, I'm sure. After all, *he* recognized me, not vice versa."

"Do you wish to tell us of him?" Godfrey inquired.

"I would rather let him speak for himself," I said firmly. "He has changed so greatly that I dare not speculate on why or how."

"What a shame!" Irene smiled tigerishly. "Speculation is one of the few truly creative entertainments left to our modern times. I have been concocting plots on an operatic scale. I would hate to have our guest destroy them with the simple, dull truth."

We finished breakfast, each in our way, and repaired upstairs to confront the invalid. There he lay, brown upon the bed linens but pale in an inner, spiritual sense. Perhaps the breaking fever had also washed away his resolve.

Sophie made a self-important to-do about fluffing pillows and propping him up against them so he could speak with us. Despite the snowy nightshirt he wore, or because of it, his skin seemed strikingly dark, though his eyes no longer had the unnatural luster of illness.

He spoke in that disconcertingly perfect English while the rest of us studied his remarkable appearance in silence. "I apologize for inflicting myself upon your household. The maid tells me that you plucked me from collapse upon the cobblestones of Notre Dame."

Irene pounced. "Then you speak French, for our servant speaks no English."

He looked taken aback at this challenging response to his apologetic beginning, but added in the language of this land, "Yes, Madame, I speak French. Yet in any language I must apologize for casting myself upon the mercy of strangers. I cannot imagine what weakness came over me."

"Can you not?" Irene did not sound even slightly merciful at the moment. "Come, come, sir. You dissemble."

"D-dissemble?"

"Or, as the plain folk put it, you lie. At the least you mean to mislead us. You have suffered from fever for some time."

"But not in this climate, not so far north. Is this what you mean by deception, Madame?" He was more bewildered than defensive.

"Not at all. There is also your insistence that we are strangers to you."

"But—" He eyed Godfrey and Irene with rather pitiful confusion. "You are."

"And Miss Huxleigh—whose name you have called out not once but several times in your delirium?" Irene pointed to me at a moment when I most would have liked to sift through the floorboards into safe invisibility downstairs. "What is she to think of you now calling her a mere 'stranger'?"

"Really, Irene," I murmured. "The gentleman is quite correct."

The man's gaunt face had stiffened like a soldier's on parade. "I may have said a great deal of nonsense in my delirium. They do not call it 'senselessness' for nothing."

"On the contrary." Irene drew a side chair to the bed the

better to interrogate her victim. "You have not forgotten an iota of what you said while raving. It is merely that with a cool head again, you are prepared to deny it."

"I cannot blame you for thinking me a liar and rogue, considering the circumstances in which you found me. Give me my robes and I'll be gone."

"Oh, I cannot in good conscience do that," Irene murmured. "You are too ill."

"And this is how you treat an ill man, Madame?"

"This is how I treat a prevaricator, sir, well or ill. If you will not answer my questions frankly, I will be forced to bully the answers out of Miss Huxleigh."

The patient's eyes gleamed with fresh spirit. "I do not know what position this unfortunate lady occupies in your establishment, but she does not have to suffer such mistreatment."

"As I thought. You seek to protect her—now, and by your continuing silence about yourself."

A silence ruled the room. Godfrey had watched the exchange with the same sharp attention he would give to a rival barrister's cross-examination, as if more were going on than was evident. I myself was embarrassed by Irene's rough accusations. Yet she had hit a nerve. For the first time I saw color flush that dusky visage.

The man sighed. "You overestimate the chivalry that I am capable of at this point in my life," he said wearily. "It is far more likely that I seek to protect myself."

"And your identity," Irene prodded. She smiled and leaned back in the chair. "My dear sir, you have in the past few hours escaped a horrible and intentional death. Can the truth of your identity be worse than that fate?"

His expression became more bitter than the black coffee Irene and Godfrey consumed so copiously in the morning. "Truth is almost always worse than death, especially to one who has lived on the other side of the veil between East and West."

"Ah." Irene settled happily upon her hard chair. "A story. Begin with who you are."

"Should you not tell me your identity first?"

"A good point. I am a dead woman, sir, but you may call me Madame Norton. And this dashing gentleman is my husband, Godfrey, also presumed dead. Miss Huxleigh you know, and her mortality has never been in question, nor has anything else about her. Miss Huxleigh is of impeccable intentions. Her position in this household is as strict guardian of propriety, and a terrible tyrant she is, too."

"You jest with me," the poor man said.

Godfrey forsook his position lounging against the bureau to approach the bed. "My wife always speaks the serious truth, but often spouts ambiguities, like the Oracle. She means that she and I are wrongfully presumed dead and that we have not sought to correct that mistake. In my case, at least, it does not matter, as I was virtually anonymous before the misunderstanding occurred."

"And"— the man looked into my eyes for the first time— "is . . . Miss Huxleigh in truth the household terror your wife implies?"

"Miss Huxleigh is a stalwart member of the company, but at times her stringent standards do terrify my wife . . . a little, as I believe Irene meant to intimidate you into saying what you may wish to keep to yourself."

"What of this deliberate death she spoke of?"

Irene wasted no words. "Poison," she said. "Borne on the prick of a hatpin. You were infected in the crowd before Notre Dame, but I believe your chronic fever foiled the toxin by forcing your body to perspire it away before it could do its damage."

The man laughed. "Yes, it's hard for civilized toxins to harm a system that has been suckled at the breast of hellish Afghan and Indian plains for over a decade. I have quinine rather than blood in my veins by now."

Godfrey frowned and drew another side chair to the foot of

the bed. "News of this attempted murder does not surprise you?"

Hazel eyes burned in the bezel of that lean, dark face. "Living in India—not as the White Man does, in separate settlements and cool hill-stations, but as the native does—is a form of attempted murder far more serious than poisoned hatpins, sir."

"Oh, you must tell us your story," Irene ordered rapturously, "but first you must explain yourself to poor, dear Penelope. She has suffered enough confusion."

I wanted to die of mortification as those hazel eyes searched mine. He seemed to look only at me, and deeply into me.

"Do you not know me, Miss Huxleigh?"

"I—I believe that I do."

"Do you wish to know more?"

"I believe that Irene is right. I believe that I must know."

He sighed, spread his brown hands on the coverlet and examined them with a kind of weary wonder. "You have before you a dead man, too, Mr. and Mrs. Norton, in everything but the fact of my breathing despite all attempts to end it—my own and others'. In my youth, I was the flower of English gentility, one of hundreds of sturdy blossoms stripped from the bush of England at their peak and exported to a foreign clime. I was sent off to war in a smart uniform with scarlet trousers, with white-gloved hands. With no blood on anything but my morning razor."

"Who were you, in this world of long ago?" Irene wondered.

He studied the figured coverlet, as if its loose-woven hummocks and valleys were an unfamiliar landscape from which he could not tear his eyes.

I found myself answering for him, saying the words he had lost the will to affirm. It has often been my role in life to act for others in this fashion, but at no time has it been more difficult. "Young Mr. Stanhope," I said, my voice remarkably clear, remarkably civilized-sounding, as if I were announcing him to the Queen. "Mr. Emerson Stanhope of Grosvenor Square."

"Stanhope." Godfrey raised a raven eyebrow. "It is an honored name in the Temple."

"And so it shall remain as long as I stay lost and forgotten. But now . . . I must venture from the foreign bolt-holes in which I have hidden for so long." He glanced at me. "And I fear I will bring pain and disgrace upon those who have known me." A flush of color surfaced again in the hollows of those sunken cheeks.

"How do you mean 'disgrace'?" Irene probed.

"That bitter battle is long forgotten. If I survived, others as deserving died that day. Others even more deserving had their reputations tarnished far beyond what the mere metal of medals and history books can honor. I was content to let the dead lie unavenged, coward that I am. Now I fear that a living man will pay the price of my stupidity and my silence, so I must return to England to set things right, if I can. Though nothing can right the perfidy of that day when men and horses died by the dozens in the dust of those brutal plains under the damned, underestimated, relentless thunder of the Ayub's artillery."

"Of what battle do you speak so harshly, Mr. Stanhope?" I asked. I confess that I have never paid much attention to these innumerable skirmishes with outlandish appellations so often fought under foreign skies by my countrymen.

"Maiwand," he answered in loathing tones, as if mouthing the devil's pet name. "A black day for England, and for Maclaine, and for a fool with the youthful hubris to call himself 'Cobra.' "

I barely recalled this engagement, but Irene raised an imperious hand, leaning forward in her chair, her eyes gleaming with dawning intelligence. "Maiwand was nearly a decade ago, Mr. Stanhope. Its name is forgotten except in the military histories, though it was far from England's finest hour. What is the present danger? What is the name of the man you seek, whose life you fear for?"

"A man who saved my own life."

"And who is he?"

Young Mr. Stanhope—and so I still thought of him, despite the lapse of years and his present, much-fallen circumstance—was strangely silent. His sun-darkened face held that inscrutability said to accompany an Oriental turn of mind. This was not the blithe youth who had left Berkeley Square in high spirits but a decade before.

"I know naught of him but those few hectic minutes we shared amid a battlefield dust storm," he finally said, picking at the crochet work—my own—on the bed linens.

Irene leaned back, looking even more inscrutable than he. "Now you truly intrigue me, Mr. Stanhope. You seek a nameless man, whose face must have been obscured when you encountered one another during the heat of battle and whose semblance is certainly time-blurred by this late date. Please tell me at least that he is English! That would narrow the field of search somewhat."

"Why should he not be English?" Mr. Stanhope shot back.

"He might have been an enemy, or an Irishman."

Mr. Stanhope laughed at her quick retort and sardonic wit. Irishmen were frequently soldiers of fortune and ever the enemy to England even as they served under British rule.

"He is European," Emerson Stanhope conceded in a raw voice of weariness, though the cautious fire in his eyes that Irene's questions had lit remained unbanked.

"I am relieved." Irene stood, catching Godfrey's eye. "Then you are in the right place. Perhaps we can help you find your quarry."

"I do not require help, save in your kindness to an ill man."

"An ill man and a hunted one, I think." He made a denying hand gesture but Irene ignored it. "It seems that the life this mysterious gentleman saved is not much regarded by its owner, for that life also appears in fresh and more sinister danger than ever on a battlefield."

"I merely suffer a relapse of fever. It is you who are delirious, Madame, with your hints of poison and conspiracy."

"I am often taken that way," Irene said lightly. "It comes of an apprenticeship in grand opera. Forgive me for harrying you at a time of such weakness. I will leave you to the tender nursing of Miss Huxleigh. No doubt you both have much to discuss."

Her skirts rustled imperiously as she swept out of the bed-chamber.

Godfrey paused by the bed. "If you feel strong enough tomorrow, we can move you to the garden for a time; fresh air should do more for fever than anything else."

Mr. Stanhope's hazel eyes crinkled at the corners. "And a smoke, Mr. Norton? I admit that I could use a decent smoke. Outdoors it would not disturb the ladies."

Godfrey laughed at that, no doubt well aware that the activity would never discomfit one lady in particular. "If you hope to hide from my wife's curiosity behind a haze of cigar smoke," he said, "I warn you that it will not do. But the smoke itself can be arranged."

I followed him out to find Irene waiting in the narrow upstairs passage like a governess ambushing a miscreant. "Nell!" Her voice was low and urgent. "You must find out more about Mr. Stanhope's mysterious mission—and his even more mysterious past."

"I must do no such thing! Irene, the man is ill. Have you no shame?"

"He is not so ill that he cannot obscure his motives and plans. Nell, this is for his own good. Mr. Stanhope has obviously been long abroad and is not well suited to conduct the sort of inquiries he intends."

"He is wise enough to dodge your impertinent questions!"

"Then you must put to him some less impertinent queries that he will not avoid. I count upon your impeccable tact, your undying sympathy and your eternal concern for an-other's own good. You must find out more about your old acquaintance—and soon. For I fear he will not live long to tell anyone more if he is not taken in hand."

Godfrey met my skeptical look with a sober nod. "Irene is

right. There is something odd about the fellow. He has obviously lived outside the pale in India and environs. Englishmen seldom turn renegade in such climes without reason.''

I turned reluctantly back to the bedchamber, my mind churning with doubt and fear. And curiosity.

"And while you are at it," Irene added in her best operatic sotto voce, which carried to me even as I opened the door, "you had best find out why he was called by that intriguing sobriquet, 'Cobra.' "

I shuddered, for I have never liked snakes.

## Chapter Eight

# PILLOW TALK

❧

"**Your** ... friend is a determined woman."

I paused in opening the shutters. If I meant to throw light on my long-ago acquaintance's situation, the actual light of day might draw forth a corresponding candor. Besides, the hushed, dim intimacy of the sickroom made me uneasy, as did the familiar but utterly altered figure upon the bed. I opened the shutters, and the clear morning light poured in.

"Irene has had to be determined," I said, taking the hard chair by the bedside with a false calm. I was not used to playing interrogator.

"Tell me about her," he suggested after a pause. "At first I thought you were employed in some manner in the Nortons' household. Are you actually mere friends?"

"Yes, I am," I said, laughing at his confusion. "And more. I assist Godfrey with certain legal matters, and—although no one can be said to assist Irene; she is far too independent—I make myself useful to her as well. I am not quite employee nor family member. I suppose you could accuse me of idleness and waste."

"You 'make yourself useful,'" he repeated soberly. "That is more than I have done in the years since I last saw you in Berkeley Square."

"Surely the wish to save a man's life is of a high order of usefulness?"

"You have not aged," he said, abruptly changing the subject.

"Of course I have. I am past thirty."

He smiled. "So am I, but a woman should not confess such things so easily."

"I am not the kind of woman who would find any advantage in coyness, Mr. Stanhope. Why would I wish to conceal my age except to deceive someone, most likely myself?"

He eyed me with some perplexity, as if he actually found me—perish the thought—fascinating in some respect. I am not used to being regarded in such a light, although I have often seen its beams showered upon Irene.

"I am quite astounded to find you here in Paris, in such circumstances," he went on.

"Indeed, Mr. Stanhope! You take the words from my mouth."

He frowned again, in the way of a baffled boy. "I do not remember you as being so quick-spoken."

"Ah." The memory of our youthful selves had induced in me a strange tongue-tied tartness that even now I could not explain. "I was far younger then, and had seen a bit less of the world."

"What of the world have you seen now?" His tone was so jocular that it unaccountedly offended me. Certainly he expected this country mouse to have ventured not much farther than the parson's pantry. Yet I knew myself to be no match for the exotic adventures that had occupied his life.

I folded my hands upon my lap, as they become restless when idle. Naturally Lucifer, who had been sitting docilely enough upon the elbowboard at the window, proceeded to loft into my lap. Mr. Stanhope awaited my answer.

"I have worked as a drapery clerk at Whiteley's and as a typewriter-girl in the Temple. I have been privileged, if you can call it that, to see several freshly murdered corpses and to have solved a cryptic cartograph that led to buried archeological treasure. I have been to Bohemia and have met a king, although I did not much like him. I have also met a princess-to-be, and came to like her despite myself. I have never liked Sarah Bernhardt or Oscar Wilde, however much they may claim to cherish me; nor do I have anything but the most profound distaste for snakes, satin slippers, French cuisine and the dreadful Casanova. Lucifer is not among my favorites, either, though I would never neglect him."

Poor Mr. Stanhope struggled more upright among his feather pillows, which were as overblown and airy as French pastries. "The King of Bohemia? A princess? Bernhardt and Wilde? Casanova and Lucifer? I fear my fever has not waned, after all."

I smiled at his agitation, a sign of recovering strength, and stroked the black cat, who at least felt amiable if he did not behave so. "This is Lucifer. He is Persian and Parisian. A gift from Irene upon my arrival here last year. Most unwanted, I might add."

"Afghan," Mr. Stanhope said in a clear, bitter voice. "The breed is Afghan. Persian is a misnomer."

"He is misbegotten, I'll give you that," said I. "But you mean to say that such cats originated in the unhappy land where you fought in that battle, My . . . My—?"

"Luckily for you, it is not 'your' anything. The battle was called Maiwand, after an insignificant village on the site." Lucifer, like all cats knowing himself to be under discussion and reveling in it, bounded soundlessly to the bed and stalked over to inspect its resident. "He's a handsome fellow. This sumptuous breed of cat is the only exportable product of that unhappy landscape, though I've spent enough years scraping over it like a scorpion. You must have been referring to domestic pets with all that King of Bohemia and Bernhardt and Wilde business."

"Certainly not! I am not personally fond of those persons but I would never compare them to animals. That would be quite . . . disrespectful. To the animals, no doubt. That would be something—"

"Something that your friend Madame Norton would do."

"Exactly," said I righteously. "Irene can, at times, be shockingly irreverent. But she means nothing by it."

"Of course not." He did not sound at all convinced, but I am used to the people around me contradicting my convictions, having resided for so long with Irene.

"Why did you take such a dislike to Mr. Wilde?" he asked. "I have overheard much of him in the cafés since I came to Paris."

"You habituated the cafés?"

"Only the fringes. But tell me how Wilde offended you."

"For one thing, he is such a man with the ladies, always throwing himself into tortured metaphors in our praise and flinging flowers and quips at our feet. I may know little of the world, but I know that nothing good can come of it. He was quite taken with Irene, I'm mortified to say that she insists he also harbored a fondness for myself."

"And Madame Sarah Bernhardt?"

"Quite an immoral woman, and utterly willful. She let Irene fight a duel disguised as her son, can you imagine it? I tried to stop it, but Sarah, of course, can be quite forceful for such a small woman. And I am not at all certain that her hair is its natural color."

He shook his head. "I fear I still suffer from delirium, Miss Huxleigh. The picture you paint is exceedingly different from what I would expect of our placid governess of Berkeley Square."

"There are times that I find my life since then a delirium, too, Mr. Stanhope. Really and truly, it is for the most part excessively dull, unless Irene becomes involved in one of her tangles."

"She has ambitions of making me into one of these 'tangles,' does she?"

"Possibly, but the tangles come to her, rather than vice versa. I would not underestimate her, Mr. Stanhope. She found a missing girdle of diamonds that belonged to Marie Antoinette. Later, she saved a young Parisian girl from disgrace and freed the demoiselle's poor aunt from a charge of murder. Ignore her flamboyant ways; Irene has done much good, despite herself."

"No doubt due to your good example."

"Well . . ." I smiled modestly. "Certainly I have offered advice on occasion. She, being an opera singer by training, suffers from an impetuous nature and requires the moderation of a cooler head. That is where Godfrey comes in so usefully, although he is so besotted at times with his bride that his normal sensible nature can be corrupted—only in the most minor ways, of course. If it were not for me, who is to say upon what questionable ventures Irene might lure him?"

"Not I!" Lucifer had settled at the invalid's side and had begun grooming his glossy black flank. Mr. Stanhope stroked the cat's flowing ruff. "You are a virtual Scheherazade, Miss Huxleigh, spinning exotic tales. I cannot believe that you are the same diffident, lonely young person I knew."

"You did not know me, Mr. Stanhope. A governess is but one step up from a servant. And I was not lonely! I had my two charges, Charlotte and Allegra—how grown they must be by now. Young ladies . . ." My sigh was echoed by Mr. Stanhope's.

"I cannot tell you how many times I thought about Berkeley Square when I was abroad," he said fiercely. "It came to symbolize the innocence of England in a world vastly more dangerous. Once I found myself captivated by that crueler, older world. Once I thought I could be at home in that landscape of clashing opposites and raw gemstones and crude hopes. Yet I always came back to dreaming of England, particularly of Berkeley Square. Remember a day when I surprised you and the girls and their friends—little wren-haired Mary Forsythe, remember her? You were barely taller and older than they, playing blindman's buff. I joined in for a few moments. Do you recall such a day?"

"I—I may," said I, brushing the black cat hair from my cream wool skirt. I could not quite look at him, so my eye focused on Lucifer, disapprovingly. "That animal is most inconsiderate of his leavings! Perhaps I could spin these wasted quantities of his hair into yarn and put some part of him to good use in my crochet work. Did they spin cat hair in Afghanistan, Mr. Stanhope?''

He was regarding me strangely. Indeed, my face had blossomed with sudden warmth. I was again that speechless girl of two-and-twenty, not a woman of the world who could regard a corpse without blanching and had resisted the overtures of such scandalous persons as Oscar Wilde and Sarah Bernhardt. Now a virtual stranger was unraveling me simply because he had seen me as I was and would not be again, and had not forgotten.

"You do remember?'' he pressed so eagerly that I had not the heart to deny him.

"Yes, I do. You were . . . amused by me.''

"Not amused. Surprised. You always seemed so grave and stern in company, like a little tin soldier sent out from your father's parsonage in Shropshire. Huxleigh, the prim and proper governess. Then there you were blindfolded, stumbling about the schoolroom like a schoolgirl yourself. How shocked you were to find me suddenly in the game.''

"Yes, I was. You played a rather . . . startling trick on me. I had not meant for any of the family to see me in such an undignified state.''

"But it was charming! I knew, of course, your circumstances. How your father's death had left you orphaned; how well suited you were to teach my dear nieces. Yet it must have been difficult for one so young and strictly reared to shepherd girls so near to her own age.''

"Not difficult at all! The girls were delightful, the situation most pleasant. I often . . . recall those days, that day, myself. We were all so innocent then.''

"Yes.'' His hazel, searching eyes turned inward again, much to my relief. "We were all so innocent then,'' he parroted in an astringent tone.

The silence grew so long and awkward that I cast desperately about for some safe topic of conversation, for a matter not rooted in the past, but the present.

"But you must tell me about yourself!" I blurted with forced brightness.

Those pale, piercing hazel eyes penetrated me as a knitting needle transfixes a ball of yarn. "Why must I?"

"It is what . . . old acquaintances do: they recall old times by revealing more recent ones. I merely wish to make conversation."

He frowned at me with suspicion. "Why should you wish to make mere conversation now? You had no time for such frivolities years ago."

"Obviously, I have consorted with the frivolous since then."

"Indeed." Amusement crimped his mouth. "I can see that you are vastly changed. As am I. There is no point in conducting a Cook's tour of my alterations; they are visible enough in my appearance and my circumstances."

I leaned forward in my eagerness to convince him. "But you left England a young officer on the brink of a brave military adventure! Your family was well connected, your future promising—er, not to say that it is no longer so, of course. What I mean is . . ."

"What you mean is that Miss Huxleigh desires to know the full extent of my fall from what this world calls position and what some might call 'grace.' You wish to satisfy your curiosity about how I have come to such a low state."

"No! Not I! I wish to know nothing of a sordid nature. Though your . . . er, circumstances, of course, are not sordid. I merely wish to offer the solicitude of one who knew you when, when—"

My blathering discomfort finally stirred him to response. His brown hand, surprisingly warm, clasped mine as he confessed, "My dear Miss Huxleigh! You must forgive a man who has led a hardened life among a foreign people for failing to realize that only Christian concern motivates your questions. Of course I see that it is your duty to learn as much of me as possible, so that you may better minister to my depraved soul. But, I warn you, my confidences may be shocking in the extreme. There are certain episodes involving the harem of the emir of Bereidah and various social practices of the Kafkir tribesmen in regard to manhood rituals—"

"No!" I snatched my hand back though his grip was disconcertingly firm. "I wish to know none of this. It is Irene who has an insatiable appetite for unseemly knowledge, not I."

"Ignorance is bliss," he quoted. I detected an unbecoming slyness in his tone that I chose to ignore.

"Ignorance is peace of mind," I returned.

"But you shock me," he went on.

"I? How could I shock anyone?"

"You underestimate yourself. For one thing, you seem utterly in the control of this American woman."

"That is untrue."

"Yet you spy for her."

"I only inquire into matters that are for your own good. How can you expect anyone to help you unless you reveal yourself?"

"I expect no help," he said in an uncompromising tone that sent chills through my veins. Gone was the merry youth who had stooped to play a schoolgirls' game. The man who spoke now could kill, I think, and he was no longer amused by me. "I did not ask to be taken to this pleasant cottage," he went on, "to be charitably tended and uncharitably interrogated. I suspect you have no personal interest in me at all."

I blushed, this time from an all-too familiar emotion, shame. "I did not wish to pry, but Irene is determined to help you. She insists on aiding anyone caught in the skeins of a puzzle that is beyond their ken. There is no arguing with such an impulse."

"Irene, Irene! You quote her as the vicar cites Scripture on Sunday. Can you not speak for yourself, Miss Huxleigh?"

I straightened. "You misunderstand our relationship. Although I have at times . . . assisted Irene in her good works, shall we say, I have never hesitated to give her the frankest benefit of my advice and opinions on any subject."

"I am sure that she is much the better for that," he murmured. "So you admit, then, that although you seek the secrets of my past on your friend's suggestion, your own curiosity—your own sense of duty, I should say—requires you to ferret out the truth."

"Of course. It is clear that you have led an adventuresome and possibly irregular life. Any decently helpful person would wish to understand the difficulties you have faced so as better to encourage you to . . . to put the past behind you and resume the life you left."

"And you always try to be a decently helpful person?"

"I do hope so."

He reached again for my hand, and indeed he was an invalid of sorts. A charitable woman can hardly withhold comfort from such a person, no matter his state of grace, or lack of it. Yet my heart began to beat most unevenly as his lean brown fingers brushed my palm and his eyes burned into mine with a mélange of amusement and keen insight and an odd flicker of challenge. I was appalled to find that during our conversation I had unthinkingly leaned nearer and nearer the bed, until we seemed to be in conspiratorial closeness, something resembling what the confessional must be for the Papists. The thought crossed my mind that whatever poor Mr. Stanhope might confide in me, I would be the judge of whether it was fitting or proper to pass on to Irene or not . . . and he had leaned toward me, as well, as the moment stretched into a strangely unsettling silence. I scarcely knew what to think, could scarcely think at all, gazing into his hazel eyes . . .

Then Lucifer, finding his luxurious position pinched as Mr. Stanhope shifted upon the bed, leaped down between us. We both started with surprise, and bent simultaneously to prevent the cat from landing askew when a sound like a sharp clap of hands exploded in my ear.

My heart spurted into a racing rhythm not at all pleasant as Mr. Stanhope seized my arms and conveyed me to the floor, falling atop me. The cat screamed like a banshee and writhed between us. Before I could catch my breath to protest this indignity as loudly and more articulately than Lucifer, the door of the chamber sprung open so violently that it clapped back against the wall like thunder. My heart pounded in the charged silence.

Godfrey and Irene stood on the bedchamber threshold, the small revolver so familiar from Irene's early adventures poised in her hand. I lay smothered and speechless in the tight clasp of Mr. Stanhope, unable to stir if my life had depended on it.

"When I asked you to entwine yourself in Mr. Stanhope's affairs, my dear Nell," Irene drawled in odious amusement, "I did not expect you to take my suggestion so literally."

While I sputtered without the breath to defend myself, Godfrey went swiftly to the window and from the side, flung the shutters closed. I cannot recall whether Mr. Stanhope helped me to rise, or I him, but we at least struggled halfway up before Irene raised a hand (not the one bearing the revolver, I am happy to report).

"Pray do not be overambitious of rising in the world just yet, my friends. At least come nearer the door."

And so I was herded like some two-legged sheep to the threshold, where Mr. Stanhope and I were at last permitted to stand upright. I put my hand through Irene's arm for support—Mr. Stanhope had offered himself in that role quite enough for one morning—and kept my eyes averted, not knowing what kind of foreign bedclothes our guest might be wearing—or not.

A whistle from the garden below caused Irene to tighten her grasp on the pistol. Godfrey cocked his head to listen intently beside one window. Then the amiable French of our coachman André shouted up the all-clear from below: *"Paré, Monsieur, Madame—paré."*

Godfrey released a breath and strode for the bed, where he began flinging the pillows about. Lucifer, on the floor, shook himself in royal outrage and strutted before us as if to demonstrate his valor, pausing only to swagger against each of us in turn and leave a swath of black hair glistening like a decorative horsehair band on our skirts and—I risked a glance—on Mr. Stanhope's quite respectable white linen nightshirt, no doubt borrowed from the coachman or Godfrey.

As Godfrey wreaked ruin on the pillows, feathers drifted over the disrupted bed's pale linen landscape like the winter's last and fleeciest snowflakes. I wondered why they had sprung a leak.

"Nothing here," Godfrey muttered. "So far."

Mr. Stanhope joined him in pillaging the pillows.

"I do not understand," I quavered to Irene.

She patted my hand where it curled around her forearm. "Someone has shot at you, Nell, or at Mr. Stanhope, rather. Or perhaps—" the stimulation of a new thought gave her lovely face a look of radiant delight "—at you both! Most interesting."

I found myself unwilling to cling to such a cold-blooded defender and moved my hand to my heart, which pumped feebly but evenly beneath my basque.

"Here." Mr. Stanhope's hand blended with the walnut finish of the left rear bedpost over which it hovered. "The bullet hit here."

Godfrey went over to look, then whistled softly again, a most vulgar habit he had acquired since meeting Irene. Certainly I had never heard him whistle so when engaged upon the practice of the law in the Inner Temple off Fleet Street.

"Went clear through," Godfrey said. "The power must have been tremendous."

Mr. Stanhope's forefinger filled the path the murderous bullet had ploughed through the wood. "An air rifle," he declared.

"Air rifle?" For once Irene sounded at a loss.

Mr. Stanhope eyed the revolver in her rock-steady hand with passing respect, then answered briskly. "A modern weapon, Madame, and deadly. The bullet is propelled by a burst of compressed air, and in the hands of a master marksman . . . Such weapons are sometimes used for shooting tigers in India."

"We are not tigers," I protested.

Mr. Stanhope regarded me—dare I say?—fondly.

"No, Miss Huxleigh, we are not." His expression darkened. "Though I was once, in Afghanistan, called 'Cobra.'"

Irene lowered her weapon but not the stern regard of her magnificent eyes. "I believe, Mr. Stanhope, it is high time for you to enlighten us all about what you have done since leaving England a decade ago."

Stillness—both of sound and motion—swelled in the small bedchamber as the tension does at the climactic moment in an opera. Then the cat Lucifer bounded across the rough floorboards, his claws skittering. Something clicked against something (I fear the chamberpot). Godfrey bent to retrieve what Lucifer had found for a plaything: a large misshapen blot of lead that even I recognized for a spent bullet of awesome and lethal size.

## Chapter Nine

# RETIRED, DUE TO DEATH

**In the** same cheery parlor where we three—Irene, Godfrey and I—had first heard the puzzling story of poor little Louise Montpensier and the odious forced tattoo, Mr. Stanhope unfolded another tale as compelling, one that would draw us from our rural Paris nest and into greater danger than any of us suspected that placid summer day.

He had dressed for the occasion in some clothes of Godfrey's that hung quite as limply on his spare frame as the shapeless foreign robes in which we had found him. Despite his privations, I sensed in this onetime acquaintance the same tenacious survival spirit I had seen in the late Jefferson Hope, the American frontiersman who had tracked wrongdoers for twenty years before seeing them punished only days before his own death from a heart condition.

I recalled Mr. Stanhope's odd comment that he had been called "Cobra" in Afghanistan, and his teasing hints to me that he knew intimately the customs of such a savage place, even those between its men and women. I really did not care to hear his tale for fear it should deprive me of a young girl's one moment of breathless admiration. Such moments were sufficiently rare in my life that I did not care to have one tarnished, not even by the person who had inspired it a decade before.

Irene had ensconced our guest in the tapestry-covered ber-gère, a kind of French easy chair, with—appropriately—an afghan over his knees. I had made it during Irene's many private singing concerts, when she was often accompanied by the parrot Casanova's razor-edged counterpoint.

Godfrey had filled Mr. Stanhope's lean brown hand with a snifter of the finest French brandy. Irene sat back, veiled in her favorite accessory for hearing bizarre tales, a haze of ciga-rette smoke. Mr. Stanhope accepted another vile cylinder from Godfrey with a faint smile of pleasure.

"Egyptian." He nodded to Irene. "Excellent taste, Ma-dame, for an American."

"I do have excellent taste, Mr. Stanhope, as you can see by the quality of my associates."

Mr. Stanhope eyed Godfrey and me in turn, then grinned. "Call me 'Stan,' I beg you. I have been too long among stran-gers, among those who would call my name only to distract me while a dagger tickled my ribs."

"Stan?" I repeated unhappily. It is a common name, more suitable for a plumber than a gentleman or a soldier. I admit that "Emerson" had reverberated in my memory and imagi-nation much more euphoniously through the years.

"An Army nickname," he explained gruffly. "It is short and it is sweet, and it does not remind me of days forever lost."

I dropped my eyes, unable to argue with the depth of emotion evident on his face.

"It began in the Army, the story you will tell us," Irene prodded thoughtfully. She was ever impatient for the meat of the matter.

"Indeed. So do most tales of death and betrayal and bloody incompetence. The details of our country's Afghanistan ad-venture from eighteen seventy-eight to eighty-one have faded already in the public awareness, and for good cause. The Great Game Russia and Britain played across the barren steppes of Afghanistan was not glorious for England."

"You refer to the eighteen-fifties' rout, the retreat from

Kabul and the slaughter of the civilians," Godfrey put in.
"The Afghans do not appear to be governed by the rules of
civilized warfare."

Mr. Stanhope gave him a sharp glance. "No nation wages
civilized warfare, Mr. Norton, though we emphasize the
atrocities done to us rather than those our own side commits."

Irene inhaled impatiently from her slender, dusky cigarette.
"Why would someone wish to kill you now, over a war that
you admit is already long forgotten?"

"Perhaps because I do not forget."

"Ah." She settled into the armchair with the innocently
arch pleasure of Lucifer curling himself up before the fire.
"Those who refuse to forget can be troublesome indeed.
What memory do you carry that is so valuable—or so inconvenient—to someone? We already know that you seek to save
the life of a man you do not know. Why is your own in
danger?"

"I still am not convinced that it is." At this assertion,
Godfrey elevated the distorted lead ball without comment.
Mr. Stanhope nodded wearily. "Hard to argue with a spent
bullet, but I think I know the marksman. He would not have
missed unless he had meant to."

"But," I put in, "we had bent down to catch the cat just
then, do you not remember? Our heads were down."

"According to where it entered the bedpost," Godfrey
added, "the bullet would have passed through your head had
you remained decently abed instead of chasing cats with
Nell."

"Nell?" Our guest stared at me with some confusion.

"A nickname," I explained a trifle smugly. "It, too, is short,
far more efficient than 'Penelope,' and Mr. Wilde cannot
make endless coy classical allusions on it."

He nodded slowly and savored his brandy. "I forget that
you have traveled far, as well. This is better than salty tea," he
declared suddenly.

"Whyever should you drink salty tea?" I wondered.

"Sugar is a rare and expensive item in Afghanistan, so precious that they drink their tea with salt. Even salt is so treasured that it is saved for only the tea."

"A most uncivil place for an Englishman!"

"You are right, Miss Huxleigh, which is why, after this second Afghanistan war, we English retreated to the civilities of India. Even the ferociously ambitious Russians appear to have tempered their hopes in regard to the area."

"Then why did you stay on?" Irene demanded.

"I could not return."

"Why not? You were unwounded, and you had a medal. That is more than most men take from wars."

"How did you—?" He attempted to rise but his weakness—or the brandy, or both—forced him to fall back.

"I searched your most intriguing apparel and found it in your shoe."

"That is no way to treat a guest, Madame."

Irene's golden-brown eyes glittered like murky gaslights through the blue fog of her cigarette. "You are not a guest, my dear Stan; you are a puzzle."

He frowned. "I begin to fear I have fallen into the lair of one more lethal even than Tiger."

"Your suspected marksman," Godfrey prompted.

Mr. Stanhope looked at me. "Your friends are formidably quick, Miss Huxleigh."

"They are curious as cats, I admit, but I do nothing to encourage their tendencies. Despite this indefensible interest in the most private affairs of others, they have been of actual assistance to some. Pray do not judge them harshly."

My comment brought a bitter laugh. "The opposite case is more likely," he said. "Very well. I will tell you what you wish to know, though it's an ugly story."

Irene held his gaze. "First, does that medal I found in your shoe belong to you?"

He started up again, fire burning in his pale eyes. "Before God, Madame Norton, you tread where the Tiger himself would hesitate. I would not dishonor myself by bearing another man's medal."

Irene shrugged. "A good part of mankind is more casual in such matters than you, and I imagine a great many of them populate Her Majesty's troops, especially in these degraded days."

He subsided, noticing that each of his aggressive gestures had caused Godfrey to sit forward in his chair with a decidedly tigerish expression. Once again he looked to me for enlightenment. "I trust that Miss Huxleigh does not suspect me of purloining medals."

"Never!" I replied. "I fear that my friends are more influenced by your present appearance than your honorable past, Mr. Stanhope."

He laughed then, softly, at himself, his hand stroking his beard. "I look a bloody wild man, I suppose. I had forgotten . . . Even when I first came to Kabul, and found myself adept at the local languages, my fellow officers looked at me aslant. It is not the done thing, you know, speaking the lingo like a native. Better to shout at them in English; they will not do what we wish in either case. But an ear I had, and few could speak Afghan or the various dialects. So they made me a spy."

"Ah!" Irene exclaimed rapturously, lighting another cigarette with a lucifer snatched from a dainty Limoges box painted with hyacinths. The scent of sulfur starched the air. Irene imbued even the most masculine occupation with an instinctive feminity—unless she wished to pass for a man, and then she doffed her ladylike habits in one fell swoop, like an opera cloak.

Godfrey nodded. By the engaged arch of his raven eyebrows I could see that the milieu of the mystery—a foreign clime, military matters, past treachery—were capturing Godfrey's interest as Irene's earlier, more domestic investigations had failed to do.

I, of course, could not have been more indifferent, save for the subject of our inquiry.

"A spy," Irene repeated in a dreamy, thrilling voice. "Sarah would love it."

Mr. Stanhope shook his head. "Grubby, thankless work, but Army life did not suit me. I liked being off on my own in the crowded native bazaars, eavesdropping among them, dressed like them, bandying a few words, as I realized that I could indeed pass as one of them."

"You must have been invaluable to the command," Godfrey commented.

"Not I. I was too lowly to report directly. I needed Tiger for that."

"Who is this Tiger?" Irene asked. "He sounds intriguing."

"I do not know. That was the point of the names, was it not? He was just Tiger, and I was Cobra."

"Cobra," I breathed. "It sounds so, so—"

"So much more dramatic than it was," he finished. "Serpents are supposed to be silent and swift, and that is what the occupation of spy demanded. My task was almost too easy," he mused. "My mastery of language is instinctive. I can hardly explain it—"

"An ear," Irene put in. "Singers call it perfect pitch. What others need to study, one can reproduce in an instant. I myself am able at languages, but you must be a born master. Do you sing?"

He looked confused, for good reason. "I've joined a chorus or two at camp. I'm reasonably true, but no soloist."

"Irene," I put in, "is an opera singer."

"Retired," she added swiftly.

He nodded. "Due to death."

"Due to *reported death*, which is much the same as the real thing."

"Naturally," I explained, "Irene has this perfect pitch she mentions. So she understands your gift."

"More of a curse," he said wearily. "It has kept me from England for a decade. But you ask about the medal. It was awarded to me for spying. That was before the court-martials came, and the charges in the aftermath of Maiwand. I might have lost it if I had stayed around, but I did not."

"You did not go home to England," Godfrey said, frowning. "Where then did you go?"

"Where no Englishman and no Russian would find me. I went the length and width of Afghanistan. To the brutal mountains of the Hindu Kush that thrust against the ceaselessly blue skies, to the farther mountains north of Kabul, through the eye of the Khyber Pass's twenty-seven miles of legend and death where brigands play gatekeeper, into the far eastern Afghan hills toward China, to the ice-bound lake along the Russian frontier. Into no-white-man's-land."

"You lived among the natives for ten years?" Irene's question was not so much incredulous as admiring. "You passed as they? You vanished, Mr. Stanhope, from the world of Berkeley Square, even deserted the comfortable hill stations of India's English settlements? What a . . . role . . . you must have played, have lived. And in all that time no one disturbed you?"

"No. Even when I visited India again, I buried myself in obscure native villages. Few civilized men ventured into that terrain. I wanted to lose myself, and it was easier than one might think."

"Why?" I asked, appalled at the waste of this fine man in that ungodly wasteland.

"I was sickened of war, of my kind, of myself. We lost at Maiwand, and there was treachery in it. Our troops took their stand in a deep ravine outside the village, but Tiger had failed to report a subsidiary ravine meeting it at a right angle. Through that sheltered slash in the terrain the Ayub Khan poured his formidable artillery. I was able to warn only one man the night before the battle, a friend, Lieutenant Maclaine. He pushed his own battery of artillery forward to cut off the Ayub's secret secondary attack, though Brigadier Burrows ordered him back to the agreed-upon battle lines."

"Where did you spend the battle?" Godfrey asked with interest.

"Unconscious near the village," Mr. Stanhope said bitterly. "I was attacked leaving camp. When I awakened, our forces were in retreat. Some British medical man came to tend my battered head. Even as he bent over me, a bullet knocked him aside. I now wonder if that ball was meant for me, even then. But I was swept up in the panic of retreat, and still half out of my head. The Afghanistan fighters harried our flanks through the mountains to Kandahar, which was the nearest Afghan city where we had troops garrisoned."

"And Maclaine?" Irene asked. "The young lieutenant who defied orders to forestall the treacherous attack. What happened to him?"

Mr. Stanhope regarded her with empty eyes, over his empty brandy snifter. "Captured while foraging for water near the village of Sinjini during the retreat. Held along with five sepoys in the camp of the Ayub Khan."

Irene winced, while Godfrey rose to refill Mr. Stanhope's glass. My old acquaintance stared into that bubble of crystal as if he saw the battle of Maiwand in it.

"You cannot imagine the heat and the dust," he said. "Our troops had recorded temperatures at one hundred and fifteen degrees Fahrenheit in June, when the *bad-i-sad-o-bist-roz*, the hot west winds-of-a-hundred-twenty-days, whip up dust devils all month, and this was almost July. We danced with dust until all was swirling, murky confusion punctuated by the screams of men and horses and camels. We had to abandon some of the field guns, abandon some of our wounded. Luckily, I had been attacked before I had managed to change from uniform back into my spy garb. I would have been a dead man for certain in my native robes amidst that mob of rampaging men.

"We stumbled back to Kandahar, an organized retreat in name only. The public soon knew the outcome: how we settled in to defend the city against siege; General Roberts's famous forced march to Kabul of ten thousand fighting men, eight thousand ponies, mules and donkeys and eight thousand followers, in three weeks, over three hundred miles of desolation at the very apex of the heat. This turning tide washed over the Ayub Khan's forces and resulted in his retreat, although he promised that the five prisoners would not be harmed. In the changing fortunes of war, soon the British were sweeping into Ayub's abandoned camp."

"And your friend, the lieutenant, and those sepoys? Were they there when our troops arrived?" I asked breathlessly.

"They were there," he answered.

"Alive?" Irene inquired sharply.

"Five sepoys were."

"And your friend Maclaine?" Godfrey asked.

"There, as promised." Mr. Stanhope sipped the brandy, then held its forbidding fire in his mouth for long moments before swallowing it in one great gulp. "Except his throat was cut. One long cut that nearly severed the head from the body. The body was still warm when our men got in."

I gasped, but no one looked at me. Mr. Stanhope stared into the yawning amber eye of his brandy snifter. Godfrey regarded his interlaced fingers; sometime during the tale he had sat forward, supporting his arms upon his legs. Irene drew on her cigarette until the ember at the tip glowed hellishly red, then snuffed it in a small crystal tray as if she found it suddenly distasteful.

"Afghan treachery," she said, but she was watching Mr. Stanhope carefully.

"No." He did not even look up. "According to the sepoys, Ayub had left instructions before he retreated that the prisoners were not to be killed. Yet a guard cut Maclaine's throat and wounded one sepoy who tried to stop it. Why would the Khan secretly countermand his orders in regard to only one man?"

"The only Englishman," Godfrey reminded him.

"No. Afghanistan breeds fierce fighters, and fiercer palace intrigues, but they are forthright folk in actual battle. Maclaine was of no danger to the Afghans."

"These five sepoys," Irene finally said. "Explain to me their part in the battle."

I was most relieved that she had asked that, as I had no idea what a sepoy was. As far as I was concerned, it could be some rare breed of lapdog.

"Native Indian troops. Noncommissioned," he said. "Good soldiers."

"They would have no reason to lie," Irene said.

"No."

"Unless—"

"Yes?"

"Unless they killed Lieutenant Maclaine. The guards had fled. There is only their word on it."

"But why?" Godfrey wanted to know.

"Perhaps they were bribed to absolve this Khan, this Ayub, of blame. Perhaps, as Stan's story implies, someone British wished to prevent Lieutenant Maclaine's testimony about his actions on the battlefield, about the unreported subsidiary ravine leading straight to the British line."

"What happened about that?" Godfrey asked, sitting straighter. "Surely there was a military inquiry?"

"There were inquiries, and a court-martial. The generals produced their reports, which varied depending on how long after the battle they were written. Much blame was laid on Mac. Of course he was the only one not there to defend himself."

"And where were you?"

He avoided our eyes. "In the Afghan hills. I did not learn of the charges, which came out a full year after the battle, until years later. By then it did not seem to matter."

"Why?" I asked. "Why did you . . . retreat so far beyond Kandahar? Into the wilderness? For all those years?"

"I was honorably discharged and free to go where I would. Native tales of treasure buried in the remote mountains intrigued me. Also, I was sickened by the method of Mac's death. If he had not acted on my information, he might be living today!"

"So you have refused to return to England and live the life you were born to because Lieutenant Maclaine could not, and you felt responsible for that." Irene spoke as dispassionately as a doctor.

Mr. Stanhope cupped the snifter in both of his bronzed hands and let the silky liquid roil like a brazen sea from side to side. "It is not so simple as that. I had reason to think that my life was wanted, too. So I saved it. By remaining lost in Afghanistan."

"Where you have been totally untroubled by anything, until—"

"Until I returned to Europe," he admitted.

Irene leaned forward, her hands taut upon her chair arms. "Why, Mr. Stanhope? Why have you returned? And why now?"

He sighed heavily. "I have learned a thing or two. I now believe that the physician who tended me in the field at the retreat from Maiwand survived also. I believe that he may be in danger. I will not have yet another man die on my account!"

"But how will you find him?" Exasperation tinged Irene's facile voice. She used it as a goad or a lure, that voice, and even when speaking she could imbue her words with all the emotional command of a coloratura soprano. "Ah. You are not quite as lost as you would have us think. You have a clue. You have—his name!"

He recoiled from her words as from a whip. "What is one name in a world full of so many?"

"A thread, Mr. Stanhope. And from a single thread whole cloth can be woven. Tell me his name."

"It will mean nothing to you! It is common beyond counting. You have no reason to know."

"We can search him out if something should befall you."

"How would you recognize him?"

"How will you, with all that battlefield dust and many years between you two?"

"This is pointless, Madame. I regret I have told you so much as my own name."

"Do you not see? It was your knowing something and

confiding it to so few that may have caused Maclaine's tragedy! Secrets aid conspirators, not truth-tellers."

"But this bloody name would mean nothing to you! None of this means anything to you. You are implacable, Madame. You are damn near Afghan."

"I reserve," Godfrey put in quietly, "the right to shout at my wife to myself."

Mr. Stanhope grew immediately silent, then ebbed back into his chair, exhausted. "Do you ever do it?"

Godfrey smiled. "No."

"I can see why not. She is . . . not to be denied."

"No," Godfrey said.

Mr. Stanhope set his brandy snifter on a side table and threw up his brown hands. "Watson," he said. "The name was Watson." He regarded us with weary triumph. "You see! The information is utterly useless. All you have learned is that curiosity can not only kill the cat, but also can be a cul-de-sac, Madame."

"Good Lord, man," Godfrey commented in awed tones. "Do you know how many thousands of Watsons there are in England? How many hundreds may be physicians?"

Nevertheless, Irene shut her eyes and clapped her hands together as if just offered a rare gem before inclining her head toward poor unknowing Mr. Stanhope.

"Ah, but you need not despair, my dear sir," Irene said, glancing significantly at me. "I may already know a most excellent place to start our search for the mysterious Dr. Watson. And Godfrey," she almost literally purred in closing the subject, "I believe that I will have some of that excellent brandy now."

## Chapter Ten

# KISSMET

**Mr. Stanhope** had to be assisted upstairs. The strain of sitting up to tell his tale had weakened a constitution already tested by years of privation and most recently—if Irene was right—an attempted poisoning. And although brandy is reputed to buttress the backbone, in this case it further sapped the system, in my opinion.

At his bedchamber door he thanked Godfrey for his support, wished Irene good night now that her questions had been answered, and requested that I remain a few moments, as he wished to speak with me.

I opened my mouth to decline—morning would do, but Irene rushed to speak for me.

"An excellent idea! You seem pale, sir, after recounting your Afghanistan ordeal. A watchful nurse for a short time would set all our minds at rest."

Her suggestion was sensible, at least, but to call Mr. Stanhope "pale," no matter how worn his condition, was a great stretch of the imagination, if not the sympathy.

So the pair of them helped Mr. Stanhope to bed, where he reclined fully dressed upon the feather quilt with a relieved sigh. Godfrey and Irene took a somewhat hasty leave, it struck me.

The paraffin lamp had been turned very low while the

chamber was unoccupied—Sophie was a tyrant about saving oil. I was expected to read and sew in a level of lamplight barely sufficient for seeing one's hands at arm's length. I went to turn up the light.

"Leave it be," he said.

At my inquiring look, he gestured to the window. "We do not wish to be too visible to the world outside."

"Oh." My hand darted back from the little brass turnkey as if it had been a viper's fangs. "Perhaps it is not safe to remain in this chamber."

"The odds are long that he will try again, but it is best not to tempt chance."

In the dimness of the tapestry bed curtains, his face was unreadable; only the extraordinary pearly glimmer of his teeth and eye whites caught the scant light. I sat on the straight-backed chair that would insure no nodding off and fell into an uneasy silence.

In my father's parsonage, visiting the sick was an obligation of the highest regard. Since a child I had sat for long hours beside many a sickbed; there I had learned patience and a respect for mortality.

Despite the nobility of the role, I found myself uneasy in Mr. Stanhope's presence. Perhaps it was the fact that he was fully dressed, oddly enough, although that should allay any notion of impropriety in my sitting up with a man in his bedchamber. Long custom makes clear that only when a man is laid utterly flat by illness can he be regarded as safe enough not to make improper advances to any nearby female.

Mr. Stanhope did not seem sick enough to erase any suggestion of scandal, at least from my mind.

"He," I said, my voice froggy from the long silence.

"He?"

"Your marksman. You know, or suspect, his identity."

"She did not pursue that."

"She?"

"Your friend. She cared only about the name of my battlefield rescuer."

"That is true, and also odd. But Irene has her instincts, and they will not be denied. Nor can I deny that such apparently wild guesses have served her well. Perhaps it is the artistic temperament."

He laughed. "Perhaps. I have not a jot of it."

"Yet you have led quite a . . . Bohemian life."

"Not at all, Miss Huxleigh. I have led an irregular life. There is a difference. That is even worse than being a Bohemian," he added mockingly. "And you . . . you surprise me. You have led an adventurous life."

"I? Not at all! I am a complete homebody. Although," I was compelled to add in all honesty, "I did once travel from London to Bohemia by train unescorted. It was highly improper of me, but the situation was desperate."

"By train? A woman alone? You see my meaning! That is the civilized equivalent of daring to dwell solitary among the brigands of Afghanistan, my dear Miss Huxleigh."

"Ah, but I have never been called 'Cobra.' "

He sobered at that; at least I no longer glimpsed the pale scimitar of his teeth.

"Although," I was again compelled to add in all frankness, "I once signed a cablegram by the code name 'Casanova.' "

"You! Casanova?" He leaned forward until the light limned his features.

At the time I had thought the ruse rather clever myself. "The parrot," I explained modestly.

"Ah, of course. A sagacious old bird. But you see? Coded cablegrams, unescorted train journeys. You have been quite an adventuress."

"Never! And only because Irene had summoned me to Prague. Even Godfrey—who barely knew her then—advised me against going, but I knew Irene would never call on me for a frivolity. And it was a good thing I went, for she trembled upon the verge of a fearsome scandal. I am happy to say that my mere presence insured that no one could speak against her dealings with the King of Bohemia. Quite a nasty little man, that, though he stood several inches over six feet tall." I shuddered in remembrance of the arrogant monarch.

"A cat may look at a queen," Mr. Stanhope said in amused tones, "but only a Miss Huxleigh may despise a king. You are so British, my dear Nell, and so innocently charming. I had quite forgotten."

I froze. "We had not agreed upon using Christian names, Mr. Stanhope."

"I asked you all below to call me 'Stan.' "

"That is a variation of a surname, not a Christian name. And even"— I took a great mental breath before I uttered it —"Emerson . . . is not a truly 'Christian' name."

"Perhaps I should not confess that my middle name is . . . Quentin, then."

"Quentin?" Alas. That, too, struck me as a highly euphonious, if unconventional, pair of syllables. "Quentin is quite—"

"A variation on the Roman Quintus. Quite pagan," he added, a teasing glint in his cairngorm eyes. "Yet I prefer it to Emerson, and was so called among my family and closest friends before I left for Afghanistan. I prefer it."

"Quentin is not uncomely," I admitted, "but it is decidedly un-Christian."

"So is 'Penelope,' " he shot back with alarming accuracy.

"Well—!" I did not know quite how to defend my poor parents' nonconformist choice of a baptismal name. "True, the name is of classical origin, but my father was highly learned, though a humble Shropshire parson. Penelope was an admirable and virtuous woman, who remained faithful to her roving husband Ulysses despite the clamor of suitors and his twenty-year absence."

"Yes, that does resemble Christian denial," he murmured, sounding alarmingly as Irene does at times.

"At least she was not consorting with some sorceress who enjoyed turning men into pigs!"

"Ulysses was a bounder to leave the lady languishing for so long," he admitted soothingly. "But if I have no true Christian name, and neither do you, is there any impropriety in using them between us?"

"I am certain that there is, but you have talked me out of it in that silver-tongued way that Irene puts to such good use. You are both too much for me."

"I doubt that, Nell. And would it be too much for you to assist me to rise? I wish to see the fabled garden that I am now forbidden to visit because of my usefulness as an apparent target. Sophie said the window overlooks it."

"Is it safe?" I looked uneasily to the window.

"Perhaps not, but it would be a shame to live in total safety. Besides, how can I sleep certain that nobody lurks unless I look?"

"You and Irene are two of a kind," I muttered as he shifted on the bed. I really had serious qualms about serving as his support. What if I could not bear up to the weight? I did not relish another humiliating tangle on the floor, this time without the excuse of an assassin's shot. But the ill often take odd notions, and I was not one to refuse them small comforts.

As he stood and lay an arm along my back and shoulder, my heart sank at the impress of alien weight. I should buckle like an overburdened banister, I feared. But then no more pressure came, and we made an awkward progress to the window, where he leaned a hand on the broad elbowboard and pushed the shutters carefully open.

It was as if a clumsy wooden curtain had been dragged away from the fairyland scene in a play. I confess I had never observed our formal French garden by moonlight, had never thought to enjoy it then. By daylight it displayed a rainbow row of hollyhock and heliotrope, larkspur and snapdragons.

But night's cool silver hand soothed the garden's fevered daytime brow, creating a pale landscape of subtle shape and shimmer and shadow. Utterly beautiful. Its perfume drifted up in a delicate, sheer curtain that was almost tangible.

We stood in silence.

He finally spoke. "When I thought of England in the ice house of an Afghanistan winter, in the sweltering swamp of

India, I pictured such serene, uncrowded beauty. I thought of Berkeley Square, teacups and crumpets, my rosy-cheeked nieces in organdy pinafores. I also thought of you, Nell, and the certainty that however the Empire sizzled abroad under brutally blue skies amid dirt and dust and a dozen vicious not-quite-wars, somewhere London fog danced a saraband on the paving stones and among hidden rosebushes in the back garden, and somewhere Miss Huxleigh was putting her charges through their gentle paces."

"And so I should have been," I burst out in frenzied self-incrimination, "save for the war which drove you from that vision! When your sister's husband, Colonel Turnpenny, was posted to India again, the family went, too, as did many such. I found myself unemployable, with governesses a glut on the market. I was forced to become a drapery clerk, and not very successfully. Had it not been for Irene, no doubt I would have starved on the streets. I am sorry to have disappointed you, but it was quite impossible for me to remain a governess. I was fortunate to become a lowly typewriter-girl, and actually was rather proficient at it, though it is a common enough skill now—"

He had grasped me by the shoulders partway through this speech, still leaning upon me somewhat and also, in an odd way, supporting me. A flutter like a caged bird beat within my breast as he spoke with rapid, even joyous conviction.

"But I am not disappointed! That is the point, Nell. I am astounded. The England I painted, that I painted myself into a far corner of the world to avoid, no longer exists except in the musty trunk of my memories. People have changed, even as I have. Times have, manners have. I have felt an outcast incapable of returning. And you, Nell, have shown me just how foolish I have been."

"Well." I could hardly take exception to serving as a model for seeing the error of one's ways. "That is quite . . . reassuring—" I decided to plunge into the deep waters I had so clearly been invited to enter "—Quentin." I would *never* call him 'Stan,' and that was that.

"You see," he said with a quite irresistible smile, "the old barriers crumble. You are not the governess Huxleigh anymore and I am not—"

I interrupted before he could finish. "—the dashing young uncle."

"Is that what you thought?" he asked.

I blushed in the dark and hoped the molten moonlight did not betray me. "That is what we all thought in the schoolroom. The girls adored you, as girls that age will."

He sighed, and his hands loosened on my shoulders. I swayed a little, surprised to discover that I had been relying upon his grip to stay upright, to find that I had willingly surrendered some of the usual effort of standing on my own two feet.

"You were hardly much older than they. That is why I will not hear talk of your disappointing me," he said, "when I have disappointed so many."

"You have not even given them an opportunity to be disappointed; you have deprived them of yourself. You must let them see you anew and judge for themselves. You have condemned yourself unheard, unseen."

"And you, Nell? How do you judge me?"

"I—I have no right."

"Forget our once-separate classes! You have opinions, that was always clear."

"I cannot say! You are so . . . different, and I have never known you, besides. You have lived a life I cannot even imagine; perhaps some of it would shock me. I would say, judge yourself. Go home! See your sisters, your old friends, your nieces."

"It would raise a hornet's nest—about the war, about wounds long healed. I fear the bad opinion of those I love more than bullets."

"Bad opinion can hurt more," I admitted, "but one thing I can tell you: whatever you have done, you do not have mine."

His hands tightened again on my shoulders, so swiftly it

quite took my breath away. "Bless you," he said in a low, intense tone that induced further threats of self-asphyxiation. "If *you* can say that, is there anyone I cannot face?"

He released one of my shoulders but I remained frozen, gazing up at his bronze face bathed in a sickle of icy moonlight. He seemed utterly familiar and utterly foreign at one and the same instant, and I felt that way myself.

In a daze, I felt his fingers pause at the point of my chin, and he tilted my face up as if to study a sculpture in better light. And then his face filled my vision. I felt a teasing tickle that reminded me of a boar's-bristle brush, his beard . . . and then his lips touched mine as lightly as moonshine. The faint flowery scent burst into full bloom around me as my closed eyes suspended me in a place with no bottom or top and no time.

How that moment—moments? minutes? eternity?—ended I cannot say. I felt myself drowning in a fragrant sea of alien yet not unpleasant sensations, so that my fingers curled into the soft folds of his nightshirt to keep myself from sinking. I was one adrift a maelstrom, embracing the strange, tender wave that sucked the very air from my soul, lost again in a suddenly adult game of blindman's buff. I recall that odd internal flutter in my chest bubbling over into breathless if belated retreat, and then a babble of parting inanities.

I next came to myself outside the bedchamber door, in the passage softly lit by the moonlike globe of the paraffin lamp. Its painted roses glowed as if alive and for a moment I held my trembling fingertips, suddenly cold, over its warmth. By its illumination I stumbled to my bedchamber, but though it was pleasant and familiar, it seemed confining. I wanted to burst outdoors, to run into the garden, but that was impractical and would cause comment, and I most of all wished to be alone, as alone as I had ever been. I rushed back into the passage. No, I must speak to someone—to Irene! I must hurry to Irene and tell her, ask her . . . but I could not rouse Irene and Godfrey at such a time, for such a matter.

I quivered in the hall like a hare frozen in the bright, silent blare of a full moon with no place to run. Then a long-ago refuge crossed my mind. I opened the door to what served as our linen closet. The space was cramped under an angled ceiling; it resembled my notion of a priest's hole from a distant century. I darted in and drew the door shut behind me. In pristine dark and quiet, I embraced a bolster smelling vaguely of camphor, and thought.

Time was irrelevant to my state of suspended confusion. The utter dark suited my mood, and so it remained for a long time, until light suddenly sliced into my surroundings—not the mellow bar of daylight dawning under the door that one would expect, but a vertical slash of lurid lamplight.

I had not thought so far ahead as to dread discovery. Its actuality stirred a mortification more profound than when I had been found raiding the parsonage tea tray at the age of four. I quailed before the questing shadow that bore the lamp, whoever it was.

"Nell!"

Irene's voice. I suppose it could have been worse, but not much.

"Nell, you were not in your bedchamber. You were not in our guest's bedchamber. You were not—"

"Why should I be in Mr. Stanhope's bedchamber?!"

"That is where I left you last," she answered reasonably. "What on earth are you doing here? And why—?"

"Must you shine that miserable light in my face?"

"No." Irene lowered it, then stepped fully into the crowded space. She closed the door behind her, taking care to sweep the lace-flounced train of her nightgown into the closet with her first. My hidey-hole glowed in all its homely clutter, lamplight reflecting from the white linens stacked around us.

Irene herself seemed a shining though girlish ghost, her burnt-honey hair backlit into an auburn aura that curled loosely over her shoulders, her snowy nightdress afoam with a phosphorescence of lace and satin ribbons.

She crouched beside me in a spindrift of silk and shook my wrist cautiously. "Are you quite all right?"

I still blinked in the sudden dazzle. "Did you need me for something?"

"No—"

"Then why bother looking?"

"I merely wanted to ensure that you had gotten safely to bed."

"Then you thought I was in some danger!"

"Well . . . a shot was fired into this house not a day ago."

"Yet you encouraged me to remain in Mr. Stanhope's chamber."

"Another attempt did not seem imminent. Was there trouble?"

"Nothing . . . of that kind."

"Ah." Irene placed the lamp on a vacant shelf and settled against a stack of coverlets, tucking her lacy hem over her bare feet.

"And you have gone roaming without your slippers!" I admonished.

"You have gone roving without your night clothes," she observed, eyeing my fully dressed state.

I suppose I did appear ridiculous, but then the look matched how I felt.

"I wanted to think," I explained in a rush, "but the garden is not safe, and I would not leave the house at night in any case. My room was too . . , familiar, and I did not want to rouse the household by going downstairs and being mistaken for a housebreaker. Besides, Casanova would no doubt squawk, and Godfrey might shoot me."

Irene received my confused recital with commendable sobriety. "Now that you explain your reasoning, I can see that the linen closet is a most ideal place to think. I am only amazed that I have not thought of it before. I have sorely wished a retreat myself from time to time."

"Oh, do not be so understanding! You know that I am in a perfectly inane position. You would never back yourself into such a ridiculous corner!" I clutched my bolster closer.

"My dear Nell, we are three unrelated adults sharing one

household, along with the servants. What is so ridiculous about seeking solitude? Even Lucifer wanders off and cannot be found at times."

"That is true. And Casanova has his cage cover to hide under, I suppose. At least he is quiet then. Usually."

"Indeed. Isolation is a rarity in modern life, yet we all need it. If nothing you wish to share is troubling you, I will leave you to your solitude." She began to struggle upright in her voluminous gown.

"That piece of frivolity is utterly impractical," I noted.

She paused to gaze at me with naked bemusement. "I did not don it in hopes of being practical."

"I can see not. You should have stayed in your bedchamber instead of hunting me down."

"Hunting you down? My dear Nell, I was merely looking— you are always exactly where you are supposed to be. Can you not see that I was mildly alarmed—?"

"No! You were merely curious. There is a difference."

She had reached her knees and was about to retrieve the lamp, but froze to regard me. "You *are* upset. You are annoyed with me."

"Not with you."

"Who then?" She settled down again, a look on her face that would not be satisfied without answers.

"With myself."

"You have annoyed yourself? How original, Nell. Most people confine their annoyance to others."

"You will quickly encourage me to reconsider," I snapped, then clapped my hands over my mouth. "Forgive me, Irene. I am frightfully out of temper. But I do think it was most . . . wicked of you to insist that I remain to talk with Mr. Stanhope."

"Why?"

"The hour was late and the circumstances most improper."

"You know that my notions of late hours and improper circumstances do not concur with yours. So how could I lead you into wickedness where I saw none?"

"You placed . . . an occasion . . . I would not have encountered by myself in my path."

"Which was—?"

"Irene, I have never in my life been alone with a man unless he was a relation, or an employer, or a member of the clergy, and it was absolutely necessary."

"Well, Mr. Stanhope is not an employer, and I doubt he will ever be a member of the clergy. But he did ask us to call him 'Stan.' "

"I have it on good authority—his—that he prefers being addressed by his middle name."

"Which is?"

"Q-Quentin," I whispered like a guilty child.

"Quentin it shall be then," she said, "and could we not consider Quentin a quasi-relation, since he is the uncle of former charges of yours?"

"No, we could not! That was far too long ago, and he has changed much. He tried to say that I have changed, which is utterly untrue. He even tried to say that I was adventurous, can you imagine? He behaved most . . . strangely, Irene. I did not know what to make of him. And then . . . then—"

"Then, Nell? Clearly something of great moment has occurred."

"No, it is nothing! It would be nothing to most women, I know that. I am being a silly goose, but I do not know what to think. I—I do not know what to feel. Except that I have the headache from not knowing anything. Oh, ignorance is not bliss!"

Irene took my hands, which were as cold as ice and knotted around each other, into each of hers. "How true, Nell; ignorance is no virtue, and to feel ignorant is a great indignity. How has this Stanhope man managed to make you feel inferior?" She sounded dreadfully angry. "What has he said? Has he had the arrogance to denigrate your former place in his sister's household? Does he dare hold to your supposed difference in stations despite his fallen circumstances? I am weary beyond words of these European notions of 'place'!

They are cruel and archaic, whether coming from a so-called king or an ex-officer of Her Majesty the Queen! I will not have such a person in my house, no matter the personal danger he faces, not if he dares to offend you!"

Irene's grip on my hands had tightened alarmingly, and she made to rise again.

"Irene, no! He has done no such thing. No offense of that sort was given. Quite the contrary. He has . . . violated the very heart of his heritage. He said that *I* was the embodiment of England, and then he—he kissed me."

"He what?" Irene sank back into her billows of nightdress, her features as slack as a drowning person's.

It was harder to say a second time. "He k-kissed me."

"Oh my." Her mouth closed again.

"You knew that something had shifted in the terms of our acquaintanceship since this sudden reunion. That is why you were always urging me to spend time with him."

"Yes, but I did not expect him to kiss you."

"I am relieved."

"Where?"

"Where?"

"Where did he kiss you?"

I swallowed. "By the window."

"Not where in the room, my darling ninny!"

"Then where . . . where?"

"Where upon your person?"

"Really, Irene. That is too . . . personal an inquiry."

"It makes all the difference."

"Truly? How?"

"In analyzing the event."

"You speak as if we were discussing one of your investigative matters."

"We are." Irene sat back, brisk and clinical. Her change of manner relieved me. Suddenly we were dissecting an interesting deviation of remote behavior. I began to believe I could learn something from my bewildering experience and my even more bewildering reaction to it.

"Quentin has been under great emotional stress." Irene began to enumerate his stresses on her fingers. "He is still ill from fever, and has recently survived an attempted poisoning and a shooting. He has encountered a figure from a past he renounced before it could reject him, at least in his own eyes. He feels he has neglected to right a past wrong that he witnessed, which now may cost a man his life. He has long lived apart from his own kind—and from all the conventions of the society that nourished him—as penance for some perceived failure, of which he will not speak. A most thoroughly romantic figure, Nell," Irene finished with a flourish. "And yet, in the midst of all this peril, he pauses to kiss you. Why?"

"Yes, why me?" I wailed. "I am the most unlikely person for such a man to fasten upon. I have led a sheltered life, despite his misguided admiration for my 'adventures.' He must be mad!"

Irene laughed. "No, you are. He does admire you, as do I and Godfrey. You are the fiber that holds our flights of fancy to earth. We rely upon you, Nell. For sense. For correction. For innocence. No doubt Quentin sees that in you also. Perhaps he had thought all that lost to him."

I nodded soberly. "Then you believe that he is sincere."

"Oh, a man may be sincere, my dear Nell, and still be dangerous. Now where did he kiss you?"

"I thought we had decided why he did. Where should not matter."

"It always matters, as does how. A man may kiss one's hand as either a social gesture or a seductive one. He may kiss one's cheek as a greeting or an invitation. He may kiss one's lips as an old friend or as a new lover."

"I see," said I, and I did.

"And?"

"And I see that such information is none of your affair, Irene." This time I struggled upright, not easy to do after hours of crouching on a closet floor. My ankles buckled but I braced myself by grasping a shelf edge. "Your comments have been most enlightening, but I really do not care to discuss the matter further. Good night." I opened the door into the darkened hall, blinking, then smiled over my shoulder at Irene.

She was still sitting on the floor, her head leaning on her hand, her arm propped on her knee. She looked most unsatisfied.

"Are you coming to bed?" I asked airily.

"No," she replied. Her tone was almost acid. "I am staying here. To think."

On that ominous note I closed the door and tripped off to bed with a lighter heart and an unspoken chuckle. I was seldom priviledged to know a secret that Irene was mad to learn.

# Chapter Eleven

# WHEREFORE ART THOU?

**A mere** ceiling is seldom praised in song or story as the source of revelation, but when my eyes opened on morning, I knew that my life had changed. At first I only sensed the miracle of daylight filtering through the lace festooning the window and bathing the rough plaster ceiling in sheen and shadow. Then, on that blank parchment, slowly, the memory of my retreat to the linen closet flashed into my mind with the starkness of a daguerreotype—along with the incident that preceded it.

Mortified, I pulled the covers over my head, forming a linen tent. How Irene must be laughing at me! And Mr. Stanhope! Quentin . . . Oh! The early birds' muffled caroling sounded like titters through my makeshift linen closet. What a fool I must seem—to everyone!

At last I crept out of bed and into my clothes. Ordinarily I arose first, save for Sophie. Neither Irene nor Godfrey was sufficiently industrious in the mornings. Indeed, both of my friends practiced the decidedly un-American and un-English inclination to linger abed well past the breakfast hour. Had they not been models of energy later in the day, I would have been forced to ascribe their habits to slothfulness.

This morning I blessed their tardiness. I had no wish to accost anyone in the passage—oh, dear. I recoiled into my bedchamber after cracking the door to the hallway. A step. Had I heard the creak of one of the ancient floorboards? I had no desire to see a single occupant of the household until I should compose myself.

The door inched open at my push. I again peeped out into the murky passage. Someone shoved the door closed. Well! I did not appreciate such games, and would confront whoever played them. I swung the door abruptly open. The passage was empty, not even dust motes dancing in the tunnel of light from the far window overlooking the stable yard.

The door wobbled on its hinges again. I looked down.

"Lucifer!" I hissed in annoyance; the name sounds especially sinister when whispered. The black cat curved around the skirts swaddling my ankles, self-satisfied Shadow Incarnate. I whisked up the surreptitious beast and closed my door, then tiptoed down the hall, pausing at every squeal of the floorboards. The dark and narrow staircase was equally vocal. My heart was pounding as much as . . . as much as it had the previous night. At last I stood on the front-hall paving stones. Lucifer billowed down from my arms and shook himself.

How peaceful it was to be up—alone—at dawn. My breathing eased to match the placid tick of the parlor clock, a rococo French porcelain affair much decorated with roses that ill suited this dwelling so humbly called a country cottage. Congratulating myself upon my discreet avoidance of any awkward encounters, I moved toward the music room and froze at a shrill squeak from my first footfall upon the flagstone. Was even mute stone to turn traitor and betray me?

The squeak repeated, though I had not moved, and declared itself: "Errrack!" drifted from the music room. "Cassie want a crumpet. Cassie want a crumpet. Yo ho ho and a bottle of rum."

I hastened into the chamber, where the parrot cage sat shrouded in chintz. Such nightclothes were supposed to silence the creature.

"Hush," I hissed again, lifting the cover to fix the parrot

with my most imposing look. "You shall get neither crumpet nor rum from me, or anyone, if you do not keep still!"

Feathers ruffled into upstanding rows of green. The bird's jet-black pupil shrank to a pinpoint as it sidled away along the wooden perch, squawking: "Cassie want a strumpet. Cassie want a strumpet."

"Now where did you get that?!" I plucked a leftover grape from the ceramic dish that served as Casanova's dinner tray and quickly silenced the bird.

He lifted a revolting foot to take the grape into his claws, tilting his head as quizzically as Hamlet contemplating the skull of Yorick. Then the fierce scimitar of his yellow-gray beak darted at the grape's ruddy surface.

I backed away, hopeful that Casanova would remain distracted, but an unholy yowl issued from beneath my feet. Lucifer, of course. So much for discreet early rising. So much for gathering my shattered nerves. So much for deciding upon a calm course of meeting the house's inhabitants.

"You are up even earlier than usual, Mademoiselle Huxleigh." Sophie stood in the doorway, and spoke with disapproval.

"So I am. I have decided to improve the parrot's language skills. Such birds are said to learn more easily in the early morning hours."

"Hmph." Sophie gave one of those Gallic shrugs that bundle indifference, skepticism and superiority into one portmanteau gesture serviceable for all occasions. "A pity that men are not parrots. My husband wishes to do all his learning at night—in the bistros."

Thankfully, she vanished before I could muster an answer to this statement. I did not wish to think of men—and the night—this morning. Lucifer had cast himself down on the carpet in a spot that in several hours would be drenched with sunlight. Evidently he preferred the afternoon. Casanova was whistling and crooning to himself as he ravaged the grape. I arranged his cage cover over the back of a rush-seated chair and went to the window. Here the interior shutters opened on the garden, which lay under a glistening net of dew, its colors lush in the returning sunlight.

I did not wish to contemplate gardens, either, so I went to the bookshelves and hunted up and down the spines until the graceful gold letters of Milton's *Paradise Lost* caught my troubled eye. I retreated to an upholstered chair and here I intended to read until the others arose and breakfast was served. If my hunger grew irresistible before then, I could always beg for one of Casanova's grapes.

Perhaps an hour and a half later the venerable boards overhead began creaking in succession. By then I was deep in *Paradise Lost*. Casanova began croaking in time with the protesting architecture. I steadied myself, preparing to look and behave with perfect calm. After reading Milton for ninety minutes I have no difficulty in miming a state of utter ennui.

Hence I was installed at our breakfast table blissfully supervising the brewing of my morning tea when the master and mistress of the house descended.

Irene honored me with her sharpest examination, all under the guise of accommodating her Paris morning gown of sky-blue silk on the rush-seated chair. Godfrey wore a maroon house-jacket over his shirt and tie, along with an air of utter innocence. But then he had been a barrister, and they habitually assume such poses.

Apparently, our guest did not yet feel well enough to join us at table. I breathed a sigh of salvation when I saw Sophie lift a laden tray and clatter into the hall passage.

"Did you have a good night, Nell?" Godfrey inquired in a robust, brotherly tone.

Irene darted him a warning glance. "Do have some sugar in your coffee, darling!" she urged with such unusual domestic solicitude that he was immediately distracted from awkward questions. Godfrey frowned as he stirred the offered sweetener into his bitter brew. I could see the moment when he recalled in whose company and in what room he and Irene had bid me good night. I had never seen Godfrey off balance before, but he gave a passing imitation of it then.

"A . . . fine morning it is," he said next. "Would you care for some coffee, Nell?"

"You know that I never drink that vile foreign liquid."

"No. Of course not." Godfrey returned the modern aluminum pot to its stand. He resumed stirring sugar with more vigor than called for, the spoon scraping the china with predictable shrillness.

"Tea is a foreign beverage," Irene observed, sipping smugly, "and some consider it vile, too. If we wanted to honor our ancestors, no doubt we'd have ale for breakfast."

"Speak for your own ancestors," I responded tartly.

"Speaking of ancestors," she added idly, "do you think, Nell, that the Dr. Watson who tended Mr. Stanhope at the battle of Maiwand could be 'our' Dr. Watson?"

My hands flew to my face. "Oh! I had forgotten in all the, the . . . excitement. I devoutly hope not."

"What Watson is this?" Godfrey asked.

I sighed. "I saw it last night when Irene looked as satisfied as Lucifer with fresh cream on his whiskers. Your wife cannot resist pursuing the unlikely, Godfrey. A Dr. Watson apparently is an associate of *the* man, but he is certainly not 'ours.' I cannot even be sure of ever having seen this person."

"So you swore not many days ago in another case," Irene put in wickedly, "and were proven spectacularly wrong."

"*The* man?" Godfrey sounded confused and a trifle worried.

"Sherlock Holmes," I said grimly.

Irene allowed me to instruct Godfrey on another aspect involving the London detective: that a Dr. Watson was listed in an early-'Eighties *Telegraph* agony column along with the address, 221 B Baker Street. That a mortally ill American murderer, Jefferson Hope, held the reins during Irene's and my first hansom ride together. After Hope collapsed and regaled us with a tale of perfidy and revenge, he gave Irene a simple wedding band that he had lost and recently reclaimed from this Dr. Watson at the Baker Street address, the residence of Sherlock Holmes. To this very address, Irene had followed the detective a year and a half earlier before fleeing England with Godfrey.

Godfrey frowned. "The early 'Eighties? Surely this Dr. Watson established his own household and practice years ago."

Irene leaped to the defense of her notion. "What of the man who accompanied the disguised detective back to Baker Street from Briony Lodge only eighteen months ago?"

"Have you ever seen Dr. Watson?" Godfrey riposted.

"No, but Nell may have!" They looked expectantly at me, Irene hoping for confirmation, Godfrey, like myself, hoping for discouragement.

I shook my head. "A third man accompanied Sherlock Holmes and the King of Bohemia to Briony Lodge when only I remained behind in the guise of an elderly housekeeper, but he could have been anybody. We have never seen more than his title and surname. I agree with Godfrey. To hunt for a Dr. Watson in England is to pursue a myriad of needles through an island haystack; we shall only prick ourselves. To suspect that the same Dr. Watson who tended Quentin nearly a decade ago in Afghanistan is also a henchman of Sherlock Holmes is utter madness!"

Irene's fingers mutely, and mutinously, drummed the linen tablecloth. Before she could argue, Sophie returned, still bearing the breakfast tray.

"Monsieur is not in his room."

"Not in his room?" Irene half rose. "But that is . . . dangerous." Sophie's look of surprise forced her to perform a verbal minuet. "I mean that is dangerous—unwise—for his fragile state of health, of course. He was not to be found in the retiring room?"

"I did not investigate, Madame. I heard no sound above stairs." Sophie set down her tray on the wooden table with an emphatic clank. There are no people like the French for resenting unrewarded effort. "The gentleman is absent. See for yourselves." Sophie's elaborate intonation of "gentleman" made plain her own judgment of our houseguest.

"Impossible." I, too, rose from my seat. "Quentin would never depart without the proprieties."

Godfrey stood last. "Quentin?"

Irene intervened as smoothly as an actress delivering a line. "Apparently the only thing of interest that Nell learned from our guest last night was his preference to be addressed by his middle name. 'A rose by any other name,' et cetera. Now we may not have a guest to address by any appellation whatsoever. We had best see for ourselves."

And so I found myself following my companions upstairs in pursuit of a meeting that I would have given anything to avoid but an hour before.

Sophie had been regrettably correct. The Stanhope bedchamber was empty; so was the bathing room tucked so cozily under the eaves. We returned to his chamber in bewilderment.

"Perhaps he is in the garden—" I went to the window. The casement was ajar; birds peeped contentedly under the eaves. The garden radiated no mysterious, misty aura in broad daylight. It seemed cold and aloof, the usual Gallic grid of walks and flower beds. How I longed for the friendly tangle of an English garden—for a vista that was not foreign!

"No." Irene sounded quite definite, and utterly serious. "He understood the danger of exposing himself."

"Then why would he leave?" I demanded, whirling on her. "*You* must tell *me*."

"I?"

"You were the last to see him."

I stared at her, then at Godfrey's innocently puzzled face, his silver-gray eyes darkened to charcoal in the chamber's dimness. I spun again to face the garden. Spears of hyacinth bowed in the breeze. Purple, orange and blue shades of heliotrope, lily, and what we English call bachelor's button ran together like flooded watercolors before my eyes. I could not see clearly, and could not say why.

"My dear Nell—" I heard the firm forward step of Godfrey's shoe.

"Godfrey, please! Stay back."

"Let us examine the chamber," Irene put in hastily, and I blessed her for that.

Behind me came the squeak of wardrobe hinges, the rustle of bedclothes. I almost laughed to think of Irene hunting under the bed for her quarry. Yet laughter seemed an alien response when all I could see were the blurred flowers melting into a potpourri of waxen blots.

"Here are my clothes," Godfrey announced from the direction of the wardrobe. "He has taken nothing."

"Only the odd garb he wore when we found him," Irene added. "And here—look!"

I almost turned but did not dare.

"In this dish upon the bureau. His medal."

Godfrey went over to examine it. "He must have forgotten it."

"Forgotten it?" Irene demanded skeptically. "With even the bedclothes straightened? No, our visitor has left this room too tidy to have overlooked anything. His military training has not forsaken him. Perhaps he left the medal as a token."

I could sense her face and voice turning to me.

Their talk, the matter at hand, drifted toward me through layers of muffling curtains. At this window less than twelve hours before I had stood with our departed guest. At this window not twelve hours before—

"Nell." Irene's clear stage voice penetrated my mental miasma. "What do *you* think? What possible reason would Stan have to vanish like this, without a word?"

"I would not presume to say, as I would not presume to still call him 'Stan.' "

"Mr. Stanhope, then," Irene said impatiently. "Something has caused him to bolt. What?"

I whirled on her, goaded beyond the wisdom to resist facing them, and facing the empty room. "Not I!"

Godfrey stepped forward, looking grave and concerned as well as puzzled. I could never resist Godfrey when he insisted on being sincere. I backed away, into the window.

"My dear Nell," Godfrey said, "what is the matter?"

"Mr. Stanhope," Irene interjected before I could answer, "expressed a small tenderness toward her last night."

Godfrey stopped moving. "What kind of small tenderness?"

"Er, in the nature of a kiss."

"Nature of a kiss?"

I could stand this speculation no more. "Godfrey, must you repeat everything Irene says? If I had wanted two parrots I would have acquired another."

"Is what Irene says true? He took a liberty?"

"Yes—and no! It does not matter. It was nothing. Obviously such a trifle would have nothing to do with his disappearance. Perhaps he has been—kidnapped."

"Without a struggle?" Irene's skepticism was gentle but unavoidable. "Leaving his borrowed clothing neatly hung and his bedclothes drawn up? A commendably cooperative kidnapping victim. No, I am sorry, Nell. Stan has left of his own free will, and you are the only person who can possibly tell us why."

"*Must* you call him that?"

"He asked us to," she reminded me. "Why do you object to the nickname so much?"

"It . . . denies his past, his place. It is something rude soldiers would use."

"He was a soldier," Godfrey put in.

"An officer," I corrected, "and a gentleman. I am the only one here who knows that for a certainty."

"You hold him to more than he claims for himself," Irene pointed out. "Is that why he left?"

"It has nothing to do with me!"

"Yet you two spoke last night, and there passed between you more than ordinary chitchat, however vague you are about the particulars. Something you said, that happened, must have persuaded him to leave—quickly, without farewell. I agree with you, Nell, your Mr. Stanhope is a gentleman still. He would never have departed without expressing his gratitude unless he felt compelled. Perhaps to save us—you—from himself," she speculated. "You must tell us what you said."

"*I* said very little! He prattled on, about the garden, about my representing England to him. And then he said that he had always expected me to be minding some charge, to be a governess. And when I explained how I had become a typewriter-girl, he behaved as if this were a kind of achievement and said that I had shown him that his memories of home had been mistaken. That we all had changed, though, of course, *I* had not. . . . He must have been feverish, though the moonlight from the window was as cool as ice water. He did ask if I judged him, which I never do. 'Judge not lest ye be judged.' And the last thing he said, the very last thing was so odd. I told him that he did not have my ill opinion. He said that then there was no one he could not face—but surely I am of no consequence to him! Why would he say such a thing? Why would he *do* such a thing?"

"What thing, Nell?" Godfrey asked.

I paused, tangled in conflicting thoughts and emotions. And then I did the unforgivable. I lied. Baldly. "Why . . . leave without a word. It is most impolite."

"A soldier cannot always be expected to be polite," Irene said with a smile. "And it is obvious that matters deeper than mere death threats trouble Mr. Stanhope."

A sudden wave of guilt engulfed me. "I—I must have behaved badly. I drove him to flee. What I said . . . I do not even remember what I said."

The strain of the long, wakeful night, of sitting up in a linen closet, of explaining what to me was still inexplicable, caught up with me in a gallop. I put a hand to my surprised mouth too late to smother a hiccough, or a sob. I was horrified to find my demeanor melting like wax, and hid my face in my hands before anyone should see it cracking.

A silence held, during which I heard the snap of Godfrey's long stride toward me. Then a hand was patting my shoulder and another stroking my hair and I was held close against his maroon satin shoulder as he murmured, "There, there."

I felt as I had at some long-forgotten childhood crisis, when I'd sought refuge in my father's gentle embrace, and heard those heartbroken sobs echoing and felt the saltwater leaking through the tight barrier of my fingers.

"We will find him, Nell," Godfrey promised in tones that thundered with resolve. "We will find him and demand an explanation, and if it does not satisfy me, I will thrash the bounder within an inch of his life."

"Should he still possess a life," Irene broke in coolly, "after facing assassin's bullets and lethal hatpins. Yes, we will find him. He must at the least explain his shocking lack of manners in the face of hospitality. And he has managed to intrigue me."

"There!" Godfrey bent toward me with a smile. "Woe to the man who intrigues Irene and runs away. She is a merciless hound on the trail and will not stop until she has her answers."

I blinked through my sopping eyelashes at my two friends. How could I tell them that learning anything more of Quentin Stanhope and his astonishing affairs was the last thing on earth that I wished?!

## Chapter Twelve

# SAVING SARAH'S ASP

**We began** our search where the man had fallen at our very feet but two days before, in the ponderous shadow of Notre Dame.

Irene visited the surrounding cafés, the greengrocers' stands, the fruit dispensers at their carts, her fluid French cascading with descriptions of the *"monsieur exotique"* and the Turkish trousers and loose jacket he wore. *"Très basané et très brunet,"* she would say, passing her hands over her face to indicate his bronzed aspect and his beard. Godfrey, presumably, was performing the same mimes in his designated territory, the Left Bank.

I was a mute witness, fascinated by Irene's endless energy. Each waiter and street sweeper was pounced upon as if he commanded the source of the Lost Chord. At every repetition, the description expanded, requiring more gestures, more discussion. *"Costume Égyptien,"* she would say. *"Nationalité, Anglais."*

At this last attribution, I endeavored to look totally indifferent to the inquiry. The French already displayed ample *hauteur* toward the English; I had no wish to encourage their unfounded prejudices by claiming this outré person Irene described as one of my own kind.

At last an individual responded to Irene's badgering with as many nods as a street puppet. *"Oui, oui,"* he squealed like a transported pig, and released a spume of French so rapid that I understood almost none of it.

"Excellent." Irene pulled me away from the vendor's river of information. "He has seen Mr. Stanhope in the vicinity—and more. He often goes to Les Halles, the great Paris market near Montmartre, and has seen our quarry about very early in that quarter. It sounds as if Quentin had rooms there."

"Montmartre? But the district is a refuge of lowlife."

"And high life, remember, Nell—if you count the fashionable Bohemian cafés."

"I count them for naught," I returned. "And Quentin did not strike me as one to frequent cafés."

"No, not in his current guise, though certainly no one in Montmartre would look twice at him. Visitors expect such examples of Bohemian dress to lounge about there. A wise address for a man who wishes to disappear." Her eyes fastened on the distance. "And *there* is a man whom I wished to appear, just when I want him. Godfrey has impeccable instincts for an Englishman."

I turned to see her husband striding across the bridge over the Seine toward us, his polished ebony cane swinging jauntily, its gleam vying with the sheen of his plush beaver top hat.

"Nothing to be learned at the bookstalls," Godfrey said as he drew near. "Evidently our friend Quentin had little time for dallying among the encyclopedias."

"Ah, but he had a definite taste for the Bohemian. Nell and I are directed to Montmartre."

"Speak for yourself," I told Irene. "I want nothing to do with such a depraved place."

"Then Godfrey will accompany me tomorrow, and you need not trouble yourself about how our search for Mr. Stanhope progresses." Irene took her husband's arm and they strolled on.

Moments later, and breathless, I caught them up as Godfrey was whistling for a hansom. "I will go to Montmartre,"

I said. "I fear that were I not present, one or the other of you might do some violence to poor Quentin."

"Very wise," Godfrey confided as he helped me into the conveyance. "One never knows what Irene will do with that discreet little revolver of hers."

Of course the day's entire agenda—from the hunt for traces of Quentin to a full schedule of social outings—was designed to distract me from my "loss." A pity we were in Paris. We were taken first to the Louvre, where I wore myself out crossing large expanses of marble floors and endless staircases to view paintings almost as large as the exhibition halls—I think of David's series on the coronation of Napoleon and Josephine—all bordered in miles of rococo gilt frame. In a short time I felt I had surfeited myself on Swiss chocolates and was glad when our party withdrew to take another cab to a fine restaurant in the Latin Quarter. There, once I had eliminated such items on the menu as tripe, octopus, squid and liver in various innovative forms, I was able to consume a *crème* soup and a small *salade*. Much of the so-called "beauty" of the French language is adding a mere fillip to ordinary English words, which last the French would no doubt spell "fillipe."

To end what had been a perfect day in Paris—that is, fatiguing and over-self-indulgent—we adjourned to the Porte Saint-Martin Theatre to view Irene's friend Sarah Bernhardt in *Lena*. A note that morning from Sarah herself had urged our attendance. I had hopes for this production, for it was based on an English novel, *As in a Looking Glass*. Alas, I would have found a looking glass far more entertaining than what transpired on the stage for several hours.

Although the Divine Sarah is famed for her death scenes, this one was most repugnant. After caressing a dagger, she snatched a nearby bottle of poison, emptied it into a rather showy goblet and consumed it. Then she sat and faced the audience. Such were her powers of concentration that I detected a green tint to her skin. I seized the opera glasses from Irene to confirm it, just in time to see Sarah mime a most unnecessarily convincing convulsion and fall face forward onto the floor. The curtain fell in great wallowing swaths of crimson velvet. I found myself heartily pleased that I had supped so lightly, especially when I noticed whey-faced gentlemen and ladies rushing from the theater for the retiring rooms after the play.

"She should have tried *Hamlet*," Irene observed, replacing her opera glasses in their velvet-lined case.

A mistress of backstage maneuvering, Irene forged a path against the current of the departing crowd, while Godfrey escorted me. The press was not as great as I expected, yet the dressing room was crowded, not only with people but with the miasma of powder and perfume that accompanied the actress as invariably as her diaphanous scarves and marabou boas. Sarah herself was the center of a frenzy of admirers, her extraordinary strawberry-blonde hair exploding from their midst like a firework.

She sizzled through them the moment she spotted our party.

"Irene! My darling child! And my dear Godfrey, how splendid you look. And Miss Uxleigh—"

Irene and Godfrey suffered her kisses upon their cheeks. The actress merely clasped my hands instead, which would have been acceptable, or at least endurable, save that I glanced down to find living green bangles circling each wrist.

I pulled my poor hands free with a genteel shriek.

Sarah regarded her embellished wrists. "Ah, Miss Uxleigh recognizes my darling little Oscar, the so-sweet snake she gave me in Monte Carlo! Do you see, Miss Uxleigh, I have found such a charming companion for the poor dear. A mate. I plan to introduce them as the asp in *Cleopatra* soon. Only one serpent will play the part at once, but the footlights are hot, the death scene much extended, and I writhe about quite intently. Each snake will alternate appearances, lest the rigors of performance overcome it. Are they not a handsome pair?"

Here she thrust her ghastly bracelets under my nose. One raised a narrow scaled head to hiss.

"Most engaging," said I, backing away. "I must not keep you from your public."

"Ah, but my dressing-room guests are always my private public," she answered. She flitted to her dressing table, opened a damask jewelry box and cavalierly stripped the serpents from her wrists into its padded velvet interior.

"They thirst for peace and quiet after their hour in the limelight. I wish I could say the same for myself. Ah, thank you, darling Maurice."

I was intrigued to inspect the person from whom Sarah accepted a flute of champagne. Maurice was her son from her illicit union with a supposed nobleman. I observed an even-featured, polite youth of twenty-some, waiting on his energetic mother like a devoted pageboy.

This paragon of young manhood appeared at my side with a companion flute to his mother's. "You are the so amusing Miss Uxleigh that Mama speaks of most fondly," he said in French. "She has many an endearing anecdote about your adventures in Monte, and is most enamored of your gift of Oscar. Few women appreciate Mama's taste in accessories."

I would have been compelled to correct this young man's lamentable miscomprehension about my opinions of his Mama and her menagerie, save that Irene, waving about one of the champagne flutes that Godfrey had procured for them both, burst forth with an announcement.

"You will never believe it, my dear Sarah. Our Nell has unearthed a most intriguing gentleman."

"Miss Uxleigh? A gentleman? French?"

"Only English, I fear," Irene returned, "but he has lived in Eastern climes."

"Ah. An adventurer. Is he rich? Has he found King Solomon's mines? Or simply a small diamond mine would do."

"We do not know. He has vanished."

"Ah." Sarah smiled knowingly at me. "Gentlemen often do. And ladies are often more grateful for the fact than they admit."

"Irene is misleading you," I said. "This gentleman is merely a member of a London family which I served as governess many years ago."

"It would not make a play," Sarah declared with a small shake of her head.

I was tempted to answer that her current property did not make much of play either.

Sarah whirled to the mirror again before I could phrase my comment in the correct—or at least comprehensible—French, though the language is never more incomprehensible than when it is spoken correctly.

"I am so delighted to see my dear friends again. How did you like the play?" she asked.

"Mere words cannot convey our reaction," Godfrey said with suave diplomacy.

"I, too, am speechless," Irene put in demurely.

"How good to be among honest friends!" Sarah declaimed. "But I am so *glad* of your presence! Irene, I have had the most marvelous news. The Empress of All the Russias, Maria Feodorovna, has expressed a desire to meet you. She has heard from her acquaintance, the Duchess of Richelieu—our friend Alice from our amusing scheme in Monte—of your singing privately for Prince Albert there. Her husband, a great stick-in-the-mire, as you say, frowns upon French and German connections for his aristocracy, and the Empress never consorts with mere artists like myself. Yet I have been assured that she would honor my salon with a visit if *you* would be there. Say that you will, and I will be the happiest woman on earth. All the other actresses in Paris will be jealous, as they should be, no?"

"No," Irene answered promptly. Sarah began to frown, but Irene laughed. "And yes. How can I resist satisfying an empress's curiosity? And I confess that the Empress has stirred mine by requesting my presence. What do you know of her?"

"How should I know anything, my dear Irene? She has held herself above me."

"Sarah, if it has to do with aristocracy, art or money, you know all. Tell me."

The actress preened, dropping her air of innocence as if it were a snake she had been toying with. "A lovely little lady, this empress. Danish by birth. Dagmar by birth name and a sister to the Prince of Wales's enchanting Princess Alexandra. She adores the dressmakers of Paris, in whom she shows excellent taste. She obeys her husband in all minor matters and rules him in most major ones. Someone must! Alexander the Third is six feet six inches tall. Can you imagine a man of such height? And a royal personage as well? That is doubly commanding, no?"

Irene kept notably still, for the czar's physical presence was a twin to that of the King of Bohemia, with whom she had such unpleasant dealings not two years before. I myself wondered if some relationship existed between the two rulers, though the Czar of All the Russias was a far more formidable regent than Wilhelm von Ormstein, King of pretty little Bohemia at the edge of the Austro-Hungarian empire. A common ancestor, perhaps?

"The Czar is a complete autocrat, I understand," Sarah said. "So rigid, these northern European men. No wonder many keep mistresses of artistic temperament—the ballerina, the actress or the opera singer. Something must melt that Nordic ice, no?"

Sarah rattled on, oblivious of Irene's sudden quiet, or of Godfrey's instant attention, as her words cut dangerously close to Irene's past.

"It would be a superb coup for me, the Empress of the Stage, to welcome the Empress of All the Russias to my salon. So you must come and sing a bit, but only a bit. It is my salon, after all. Say you will! And bring the adorable Godfrey, of course. And your Miss Uxleigh of the intriguing but lost gentleman. I must hear more of this fellow. Perhaps I can locate him. There is not a man worth knowing in Paris who does not find his way to my doorstep on the boulevard Péreire."

"That is one place, I venture, where we will never find him," I murmured, "nor anything that will aid our search."

"What do you say, Miss Uxleigh? Speak up!"

"Nell says," Irene interjected tactfully, "that she is fever-ishly awaiting this next occasion to visit you at home. She had feared that she would never encounter such an opportunity again."

We left soon after on another wave of social insincerities, which are to theater people as air is to the rest of humanity.

## Chapter Thirteen

# HISSTERIA

**Moving from** the tawdry glitter of the dressing room to the decadence of Montmartre resembled a plummet from the gargoyle-ridden spires of Notre Dame into the rank river that lapped at its foundations. So Irene and I were hurtled after luncheon the next day as our open carriage bore us up to the infamous environs of Montmartre.

Oh, both the Seine and the Montmartre window glass sparkled in the sunlight of a Paris afternoon. So did the rooftops of the city visible below the *Butte*, the highest part of Montmartre upon which shone the white bulwarks of Sacré Coeur, still under construction. Far away and below us, the rusted steel pin of the audacious tower of Eiffel, also under construction, poked into a ragged pincushion of clouds. It reminded me of some monstrous modern bridge piling bereft of its span.

Godfrey did not accompany us. Irene had suggested that he inquire into certain immigration matters at the embassies. He was at first loath to allow us to venture unescorted into such a notorious section, but Irene insisted it was safe by daylight.

She also had pointed out that since he had detected the King of Bohemia's incognito entrance into England and made possible their flight (not to mention their marriage) in the nick of time, his talents were needed more at the bureaus than in

the bistros. I knew from my time as his typewriter-girl in the
Inner Temple in London that Godfrey suffered from the barrister's love of obscure and hard-to-ferret-out information.
He was one of the few men in the world who would take such
a humble quest as an opportunity for a romp through the
official records. He often claimed that entire novels by Dickens lay tacit in the entrails of the French bureaucracy, and he
relished following these paths of paper to their unexpected
endings.

So off he went, and thus Irene and I broached this legendary
and shocking "mountain" unescorted. It is seldom the case
that the higher one ascends in any landscape, the meaner
become the dwellings, the shops and the populace, but such
was the perverse way of things in Montmartre. Our carriage
climbed the rue de la Chaussée d'Antin and the boulevard de
Clichy, and the surrounding view degraded. Unkempt, long-
haired men shambled alongside us in the streets. Women of
a certain kind lounged in doorways, regarding us with bored,
hostile eyes imbedded in lampblacked smudges. Articles of
clothing seemed little more than discarded rags woven into
some fanciful new application.

Modest two-, four- and six-story buildings offered little
architectural detail save askew shutters hanging by one hinge.
Although geraniums bloomed in the window boxes, slop
stains drooled down stucco walls. The odors of onion soup
and ownerless dogs overwhelmed any perfume the cheerful
red blossoms could offer. Cries rang off the nearby walls—
screaming children, caterwauling hawkers, even carousing ha-
bitués of the bistros, lurching about the streets in broad
daylight.

The ubiquitous loaves of French bread thrust from the
figures of passersby like umbrellas. He who was not carting
about his bread—or wine—would bear a wrapped canvas
under one arm. Few men wore hats. (I hesitate to describe
them as "gentlemen.") Their uncut, unkempt hair perhaps
explained the omission.

"Here!" Irene commanded our coachman to a stop with

vocal gusto. She surveyed the daunting surroundings like a general overlooking a particularly well-situated battlefield. "We will walk from here and meet you in this square later."

The driver drew our open landau under the shade of a queenly chestnut tree and dismounted to help us alight. I smiled to guess the impression we made upon Montmartre residents: Irene in her Worth gown, a Nile-green-and-tea-rose striped silk visiting dress with a rosette-edge hem and pointed Vandykes of Irish lace girding bodice and sleeves; I in my Bon Marché blue-and-cream lightweight wool gown with the broad sash of Republican red, also available in Empire green and cream, or rosewood and white. Even Paris department stores emphasized whimsy and extravagance.

Yet I spied some redemption in the surroundings. Above us windmills churned lazily in the breeze and cows grazed on green pastures. In some ways, Montmartre was still the picturesque village it had always been.

Irene eyed this bucolic scene. "A pity we do not have time for a picnic. Come, we must survey the neighborhood."

I was relieved to see that the strolling crowds included shopkeepers' wives and even members of the French aristocracy, whose delicacy of dress and manner contrasted with the boisterous common folk around us. Irene took my arm, whether for her protection or mine I cannot say.

"You see, Nell," she confided, leaning close as if to exchange a girlish confidence, "your Mr. Stanhope would be quite unnoticeable here."

"Indeed." I would not give her the satisfaction of again protesting that "your."

"And this is nothing," Irene went on, "as compared to when the quarter throngs with merrymakers of an evening, and the cafés are alight and the *cancan* dancers perform their gymnastics."

I eyed the tawdry café fronts. "Are these *cancan* dancers truly as scandalous as they say?"

"It depends upon who is doing the saying. However, I say—" Irene leaned inward to confide again "—that women so swathed in petticoats and ruffles as these can hardly manage all that yardage and be scandalous at the same time."

"Still, they show their knickers," I sniffed.

"And dingy ones they are, too, I hear. Odd that a washer-woman is the most famous of these *cancan* dancers."

"A washerwoman! Where do you learn such things, Irene?"

She shrugged in a suspiciously Gallic way and stopped to unfurl her parasol. "One hears things."

"Hmm." With Irene, such eavesdropping was likely to be done in person, if not always in her own guise. "I should be most disappointed to learn that you had been visiting these low cabarets."

"Then I shall try my best not to disappoint you," she promised. Whether she meant that she would avoid such places, or merely avoid telling me that she had visited them, was not clear. Such matters never were with Irene. To me, truth was as obvious as an ax; to Irene, truth was like the wood chips that splintered from the ax blade: it changed, depending on which piece of it you grasped at the moment.

"We must inspect the work of these Montmartre artists," Irene suggested, pointing her parasol ferrule in the direction of a shabby cafe whose exterior walls were papered with ragged posters. Under the cafe's tattered red awnings sat even more tattered men surrounded by sketch pads and canvases.

I liked their looks no more than I did the district's. "Why?"

"Because artists use their eyes. While we examine their wares we can cross-examine them. Surely Quentin's Turkish trousers would have been worthy of note, if nothing else."

I studied the baggy-trousered men shambling over the cob-blestones. "I doubt it, among these clowns."

"Still, we must begin somewhere. Humor me, darling Nell. I am trying to be logical."

"I see very little of sense in such rude dabbles. These men must be mad. Nothing looks like anything at all in their paintings," I grumbled as we approached the tables.

That they aspired to be artists of a sort was obvious. Their fingers were stained with oils, pastels, watercolor and charcoal. Many sketched passersby as they sat beside their unappetizing wares, which included tasteless depictions of young women casting their black-stocking-clad legs into the air against frothy clouds of petticoats. Whether these articles of underwear were indeed dingy, or merely ill lit by the murky gaslight of the dance halls, was difficult to tell. In fact, I was extremely dubious that the human form could assume such outré positions.

"Their mastery of anatomy is pathetic," I murmured to Irene as we strolled past a brotherhood of artists all engaged in depicting the same sordid subject matter. "Look! That poor sitting girl's legs go in two different directions—not only an unladylike posture, but also utterly unlikely."

"The position is called 'the splits,' Nell, and it is astounding what feats a devoted dancer may assume. I myself have been required to attempt unlikely—not to mention unladylike—positions during my performing career, though I am far from a dancer. Have you never seen a ballet?"

"My father frowned upon theatrical mummeries."

"You must see one, then," Irene declared, blithely dismissing my late father's wishes. "The Paris ballet is not what it was—the blue ribbon in ballet now goes to St. Petersburg—but some small spark remains. We will attend the ballet at the new Paris Opera House as soon as we retire the mystery of Mr. Stanhope's whereabouts."

"I really would rather not find him, Irene! If he chose to withdraw he must have some reason."

"Of course, but what?"

"That is his affair."

"Not any longer. Now that we know about it, we are obliged to assist him. The benighted man has not lived in civil climes for nearly a decade."

I examined the scene. "If he has been residing here, that certainly is true."

At that moment one of the grubby artists took a large cigar

from his lips, balanced it on the edge of his small round table and eyed Irene.

"Madame seeks a Paris scene to take back to England?" he asked.

She took the small canvas he extended in her gloves—lily-white today—and tilted it so the daylight should catch the blotches of blue, yellow and orange in their blurred glory, apparently a garden.

"I was looking for something colorful, in the way of street scenes," she said. "With figures."

The cigar was plucked up again, and the canvas rudely reclaimed. "See him, then." The cigar jerked toward a fellow smoker among a farther grouping of artists. "I never paint human subjects. They only trivialize the truth."

"I fear that I am always in search of such trivial truths," Irene said. "My companion seeks a dear friend who has been lost to the spell of foreign climes. He is European, but dusky of skin and dresses in the eccentric manner of the East."

"You have come to the proper quarter for the eccentric, Madame." The painter spread his arms, displaying a coarse shirtfront decorated with food and wine. In my opinion, it offered more artistic promise than his miserable paintings. "Here wander poets, painters and scribblers of every sort among shopgirls, bakers and street-sweepers—and sometimes ladies and gentlemen in search of originality. How should one man stand out among so many?"

Irene replied with a most eloquent Gallic shrug and moved on.

"That painter is correct, no matter how personally repugnant," I pointed out. "How can we find one man amid this mob?"

"Our search is not as random as it may appear." Irene's parasol tip indicated the windmill topping the hill ahead of us. "I found a matchbook in our guest's pocket from the Moulin de la Galette, the most famous music hall in Montmartre, and wellspring of the scandalous *cancan*."

"You did not tell me!"

"Why? It was his affair," she said, repeating my earlier answer with a mischievous smile. "I dared not tell you. No doubt you would have objected to the idol of your youth visiting a common French dance hall in order to eye dirty laundry, no matter how artistically presented."

"A man," said I slowly, "must have his amusements."

Irene stopped abruptly, causing a swarthy urchin to careen into us. "A most tolerant sentiment, Nell!" She whirled to watch the rude child stumble away. "You still have your reticule?"

"Of course. I am no foolish country girl now. I have been wary of such pernicious little street thieves since our fortuitous meeting at the decade's other end." In demonstration I lifted my right forearm, from which dangled the green satin strings of my . . . missing reticule!

Irene was already plunging into the crowd, shouting "Ar-rêtez, voleur!" in a voice that would have awakened Napoleon in Les Invalides. It was not sufficient, however, to halt a cutpurse. Her parasol, raised like a lacy lance, beckoned from a swirl of figures. I scurried to join her, finding Irene at last amid a melee of Frenchmen with the very urchin we sought. The boy tried to eel away, but Irene thrust her parasol between his legs. He tripped, scrabbled under an artist's table and at last collapsed under an avalanche of canvases.

"Ici, Madame." The artist was the very one indicated earlier, a bearded dark-haired man with coarse features that well suited the cigar smoking noxiously in a small porcelain dish beside a bilious green glass of absinthe. He was dressed well enough: wide-brimmed straw hat, spotted tie, vest and even a coat despite the warm day. Nevertheless he cut a slightly sinister figure as he dredged up the lad, and my reticule. "I doubt this rascal needs such a dainty accessory." The vile man winked as he extended the article to Irene.

She promptly passed it to me.

"What to do with this rogue?" the man debated.

"Let him go," Irene said. I was about to make an uplifting comment on the quality of mercy when she added: "We have no time to waste on guttersnipes. We are after bigger quarry."

"So I see," the man replied, staring rather too long and too intently at Irene. "Madame is a formidable hunter. Pause a minute, and I will sketch you."

She was already dusting off her abused parasol and righting her bonnet. "I have been sketched before," she said, turning away.

"But, wait! I must capture this thing I see. You have an impressive face, Madame. It belongs on canvas."

Irene paused, trapped by her vanity. Her vanity had nothing to do with her beauty, which she took for granted and thus forgot. No, the canny painter had snared her attention by ignoring her beauty, instead perceiving her unusual will and intelligence. The result was the same; his charcoal was scratching over the sketchpad even as hesitation gave Irene's features a rare look of distraction.

I bent to restore order among the tumbled canvases. I found what Irene sought, charcoal sketches and portraits whose paints had been watered down to transparent, ghostly slashing lines: an old woman with a face as fine as Spanish lace, an urchin as impudent as our thief, a vulgar blonde dancing girl: these played through my hands like the face cards from an ancient deck as I tidied the mess. He had skill, the man with the face of a comic professor, but all of his subjects seemed to be wearing masks that were melting. I feared that his likeness of Irene would offer the same jaundiced distortions, a far cry from the pretty, facile pen-and-ink portraits of the newspapers.

This artist's eye was utterly democratic, almost perverse: the faces of debauched aristocrats, haughty, top-hatted beggars, worn shopgirls and dissolute *cancan* dancers peered back from his small canvases. Then I uncovered one with a jolt of recognition! Quentin Stanhope, as we had first encountered him near Notre Dame—bearded, bone-deep desperate, sitting in some murky café with a glass of opalescent, poison-green liquor before him, a burnt-out cigar on a chipped plate and a small box of matches between his fingers.

I crouched there, staring at this seeming apparition from the attic of my mind. Ordinarily I was one to announce a discovery to the world; yet I was not often privileged to be the exclusive caretaker of anything, even knowledge.

Now I froze in contemplation. Why should not my fingers let the canvas fall face-forward into the pile I had already examined? Why should not Quentin Stanhope remain buried in his unconventional past? More to the point, why should Irene pursue him until he ran where he did not want to go?

Whether I would have concealed this find from my friend, and whether I would have kept that secret for long, I cannot say. A pair of disembodied gloved hands reached down to gently extract the work from my grasp.

"Now this is a fine piece," Irene said in bartering tones as she straightened again. "Exotic. Do you know the subject? Ah, merely another anonymous face captured in the bistros. Recently? Seen once, and never again? Oh, yes. Around Montmartre. How much?"

"Irene, I—" Perhaps she did not hear me. I had not yet managed to rise.

"Forty francs, Monsieur—!" her artful voice rebuked above me. "Twenty. Thirty if you can tell me where to find the gentleman. Ah, it does not matter. Art is supposed to be elusive, is it not? Twenty-five, then."

The clink of coins reminded me to ensure that my reticule was firmly clasped in my hand. I would have to carry it about like a dead rat until I could return home and repair the broken strings.

"No, no wrapping, Monsieur," Irene insisted. "This piece is too fine to hide. We shall take great care with it, I assure you."

By the time I rose and straightened my skirt folds, Irene was holding the canvas at arm's length, dreamily studying its subject. The artist himself had risen to conduct the transaction, and stood no higher than five feet! I blinked. He resembled a nasty, masquerading boy, with his beard, cigar, hat and—I cannot describe it any other way—the appreciative leer that he fixed upon Irene, and . . . as I rose, myself!

Grinning, he tilted his sketch pad so that only Irene could see it. She lifted one eyebrow. "An original approach, Monsieur; I have never before seen myself portrayed as an advertisement for absinthe. I look as deadly as *La fée verte* herself."

Thus the French characterize this lethal liquor of the bistros, as the Green Fairy, a femme fatale of addictive, toxic beauty. I snatched a glimpse of the sketchpad: Irene's features looking quite wicked. She remained nobly indifferent to the familiar fellow as we strolled away. Little did he suspect that Irene had bought his work for its subject rather than its feeble execution, this cheeky creature who signed his work by the overlong name of Toulouse-Lautrec. I hoped never to see such a signature, or its owner, again.

"A splendid likeness, Nell," Irene rapsodized over Quentin's sordid portrait as we strolled away. "A mere phantom of loose lines but quite an uncanny evocation. This artist will make a name for himself. I knew we should find some trace of Quentin in the district, but to unearth a portrait—*quelle chance*, as our French hosts would say. Now we will certainly find him!" She turned a discerning eye on me. "Do not fret about the urchin; they are as common in Montmartre as fleas. Oh, and I have not given you proper credit for finding Mr. Stanhope again. You show a positive genius for stumbling over him in one form or the other. Certainly we will encounter some genuine clue to his whereabouts before the day is over! Well, what do you say to that? Is it not marvelous?" She tucked the portrait under the arm not occupied with her reticule and parasol. Its addition to her accoutrements made her an instant *habituée* of Montmartre.

Irene's high spirits only increased my vague feeling of dread. Why was I so reluctant to see Quentin again? His flight should have buried forever any illusions I might cherish about his character or his seriousness.

Irene's shrewd gaze waited upon my response. I saw in an instant that her chatter was no more than compensation for my introspection, my odd momentary paralysis. I straightened my shoulders and reached up to do the same for my bonnet. Quentin believed that I had developed an adventuresome nature. Today, in Montmartre, we would discover just how adventuresome I was. I nodded to the crooked, climbing path ahead, and we walked on.

The afternoon grew long, and warm, and interminable, and then hot. I donned my pince-nez to consult my lapel watch. Surely there was a limit to how long respectable women could linger in Montmartre, and twilight was its borderland. At the least Godfrey would fret.

"Irene, we must return to the carriage," I protested as we climbed yet another winding lane to yet another row of shops and lodgings. The aged stucco cracked away from the corners of the buildings, so that they seemed to have a skin disease. In these shadowed streets the scents of garlic and human excrement mingled uneasily. Cats were thin and wary. Hoarse dogs barked.

Irene flourished her painting like a badge. "Here, Madame? This gentleman? Have you seen him, Monsieur? Our poor friend. Yes, much fallen in the world. He may be ill."

Our search met indifference unless Irene evoked cooperation with sou coins. I began to squint toward the roofline; by the sky's paler hue, daylight must be slipping out of sight behind Sacré Coeur. My thin boot-soles burned at the long admonishment of the cobblestones, but Irene on a hunt felt no fatigue.

"When you are searching for a needle in a haystack, Nell, it is utterly necessary to inspect every shaft of straw."

She paused at a surprisingly respectable door and pulled the bell. A pansy-faced maid answered, listened politely, glanced at the painting and nodded cheerfully.

"*Oui.*"

One word, but it proved Irene's stubborn optimism and put a dampness in my palms that gloves of the sturdiest Egyptian cotton could not absorb.

"Above," the little maid added, "the attic." I gazed up past the house's steep peak, six stories above us. The sky had paled to an anemic aquamarine color, a blue so bland that it seemed no more than dissolving watercolor.

Irene handed me the portrait. "You can be trusted to take proper care of this, I think, Nell." We began to climb the common stairs at the girl's innocent invitation. "*Monsieur l'Indien*," she had said. As we left the maid's sight, Irene produced her revolver from her reticule.

"Surely we do not need that, Irene?"

"When one is sure that one does not, the need is greatest." She spoke softly.

"What kind of place is this? The entrance, the maid—it seemed respectable."

"It is. Some of the bourgeoisie find it fashionable to live in Montmartre now, but such folk occupy the lowest level. The longer the climb the poorer the occupant." Irene nodded to a nondescript door on the next landing. "A washerwoman lives here, perhaps, who dances the *cancan*. We must reach the last floor."

The stairs grew steeper. I clutched the portrait to my side, wondering what our quarry would think of our purchase, of our pursuit. I had lost count, but my protesting lower limbs screamed that we must have climbed five flights by now. The street din faded as we rose, the paint thinned on the walls and disrepair became utter neglect.

It was again an ascent into greater deprivation. Irene had paused, obscuring my view. Or shielding me with her body.

"Carefully, Nell," she whispered, nodding to the mean little door before us. There the stairs ended. There we must enter, or leave unsatisfied.

Irene listened. Others may pay attention, but Irene had made listening into an art. Perhaps it was due to her musical training, for she gave the appearance of hearing on several levels at once—hearing not merely the footfalls or voices or the creaking furniture springs that one would expect, but sensing movement, sensing presence as an animal might. Her entire attention was devoted to listening so fiercely that she seemed to see beyond the wretched wooden door. Only when her posture subtly relaxed did I believe that there was nothing to hear.

Still, her glance cautioned me as she tried the latch.

It squealed like a piglet. I nearly dropped the canvas, which would have added to the explosion of sound in our tiny cul-de-sac. The stairs narrowed into plunging grayness below us. We seemed to be balanced atop a soaring tower.

Irene listened again, then pushed the door fully open. The flimsy wood banged to a stop on some piece of furniture behind it. I wanted to push past the uneasy perch of the stairs, but Irene did not move. I sensed her surveying the room in the gathering twilight. We had stayed too late in Montmartre. This was worse than the eerie Old City in Prague!

"I-I—" I began, meaning to intone her name, not express an opinion.

"Shhh!" She edged finally through the door.

I followed, glad to have my feet on a level, even if it was raw wood undressed by so much as a rag rug. A meager row of windows spit blurred squares of ebbing daylight onto the floor. The smell of old, and distinctly odd, food lingered like rank perfume. I sensed other odors, vaguely animal, definitely wrong.

Irene moved silently to where the raked attic ceiling almost met the floor and swung the casements as wide as possible. Light like skimmed milk pooled on the floorboards. I saw two narrow cots against the opposite wall. A chest. A basin on a small table between two casements. A slop pail. I had not yet left the doorway. There I stood, dangling between two alternatives equally loathsome: that rude, unlovely room and the twisted stairway that led to it.

"He is gone, Nell." Irene's normal speaking tone nearly startled me into leaping off the threshold and down the yawning throat of steps.

"You are certain?"

She nodded, the revolver still loosely clasped in one hand.

And then I heard a rasp, like a fingernail being drawn across faille silk. "Oh, Irene . . ."

"No one is here." She sounded almost angry in her disappointment. "Nothing remains. Except for that bundle of discarded rags—" She moved toward it.

I heard again—no, sensed—movement. Subtle, hidden, threatening movement. "Irene—?"

"I know, Nell." Her voice was taut, in a higher register, thin, anxious. "I have heard it from the first moment we entered."

"What . . . is it?"

"I do not know, but I doubt that it is human."

"Ohhh!" If she expected *that* intelligence to reassure me she was mistaken.

"Rats, perhaps," she speculated casually.

I leaned against the filthy doorjamb, my knees suddenly as supportive as water. "Shoot them!"

"Nell." Irene sounded amused, even relieved. "They cannot hurt us. I will just inspect that bundle, and perhaps the trunk, and we can leave."

She walked briskly toward the cots while visions of fleas and even more disgusting vermin hopped in my head. My skin crawled. My hair itched. My hands burned on the edges of the canvas, so tightly did I hold it.

Something moved again, at every step Irene made, an unseen mirror of her motions. Something slow, hidden . . . and intelligent.

She bent over the uncertain darkness on the floor, pulled up a length of cloth, and drew back then against a cot, a recoiling melodrama heroine. The gesture was madly unlike Irene.

"W-w-what?" My teeth chattered now, although it was hot under the eaves and perspiration trickled invisibly down my spine in an unpleasant serpentine tracery.

She was backing away as if she did not hear me. "A dead man," she muttered. "Dressed as a native of India. A terrible death."

Speechless, I clung to the portrait, rejecting time and truth, refusing to believe that a man I had seen only two days before should lie lifeless in this squalid attic.

Irene glanced at me, her pale face pocked with the holes of her eyes and mouth and not beautiful at all, unless a skull is so. "Not . . . him. The beard is white and the face so swollen and dark, my God—stay back! It could be . . . plague."

"Quentin was ill even before the poison," I began, appalled at the specter she had raised: an alien disease, with all of us exposed. One man dead of it, and Quentin gone, unable to be told. Unable to tell us what it might be. Plague. "What can we do?"

"Remain calm." Irene seemed to be advising herself as much as me. I had never known her to be so uncertain. It was like seeing Queen Victoria screaming at a mouse—unlikely and frightening.

"I *am* calm," I said with an emphasis that I am sure fooled no one for a moment, not even the . . . corpse. "But I still sense something here—"

"Rats," Irene repeated. "The man has been dead for some time. Rats will come, especially to a garret like this. He looks so ghastly. Perhaps they have been here already." She edged away, toward the sad puddles of waning daylight, toward the stairs.

A rasp again, across the wooden floor, similar to a heavy damask train dragging, snagging on splinters and still being drawn along. A womanly ghost in a court gown? I stared into the haze that heat and unfamiliarity and twilight made of this place. Then I saw something rising, something . . . probing the air. Something that lifted of its own accord, and lifted long, supple and rasping. Irene was backing directly into it.

I had no voice. I had no voice! My throat, my lips moved. My fingernails thrust through the stretched canvas with a wrenching sound. My foot had stepped forward without my willing it, but still I could not speak.

Irene turned toward my motion, turned away from the

silent shadow at her rear now looming as high as her hand, then her waist.

"There!" I screeched at last, pointing. "Shoot! Shoot!"

She whirled. Her silk skirt brushed, actually brushed the swaying shadow. What poised there was no thicker than her furled parasol, which suddenly thrust out like a rapier to engage something long and lethal. At the same time, the pistol spat red smoke in the dusk. Clap, clap, clap! A sound of admonishing hands. Her parasol hurled something limp into a shaded corner. I would have rushed to her side, but she flung a hand behind her to stop me.

For a long while I heard nothing but Irene panting softly and my blood thundering in my ears until these sounds were slowly snuffed by the spreading darkness. I could still see the pale edges of Irene's gown, a bit of light threading through her hair and edging her profile. Her voice came husky, almost hoarse.

"A lamp sits on the table by the door, Nell. I'm going to throw you a box of lucifers. Stanhope's box," she added ironically. "I want you to light the wick and turn it up. Stay as close to the door as you can, but be quick and quiet about it."

Something hurled toward me; I fought the impulse to dodge. The object hit the canvas I clutched to my bodice and slid down until my hand caught and cupped it against my skirt. I set the portrait against the wall and worried the small cheap paper box open. The wooden lucifer was tiny, fit for a doll's hand. I struck it on the tabletop, breathing easier as warmth and light flared. It flickered out before I could even find the lamp Irene had spied on the way in.

I underwent a second struggle to extract another miniature wand and produce another burning flare. This time I touched it to the wick, but it seared my fingertips and I dropped it. Irene said nothing. I heard nothing. I saw little beyond the hot circle of my struggle. I must not fail. The next lucifer licked at my fingers, but I held on until sparks spawned light. When

I dropped the lucifer, the lamplight remained and grew as I turned up the key.

"Bring it here."

I approached Irene as if fearing to wake an infant—or a fiend. Irene handed me her parasol and took the lamp. She moved forward, putting me in darkness that iced my soul. Something on the floor commanded her attention. I edged nearer to view a dark, mottled, sinuous form coiled like massive loops of nautical cable. She bent down, the revolver at the ready, then straightened suddenly.

"Yes, thoroughly dead." She moved more briskly to the bundle she had identified as a dead man, a possible plague victim.

"Irene—?"

She sighed. "Now I understand. Venom. Snake venom. Quantities of venom, from an indecently large snake."

"Not like . . . Oscar?"

"Not like any serpent even Sarah Bernhardt dares to keep. A cobra, I think, but I will let someone else identify the species. And its presence explains that." She stopped by the table where the lamp had rested. "I noticed it when I entered."

I had not, but my eyes now took in all its sinister implications. Some sort of abandoned chest, I would have said but minutes before. Now I saw that it was a cage, perhaps two feet long, pierced with tiny air holes, a small door eloquently ajar. A scum-slimed saucer sat beside it.

Irene sniffed the contents fastidiously. "What did Oscar drink, before you bestowed him on Sarah?"

I shuddered. "Milk. A small saucer of milk."

"Empty, save for dirty residue. The serpent must have been neglected these last days, been hungry."

"But the dead man?"

"Did not live here. He came here. Perhaps he knew of the snake, perhaps not. The maid spoke of only one occupant."

"But, Irene, Quentin Stanhope *lived* here, according to your investigation. Quentin Stanhope—and cobras, assassins? I cannot credit it. It makes no sense. This cannot be the same man I knew in London, though I barely knew him."

She looked at me, all insouciance fled, and nodded grim agreement as she replaced the revolver in her reticule and drew the strings securely shut. "I know, Nell. I know."

## Chapter Fourteen

# SLEEPING SNAKES LIE

"**If our** main objective, Irene, is to find Mr. Stanhope—and I am not at all sure that it should be—then why are we rattling across the cobblestones of Paris en route to a soirée *chez* Sarah?" I inquired with what I thought was admirable restraint.

"Because," Irene answered imperiously, "I wish to meet the Empress of All the Russias."

"Truly?" returned I. "From your costume, I had concluded that you were intending to *play* the Empress of All the Russias."

"That she could." Godfrey's smile looked doubly dazzling under the dark portcullis of his mustache. He eyed his wife with an approval that I could not fault, for Irene did indeed look fit to hobnob with an empress, if not to be one herself.

"I have renounced thrones for more interesting pursuits," she said, unfurling her gauze and ostrich-feather fan rather theatrically. Her evening jacket was a transparent affair of black lace and jet that glittered like fairy netting in the soft light from the carriage lamps. "For the time being," she added wickedly. "Besides, I am most curious to know why the Empress of All the Russias acquired such a sudden desire to meet me that she would break long custom and deign to visit Sarah's salon."

"We know why," I put in. "The Czar is fond of opera. No doubt he has heard of your private concert in Monaco—Sherlock Holmes himself warned you then that you had become too public for one supposedly dead—and recommended you to his wife."

Godfrey's smile had grown dubious, perhaps at mention of Sherlock Holmes. "And for this the Czarina violates her customary refusal to mingle with commoners and begs an invitation to one of Sarah Bernhardt's notoriously Bohemian soirées? No, Nell. Irene is right. Something more lies behind this invitation."

"I am always right, except when I am wrong." Irene regarded me closely. "Why are you so reluctant to visit the boulevard Péreire again, Nell? You know that Sarah is especially fond of you, and, more importantly, all the men in Paris eventually turn up at Sarah's," she added with a particularly sly smile.

"I rather doubt that! Even the Divine Sarah's appetite for novelty must have limits. And the woman barely knows me! How can she be so 'fond' of me for so little reason? It is most illogical, even perverse of her."

"Are you saying, Nell," Godfrey said with lawyerly patience and a hint of laughter in his voice, "that to like you one would have to be perverse?"

"I am saying that . . . That Woman persists in paying me more attention than I welcome. And after our adventure in Montmartre today, I am not excessively enthusiastic about encountering any more . . . serpents."

"Not even poor little Oscar?" Irene asked.

"Not even Oscar," I answered. "And I resent that actress treating me as another exhibit in her menagerie."

"Sarah means nothing by it, Nell. She merely finds you fascinating. She can never resist the exotic, even when it is so merely domestic."

"I am *not* fascinating! I am not adventuresome. I am English."

Too late I saw the corner into which I had painted myself

and my entire race. Luckily, my two friends had amused
themselves sufficiently at my discomfiture and did not press
their advantage.

So Godfrey joined us at last in passing under the engraved
*S.B.* over the door. From the murmur and clink emanating
from our hostess's salon, other guests had already arrived. A
manservant took Irene's lacy jacket and my fitted black silk
jacket with the ruffle of black lace under its wide reveres.

"Why, Nell, you look quite empress-worthy yourself tonight." Godfrey turned me like a top by the shoulders. "I
could not see by the dim hall light of the cottage how splendidly you were gowned."

I flushed, as I always did when a gentleman noticed my
attire, which was a bit excessive this evening: Nile-green China
crape sashed with black watered silk. A rosy epaulet of flowers decorated my left shoulder and more roses perched at the
top right of my coiffure, a most pleasing and subtle touch,
Irene assured me. "Opposing sides, my dear Nell," she had
said while torturing my hair into ringlets with her curling
iron. "Flowers or jewelry best play off each other when
mounted on opposing sides. It is a question of balance."

"So are my slippers," I had complained then, for her own
Nile-green shoes and stockings clad my feet. The two-inch
heels were more than I was accustomed to, especially if I was
to curtsy to an empress.

I still was uncertain that the lily of the valley scent she had
sprinkled liberally on me had overcome the lingering singed
odor of the curling iron. It did not matter. The Bernhardt
rooms sprouted heavy aromas the way they did tropical
blooms and exotic wildlife.

The first trophy I glimpsed in the salon ahead was the
brown bearskin rug that had nearly devoured me on my first
visit. The huge, ferocious head confronted all guests with
glassy staring eyes the size of monocles, and bared fangs set in
massive jaws a full foot apart. One misstep into the maw of
this mighty floor covering, and Irene's silken Nile-green
stockings would be reduced to threads.

"It does pose a problem for trains," Irene murmured, having followed the, ah, train of my unspoken thoughts. "Luckily, neither of us is wearing one."

She bearded the bear first, sweeping ahead of the ever-courteous Godfrey and my ever-reluctant self. Into this hothouse of Oriental decadence Irene wore an insouciant gown of Rose Dubarry, the skirt and bodice draped with pink tulle dotted with black velvet and touched at the shoulders, décolletage, waist and bustle with black velvet bows tipped in gold. The Tiffany necklace of diamonds mounted between opposing rows of pearls circled her neck, and affixed to it was the Tiffany pin Godfrey had given her: the diamond-studded clef and key device, signifying her twin interests of music and mystery. This was Irene's commoner coat of arms, signifying an aristocracy of wit and talent that no amount of blue blood could contest.

Her dark hair was banded by a narrow fillet of gold over the forehead. A high panache of pink ostrich tips vibrated above her topknot like an amusing crown. Long flesh-pink gloves of undressed kid gave her arms a scandalously unattired look. She stepped over the snarling bear head in this most dainty of costumes, pink silk slippers with black velvet bows on the toes mincing expertly around the fearsome impediment.

Irene's entrance was not unobserved by the two dozen guests present, although some were no doubt expecting the Empress. Men in formal black-and-white stood interspersed among a glittering flower bed of pastel evening gowns. Heads turned and lifted, cigarettes paused midway to mouths, conversation faded as Irene became the focus of all eyes. In the hush, I found my gaze focusing on a regal blonde woman opposite us. This commanding creature, as statuesque as a Greek goddess, wore a violet taffeta gown so lavishly encrusted with turquoise, copper and silver beadwork that it formed a rich, Oriental carapace. I wondered if she would crackle when she walked.

For a startled moment, I thought we faced the Empress of All the Russias and fought a mad impulse to curtsy. Then the guests' chatter resumed and their ranks closed, removing this savagely attractive figure from view. Her presence had not escaped Godfrey's notice.

"I know," he bent to confide as he followed me into that crowded chamber of crimson walls and caged birds where scent and smoke mingled into a heady fog, "that you will record every exotic detail of this evening in your diary, including Irene's ensemble. Do you ever report my mode of dress?"

"Well . . . not often. It is not so interesting."

"Thank you."

I belatedly eyed him. He looked handsome enough to be a play actor, as usual, the severe black-and-white of evening dress emphasizing his almost-black hair and pale silver eyes. Had he not been my employer, and now my dearest friend's husband, of course, I might once have cherished illusions on his account. But to record the details of his attire—

"I am sorry, Godfrey, but this is a restrained age. Men dress as they should: with little vanity or display, in unchanging style. You will forgive me if I speak plainly. Men are judged more for what they do than for what they wear."

"Yet I had to don a horsehair wig and antiquated robes to practice law," he mused with a glint in his eye. "It seems that when men do really serious things, such as wage war, they must resort to silly attire. And consider that models of uniform dress, like our former military man Stanhope, often adopt the exotic, free-flowing wardrobe of the East. It speaks of male dissatisfaction with dull tailoring. Perhaps you could note that observation in your diary."

"Perhaps," said I, making no promises. My diaries were one area in which I was the final judge and arbiter, a deity unto myself on a modest and private scale.

We had maneuvered around the bear and past a buffet table laden with the usual (and often inedible) excesses of French cuisine and spirits. This cornucopia of the unappetizing was implemented with such barbaric fare as raw oysters and mounds of Russian caviar shining like beady black little serpent eyes.

We next confronted the richly carpeted dais upon which our hostess reclined on her famous divan, in a loose gown of Chinese brocade with a great billowing train of heavy smoke-blue velvet. None of the windows were open, for Sarah's multitude of wild pets might escape, so the atmosphere was warm and soporific.

Madame Sarah herself wielded a massive peach-colored ostrich fan which clashed violently with her masses of red-gold hair. It nearly made me sneeze to look at her, though I did not dare, for fear I should undo my coiffure.

She saw us immediately.

"Irene!" Kisses cheek to cheek, Irene's delicate ostrich headdress almost colliding with a sweep of Sarah's intimidating fan.

"My adorable Godfrey!" A kiss (his) on the hand; a kiss (hers) blown over the trembling horizon of the fan.

"And the amusing Miss Uxleigh!" A nod (mine) and a playful, admonishing finger-wagging (hers). "But where is your vanished gentleman?"

"On canvas," I replied.

She turned immediately to Irene with a shocked expression. "He is one of these brutal pugilists?"

Irene smiled. "Nell means that she has only a painted portrait to remember him by."

The Divan One turned to me with a conspiratory leer. "Sometimes I think that this is the ideal place for men—in oils, preferably burning." She examined my attire with mercurial speed. "But you look ravishing, my dear Miss Uxleigh, in green. Nile green like a queen. You require an asp for the evening. If I can find Oscar you may carry him for the night—"

She began uprooting brocaded pillows, and I am sorry to say that something long and sinuous stirred amid the patterned cloths. I felt a sudden panic.

"Let sleeping snakes lie," Irene urged. "Our poor Nell had a rather upsetting encounter with a reptile today."

"Upsetting? Snakes are the soul of tact. Where is the naughty serpent that has upset my adorable Miss Uxleigh? I shall tie it in a knot until it promises to be good."

"I am afraid that I cannot produce it," Irene admitted. "I was forced to shoot it."

"So sad," Sarah hissed sympathetically. (Lest any suppose me so prejudiced against the actress that I exaggerate, I must stress that the French word for "sad" is *triste*, and Sarah lisped it, thusly: *trisssste*.) The actress made sure that all eyes in the salon were fixed on her before speaking further. "I also was forced to shoot a snake. Otto was eating my sofa cushions. He went quite berserk."

"This snake did not have a name that we know of," Irene said, "other than cobra."

The Divine Sarah sat up amid her cushions. "A *cobra*? You shot a venomous snake? Otto was merely a boa constrictor; like most men, he was not dangerous unless one wished to embrace him. But a cobra—again you amaze me, my enterprising Irene. I salute your marksmanship. A cobra is a much smaller target than a boa." She pointed to a lengthy pair of loudly patterned serpents as thick as top hats that coiled decoratively around an ironwork torchère and a potted tree.

"The room was dark," I added.

Sarah fanned herself in agitation. "And in the dark! Even more astounding."

"Not really," commented a new voice in impeccable French. "I imagine the lady aimed for the hood, which would be fully fanned if the snake were raised to strike. The head is the only place to shoot a snake."

We turned to face a gentleman in evening dress. For all his refined garb and perfect French, I should not have judged him a gentleman in the oldest sense of the word. I have never regarded a pair of blue eyes that seemed colder. Despite his fifty or more years, his features were energetic, with a jaw so powerful I was immediately reminded of the bear at our feet.

His white hair had receded from his brow, but baldness did not make him a figure of fun. Rather, it stripped away all softening influences from those pugnacious features, and seemed an affront rather than an accident of nature. His baldness resembled the tonsured sleekness of a fanatical monk. I am not often aware of men as men, but this one struck me as wielding an innate power over his fellow creatures, as if he were a law unto himself. His effect on the others was as potent. Irene had not changed outwardly, but I saw that she had gathered her most incisive instincts about her like a cloak. She radiated an air of instantly rising to the occasion, like a hunter who, stalking dangerous prey, suddenly finds it before her eyes.

Godfrey was no less wary, although one who did not know him would not see that fact. His expression grew noncommittal, guarded. He, too, was concentrating all his faculties on this stranger.

"My dear Captain Morgan!" Sarah actually rose, her gown coiling around her in folds of taffeta and velvet, and advanced—rustling in a way that set my teeth on edge—down the dais steps to offer her hand.

Captain Morgan bowed over it like a Bohemian princeling, which breed I have observed, in a stiff salute, though the kiss was perfunctorily proper. Certain recent events had made me newly aware of the nuances that may be hidden in a kiss.

"What have you brought me?" the Shameless Sarah purred deep in her throat.

"If Madame wishes me to present it in the presence of her guests . . ." He clapped his hands.

Two turbaned servants, their faces the color of *café au lait*, came bearing a great furry bundle over the prone bearskin on the floor.

"This is . . . magnificent!" Sarah exclaimed when the men knelt to unfurl the bundle at her feet, a mammoth pelt. The three of us edged back to avoid the tide of white fur lapping at our shoe tips. "Extraordinary!"

"No more than the mistress of the world stage deserves," Captain Morgan said grandly.

As the bearskin foamed over his feet I noticed that he wore black boots with his evening dress—polished to obsidian sheen, but boots, not shoes! I was beginning to revise my notions on the unimportance of men's dress. Certainly this man's boots spoke of a disregard for civilized niceties.

The huge white pelt ended in a head larger than that of the brown bear, with even sharper teeth. We all gazed speechlessly at this incredible hide.

"I shot it once," the captain boasted idly. "Through the eye, so the skin should bear no mark. Of course a glass eye now covers the bullet hole."

"How clever of you," Sarah said. "But where—?"

Captain Morgan altered his face in a way that might have suggested a smile to the undiscriminating, revealing teeth as yellow and prominent as his massive prey's more pointed armament. "As you know, I hunt the brown bears in Russia. In the northern reaches of that land, where the glaciers creep south toward the tents of man's farthest-flung outposts, the great polar bear rules, virtually invisible against an endless carpet of ice and snow. They call the place Siberia. I donned the hide of a seal, skin-side out, so I wore the bone color of that icy wasteland to stalk these great white bears."

"You took more than one?" Irene asked quickly.

Captain Morgan bowed his bald head in mock-humble pride. "The Czar permits my Russian hunting expeditions; I am privileged to reward my host." He turned to Madame Sarah. "This is the only polar bear pelt I have brought further than St. Petersburg."

"You will be outrageously rewarded," she promised with a happy pout, "much to the displeasure of my manager, Herr Heine. This is too wonderful to resist. Lay it upon my divan."

The turbaned servants understood French, for they instantly bent to lift the heavy bearskin into place. There it lay in barbaric splendor. Sarah reclined upon it in calculated inches, finally pushing her hands into the thick fur to the wrists.

"To think that I will be honored in the same night with the presence of the Empress of Russia and the emperor of polar bears. You are a peerless hunter, Captain. I quite quiver for your prey."

He laughed, a harsh, humorless sound. "And so you should, Madame."

He withdrew to our side as Sarah's other guests came to examine her prize, then turned to Irene. "I would be interested in your cobra skin—Madame, is it?"

"It is," Godfrey answered in French so blandly that the man whirled as if confronted by an enemy from ambush. He was a good judge of character, that hunter, for I have never known Godfrey to be so dangerous as when he is quiet.

"*Monsieur—?*" the captain began, seeking his identity.

"Godfrey Norton," Godfrey said sharply in English.

The captain's strong jaws snapped shut, as if he had been struck an invisible blow. Then the fierce blue eyes narrowed and focused on me. "And Mrs. Norton—?" he asked in a perfectly proper British voice.

"Mrs. Norton is the lady behind you," Irene said in her impeccable French, "who shot the snake. This is Miss Huxleigh, our friend."

"American!" He turned, unfooled by her perfect French, and his blue eyes drilled into Irene like bullets. "You are merely visiting the Continent, then?"

"I am a bird of passage, Captain," she said airily, "as are we all."

"But your home is in America."

"One of them. Once."

"I am serious about the cobra. I have a large collection of cobra skins."

Irene considered, casting her eyes down to her fan and biting her lip in mock-girlish fashion. "I cannot swear that I shot it precisely through the eye, sir. It might not be suitable for your collection."

"I do not require snakeskins to be whole. I rather enjoy shooting cobras. I like to see the evidence of it."

"It would have killed me," Irene answered. "That is why I shot it. And the Paris police are as interested in the skin as yourself. Perhaps you should inquire there."

"Perhaps." His icy gaze regarded us all. "I did not mean to interrupt your discussion. Pray continue."

With another bow so smart it seemed an insult rather than a courtesy, he left the dais.

Sarah looked up from caressing her new pet to address us. "I must confess—" her large, blue-green eyes drooped into Lucifer-size slits "—that few Englishmen impress me. That one does. He has passion. Unfortunately, the game that obsesses him is not human."

"Who is he?" Godfrey asked.

"Captain Sylvester Morgan, late of Her Majesty's forces in India. He has brought me all these lovely bears. I will not have heads of the big cats mounted about me; those I can import to my salon alive, like Minette." She nodded at the tiger cub clumsily cavorting in one corner of the salon. "But bears— they are too big for domestic pets."

"How did you meet him?" Irene wondered.

"He is not a man to trust to chance. He introduced himself, as an admirer."

"How long ago?"

"Does any truly intelligent woman keep count of such things? As well ask me to number my lovers, dear Irene. It is impossible! One must live life so that it cannot be caged behind mere dates. But for some years I have known him. He comes and goes. I hear that no tiger in India is safe from his marksmanship, but of course he knows better than to confront me with his tigerskins." She absently stroked the bear pelt.

"I imagine," Irene said after a slight pause, "that specific times are equally tiresome to the truly intelligent woman, but can you venture to say when the Empress will arrive?"

"Oh, that, yes! Her equerry was most officious about it. She will arrive at nine and depart within half an hour. You must sing in that interval. I trust that you have selected something brief. The instrument is there."

Her furled fan indicated something huddled in a corner of the room. It could have been a draped tiger cage. It could have been a piano. Irene glided over to it, Godfrey and I following.

She lifted the thread-encrusted throw, which was emblazoned with the actress's ubiquitous motto: "*Quand même*," Despite Everything. "Here, I think, is Oscar, Nell. Sarah is right; you should carry him as an accessory."

Irene lifted the coiling Indian green snake from the dusty key cover with one hand. He responded by winding himself several times around her forearm. Her flesh-colored gloves too artfully mimicked bare skin. I repressed a shudder at the picture the pair presented, reminding me of a foolish Eve in a lethal Eden.

Godfrey peeled Oscar from Irene and draped him over a twittering, thick-leaved plant. In fact, the twittering came from the contents of a birdcage concealed by the foliage.

Irene lifted the key cover and struck a note. "I doubt it is in tune. Music is not Sarah's forte. This will be a poor excuse of a concert."

"It *is* an excuse, Irene," I reminded her, managing not to sound at all sympathetic.

She smiled. "Quite right, Nell. What does Madame Norton's musical reputation matter, if she satisfies her curiosity?"

"There is more to it than that." Godfrey withdrew a pair of dusky cigarettes from his gold case and offered one to Irene.

A moment later a lit lucifer twinkled in our shadowed corner of the salon, and then two scarlet embers burned as bright as animal eyes in the dark. The charred lucifer made a burnt offering for the shallow porcelain dish atop the piano.

"Yes," Irene agreed at length, gazing toward the guests through a contemplative curtain of smoke.

I followed her example, recognizing no one but the noxious bear-killer, and then only by his bald head. The salon had become as mysterious as any Montmartre bistro, so fogged was it with smoke. I am sorry to say that cigarette smoking, even by women, had become the fashion at artistic assemblages such as this. Few objected to the petite cigarette as strenuously as they might to a cigar; certainly the odor was milder. And more than the occasional woman carried a bejeweled cigarette holder in her reticule, as Irene did. It occurred to me to wonder if the Empress of All the Russias would smoke.

"Godfrey," Irene said of a sudden, "you pore over the political columns in the newspapers. What do they say of Russia and its royal family?"

"A large subject for a summary."

"You summarize divinely," she said, smiling. "Pray do it."

"Alexander the Third is said to be an utter autocrat."

Irene nodded. "And his wife?"

"The mother of his six children. Much loved. Her only flaw is a fondness for Paris fashion."

"An utter paragon, then."

"So it seems. But czars' heads rest uneasily on their shoulders. The Romanovs have a history of internal treachery and outside assassination for possession of the throne. Germany is nibbling at the Russian bear's borders. England bristles over Russia's intentions toward India, past and present."

"So France is Russia's most obvious ally."

"For now."

Irene straightened suddenly and extinguished her cigarette in the small dish. "Politics is so dull, Godfrey! But, look, here comes royalty and fashion to rescue the evening. I predict that the reception is about to become far more interesting."

Indeed, a flurry at the doorway resolved itself into an ornately bemedaled Russian officer, who announced: "Her Imperial Majesty, the Czarina Maria Feodorovna, Empress of All the Russias."

"I should think, Godfrey," Irene commented sotto voce, "that, from what you have said, one Russia is enough to lord it over, just as a single cobra is sufficient for target practice."

"Indeed," I said, gathering myself to observe the progress of my first empress.

Imagine my surprise to see a tiny, dark-haired woman as slender as a schoolgirl enter the chamber. Her exquisite gown and jewels, however, commanded a respect her diminutive person could never enforce alone.

She illuminated that smoky, decadent salon like the sun bursting full power upon the sulky shadows of a swamp. Her yellow taffeta gown dripped blonde lace. Canary diamonds circled her neck and wrists and glittered in a tiara against her raven hair. Most glorious of all was the cheerful smile on her face.

Sarah had risen and curtsied deeply to this doll-like figure. After exchanging a few, unheard words, she turned to present Irene, who had appeared behind the actress. Irene sank into her rosy skirts in a profound but less effusive curtsy than Sarah's.

Godfrey was presented next. I had never seen him bow from the waist, but he managed it quite nicely. Then I, oh dear . . . I hardly recall the actual moment, a propensity of mine under great stress. We Shropshire girls had always practiced our curtsies in the unlikely case that we ever "met the Queen." I had never expected to meet an empress, but gave her slightly less than the same curtsy I would our own Queen, and thought that should suffice. After all, Godfrey had described the relations between my country and hers as "uneasy." A bit of coolness seemed appropriate. I most remember her remarkable eyes, darker than Irene's, but bright with amiable pleasure.

Others were presented, as well as the six or seven with the Empress—large, blonde, uniformed men like the King of Bohemia, tall women glittering with jewels and foreign eyes whether blonde or dark. The faces are a blur, save for the tall blonde woman I had noticed earlier; so she *had* been Russian! I asked Godfrey for the time, to which he produced a gold pocket watch and the answer, "nine-fifteen."

I suddenly found Irene at my side. She took my arm while

Godfrey took the opportunity to pay his respects to the barbaric buffet table, much to my surprise. Irene never ate before a performance, and Godfrey knew that I would never consume a crumb from the Divine Sarah's table; some men, however, can eat anything, anywhere. It made me speculate unpleasantly on Quentin's past eating habits.

"Now, Nell," Irene told me, unworried by Godfrey's culinary intemperance. "You must sit at Sarah's rather decrepit piano and play an F-minor chord."

"I? You mentioned no such necessity before!"

"I expected to accompany myself, but had not inspected Sarah's piano before. Utterly unreliable. Do not fret. I anticipated as much and came prepared to sing a cappella, but I must start someplace. One chord. Surely you can manage that."

"F-minor?"

"F-minor."

"I . . . believe that I remember where that is."

"I will show you before we start."

"And then what do I do?"

"Remain seated and try not to draw untoward attention to yourself," she answered dryly.

"F-minor?"

"Yes!"

"I did play a bit of piano as a child."

"I know."

"But I've never *performed* before."

"This is not a 'performance.' Casanova could do as much. With two feet. I only need one hand."

"How long should I hold the chord?"

"Until I start singing."

"Oh." I was being steered to the piano corner and seated on the small stool upholstered in leather—leather well scored by rather large cat claws. "Oh!"

"Never mind, Nell." Irene placed my right hand on the keyboard and guided my fingers to the appropriate keys.

"There. Simply press down, hold and then—gently—release."

How gently? I was going to ask, but Irene had turned to face the salon. I looked beyond her to see that during our intense discussion the Empress and her entourage had been seated in a semicircle around us, to see even Sarah Bernhardt sitting on an ordinary upright chair! I glanced quickly to my fingers. They had not moved. Apparently. Unless a finger had slipped onto an adjoining key when my attention had been distracted and I would strike a disastrously off-key chord . . .

Irene stood but two feet from me, calmly shaking out her skirt folds and clearing her throat. I had meant to tell her: smoking could not be doing her voice any good. I would misstrike the keys, and she would croak, and that would be the end of this little charade chez Sarah!

Several gentlemen were standing at the back of the room among the parlor palms, birdcages and hidden snakes, among them a flash of flesh-pink bald head and relentless blue eyes. In their evening dress they resembled a phalanx of penguin-like little tin soldiers. That comparison immediately made me think of the purported reason for this expedition, the abruptly absent Quentin Stanhope. Could he possibly resurface here, now? Would I truly see him again . . . or would he see me making a fool of myself at the keyboard of a neglected piano? Oh, dear . . .

"My most honored guest and her companions, and my dear friends," said Sarah, rising to stand beside her chair. "I present at Her Majesty's request my own friend, Madame Norton, performing a song of her selection. She will be . . . ah, accompanied by her friend, Miss Uxleigh."

I shook my head violently, but Sarah was sitting down with the blithe satisfaction of one who has performed her duty.

The striking blonde woman broke from the knot of the Empress's attendants and came crackling toward us, her glittering bodice clicking violently.

"Her Imperial Highness is ready," she told Irene in French

with a throaty accent. "I myself anticipate your performance. I have heard your talents spoken of most highly."

"I hope you will not be disappointed." Irene answered the odd undercurrent in the other woman's voice. "I am but a modest avocational singer," she added lightly.

"Oh, you do yourself an injustice, Madame," the woman returned, her eyes the color of Russian cherry-amber glittering in tandem with her gown's beadwork. "Begin when you are ready." She clicked and rustled off . . . to join Captain Sylvester Morgan at the back of the salon!

Irene had not followed her departure, instead reaching inward. A moment of concentrated quiet always prefaced a performance. Then she glanced over her shoulder at me and nodded.

My miserable hand pressed down the miserable keys upon which my fingers rested. The chord that rang out was certainly minor, but where one might find a starting note in it I could not imagine.

Then Irene's voice began, deep and mournful as a bell. She poured out pure sound, not song. Melancholy, ponderous sound, mourning made music. I cannot say how long it was before I realized that the sound had become words, and that those words were not German or French, or even Bohemian, but something very near the latter—Russian! When had Irene learned Russian? And when had she mastered this alien piece, which was a far cry from the robust peasant melodies of Dvořák?

While I pondered the strange new music, I kept my fingers tensed upon the keys. I was terrified that taking my hand away, even though the chord had long since faded, might disrupt the song. Yet my hand protested its unnatural position. Just when I decided to ease one finger from the keys at a time, a motion on the piano top caught my eye.

The fringe of the piano scarf that draped the closed top and dangled over the front and sides was wavering. While Irene's voice seemed at times to make the walls vibrate in sympathy, I seriously doubted that silk should follow suit . . . especially since the area that trembled now *migrated* slowly from one side of the piano case to the other.

I remained unmoving, my right hand crippled into its awkward position, my eyes never daring to leave the cloth as its horrid undulations seemed to sink and swell in response to the expression in Irene's voice.

Where was little Oscar? More to the point, where were the larger snakes that Sarah Bernhardt kept: the huge muscular spotted species familiarly called boa constrictors? I had heard of snake charming; was it possible that Irene was a born snake singer? That I would be the first "accompanist" to perform in tandem with a reptile?

I eyed my general vicinity for a discreet means of escape. None; I had no recourse save tumbling over backward on the stool and hoping to arise from the tangle of my gown in time to avoid the snake's following me into disgrace.

Although Irene's voice throbbed with the pathos of a violin while delivering the strange, thick-throated words she sang; although one part of my mind noted that she was giving a magnificent and moving performance, and that her unaccompanied voice had a rich power I had scarcely suspected before; although I had to concede that her musical selection was brilliantly chosen and was delighting her audience, I simply could not sit here mesmerized by the ever-nearing manipulations of a snake, no matter what it was wearing!

I lifted first my forefinger. Then my ring finger and my smallest finger. It only remained for me to remove my thumb from the ivory and I would be free of the piano. Perhaps tiny pushes of my feet could ease the stool backwards, and then I could unobtrusively edge sideways, jump up and run!

Sound exploded around me, and I did exactly that in a flash, save that I could not run. Everyone was standing to applaud Irene, except the Empress, who would have stood had she been sitting where I was, even if she *was* an Empress.

"May I?" came a male voice from much closer to me than it should have been.

I glanced toward the piano to find the odious bear-slayer awaiting my permission for something. I nodded numbly.

He tore back the cloth.

I gasped and covered my mouth to muffle the sound.

A long, dark, furry . . . appendage writhed on the polished wood.

Captain Morgan smiled that mirthless smile of his and lifted the slightly open piano top. From within he extracted a hairy little gnome of a creature.

"A Capuchin monkey," he said. "A good thing that you did not actually play the instrument. The rascal was inside, with only his tail—keeping time to the music, I think—protruding. I trust that he did not disconcert you."

"Not in the least," I managed to croak.

Captain Morgan let the creature run up his arm to his shoulder and loop its extraordinarily long tail around his neck. He looked to Irene, who had been called over to receive the Empress's congratulations.

"She is a politician, this Madame Norton," he mused, oddly, since Irene had earlier professed finding politics dull. "Beautiful women make very dangerous politicians. Tell her that my interest in the cobra remains keen. Tell her that she should surrender it to me."

" 'Surrender'? A most odd phrasing, sir."

"Tell her exactly what I said. Can you do that?"

His condescending question reminded me that in some quarters I was considered an adventuresome woman. I drew myself up. "I will report your words precisely."

He nodded, that awful man, with the monkey cradled around his head, its clawed paws curving over his bald scalp. For a moment, the two seemed a hellish hybrid of man and beast.

"You had better," said he curtly, and left me.

## Chapter Fifteen

# HOMEWARD BOUND

"**I have** only one question," Godfrey said on the morning after our command performance on the Boulevard Péreire.

We were gathered after a late breakfast—Irene's and Godfrey's had been taken in bed—in the small front parlor that served as music room. At least Casanova's cage shared the space with a handsome, square grand piano, on whose shawl-strewn top he was forever casting grape stems and seed hulls.

"What is that, my darling?" Irene asked lazily. (Though she usually possessed an almost demonic energy, she all too easily evinced that post-performance sloth so deplorably common to those of a theatrical bent.)

Godfrey put down the Paris papers, which were printed on exceedingly thin tissue, like that which wraps pastries. I often suspect that the word "insubstantial" was invented in Paris.

"What was the name of the piece you sang for the Empress last night?" he queried further.

Irene wrapped herself tighter within her violet taffeta robe with a self-congratulatory rustle. Her feet, clad in purple satin slippers, were crossed upon an ottoman.

"I am so delighted that you asked. It was an aria from the most recent Tchaikovsky opera, *Eugene Onegin.* Melancholy stuff, but then there is so much of Russia, and so few Russian cities of gaiety and style. No wonder that everything composed there sounds like a dirge."

"Melancholy suits you," Godfrey replied, "or, rather, your voice. Not a soul in the salon moved an eyelash while you sang."

Irene sat up to regard me over her balloon-sleeved shoulder. "Our dear Nell, I understand, was a veritable pillar of salt during my rendition: so smitten that she could not even lift a finger to remove it from the keyboard."

"I did strive to prevent any distraction," I replied, rising from my chair to approach Casanova's cage.

The bird waddled over to the brass bars, actually welcoming company, especially when it bore an olive branch of plump Muscat grapes.

"You succeeded admirably," Irene admitted, sipping from the coffee cup that accompanied her from rising until noon on mornings after such late evenings. "What did Captain Morgan say to you? I saw him showing you the clever little monkey."

"Eerie beast!" I could not help shuddering when I recalled the creature clasped in that man's arms like some demonic infant. "And Captain Morgan made no sense, though he insisted that I convey a message to you. I am thinking better of it this morning."

Godfrey and Irene exchanged a glance. "You had better do so," he said.

"But Captain Morgan is an odious fellow! Why should I serve as his messenger? And why should Irene be of interest to him?"

"Exactly, my dear Nell." Irene's eyes shone like the almost-black coffee that filled her cup. "Once again you state the obvious with scintillating originality. And you are quite right that I am utterly insignificant. Still, I would like the captain's message."

"Cut the cackle!" croaked Casanova, thrusting his ruffled head forward for another grape. I had neglected his supply in the heat of the discussion.

He got his grape and Irene got her answer.

"Captain Morgan was most rude," I said. "He insisted that he was still interested in the skin of the cobra that you killed. He said that you would do well to surrender the skin to him."

"That is exactly what he said?"

I sighed. "If you wish me to go upstairs and consult my diary—?"

"I do," she answered. "There is nothing for accuracy like the words when they are first set down."

I forsook Casanova, who kept calling "Cassie want a crumpet" after my departing figure, and thumped up the stairs to my bedchamber.

Irene was still lounging in the upholstered chair, feet up, when I returned, except that a cigarette was decorating her small enameled holder and filling the room with tendrils of smoke. "And?"

I stood before them like a well-drilled schoolgirl and read from my own hand: "The Awful Evening ended with the removal of the monkey from the piano chamber. The dreadful bear-slayer said, 'She is a politician, this Madame Norton. Beautiful women make very dangerous politicians. Tell her that my interest in the cobra remains keen. Tell her that she should surrender it to me.' "

I shut my diary, pursed my lips and waited.

Irene looked at Godfrey, who looked at me.

"That is exactly what he said—his interest in the cobra remains keen?" she asked.

I nodded. "It could not be clearer."

Irene laughed then, a cascading gale that somehow made my taut lips want to twitch. "Oh, Nell, much about this affair could be made a great deal clearer, but I am glad that you are here to take such convoluted matters at face value."

"Captain Morgan was *not* speaking literally?"

"Captain Morgan was warning me. His 'cobra' is *your* 'Cobra.' "

"I have no such thing as a snake!"

"He spoke of a man, not a man-biter. Quentin Stanhope.

Remember? He used the spy name 'Cobra' in Afghanistan.''

I looked back to my diary pages, and the neat ink-blue words took on a sudden sinister significance. "Then the 'cobra' in which Captain Morgan remains keenly interested is . . . Quentin. And he wants you to surrender Quentin to him!"

"As if I had Mr. Stanhope to do so," Irene pointed out good-humoredly.

I clasped the open diary to my bodice. "You would betray him?"

"No, but I do wonder what Captain Morgan would attempt to do if he knew Mr. Stanhope's whereabouts. Do not worry, Nell; at the most I would use your Mr. Stanhope as a Judas goat."

"The poor man! No wonder he fled this cottage as one might a trap."

"I think his flight had more to do with Captain Morgan—perhaps the possessor of an air gun, do you think?—and a great deal to do with you."

"Myself? But I am of no significance in this matter."

"At the moment you are a go-between for hunter and prey."

"And what role do you play in the game of cat-and-mouse?"

"Ah." Irene inhaled the smoke from her cigarette as if it were food for thought, and expelled a dreadful one. "Call it, rather, a game of cobra-and-mongoose—or tiger. I am convinced that Captain Morgan is the person that Mr. Stanhope knew as 'Tiger' in Afghanistan."

Even Godfrey sat up at that. " 'Tiger'? Are you certain, Irene?"

"I am, but my facts are not. I will have to ask you to do more pottering amongst the official papers."

"There will be no record of the English-Afghanistan War in Paris!" I pointed out triumphantly.

Irene regarded me as if I were auditioning for the role of a madwoman. "Of course not. In London."

"You are sending Godfrey to London?"

"No, I am going with Godfrey to London."

He laughed softly, obviously hearing for the first time this latest intemperate scheme. Unfortunately, Godfrey was a good deal more accommodating than myself.

"Well, Irene, you cannot go to London!" I said.

"It may mean Mr. Stanhope's life," she advised me.

"I am sure that he is well suited to preserving it himself."

"Matters must be investigated there if we are to get to the bottom of this."

"I am not at all convinced that I wish to get to the bottom— or the top—of this. And certainly *you* cannot go to London!"

"Why not?"

"Irene, must I constantly remind you of the obvious? You are presumed dead. You are living in virtual anonymity by your own wish. You are known in London. If you go there, you will betray your existence. You may attract the attention of the King of Bohemia's agents—who may not truly have given you up. And you will certainly risk drawing the notice of Mr. Sherlock Holmes of Baker Street."

"He knows that I am alive."

"But he warned you in Monte Carlo to avoid the kind of matters he delves in. I know what you are up to, do not deny it! You will immediately seek out the Dr. Watson who is associated with Mr. Holmes. In so doing, you will stride right into the serpent's jaws. You will ruin your anonymity!"

"Goodness," said Irene calmly. "Quite a case you have built up. Indeed, it is awkward for me to venture from the Continent. You are quite right, Nell," she added with becoming contriteness. "I would, of course, immediately find this Dr. Watson to learn whether he is Mr. Stanhope's Dr. Watson, although the likelihood is . . . well, unlikely." She sighed and was silent.

I closed my diary and glanced at Godfrey, who was regarding Irene's bowed head with concern, or at least surprise. She sat up abruptly, her entire manner animated for the first time that morning.

"But of course! That is the solution! Once again, Nell, your inescapable logic has shown me the way. *You* must go to London with Godfrey while I remain safe and undetected in Paris. How could I miss such an obvious conclusion?"

"I? And Godfrey? But—"

"*You* are not in danger of detection; nor is Godfrey. Neither of you had a public reputation in London, as I did. Unless you led a double life—? No. Certainly you can both be more discreet than I. And since Nell would worry during my absence in London—"

"I would indeed."

"I will remain at home here in Neuilly and worry about *you!*"

Irene sat back with the happy expression of a child who has successfully protested a bedtime by persuading the governess to stay up with her.

"Why must anyone go to London at all?" I muttered.

"Because, dear Nell, Captain Morgan is a very dangerous man who is not only on the trail of poor Mr. Stanhope, but also of the man whom Mr. Stanhope hopes to protect. And now Captain Morgan is convinced that we are involved in the matter. We must delve deeper into the affair for the sake of our own skins, if nothing else. Is that not true?"

"I do not like your figure of speech."

"Which figure?"

"Skins," I intoned. "I have had enough of bearskins. Nor do I care to encounter snakes in any form, even metaphorical, as in this Captain Morgan's case."

Godfrey laughed. "We must, dear Nell. Irene has requested that the Paris police surgeon inspect the, er . . . form . . . of the deceased cobra as well as its victim. He promised to call tomorrow, and I suspect that he will."

"You agree with this scheme, Godfrey?"

He thought for a moment, while regarding Irene fondly. "I agree that we must take action. Whether we like it or not, our taking in Stanhope has attracted the attention of those with the most noxious motives . . . to Stanhope himself—and to us all."

"Then it is settled!" Irene rose and shook out her taffeta robe until it crackled. "I will remain here and pursue snakes, of various sorts, while you two will visit London and interview medical men named Watson who served in Afghanistan." She sighed and gave me a grave look. "I think, my dear Nell, that you have chosen the better part."

"All the world's a stage," the parrot proclaimed as if cued. I suspect that he was.

One good thing can be said about preparing for travel: it so occupies the mind that the ordinary shocks and surprises of life seem strangely muffled.

Thus I was like a person moving rapidly through a fog in the two days preceding Godfrey's and my untimely departure. Thoughts of Quentin Stanhope collided in my mind as I dealt with shirtwaists and stockings, corsets and collars.

Though I well knew that this trip—like all of Irene's schemes—was designed to distract me from the case of reason and restraint, I also sensed a hidden purpose. Yet I could not argue with her intent to safeguard Quentin, no matter how rudely he had behaved toward me. I was so triumphant at having persuaded Irene to remain safely behind that I did not contemplate one obvious fact until I was alone with my thoughts and my wearables: by going to London, I would almost certainly encounter Quentin again, should Godfrey and I have any success in our inquiries.

So I often found myself standing with a knot of petticoats clutched to my bosom, my heart pounding. I moved my latest diary from one hidden place to another, and finally burdened my trunk with the volume. If anything should happen to me, if the steamer should sink in the Channel, so too would my tenderest thoughts.

I did not give much thought to Irene or to my traveling companion, Godfrey. For the first time, I faced a matter so pressing that my own affairs, such as they were, took precedence over my lifelong dedication to the welfare of others. I had not the slightest thought to spare for the most commonplace things around me. Even Lucifer had a downcast look as he lounged on my counterpane and watched the contents level of the trunk rise. Casanova serenaded me with such innovative variations as "Cassie want a trumpet" to catch my attention, in vain.

With customary efficiency, Godfrey had dashed out to book our passage from Calais. We faced a short train journey followed by a hopefully calm crossing and another short train journey at the other end. I confess that the notion of seeing London again, of breathing British air, quite excited me. Certainly it was only that which caused my heart to give little, breathless skips now and then.

"He is here!" Irene announced the next day, pausing breathlessly on the threshold to my bedchamber.

Only one type of personage (excluding Godfrey) could cause that sudden exuberance, the pink on her cheeks and the fire in her eye: an emissary from the realm of crime and chaos beyond the ken of most gentlefolk.

I set down my small pile of handkerchiefs and went below, where our parlor housed a representative of the Paris Prefecture of Police.

Godfrey paused in the pouring of a sherry—these Paris police are ever ready to mix business with pleasure—and nodded to me as I entered after Irene.

"Our dear friend, Miss Huxleigh. Dr. Sauveur."

I nodded at a hedgehog of a man with a quantity of unruly brown hair erupting around bright brown eyes and an unfortunate, though imposing, nose.

"Dr. Sauveur is associated with the Paris police," Irene explained unnecessarily. I can make some deductions quite unassisted. "He has examined both the unhappy Indian man who perished in Montmartre and the cobra I killed."

"How fortunate," I murmured as I sat.

"Most unfortunate," the doctor contradicted me. "This incident is a complete puzzle." He flipped up his coattails and sat, cradling his glass in both hands with a familiarity all too common to the French when it comes to alcoholic beverages. "I am more baffled than when I first heard of the case."

"Perhaps," Godfrey suggested after he had brought me a glass of Vichy water, "you could begin by telling us the condition of the man."

"Dead." The doctor laughed. "And by cobra venom, though there were no fang marks upon the body. Most puzzling."

At this Irene nearly leaped out of her chair. "No bite marks? But the snake I shot—"

"Was venomous, Madame. You did well to dispatch it. Yet it was not the means of the Indian gentleman's death."

"Do you mean to say, Dr. Sauveur," Godfrey demanded, "that my wife and Miss Huxleigh found a man dead of snakebite alone in a room with a poisonous snake—and the snake was innocent?"

Dr. Sauveur shrugged and sipped sherry. "That is what Inspector Dubuque asked. But facts are facts. There were no fang marks on the dead man."

"Were there any other marks upon him?" Irene inquired.

The doctor looked up with a moue of distaste. "I understand, Madame, that in your . . . past you were a theatrical performer and were thus accustomed to arming yourself as you went to and fro at night. Or so Inspector Dubuque tells me that you told him."

Irene smiled mysteriously at his disapproving tone. Once she would have told him sternly that she had been a prima donna, not some obscure supernumerary one corset-cover removed from scandal. Now she dared not advertise her past respectability without betraying her past identity.

"My wife," Godfrey put in for her, "is American. It is not uncommon that respectable women there carry weapons for self-defense."

"Ah, America. Always the Wild West Show, no? So the Inspector told me that he was told. Still . . . for a woman to go armed in Paris is as unusual as for a man to die of snakebite without a mark upon his skin."

"Unusual," I put in despite my uncertain French pronunciation, "but fortunate in this case. The creature was preparing to strike Irene."

"It was frightened, Mademoiselle," the doctor began.

"So was I!"

"Miss Huxleigh is not terribly sympathetic to snakes," Irene said, "and I do not blame her. What have you learned, then, of the man and the snake, beyond the intriguing fact that they had nothing to do with one another despite a common Indian origin and their admittedly . . . close association in death?"

"From what the inspector tells me, the Indian is unlikely to be identified. Such men are nameless, usually of the servant or sailor class. They come and go as their masters and ships do; few know or note their progress. The cobra is as common, at least in its native land. An Asian cobra is only one and a half meters long—some five feet in your measurement in England, or America, Madame 'Sharpshooter'—" the last word was delivered in English with a pronounced French emphasis "—no very great length as cobras go. It is not as if it was a king cobra. Now those reach—you would say?— eighteen feet."

I must have made a whimper of distaste, for all regarded me attentively.

"A most royally attenuated serpent," I admitted. "Madame Sarah would adore it."

Dr. Sauveur shook his grizzled head at me with some sympathy. "What eccentrics, these performers, eh?" He smiled unctuously at Godfrey, who regarded him with the cold, cobralike stare that a good barrister can produce in court.

The physician swallowed the last of his sherry in one greedy gulp and rose. "There is little more to say. I was asked to report and have done so. The man is dead by cobra venom. The cobra was not the source and it is also dead, by pistol shot."

"Have you no speculations?" Irene asked incredulously.

The doctor's lip curled. "No, Madame. I am not paid to

speculate, only to examine. However, a colleague of Inspector Dubuque's, Inspector Le Villard, suggests that only one man may be able to unravel such a conundrum, a Mr. Sherlock Holmes of London. He is an English amateur who has written monographs on various matters. Le Villard is translating them to our language. Perhaps you have heard of this man?"

"No," said Godfrey quickly, as quickly as Irene said "Yes."

It was left for me to tread the thin line between truth and self-interest. "Perhaps," I said airily. "Theatrical people can be so eccentric."

Dr. Sauveur frowned, as if unsure how to take my meaning. Indeed, I was uncertain of that myself. Then he picked up his top hat and bowed sketchily before leaving the room. Sophie waited in the hall to let him out.

"Well!" Irene's ambiguous eyes sparkled with the pure honey of speculation. "I am minded to reconsider and journey with you. Perhaps this Mr. Sherlock Holmes we 'perhaps' have heard of should be consulted in the case! Quite a pretty puzzle."

Godfrey frowned and lit one of his cigarettes, dropping the lucifer into a crystal dish. "What do you think, Irene? Victim and weapon in the same room, but not related."

She tented her long fingers and rested her chin upon them, a pose that would have been piquant had she not been thinking so hard.

"Could there," I suggested tentatively, "have been another snake?"

"Another snake!" Godfrey nodded approvingly at me.

"That is the heart of the problem," Irene said. "Where did the snake come from, and were there two? We have assumed that the snake was an occupant of the chamber, because its cage was there. But was the Indian also an unacknowledged lodger? We cannot know for sure until we find Mr. Stanhope and ask him."

"Until *we* find Mr. Stanhope," I corrected. "Godfrey and I. You are remaining here in Paris."

"Ah! So I am. And a pretty puzzle remains here in Paris with me: the two snakes, the mysterious dead Indian who may or may not be acquainted with Mr. Stanhope, and the sinister Captain Morgan." Irene rubbed her hands together in anticipation.

"Godfrey!" I demanded. "Do you think we should leave her?"

"We have no choice," he retorted cheerfully. "I hazard that the London end of the matter will be fully as nettlesome. But the questions Irene raises are fascinating. Did the Indian bring the lethal snake—or snakes—to Stanhope's garret intending to kill him? Did one bite his trainer and escape—you said there were several open casements? Did Irene shoot an innocent bystander?" Godfrey laughed and rubbed his hands in imitation of his wife.

"Or . . ." Irene sat up with a demonic expression. "Was the Indian a manservant, even a friend of Mr. Stanhope's? Was the snake his, and did someone, not knowing of either the Indian's or the snake's existence, import his own snake to kill Mr. Stanhope? Only the lethal snake escaped, after ridding itself of its venom. But no matter how many snakes we import to the scene, we are missing something. The man was killed by snake venom . . . administered somehow. Not necessarily by a reptile. Did the same venom coat the needle that pierced Mr. Stanhope, I wonder, only in that instance, in an insufficient amount? Inspector Le Villard was right. This case requires some sophistication in chemistry. I will have to persuade the inspector to let me see whether the English detective's works include any methods of transmitting venoms. Perhaps the good inspector could use a proofreader for his translations?"

"Irene, even you would not dare!"

"Why not, Nell? One can always learn from a rival."

"You and Sherlock Holmes are not rivals."

"We are certainly not allies."

"I hope not," Godfrey put in significantly.

Irene eyed him. "Surely, Godfrey, you have not resided

near Paris long enough to contract the French national disease?"

"And what is that?" he asked.

"A rivalry of your own."

He was quiet for a moment. One of Irene's eyebrows arched in surprise. He said slowly, "I agree with Nell. You are like a moth playing with the fire. I understand that for you it is an amusing game, but it makes me uneasy at times. There is the matter of the King of Bohemia as well—"

"That, too?" She, also, had become unnaturally quiet.

"Only in that he is not likely to have forgotten you so quickly. He is an autocratic, unpredictable man, and a spoiled ruler. It is best not to tempt him into something rash. The more you plunge yourself into sensational matters, my dear Irene, the more likely you are to attract unwelcome attention, even exposure."

"Oh, pooh, Godfrey! You are sounding like Nell. Shortly Casanova will be carping at me, urging caution. The King is in Prague and Sherlock Holmes is in London. I will be in Paris, will I not?" she added almost coquettishly. "What harm can come of that? Better you should worry about the safety of Quentin Stanhope and his long-ago friend, Dr. Watson. Better you both should fret about the explanation our former houseguest owes to us all, and especially to Nell."

Once more all eyes fastened on me, as Irene skillfully turned an inquiry into her own situation into an unwanted and intimate examination of mine.

## Chapter Sixteen

# INNOCENT UNRELATED ERRANDS

**England lay** ahead, visible on the heaving silver breast of the sea. How was it that the land that I approached with so much fond eagerness should strike me as ominous when I saw the chalk cliffs of Dover rising like a ghostly barrier from the crashing sea?

Godfrey stood beside me at the rail, his feelings perhaps as mixed as mine. Neither of us was used to traveling without Irene, and we were both forlorn, yet relieved that we need not worry about her.

"I have not forgotten," Godfrey remarked.

"Forgotten what?"

"My promise to you."

"Oh, please, Godfrey, it is not necessary to speak of it."

"Yes, it is. You must not think that either Irene or I take you for granted. You are our friend, and we cannot allow this man to take advantage of you—"

"No such thing happened!"

"Or allow him to renew a friendship and then leave so callously, without explanation. Gentlemen do not do such things."

"I do not think he had any choice. If the man who died in his rooms was a friend or acquaintance, perhaps he feared that same fate for myself—for you and Irene, who had only tried to help him. An honorable man would have no choice but to flee."

Godfrey nodded slowly. "I hope for your sake that he is honorable still, Nell. If he is not—"

"Then we shall know, shall we not? And I suppose that knowing is better than . . . not knowing."

He suddenly smiled down at me. "So serious, Nell, for a lady under a Paris bonnet. You have changed, you know. Stanhope was right about that. And now you espouse the motto that drives Irene, and sometimes myself and most of the human race."

"What is that?" I asked, unaware of any recent profundity that had dropped from my lips.

" 'Knowing is better than not knowing.' I trust we shall soon know more about this tangle than we did."

"What if 'Dr. Watson' is the Dr. Watson?"

Godfrey's gray gaze suddenly twinkled like the water around us. "Then we will have a most interesting puzzle piece to deliver to Irene. Perhaps we will even surprise her and solve the puzzle altogether on this end."

"Oh, do you think so, Godfrey?! That would be . . . amusing, would it not? That would be adventuresome."

"Yes, my dear Nell, it would. Even my incomparable Irene can benefit from an outwitting now and again."

I would have never believed that London could strike me as terra incognita, yet it looked like an utterly unfamiliar charcoal sketch through which we rode by some magical means of progress—though a four-wheeler has seldom been mistaken for an altered pumpkin. The soot-blackened buildings seemed limned by some absent artistic hand rather than by reality. Viewed in the high noon of summer rather than through the romantic misty lens of gaslights and fog, the streets appeared cramped, commercial and tawdry compared to the broad, tree-strewn boulevards of Paris. The constant clatter of omnibuses and carriages, the calls of street mongers through the narrow lanes, quickly gave me the headache.

Godfrey directed the driver to Brown's Hotel.

"That sounds a rather common establishment," I commented.

Godfrey merely smiled. I had long ago learned to interpret that response: he knew something which I did not.

As our vehicle drove past Green Park to Dover Street, I realized that we had crossed into Mayfair, which made me lilt my eyebrows as Irene often did. "Is this not an excessively extravagant address?"

"We have an extravagant amount of money from the sale of the Zone of Diamonds," he replied.

I could not argue with fact, however much I might wish to. Brown's Hotel appeared as respectable as the Duke of Kent's country house, not that I have ever been a guest at such an establishment, but a governess does hear things, and I had forgotten nothing that I had heard during those days. And, of course, even then I kept my diaries, though they were not so interesting as they had become since my involvement with Irene, and now Godfrey.

For me the greatest obstacle to Irene's scheme of sending Godfrey and myself a-hunting medical Watsons in London was not the formidable consulting detective sure to be lurking there. No, the most dreaded barrier now rose up before me in a wall of coffered mahogany: the embarrassment of registering at a hotel.

Although some benighted young women nowadays, who consider themselves thoroughly modern, think nothing of remaining unchaperoned with a man for whole hours at a time, the true gentlewoman cannot permit the slightest miscomprehension of her position vis-à-vis any male person at any time. Dear as Godfrey was to me as both employer and friend, I could not bear to have a hotel clerk reach any wrongful conclusions about our relationship.

Godfrey broached the main desk. "I have made reservations for a pair of suites," said he, very commandingly, I thought.

"And the name, sir?" inquired the man on duty. The wall

behind him resembled a gigantic pigeonholed desk bristling with messages, mail and unclaimed keys.

"Feverall Marshwine," said Godfrey without batting an eyelash. "Of Paris."

"Feverall Marshwine of Paris," repeated the clerk without a pause. "Here it is, sir. And a two-room suite for Miss Lucy Maison-Nouveau."

"My cousin," Godfrey said with a courteous nod at me. The desk clerk inclined his head politely. He eyed the trunks a man had deposited in the lobby and rang for a manservant.

Shortly after we and our baggage were escorted by a modern lift to our rooms high above Old Bond Street. They were adjacent, but no one could accuse us of cohabiting without a lewd imagination.

It was not until Godfrey had paid our baggage toter an unholy amount of coinage for the herculean task of conveying our baggage up six flights in a lift that I was able to doff my bonnet and gloves and speak my mind.

We stood in the sitting room of my suite, where my trunk had been deposited until a maid could unpack it.

"This is splendid accommodation, Godfrey," I admitted, "but it is shockingly extravagant for us to occupy two rooms each. I could do quite nicely with one."

"Surely, Nell, you do not wish to be perceived as entertaining gentlemen in your bedchamber? And I will find it necessary to visit you, or vice versa, so we can compare notes on the day's investigations."

"Yes," I agreed, "but you are my 'cousin.' And what do you mean by 'gentlemen' plural? Surely my rooms are not to become an interrogation center for cabmen and snake charmers?"

He smiled. "How quick you are. I was thinking, of course, of Stanhope. Well, Nell, if—when—we locate him, it is possible that we will need to offer him the discretion of a private talk. So you see, our parlors are needed as interview rooms, so to speak, as well as for our own consultations."

"A long way around to justify extra expense," I said. "And

where did you come by those ridiculous pseudonyms? Irene, no doubt?"

He bowed. "Irene had nothing to do with it. I am in charge of this expedition."

"Feverall Marshwine?!"

"It leaped into my mind at the cable office. Have you never wanted to pretend to be someone else?"

"No, I have not. I know what I myself have been up to, but some other identity may be another case entirely. And how did you come by 'Lucy Maison-Nouveau'? Do not tell me it was another inspiration of the cable office."

"But it was! Based upon your sterling example, as always. I recalled the cable from Belgium you signed with the code name Casanova."

"Oh. I see. Maison-Nouveau is French for the same thing. In English it would be Newhouse. Perhaps the better choice, Godfrey. No one will ever mistake me for a Frenchwoman. And the 'Lucy'?"

Like many a delinquent charge from my governess days, Godfrey guiltily eyed his boot tips, polished to as glossy a black as Lucifer's fur after an hour's licking.

"*Lucifer!* Godfrey, how could you?" I managed to avoid laughing.

"A hasty and desperate invention, Nell," he said contritely, "and 'Lucille' is a French name. Forgive me, but I thought it better for us to travel incognito."

His apology was approximately as sincere as Irene's respect for the literal truth. At least no one in London who had known me would suspect that I was masquerading as a French female who had no objections to engaging a suite adjacent to that of an unrelated man, which, I admit, was decidedly "French" behavior.

"Now that we are here, what is our plan?" I asked.

"First, to eliminate the obvious."

"You mean this 'Dr. Watson' who Irene is convinced shares rooms with Sherlock Holmes?"

"Irene saw *two* men entering 221 B Baker Street late at night after the rather underhanded charade in St. John's Wood."

"I agree with you on the underhandedness of Mr. Sherlock Holmes, Godfrey. I cannot comprehend how Irene can profess such admiration for a man who would stoop to impersonating a clergyman while attempting to trick a helpless woman out of the sole artifact that defends her from another man's unwanted attentions, and a king's at that!"

"I agree with you," he said, "except for the 'helpless.' In fact, I consider it highly charitable of you, Nell, to campaign for the life of a man who very likely pitched the plumber's rocket into our drawing-room windows at Briony Lodge. It was a shabby if all too effective ploy to trick Irene into revealing the hidden chamber in which lay the photograph of her and the King of Bohemia."

"You think that Dr. Watson did such a despicable thing? He is a medical man."

"You are a former governess, but I believe that you have essayed a deceptive mission or two for Irene's sake."

"That is quite different! Nothing I have ever done could possibly be construed as malicious mischief."

"Oh? What of your masquerade as Irene's housekeeper, gloating over Mr. Holmes and King Willie when they found their trap sprung and their quarry gone?"

"Perhaps that was the tiniest bit mischievous, but it was hardly malicious, Godfrey. No, you will have to find a better apologist for Dr. Watson's failing than myself. Irene's freedom and happiness were at stake then. Sherlock Holmes had nothing to gain but a mere fee. His only interest was financial."

"Odd that he has not pursued the Zone of Diamonds now that he knows Irene is alive. . . ."

"Nothing odd, only ignorance. He knows nothing of the Zone!"

"He knows it existed, for Tiffany himself said he hired Sherlock Holmes as well as Irene to look into its whereabouts. And from your own account of the trio's visit to

Briony Lodge, it is obvious to me that Mr. Holmes had hoped to find a far more glamorous prize than a photograph, or even Irene herself."

"Obvious? To you? I wrote the account to which you refer, and it was more than obvious to me that no such undercurrent existed."

"Ah!" Godfrey spread his hands in surrender. "Useless to argue with the author of the document in question. Perhaps I am seeing undercurrents on dry land. So you are convinced now that Sherlock Holmes's Dr. Watson—should he prove also to be Quentin Stanhope's Dr. Watson—is a heartless trickster and a lying lackey not worth the effort of saving?"

"If we doled out our acts of charity according to who is worthy, we might have no objects left for our concern," I said stoutly. "And if Quentin thinks it worth risking his life for this man who saved him in Afghanistan, I can only do my best to aid in this enterprise. Besides, I am convinced that the Dr. Watson from Afghanistan in eighteen-eighty has never set foot in Baker Street except for innocent, unrelated errands! He may not even be in London, or England."

"Then the only thing to do is to test your—I hesitate to call such a rousing opinion a mere theory—assertion, shall we say?"

" 'Assertion' is a fine, forthright word that does not shilly-shally. So shall we sally forth?"

"First we have two separate duties to perform."

I grew instantly serious, as the word "duty" invariably encourages me to do.

Godfrey smiled in a way that was eerily reminiscent of Irene. "I must repair to my suite and make some alterations of a personal nature. Irene, I believe, equipped you for slight disguise?"

I produced a length of heavy black veiling, diligently spotted with velour, from the upper shelf of my trunk. "Not efficient for seeing, but most appropriate for mourning—or for not being seen."

"Excellent. And I believe now would be a good time for

you to take the hotel stationery in hand and pen a note to the family of your former employer. Mrs. Turnpenny, was it not?"

"The Turnpennys left Berkeley Square for India. I have no notion where they might reside today."

"I refer to Mrs. Turnpenny's family—the Stanhopes."

"The Stanhopes of Grosvenor Square—Quentin's parents? You expect me to address them at this late date? I have never met them!"

"But you have encountered their son recently, which may be of some interest to them if he has not already returned to England and made himself known. Merely send them a note identifying your earlier connection with the family and expressing your desire to visit them on a matter concerning their son, et cetera. You composed such communications for me innumerable times at the Temple, dear Nell. What makes you pale at the idea now?"

"They are . . . well-placed people. I cannot intrude . . . they would not see me."

"You underestimate yourself, as usual," he said with a smile. "Simply write the note, and we will leave it at the hotel desk for a messenger to deliver. And do not look so appalled! Not even Mr. Sherlock Holmes can investigate a mystery without rushing in where he is not wanted; consider his surprise descent on Briony Lodge."

"Yes, that was cheeky. Very well, I will write the Stanhopes, but I cannot guarantee any response."

"Who can in this hurly-burly world, Nell?" Godfrey said cheerfully, bowing out of my sitting room.

I spent the next half hour penning the wretched note. Several versions lay crumpled in my wastepaper basket, a pitiable waste of Brown Hotel's stationery, which was exceptionally fine cream parchment-paper. Finished at last, I struggled to affix Irene's disguising veiling to my bonnet, a process that involved several short hatpins and even more prickings of my poor fingers. Thus far I was not impressed with the business of being a private inquiry agent.

When Godfrey rapped upon my door, I opened it in not very good temper. The sight that greeted me did little to amend my mood.

"Godfrey?! What on earth have you done to yourself?"

He stepped in past me and ducked to regard himself in the small oval mirror near the door. "I have removed my mustache. Does it alter my appearance?"

"Indeed it does! And I am not sure for the better."

"I thought that you disliked facial hair upon men."

"Yes . . . but I had become accustomed to yours, and it was just a mustache, after all. Oh, what will Irene say?" I was suddenly reminded of the more intimate effects of mustaches, and blushed furiously.

"We will find out when we return to Paris. In the meantime, I congratulate myself upon the idea. At least I have changed my countenance enough to deceive Sherlock Holmes if we encounter him, for I doubt he ever much noted my appearance," Godfrey added dryly.

"You expect to encounter *the* man? Really, Godfrey, I have no desire to come that close to him again. He quite terrifies me."

"The person I expect to encounter is Dr. Watson, of whom I have never seen hide nor hair, and of whose existence and exact relationship to Holmes even you cannot be certain. Perhaps he is a figment of Irene's imagination, or a blind that Holmes uses for his advertising convenience in the agony columns, hm?"

"A third man accompanied Mr. Holmes and the King to Briony Lodge. It could have been—"

" 'Could have beens' are not evidence. We must venture to Baker Street to test our theory, and we must be prepared to elude the master detective. There, now that you have donned your bonnet and I have doffed my mustache, we look quite unlike ourselves, do we not?"

Godfrey bent so that his face and mine were both visible in the mirror.

"I look like Her Majesty in mourning," I murmured unhappily from behind my layers of veiling, "and you look like"—now that Godfrey was clean-shaven the resemblance suddenly struck me—"a rather handsome Sherlock Holmes."

Godfrey recoiled as if snake-bitten, finding the comparison too close for comfort. Yet both men were more than six feet tall, dark-haired and the same age. If both wore top hats, it would take an artist no great skill to sharpen Godfrey's nose, thicken his brows and produce a creditable simulacrum of the famed detective. I could not help smiling to myself at his discomfort. He took much harmless amusement in nudging me beyond the bounds of my strict upbringing, but the shoe distinctly pinched the other foot when I pointed out that he and his rival for Irene's professional interest bore more than a passing similarity in form.

I gave Godfrey my note, addressed to the Stanhopes of Grosvenor Square, then offered my brightest smile. "Shall we sally forth, as I said before?"

Godfrey drew my hand through his arm and we left, stopping at his rooms to gather hat, stick and gloves. The man at the desk assured us that the note would be delivered by the afternoon. I watched it vanish from my care with regret. So much can be set in motion by an innocent note. Perhaps Quentin did not wish his family to know of his return. Or perhaps he did not wish them to know of us. But at least with Irene absent, Godfrey and I were proceeding in a logical manner, rather than rushing into the unknown on pure instinct and panache.

Thus it was with some surprise that I heard Godfrey direct our cabman to "Madame Tussaud's Wax Museum on the Marylebone Road."

"Godfrey, why are we going to that awful place?"

"It is not far from Baker Street, and until recent years occupied a Baker Street address," he replied.

"That would apply to a great many other less loathsome establishments, I would suppose."

"But none draw as many sightseers. A visit to this attraction will allow us to survey the neighborhood before we concentrate on our quarry at 221 B. I suspect even the Great Mr. Holmes first reconnoitered the Serpentine Mews when he was spying upon Irene."

"Why, Godfrey, I believe that you *do not* like him at all either!"

"Why should I? He attempted to wrest from Irene her one means of protection against the King; he was willing to confront her with the King again, despite all her efforts to prevent contact. In addition, despite your opinion, I suspect that he knew of the Zone of Diamonds and hoped to capture that, as well. I cannot think of a single good turn the man has done us, save for keeping his peace about Irene's and my survival after our supposed deaths. Even there he may have some self-serving motive. He is, after all, available for hire. Irene offers her . . . diagnostic services for nothing."

"You *are* indeed a bit jealous, as you said in Monte Carlo!"

"A serious charge, and nothing to smile about, Nell, I assure you." Godfrey idly rapped his cane tip on the hansom's wooden floor. "Say rather that I am uneasy. We do not really know where this Holmes sits when it comes to secret knowledge and profit."

"That is why I am relieved that Irene remained abroad," I put in. "I feared she could not resist the opportunity to engage a foe of such caliber again. She does relish challenge," I admitted, "to an alarming degree. Now there is a woman that Mr. Stanhope could honestly call adventuresome, although he has not seen her in action."

"Hopefully, he has left France and will not. And hopefully the sinister Captain Morgan has left France also. I did not fancy leaving Irene behind with that man circulating. Please do not attribute my concern there to jealousy also, Nell. A husband may worry, that is all."

"That is most becoming, Godfrey. I can imagine no greater good fortune than that someone would worry about me one day."

"There are other emotional apexes than worry, my dear Nell."

"Such as—?"

Godfrey looked about to say something, then shook his head. "Some things one must discover for oneself. Look at the lines! We have arrived at the temple of La Tussaud."

How amazing that so many people should queue up to see some dressmaker's dummies, I thought as Godfrey helped me out of the cab and paused to pay our driver. Once we were ushered into the dim-lit building, my tune changed. Perhaps it was the cleverly manipulated lamplight and settings, but many of the waxen figures seemed eerily real, especially those in the horrific tableaux displayed in "The Chamber of Horrors."

Godfrey and I emerged into the daylight blinking, and London came into clean, bright clarity for the first time since my return.

"How wonderful to view a street crowded with carriages and horses, and omnibuses topped with signs and people, and peddlers and pedestrians," I said. "I had no idea that so many dreadful historical events required memorializing in wax. Those guillotine scenes—"

Godfrey nodded. "That is the real reason I wanted to view this exhibit. Lives are at stake in this matter we meddle in. Who can say what really happened in Afghanistan so many years ago? Yet I believe Stanhope when he says that Maclaine was brutally killed and as brutally libeled after his death, that Stanhope's own life has never been the same, and that at least one other, innocent life stands in danger today from the repercussions of whatever conspiracy unwound then."

"When you put it that way, I feel quite foolish for presuming to play a part in this drama."

"You are foolish." Godfrey looked as serious as I had ever seen him. "So is Irene, and so am I. Danger comes to a boil in the world around us. Your chance acquaintance with Quentin Stanhope—not to mention your unexpected reunion—has immersed us in the nastiest cauldron we have stirred up yet. Remember that in the days to come. Our guard must be up constantly. Nothing is more dangerous than old secrets that span many borders."

"You think our world is as ugly as the one depicted in the wax museum's Chamber of Horrors?"

He nodded. "Sometimes, Nell, it is. For the most part it presents a fairer face, but we must not allow that benign visage to lull us."

"What now, then?"

"Now that we are suitably impressed with the seriousness of our task," said he, hailing a cab with his lifted cane, "on to Baker Street and the trail of the mysterious Dr. Watson."

## Chapter Seventeen

# WATSON'S FEVERED FRIEND

"**What is** it, John, dear?"

"A matter for Holmes, I am afraid."

"Afraid? When something turns up that could benefit from Mr. Holmes's talents you are more often intrigued than regretful."

I handed the letter across the toast rack. My wife accepted it with her usual grace, preventing the lace-trimmed sleeve of her combing gown from trailing in the clotted cream, while never taking her eyes from the letter in her hand.

"Oh, how sad!" she exclaimed after reading it.

Holmes's evaluation would be far more forthcoming about the nature of the paper and penmanship, but Mary's sympathetic response echoed my own immediate reaction. Well I remembered the writer from our school days: Percy Phelps, known rather more familiarly as "Tadpole." A bright if somewhat fragile boy, he had gone on to a glittering Cambridge career, followed by a Foreign Office appointment, while I was still wallowing in enteric fever in India.

"Brain fever for nine weeks!" Mary shook her head. "The poor man." A woman's compassion is a wondrous thing. There is no man, even one hardened by life and its disappointments, who will not stir some woman to pity when he is truly down and out.

178 Carole Nelson Douglas

"I can well sympathize myself," I added, grimly recalling my own months of fever and forgetfulness nearly nine years before.

"What disaster can he refer to in his letter?" Mary wondered, her large blue eyes all concern.

"That is for Phelps to say, or, rather, for Holmes to discern."

"Yes, you must present the matter to Mr. Holmes at once! No one can dissect the unthinkable as he can."

"You are certain that you will not mind my running off for the day, Mary? Phelps gives his address as Briarbrae, Woking, and Woking is far from the city smokestacks."

"Nonsense! The poor man has asked you for help. I have never known you to refuse it. Besides, a jaunt to the country will be good for you."

Blessed the man who is joined to a compassionate woman! I kissed Mary good-bye and within twenty minutes was bound for Baker Street. If Mary's company was a balm, Holmes's was sure to be an astringent. Of that I was soon reminded when I arrived to find my friend hunched over one of his chemical experiments.

"Ah, Watson, the married man!" he greeted me without surprise. He went on to warn me that should the chemical solution turn the litmus paper red, it would cost a man's life. I watched the paper suffuse into a telltale maroon the moment Holmes thrust it into a test tube.

Holmes spent the next moments scrawling telegrams for the pageboy. "A very commonplace little murder," he commented before settling into his favorite velvet-lined armchair and giving me his utter attention, his gray eyes keen with anticipation.

I produced my mysterious letter with a tinge of hesitancy. Phelps's dilemma seemed mild in comparison with murder, no matter how commonplace. Indeed, Holmes found nothing of interest in the missive besides the fact that it had been written for my friend by a woman—a woman of extraordinary character, Holmes claimed airily without further explanation.

Yet this poor, vague spoor was enough for the hound always lurking within him. Despite declarations to the contrary, he harbored a drop or two of the milk of human kindness; in minutes we were off for Waterloo and within an hour walking toward the large house and lavish grounds at Woking where my former schoolmate lived.

We found my friend Phelps, looking pale despite the summer sunlight pouring in from the garden window, with his fiancée, Annie Harrison, a handsome, tiny woman with a madonna's eyes and a diva's glossy black hair.

Phelps's tale was sobering. He had been asked by his uncle, the Foreign Minister, to transcribe the original of a secret treaty between England and Italy, whose contents "the French or the Russians would pay an immense sum to learn."

Percy had retired to his office and stayed late in order to accomplish the task in privacy. When he went to inquire after a cup of coffee he had ordered from the commissionaire's lodge he found the old soldier asleep at his post.

At that moment, a bell rang from the very room poor Phelps had left unattended.

He dashed back to the chamber, seeing no one in the hall or its intersecting passage while coming or going. Yet Phelps found the original treaty gone. Only his copy of eleven of the twenty-six articles remained.

Although in the nigh ten weeks since the tragedy not a whisper indicated that the treaty had reached the wrong hands, be they French or Russian, this fact was small comfort to my friend. He had collapsed completely at the discovery of the theft, and only now had emerged weak and anxious from lost weeks of delirium, spent in the ground-floor bed-sitting room at Briarbrae, from which his sudden illness had evicted Miss Harrison's brother Joseph. Miss Harrison had come to Briarbrae to meet her fiancé's parents, with her brother as escort, when the tragedy occurred. Despite a sickroom bedecked with dainty bouquets from the tending hand of Miss

Harrison in every corner, despite her brother Joseph's cheery optimism, I could see that the only thing that heartened Percy's spirits was the intervention of my friend Holmes.

Yet Holmes offered no false hopes during the interview with Percy and Miss Harrison, pronouncing the case very grim indeed. We returned to London. A call on Inspector Forbes at Scotland Yard produced no obvious direction to the mystery. At least Percy's eminent uncle, Lord Holdhurst, the Foreign Minister, at Downing Street confirmed that France or Russia should have acted by now had either nation obtained the treaty.

Imagine Holmes's chagrin, after we traveled again to Woking the next day, to learn that Phelps had surprised an intruder at his window the previous night. Truly, the mystery had deepened. Holmes responded by ordering the recovering Percy to come to town with us. Holmes's actions took a further odd turn at the train station in Woking, when he left Phelps and me to proceed to London while he remained behind on errands of a peculiarly vague nature.

I had rarely been so annoyed with Holmes during our acquaintance. I would be forced to spend the entire day with Percy, a fine enough fellow but one in a strained and nervous condition.

"If your Mr. Holmes remains at Woking to trap last night's burglar, his efforts are vain," Phelps confided as we rattled along toward London.

"Why do you think so?"

"Because I am no longer at Briarbrae. Oh, you may eye me askance, Watson; you never were a decent mummer even at school, but I am not still off my head. I tell you that no common burglar broke in with that long knife last night. And if I am the target of this mania, now that I have left Briarbrae there will be no further incidents."

"Holmes does not usually act against the grain of the situation."

"He underestimates the political depth of this conspiracy."

"Perhaps so," I said mildly, "but why are you the focus of

such a grandiose scheme? Who would have cause to destroy you?"

"I do not know," Phelps said despondently, lapsing into a silence all the more unnerving because his hands and feet were never still.

By late afternoon we returned to Baker Street, where I sent a message to Mary that I would be staying the night with a sick friend. As a doctor's wife, she was accustomed to my extended absences. We shared one of Mrs. Hudson's substantial dinners—roast beef—then settled in for a worrisome evening. I attempted to distract my charge from matters that upset him.

"I must say, Phelps, we have come again to a common path by unfortunate events, but I have faced more dire circumstances than this and come through."

"You, Watson?" His hand patted nervously at his face in the pallid gas light. "How could anything be more dreadful than this pall over my life and reputation? Nine weeks of my life unremembered; my career in limbo, awaiting only an awful disclosure to complete my ruin; my fiancée, the sweetest woman who ever stood by a man, facing only shame and revilement for her loyalty—"

"You are not dead yet, man! And Holmes is helping you. I would that I had acquired such assistance at Maiwand."

"Maiwand?" Phelps looked totally mystified and bit at his lips. I could as well have spoken of Katmandu.

"Yes, the battle of Maiwand in Afghanistan in 'Eighty. I joined as an assistant surgeon with the Northumberland Fusiliers, but when I arrived in India the Afghan war had broken out, so I was assigned to the Sixty-sixth Berkshires at Kandahar under Brigadier General Burrows. At Maiwand I took a jezail bullet in the shoulder. . . .

"You were wounded, Watson?"

"I seldom speak of it, but I was very nearly killed, Phelps, and suffered enteric fever for weeks afterward, during the entire month-long siege of Kandahar, before Roberts's troops came marching to our rescue. Then we turned and drove the

Ayub Khan's men back into the Afghanistan mountains. So, you see, I know more of brain fever than even my medical degree would attest."

"You, too, forgot everything while you were ill?"

"My dear fellow, you must keep this to yourself, but I never even remembered taking a second bullet in my leg, yet that is the inexplicable scar that reminds me of itself every rainy day, though it has been less bothersome of late."

"I was never military material, Watson," Percy said with a wan smile. "It is hard to imagine you in such a shabby fray. One does not hear much about the Afghanistan adventure these days. I had forgotten all about it."

"So have most people. I do not fancy many military reputations were polished in that rough arena. Of course, I was just doing my duty and seeing something of the world, a lad in my twenties. And there is much to see in that quarter of the globe, exotic bits, Phelps: snake charmers and belly dancers and some astounding mating rituals—"

Phelps suddenly clasped a hand to his mouth. "What do you suppose Holmes is doing all day at Woking?"

"Walking," I suggested shortly.

"I am sure that he underestimates the influences at work here." He rose to pace the chamber anxiously, his fingers twitching. "It could be foreign spies; the interests of strong nations are at stake."

"Holmes is aware of such influences. He has often represented the reigning houses of Europe in matters of such sensitivity that they are far too dangerous to speak of even now."

"Perhaps he has served the interests of the French and the Russians in those matters," Phelps said darkly.

"He serves his own country first and foremost," I admonished gently. The man's melancholy grew wearing. At that moment I could have done with a dose of Mary Watson's patient kindness. "When Holmes can assist a foreign personage without harming England, he does—there was the scandal involving the King of Bohemia, for instance, and the astonishingly beautiful I—"

"Bohemia is a pretend-dukedom sewn onto the selvage of Austro-Hungary!" Phelps interrupted petulantly. "This stolen treaty could irritate a Russian emperor and the ruling body of all France!"

"Holmes has been of service to individuals as highly placed as those," I replied a trifle stuffily, "though I can say nothing of the specifics. You underestimate him, and myself, Phelps. I am not merely a dull and domestic London physician. I have aided the world's first consulting detective, and am a veteran of one of the most grueling conflicts of the past decades."

"It is true, it is true!" Phelps cried pathetically, pressing his trembling hands over his pale face. "Pray excuse me. I am distraught. Of course your friend Holmes is my only hope! Of course you are an absolutely splendid fellow to come to my aid! But, Watson, I am sorry, I have been through too much of late. At the moment, I simply am not up to hearing your war stories."

"Oh. I see." Certainly I had heard enough of his difficulties all the day.

"I cannot concentrate on anything trivial when I am bedeviled by larger issues. Where has the treaty gone? Who removed it in such a devastating manner? And what is your Mr. Holmes doing in Woking?"

Trivial! "I am only trying to distract you. I have told you before that you must remove your mind from this current puzzle. Such fruitless speculation will only excite your nerves—and mine. You must retire and manage a good night's sleep, dear fellow. I beg you to rest and think no more about it. In the morning we will know more."

I finally persuaded him to lie down in the spare bedroom, though he was still visibly fretting. I myself did not find Morpheus easily that night. My attempts to show Phelps that others had survived circumstances as difficult as his had only revived my few memories of Maiwand and the fever.

I found it hard to lie upon my left shoulder and seemed to sniff Afghanistan's dust-laden air in the high summer of July. It was the same month, nine years later. Phelps had suffered from brain fever for nine weeks. A woman bears a baby for nine months before it is delivered fully formed. For a moment, I glimpsed fragments of Maiwand I had not recalled before: wounded faces beseeching me for aid; a sudden dull shattering sensation in my shoulder; a bone-rattling ride over a packhorse led by the loyal Murray; delirious days and nights on my back in some makeshift dispensary, during which I imagined poisonous serpents writhing around me and my comrades on the adjoining cots.

I knew that I had made the unpleasant overland trek to Sinjini where the new railway began after the siege of Kandahar was lifted at the end of August, but I remembered nothing of it. My memories of the difficult train journey from Sinjini to Peshawar in India were fuller, and unappetizing, especially in regard to the scanty sanitary arrangements. I certainly recalled my relapse into fever once I reached Peshawar, where the bitter taste of quinine baptized all my liquid intake.

For the first time since I had received Phelps's letter I began to regret my involvement in the case. For the first time since my association with Holmes I was moved to wonder if a middle-aged doctor belonged at home with his wife, rather than nursing querulous acquaintances in questionable circumstances and reviving old campaign days long gone and forgotten.

## Chapter Eighteen

# THE THIRD MAN

In a great, humming metropolis of four million persons it is possible to live for many years without traversing every street. I approached Baker Street for the first time with a sense of visiting an alien locale, and yet, the sensation of finally seeing what I had always known. Godfrey's companionship in the hansom cab was little comfort.

Our sturdy horse's hooves clattered on the pavement, a sound magnified by dozens of drumming hooves. Around us, the very air dispensed the mingled odors of horse and hazy summer heat. The interior of the hansom cab, the shopfronts and signs passing beyond the windows, the sounds and the smells were all as familiar as tea. Yet . . . yet.

Baker Street.

Those words were inextricably associated with the key event of my life, my chance meeting with Irene Adler outside Wilson's Tea Room in 1881. Never mind that I was homeless, hungry, unemployed, desolate. Perhaps that merely sharpened my senses, for every detail of the following twenty-four hours is engraved upon my brain: Irene, in all her intimidating, energetic splendor, which I soon discovered to be gallantly counterfeit, for she was as impoverished as I, had seemed like some glamorous machine, an urban Titania descending upon a lost child in the forest of the great city.

I had followed her, benumbed, into a world of ghastly figures (consider the tragic Jefferson Hope, doomed murderer and avenger, who had driven our first shared, extravagant cab) and treachery hidden in homely symbols (consider the unholy wedding ring that was the sole souvenir of that episode).

Thus I had come in a sinister London twilight to the modest but eccentric rooms Irene rented in Saffron Hill, the Italian district, where arias and sausages scented the everyday air. I remember Irene's purloined pastries toasting on the fireplace fender that evening, and her faded, crackling Oriental robe; a bottle of wine prized open with a button hook.

My confusion, my concern, my disorientation at the unaccustomed wine. My relief at being in hands as certain as hers, however Bohemian. And later, the newspaper column announcing the death of Jefferson Hope. And Baker Street, 221 B Baker Street, where dwelt the amateur detective, Mr. Sherlock Holmes, was where Jefferson Hope had sent a crony to collect the unholy wedding ring from a certain Dr. Watson only days before his death. . . .

So, Baker Street. From the first mention of that locale my life had changed, and so had Irene's, and ultimately, Godfrey's. We were all three hopelessly entwined with that plain address, and *the* man who lived there. Now I was, at last, to see it.

Godfrey was watching out the hansom window with an intensity so like Irene's on a quest that I smiled. He seemed consumed by an unadmitted curiosity about the man who had piqued Irene's competitive instincts.

Baker Street itself was commonplace—a series of functional four-story Georgian facades, some performing as shops on the street level, other as entries for offices or lodgings. Wrought iron fenced the fronts, bracketing doorways and guarding windows and below-street trade entrances.

"There!" Godfrey said, a trifle tensely. His cane urgently rapped the ceiling to signal the driver to stop. "I want to approach on foot."

We disembarked upon a well-maintained pavement, and I

gratefully took Godfrey's arm. For some reason I needed moral support. We ambled along in a current of hurried passersby. Brass numerals and a letter flashed into my mind like daggers. Two. Two. One. B.

"There it is," Godfrey said unnecessarily in a low tone.

We strolled past a perfectly ordinary entryway: two stone steps, a graceful break in the wrought-iron railing, a fanlight over the door greeted us.

In only a moment, we had walked past it.

"Well," I said, sounding breathless.

"An ordinary address," said he.

"I could not agree with you more. What do we do next?"

For the first time in my experience, Godfrey seemed uncertain. He examined the street both ahead and behind us, then nodded at a shop across the way.

"There is an ABC tearoom, Nell. We can quite properly stop for refreshment there, and keep watch on the address we are concerned with."

"Oh, tea should be quite proper," I answered, "but can we ensure a proper view?"

"We will," said he, guiding me across the street with nary a brush with a hansom or a misstep into the unfortunate residue of an equine engine.

And so we settled in for the afternoon. Godfrey had requested, nay demanded, a window table. Men do have their uses. Ensconced in it we had a fine view of bustles, canes, horse hindquarters and, when the intervening traffic permitted, the entrance to 221 B Baker Street.

From all that we could survey in the first hour, no one came or went from that benighted address. Finally Godfrey expressed a pressing need to visit the tailors of Regent Street, so I occupied the window seat alone for another two hours, dutifully noting any who came and went from number 221 B.

A resident left just after Godfrey did, a white-haired old lady in a violet cape somewhat out of fashion, with a straw bonnet tied firmly under her ample chin. Remembering that *the* man had once deceived us in the guise of an elderly clergyman, I placed a faint question mark next to the description. Irene had warned me to overlook nothing with an adversary of Sherlock Holmes's caliber.

A rough-looking boy in a tweed cap several sizes too large came along twenty minutes later. He rang the bell, to no avail, leading me to speculate that the old lady was a housekeeper off on her day's errands. The lad jigged his feet, turned his cap this way and that, and generally fidgeted until it was obvious he would get no response. At that he drew away from the doorway, looked cautiously in all directions, then jerked on the bill of his cap and leaned back to hurl something from his pocket up at the first-floor bow window.

I could not hear the impact, but saw a fistful of small stones rain down from the glass. "The ruffian!" I muttered, looking about for a constable. But no such person appeared, and the rude boy was off, tossing his cap in the air and whistling quite boldly.

I noted the incident and his description, in case a constable should arrive on the scene later.

"Well, miss, and you've a right lot of work to do there." The serving girl nodded at my notations as she brought a fresh pot of tea.

I shifted the papers discreetly out of view. "Merely catching up on some entries in my diary."

The girl's blue eyes widened to match the Delft saucer under my cup. "Lor', miss, an' you must lead an excitin' life, with so much writin' to do about it!"

"I manage," was my curt reply. I kept her gaze until she bobbed a slovenly curtsy and went about her business.

Shortly after that an elegant equipage drew up to disgorge a heavily veiled lady attired all in summer white. She poised upon the stoop of 221 B like a bride; one small gloved hand reached out three times to ring the bell. The door was as indifferent to this intriguing figure as to the others. She retreated to her carriage and was barely out of sight when the old lady waddled back into view, bearing a number of brown paper parcels tied with string.

This, too, I noted down, along with my guesses as to the contents of the parcels. Lemon curd for tea tarts, I decided, and perhaps some crochet string. That is where I wished to be: at home having tea and doing my crochet work, even with Casanova and Lucifer at hand.

I began to keep a worried eye out for Godfrey. We had not been in London for more than a year. I was not anxious to lose him. Just then a hansom cab drew up across the thoroughfare, obscuring the entry. I sipped my Earl Grey in great impatience, but the hansom crouched before the door like a great shiny black beetle too lazy to move.

At length the driver bent down for his pay and the cab crept off, revealing two men by the door. Both wore soft country hats, but one appeared rather pale and weak. The second was a sturdy man with a mustache. The old lady, sans bonnet, cape and parcels, opened the door and they vanished within. And that was that. Surveillance work, I concluded, could be quite boring.

I ate an inordinate amount of tea cakes, then removed my pince-nez and settled in for a good bout of worrying.

"Well, Nell!" Godfrey arrived at half-past four in a flurry of top hat and cane, looking flushed. "The traffic seems to have increased since my departure. What have you observed?"

"A good deal of nothing," said I, turning my notebook around.

He frowned at the entries. "None of these visitors looks like Mr. Holmes. So you have not seen him?"

"Not in his own guise, certainly. But he is a 'consulting' detective; perhaps he seldom leaves his domicile."

"He got about well enough in St. John's Wood," Godfrey said ruefully. "So no one was admitted until the two men. . . . Your notes express suspicion of the old lady and the young boy."

"Either could be a disguise, since both are the sort of persons often overlooked, as no one expects much from either."

Godfrey laughed as he drank the tea the serving girl had rushed to him upon his arrival. Men, even of the most superior sort, are invariably oblivious to how thoroughly they are catered to.

"You sound like Irene," he noted.

"That is where all resemblance ends," said I. "Despite drinking four pots of Earl Grey and consuming as many tea cakes as Irene once kidnapped from Wilson's in lieu of lunch, the static nature of my vigil has not altered. Irene would never have stood for such a tame train of events."

"Then—" he obligingly gulped down the rest of his tea and rose to draw back my chair "—we must accelerate matters."

As Godfrey paused to pay the bill the serving girl brushed past, leaned toward me conspiratorially. "Now I see why your diary takes so much writing," she whispered in a forward but mystifying way, casting her eyes toward Godfrey.

I blushed, not quite sure why, but I had been well reared and knew when I ought to. Soon we were on Baker Street again, facing the enigmatic facade of 221 B.

"I had expected a famous detective's door to be a modicum more busy," Godfrey admitted. "If you tire of surveillance, there is only one course left to us. We must inquire within."

"Ring the bell?" I asked incredulously.

"It would seem so, Nell," he conceded sadly. "I realize that Irene would never resort to so simple a stratagem, but I am, after all, a barrister, and used to taking the direct route."

I was not so sure. Never had the door to 221 B been so forbidding. Never had I felt more obvious. Nevertheless, we marched up to the establishment. Godfrey rang the bell with a fine, determined flourish.

The plump, white-haired woman answered. "Yes, sir?"

Godfrey presented this simple soul with a dazzling smile. "We seek the residence of Dr. Watson."

"You would have been successful, sir, only months ago, but since his marriage, Dr. Watson keeps his own establishment in Paddington. Is it Mr. Holmes you would wish to see instead?"

"No," said I firmly, before Godfrey could say the opposite. "It is a medical matter."

"Paddington, you say," Godfrey added politely, at which prompting the woman disgorged the doctor's new address.

We withdrew with murmured thanks.

"Well," said Godfrey ten paces down Baker Street. "I had not anticipated that the doctor would be on his own."

"All the better for us. We can inquire forthrightly into his past without fear of *the* man interfering."

"Still . . ."

"Godfrey! You are fully as fascinated by *the* man as Irene is. You should be grateful that we can conduct our inquiry without having to tread near Mr. Holmes again."

"You really think that she is so fascinated by him, Nell?"

I sighed. "A figure of speech, Godfrey. You know that Irene is devoted to you. It borders upon the sickening on occasion."

"Really?"

He sounded most interested, but exploring such topics now would not advance our inquiry. It was too late to call on Dr. Watson in Paddington, so Godfrey quickly hailed a hansom and was amenable, if silent, on the journey back to Brown's Hotel, where we received another surprise of the day.

Our routine inquiry at the desk produced a communication on pale-blue parchment paper addressed to me in a hasty hand. The return address was Grosvenor Square.

"Excellent!" Godfrey chortled in the lift, eyeing the communication.

I attempted to calm myself in the face of my most immediate concern: being in the interior of an overdecorated moving closet.

Godfrey had been correct about one thing. We required a discreet place to repair and compare notes—or at least peruse notes. My sitting room proved to be ideal.

"Well?"

"Please be patient, Godfrey. I must remove this rather smothering bonnet and veil, and my gloves first."

He was so impatient that he seized my hatpin as soon as I had released it and began stabbing at the envelope.

"There is an opener here," said I, taking the now-mangled correspondence to the small writing desk. Godfrey had never shown a subtle hand with the correspondence in chambers. I neatly slit the seam and pulled out a folded paper.

"Very fine quality," I noted, as Irene might.

Godfrey sighed. "What does it say?"

"It is from Mrs. Waterston. Quentin Stanhope's married sister, as Mrs. Turnpenny was."

"What does she say?"

"Only that . . . my goodness!"

"Nell!"

I sat down. "She recalls me as her sister's governess—is that not nice?"

"Wonderful! Sublime! What does she—?"

"She wants us to call as soon as possible. This evening if possible."

"Marvelous!"

"She says that her aged mother is most interested in news of her long-lost, dear son Quentin . . . Oh, Godfrey—"

"What?"

"She does not know of his . . . condition. We cannot disabuse poor old Mrs. Stanhope of her illusions."

"We will not. We will relieve his relations of the information we require and give them next to nothing in return."

"Is that fair?"

"No, but it is useful."

"You sound like Irene!"

"Thank you."

I sank unhappily onto the Louis XIV chair before the escritoire.

"We are here to serve the greater good, Nell. That may require . . . compromise."

"I am not used to compromise."

That gave him pause. "Neither was Quentin Stanhope. Until Afghanistan."

"Oh!"

Godfrey came and leaned over me in a most emphatic manner, his hands braced on the chair arms. "Nell, we are thrust into matters of great moment. Nicety has no place in our calculations. We must steel ourselves to serve the truth, and hope that it will hurt no one for whom we care."

"I do not even know these women."

"No, but you know their lost loved one. Irene would never have let you come if she had suspected that you would succumb to such qualms of conscience."

"*Let* me come! Irene cannot come because she is known here!"

"Would that stop her? She thought that the trip would do you good."

"Do me good? Why?"

Godfrey withdrew, suddenly subdued. "You are the springboard of the current puzzle. Irene thought you deserved the opportunity to investigate your own mystery."

"I see."

"Do you?"

"You need not glower like the Queen's Counsel, Godfrey. I understand that I am broaching my past, and Irene's past as well, in this affair. Very well; I will call upon Mrs. Waterston and endeavor to learn what we must know in order to best serve her true interests, even if we cannot confide fully in her."

"Brava, Nell." He smiled like a man relieved of a burden not his.

Godfrey glanced at my veiled bonnet lying like a wounded pheasant on the pier table. "And I think you can dispense with that bonnet. The idea is for you to be recognizable in Grosvenor Square."

## Chapter Nineteen

# A NOSY NIECE

**Godfrey again** perused my list of Baker Street visitors in the cab en route to Grosvenor Square, shaking his head. "Not promising, Nell. Obviously Holmes is either gone or keeping to his rooms. None of the visitors is a candidate for the doctor, except this stocky chap who arrived with the pale-looking man. The old lady is likely the housekeeper, or land-lady, as you surmise. When our interview on Grosvenor Square is done, we shall have to take steps."

"What do you mean?"

"I mean that we will have to inquire after Dr. Watson ourselves," he said.

"I as well? Mr. Holmes could be lurking about, and I have been seen by him."

"But in circumstances in which he would be likely to over-look you."

"I thought he was a formidable detective. How should he overlook me?" I asked.

"Irene has said that he has a weakness for women."

"Indeed! That is the first that I have heard of such a fail-ing."

Godfrey smiled. "Not in the common way that the phrase is meant. She claims that he is uninterested in women to a fault, so that he is forever underestimating their importance and wit. That gives women a kind of invisibility."

"He appeared perfectly capable of noticing Irene, and found her on the crowded terrace of the Hôtel de Paris in Monte Carlo."

His smile faded. "Ah, but that was Irene. Irene is always noticeable unless she is taking especial care not to be. Here is number forty-four."

Anyone who has lived in London is well aware that Grosvenor numbers among the city's most lordly squares. Our cab drew up before an imposing stone fence. A piece of antique statuary peeked from beyond the manicured greenery of high summer.

"In truth, Godfrey," I said, my eyes surveying the blank expanse of windows lining the great house, "I dare not confront this family again. I am but a mere mote in their memories . . ."

"Fortunately their son and brother is not," he said in firm tones, stepping down from the cab to help me out before he paid the driver. "And we are expected."

I sighed. "I suppose it is my duty."

"Of course it is." He drew my hand through the crook of his elbow. "Yet it would be more amusing to regard this as an adventure."

His use of that particular, overadvertized word reminded me of Quentin. How could I tell a man who had faced the unthinkable in India and Afghanistan that I was reduced to a quailing girl by his own family? Not that I was ever likely to see Quentin Stanhope again. Still, passing up that long, formal walk into that long, formal house was for me a return to a once-pleasant past that now seemed beyond reach. I was nothing to these people except a link between our common history and their lost member.

The butler who answered the door was impeccably non-committal. I felt like a pair of galoshes that had been inadvertently left on the steps. Godfrey's hat, stick and gloves were swiftly stripped from him; at least women could retain the accessory armor of hat and gloves indoors.

We were shown into a front receiving room full of strangers.

"Please, come right in!" cried a pretty young woman in a buttercup-yellow mousseline tea-gown, rising to draw us in as we paused politely on the threshold. "Why, Miss Huxleigh, you have grown so smart!"

Her words astounded me, but her identity amazed me even more.

"And you have simply grown! Miss Allegra?" I asked rather than exclaimed. "Miss Turnpenny now, rather."

"No, I am Allegra still," said this ingratiating creature, taking my hands and laughing. "But what has happened to Miss Huxleigh's mouse-gray skirts and cream cotton shirtwaists?"

"I have . . . changed," I said, "and so have you."

"And are you still Miss Huxleigh?" inquired the impertinent young person, eyeing Godfrey with an interest unbecoming to a well-brought-up girl.

"Indeed," I said hastily. "That has not changed. May I introduce Mr. Godfrey Norton, a barrister who practices in Paris? He, too, is aware of the news I have come to convey." At least here we could use our true identities.

"Then you must meet the others."

The young woman spun to introduce the array of middle-aged ladies seated behind her: her aunt, Mrs. Waterston; her mother, Mrs. Codwell Turnpenny, who had grayed greatly since Berkeley Square; her other aunt, Mrs. Compton. These three women were Quentin Stanhope's older sisters, I realized with a jolt. Looking into their genteel, concerned faces, I wondered what on earth I should tell them about the fate of their baby brother.

We were seated and plied with tea and crumpets of a vastly superior variety. Godfrey accepted the female doting they bestowed with calm good grace, refusing all offers of cucumber sandwiches until the social flutter had died a natural death.

"It is wonderful to see you, Miss Huxleigh," Mrs. Turnpenny finally ventured over her cup of tea. "You do not look a day older." I could not truthfully say the same of her, so remained attentively silent. "Now, please, you must tell us what you know of Quentin."

"Perhaps," Godfrey intervened, capturing their instant attention by being both handsome and a man of affairs, "you should tell us what you know first."

Their eyes, all pale watercolor shades of blue and gray, gently consulted each other. I imagined a family portrait— perhaps by the Florence-born American, Singer Sargent, who in his London studio attired his female subjects in such a swooning shimmer of pale paint—with the sisters portrayed as the fading Three Graces. I then pictured the brother and beloved uncle we had first seen in Paris—bearded, bronzed, berobed, ill—thrust into their midst. No. Quentin Stanhope as he now was made a more proper subject for one of those Bohemian bistro painters of Paris—a Mucha or a Chéret.

Mrs. Turnpenny spoke. "I am a widow. Yes, my dear," she explained with a glance at me, "Colonel Turnpenny died in Afghanistan. Not at Maiwand, but ironically in the victorious battle that followed it."

"I am so sorry," I murmured.

"Our elderly mother is a widow also," Mrs. Turnpenny added. "She is upstairs in her rooms. We did not wish to upset her unnecessarily. We knew Quentin had been wounded at Maiwand, and that he had been reported missing or dead. Later, the Army insisted that he was alive, and indeed, we finally received a letter in a shaky hand that was certainly his. So we waited for him to recuperate and come home."

"He never did!" Allegra interjected this in the aggrieved tone of a disappointed child. "Uncle Quentin never came back. The others had given him up, and certainly it was better for Grandmama to think him dead if we had no word or sign of him, but I have never understood why he left us. Do you know something more, Miss Huxleigh, please? Can you tell us something more?"

"Allegra!" the young woman's mother rebuked softly, turning to us. "She remembers him with a child's freshness. You must forgive her enthusiasm. I would be most grateful for any information you could offer us. We had hoped when the other gentleman called—"

"Other gentleman?" Godfrey asked.

Mrs. Turnpenny paused at the urgency in his tone. "Yes, a war veteran, like Quentin. A former member of his company."

"When did this gentleman call?" Godfrey wanted to know.

Again the three older women silently consulted one another, both to bolster their common recollection and to protest Godfrey's intrusive curiosity.

"In May," Mrs. Waterston declared in a no-nonsense voice. "It was my wolfhound Peytor's birthday."

"May," Godfrey repeated without further comment, in the irritating way of barristers everywhere.

"*Do* you know anything of Quentin, Miss Huxleigh?" Allegra beseeched me.

Suddenly my qualms tumbled like a wall of stone turned to sand before their heartfelt concern.

"We know that he is relatively well, and alive," I said briskly. "We encountered him in Paris last week. He has lived in the East for many years."

"He was well?" Mrs. Turnpenny demanded. "Why did he not contact us? Why has he not come home, then?"

"He was not well," Godfrey put in quite rashly. "We think he had been poisoned."

Shock sighed through the room, and their pale powdered faces grew more ashen.

I said quickly, "Quentin had reasons for staying abroad. There may have been danger to those he came too near. He is quite all right now, save for a troubling touch of fever now and then."

"Quentin?" Mrs. Turnpenny repeated with a polite frown.

Godfrey regarded me with a deeply interested expression, like any barrister curious to see how a witness would extricate herself from an unpardonable blunder.

I flushed as scarlet as the velvet footstool at Mrs. Turnpenny's aristocratic feet.

"Oh, Mama, don't be a stick!" young Allegra urged with flashing blue eyes. "Miss Huxleigh has known me since the schoolroom, and Uncle Quentin was a favorite visitor there."

"It was Nell who roused Mr. Stanhope's memories of home," Godfrey added in my defense at last. "He recognized her in Paris."

"Nell?" Mrs. Turnpenny murmured again, this time faintly, as if confused beyond the point of fretting about it.

"That is how my wife and I call Miss Huxleigh," Godfrey explained.

Mrs. Turnpenny nodded, reassured that Godfrey had a wife. If only she had met Irene! "And Paris is where Quentin was . . . poisoned?"

"We think so," I said, "or rather Irene does." A silence. "Godfrey's wife. Irene. She has remained behind in Paris. It was not serious, the poisoning, only Qu—Mr. Stanhope feared for our own safety and vanished. We thought he might have come here, but of course if he fears that whoever he approaches is endangered—"

"Quite a tale, from what sense I can make of it," the formidable Mrs. Waterston noted. "Yet it might explain the gentleman caller in May if Quentin has been seen in Europe."

"Indeed," said Godfrey. "So while we can offer no particulars about your loved one at present, we can tell you that he was well not many days ago, and that his long absence has apparently been forced by circumstance, not inclination. But take care to whom you speak of him."

"He has always kept you in his mind and heart," I added. "You must not think that he has not. I hope that one day he can tell you so himself."

"As do we," Mrs. Turnpenny said feelingly. "And what

has brought you from Paris to London, so that you could deliver this news?"

"Shopping," said Godfrey promptly and somewhat truthfully, given his afternoon activities. "The French are quite inferior at men's tailoring, but excel in women's styles. As you can see, Miss Huxleigh has become a formidable fashion plate since her sojourn in Paris."

The older ladies blinked politely at his mock-serious tone, but Miss Allegra laughed until her eyes watered. "Oh, you remind me of Uncle Quentin, Mr. Norton. He was such an unreformed tease! What fun we had when I was young."

"That is usually the case, miss," I reminded her primly.

"In some ways you have not changed at all, Miss Huxleigh," she answered, "and I am glad."

I smiled at the dear child, who reminded me of her uncle, though she found me less changed than he did.

The rest of the tea was spent in polite chitchat, which Godfrey handled with masterful blandness. As we rose to leave, Godfrey inquired casually, "By the way, what did the gentleman who asked after Mr. Stanhope look like?"

The ladies exchanged another blank glance.

"Quite unremarkable looking," Mrs. Turnpenny said, consulting her sisters. "Middle-aged, respectable." Mrs. Compton nodded soberly.

"I was not at the house at the time," Mrs. Waterston declared, and that was that.

"I will see them out, Mama," the charming Allegra offered, frothing to my side in her jonquil gown to lay a hand on my arm like a favorite niece.

As we walked into the tiled entry hall, Allegra spoke in a voice lowered to an excited whisper. "Not so tall as Mr. Norton," she said, slipping her arm through his so we three were conspiratorially linked. "Bald as a cue ball. Fierce lapis-lazuli eyes, cold as stone. A most sinister individual. Mama has absolutely no powers of observation," she added sadly.

She delivered us to the cruising butler, who circled us like a shark, so eager was he to rid the house of its unconventional visitors.

"Do find dear Quentin," she finished, shaking our arms in light admonishment. "He is quite my favorite uncle."

"I am afraid," said I, "that you take after him a great deal."

"Thank you, Miss Huxleigh," she said with a last, roguish smile and a curtsy, before melting down the hall.

Out in the square we paused, staring across the vast garden to the line of stately houses beyond.

"Quite helpless and unforthcoming, the ladies of the house," Godfrey mused as he smoothed his French kid gloves over his knuckles, "but your former charge is a charmer. She reminds me of Irene."

"I did not have a very long time with her in the schoolroom," I admitted. "She does take a great deal upon herself."

"Someone must, in that household." He sighed. "So Captain Morgan was already hunting for Stanhope in May. Why?"

"Of course! *That* is who the inquiring gentleman was!"

"The real question is what the devil—sorry, Nell—was Stanhope involved in, and why has it turned so urgent now?"

"Oh," I said without thinking, "I wish Irene were here. She would know what to do."

Godfrey smiled fondly. "We can cable her, if you like, in the morning, to tell her what we have learned."

"Oh, yes! But Godfrey—"

"Yes?"

"We must use a code name, in case that odious man Morgan has henchmen in Paris."

"We already have one," he pronounced as we strolled toward New Bond Street, where we could more readily hail a cab.

"What is that?"

"Lucy Maison-Nouveau."

"Oh."

## Chapter Twenty

# SHE SNOOPS TO CONQUER

𝔈

**At last** a Watson in the flesh!

Godfrey and I had decided that we would have more luck finding a physician free later in the day, so we stood before the doctor's door in Paddington at four o'clock the next afternoon, I in a froth of excitement at finally meeting the figure who might serve as the key to Quentin Stanhope's dilemmas. We confronted a semidetached brick residence that sat close to the street but was domestic enough in appearance to promise a garden in the back. A brass lozenge attached to the brick wall read, JOHN H. WATSON, M.D. Was he the same Dr. Watson who had aided Quentin Stanhope on the blazing battlefields of Afghanistan?

The door opened. Instead of a gentleman who had consorted with *the* man of Baker Street, a lady stood in the doorway, regarding us with an air of pleasant but unsurprised inquiry.

"We are here to see Dr. Watson," Godfrey said. "This is Miss Huxleigh and I am . . . er, Feverall Marshwine."

"I am Mrs. Watson. The house girl has the day off. Have you an appointment, Mr. Marshwine?"

"No," he admitted, "but we will wait."

"You will wait in either case, for the doctor has been called out suddenly," she answered with a slight smile. Then she stepped back to allow us in. Mrs. Watson was a dainty, self-possessed woman, whose vivid cornflower-blue eyes eclipsed any plainness in her refined face.

We followed her down the passage, which was dim, as such hallways usually are, into a back parlor that had been furnished as an office with a large mahogany desk and several leather upholstered chairs. An open door to the room beyond showed a cabinet filled with medical preparations.

"Can you say when you expect him, Mrs. Watson?" Godfrey asked.

"Hardly. Like most physicians', my husband's days are filled with long, empty hours broken by sudden flurries of patients or the emergency call."

"No doubt such enforced idleness encourages a taste for other pursuits," I commented.

"Why, yes." The lady glanced rather fondly toward the desk, where some papers lay piled near a crystal inkstand and a Gray's *Anatomy*. "As a matter of fact, my dear husband has a literary bent. Unfortunately, I cannot guarantee his prompt return. He has left the town."

I glanced doubtfully at my lapel, about to consult my watch, when Godfrey spoke.

"Thank you, Mrs. Watson. We will wait nevertheless."

She nodded and left us, closing the passage door behind her.

"Why did you use that ridiculous name?" I demanded.

"Marshwine?" Godfrey seemed genuinely hurt. "I thought that Dr. Watson might recognize my own name. Remember, Sherlock Holmes implied that he knew of Irene's marriage to me when they all descended on Briony Lodge to trap Irene."

"Then . . . why use my real name?" I demanded with some agitation.

"Because, dear Nell, I believe it is always better to tell the truth than to lie, and surely neither Holmes nor Watson can know your name."

"At any rate," I declared, "the doctor may be gone for hours—for the day."

"I sincerely hope so," Godfrey replied, going to the passage door and listening intently. "We could not have arranged a better opportunity to learn a thing or two about Dr. Watson." He had paused before a photograph of a gaunt, medal-decorated man framed on the wall. "General Gordon of India. An Afghanistan connection already. I wonder what others may be hidden in drawers."

"Godfrey! You would use this occasion to spy?"

"Yes, and so will you. Have a look at the desk, will you, Nell? You have a sublime instinct for paperwork."

Godfrey darted into the neighboring chamber, leaving me no time to object. I gingerly approached the doctor's large mahogany desk decorated with Chippendale fretwork, still unsure that I would actually stoop to the act required.

A small red Turkish carpet, perhaps two by five feet and somewhat worn, ran from the chair between the desk's flanking pedestals of drawers, ending at the pair of side chairs for guests. Obviously intended to protect the chamber's overall Axminster carpeting, the Turkish rug reminded me of a royal runner, which the desk straddled like a throne to be approached at my own risk. It made the desk look as tempting of exploration as a covered candy dish set upon a brightly colored doily.

My gloved fingers trailed along the desk's exposed wooden top, then paused at the piled papers. A casement window behind the chair wafted the drone of bees from the honeysuckle bush flowering beyond it. If I wished to investigate, I would have to remove my gloves. Proper paper shuffling requires agile fingers. I tugged the tight cotton off my right hand and soon was riffling through the pile.

As quickly I discovered that this was not the usual stack of unconnected documents, but rather a continuous narrative. I could not believe my eyes, even as they read the opening sentence: "To Sherlock Holmes, she is always *the* woman."

I sank onto the huge chair behind the desk, though its upholstery was lumpy and its legs were mounted on little wheels that gave me an uneasy seat, like a nervous mare. The shocking words leaped into stark emphasis before my eyes, all the more horrible for being penned in a neat, quite legible hand.

*In his eyes she eclipses and predominates the whole of her sex. It was not that he felt any emotion akin to love for Irene Adler. All emotions, and that one particularly, were abhorrent to his cold, precise, but admirably balanced mind.*

More than ever was I convinced that *the* man was a monster who, as his biographer admitted, "never spoke of the softer passions, save with a gibe and a sneer . . . who loathed every form of society with his whole Bohemian soul," and who, buried among his books in his Baker Street lodgings, alternated "from week to week between cocaine and ambition. . . ."

My feet had pushed forward on the rug as I read. Beneath my boot soles, the material had rolled into a hard hummock as adamant as a doorstop, which made a useful footrest as I read the awful words before me.

"And yet there was but one woman to him, and that woman was the late Irene Adler, of dubious and questionable memory."

*She?* Dubious and questionable? My gasp was echoed by the breeze sighing through the casement and buffeting the flowered curtains, as my hands—one gloved and one ungloved—made outraged fists.

The narrator, surely the selfsame doctor in whose rooms Godfrey and I now pried to our joint shame and my sole and swiftly receding regret, recounted how his recent marriage had created "complete happiness, and the home-centered interests . . . sufficient to absorb all my attention." To this I could not take exception.

Then, one March night a year ago, this same upright doctor wrote, he was returning from a journey to a patient when his path led him through Baker Street. The events could have been set down in a modern *Faust* or perhaps in *Dr. Jekyll and*

*Mr. Hyde*, as the ordinary physician finds himself drawn again into the web of his evil genius: He finds himself passing That Doorway, which first recalls the circumstances of his wooing the woman now responsible for his bliss. But unhappy chance also reminds him of "the dark incidents" of the case during which the blissful couple had met. Soon the doctor is "seized" by "a keen desire" to see *the* man again and discover how he is using his "extraordinary powers."

And there, within, he did indeed find *the* man "at work again. He had arisen out of his drug-created dreams, and was hot upon the scent of some new problem."

A noise behind me made me start so guiltily that my foot kicked the rumpled rug with a dull thump. Something about the hummock was oddly . . . pliant. Godfrey was emerging from the inner room, frowning.

"Nothing in the consulting room but the usual remedies and supplies. Have you made any progress with those papers, Nell?"

"No!" I shouted, collapsing them back into a single pile like a flimsy deck of cards. "Ouch!"

"What is it?" Concern brought Godfrey even closer, when I wished to prevent him from seeing the outrageous papers beneath my hands.

"Nothing, Godfrey, nothing," I said, rising awkwardly. I always have been a most unconvincing prevaricator. "Only . . . my foot has struck some untoward object under the desk."

"Oh?" At least Godfrey was peering now at the carpeting and need never read: "And yet there was but one woman to him . . ."

I turned the papers upside down and weighted them with the Gray's *Anatomy*. "It is nothing, really, Godfrey, merely some household appliance that I stubbed my toes on."

"Why were you sitting at the desk, Nell?" He had bent to inspect the area beneath it.

"I was . . . feeling faint."

"But the casement is open. Surely there was sufficient fresh air."

"I, ah, am not used to criminal activities."

"Hardly criminal, Nell." Godfrey's voice was muffled now as he burrowed under the desk. "Yes, there's something here—and heavy. Stand by the other side of the desk and I'll push it through. That will be easier."

I took my position as requested. The papers were safe beneath their bookish disguise. "You really ought not to disorder the office, Godfrey. Dr. Watson might notice."

"This is extremely odd," he said in an annoyed voice, ignoring my advice. "There!" He grunted, and something long and heavy rolled out from under Dr. Watson's desk and onto my boot toes.

"Well?" Godfrey, somewhat flushed in the face, popped his head above the desktop.

I looked down.

I would have screamed, save that I did not have the breath for it. I stiffened as if turned to stone by a Medusa.

"Nell?" Godfrey rose and came around the desk. "Nell—?"

I could not find words, or the breath to speak them.

He looked down.

Then he bent, cautiously pinched the rug into a pair of folds and gingerly eased the five-foot-long cobra from my feet.

"I believe that it is dead, Nell."

"Believe?" I began to breathe again.

"Hope and pray, rather. It has not moved except by my exertions."

"How reassuring."

"It cannot be long dead," he mused, "for the body is still amazingly flexible."

"Godfrey! Please keep such revelations to yourself."

"It could be the twin to the one Irene shot in Montmartre."

"Good. We can call it the one my feet pummeled to death in Paddington."

"I mean that it seems more than coincidence to find two dead Asian cobras of similar type in Paris and London."

"Of course it is more than coincidence. It is appalling!"

He knelt over the long form on the rug. "The head seems almost jointed. I believe the neck is broken."

"Can a serpent be said to possess a neck?"

"Certainly. A serpent is all neck."

"I see. Godfrey?"

"Yes, Nell?"

"I appear to have dropped a glove under the desk. Could you—?"

"I am not anxious to explore and find another cobra."

"Please."

He sighed, returned to the desk's other side, and vanished beneath it.

Moments later he surfaced, waving a white glove of surrender. "No nest," he reported cheerfully.

I regarded the mottled corpse. It all too precisely matched Dr. Sauveur's description of the Asian cobra Irene had shot in Montmartre: perhaps five feet long but thick as a table leg, a speckled pattern of scales tapering to a tail end as delicate as little Oscar's entire body. A depraved mind might find beauty in its lethal, whiplike pliancy.

"Perhaps Dr. Watson was going to have it stuffed, *à la* Sarah Bernhardt," I suggested.

"I think not. I believe that someone intended to have Dr. Watson stuffed full of cobra venom."

"But who?"

"Come, Nell! Obviously the person that Stanhope wished to warn Watson against. Our outing is a success: we have found the very Watson we wanted."

"I am most relieved," I said faintly. "I doubt I could invade doctors' consulting rooms on false pretenses indefinitely." A thought came to me. "Godfrey, if cobra venom is so deadly, why are we coming upon dead cobras instead of dead victims?"

"Put like a prosecutor, Nell," he congratulated me, bending to take hold of the carpet, which I was all too happy to vacate.

A few vigorous shakes of the rug and the cobra was once more concealed beneath the desk. "There, tidy again."

"You are not going to simply leave it there?"

"It is not my desk, and certainly not my business."

"But what shall we do, then?"

Godfrey grinned and smoothed his hair. "Wait for Dr. Watson, as we intended, and ask him some questions about Afghanistan."

## Chapter Twenty-One

# DOCTOR'S DILEMMA

**After forty** uneasy minutes, during which I watched Godfrey snooping about the premises when I was not eyeing the carpet beneath the desk for signs of movement—after all, some snakes hibernated, I understood, and there was no guarantee that this one should not rise from the dead—the door opened.

I do not know what kind of man I expected. A rather weak one, perhaps, to be so easily led from domestic and professional rectitude by an individual as apparently erratic as this Sherlock Holmes. Certainly I had wondered whether Watson had in fact visited Briony Lodge in company with the vaunted detective and the foiled King. I remembered the detective's companion as an ordinary, quite overlookable sort of person. I had not anticipated the solid citizen who now stood before me, a man not yet forty who was built like a boxer and possessed of a certain symmetry of feature as well as an unassuming mustache that made me miss Godfrey's adornment.

"Mr. Marshwine?" the gentleman inquired. "Miss . . . er, Buxleigh?"

"Indeed," said Godfrey as he rose, thereby avoiding an outright lie.

I myself was pleased to be mistaken for the fictional Miss Buxleigh, given our violations of hospitality in our host's absence. This Dr. Watson certainly did not look like a writer, nor like a person who could be led willy-nilly by an extravagant but strong personality. He had the demeanor of a physician—and a former military man.

"What may I do for you?" the doctor inquired as he started for his desk. My eyes flew to the rug.

"Actually," Godfrey began easily, "we are not here to consult you on a medical matter."

"Oh?" The doctor sat, and yawned. "You must forgive me. I have been attending a nervously exhausted individual." I heard his feet stretch out beneath the desk as he leaned back in the chair, which creaked.

The rug before the front of the desk wrinkled in response. I bit my lip.

"We are here on a personal matter," Godfrey went on. He was being alarmingly frank for a person who only minutes before had been searching the premises.

"And that is—?" Dr. Watson's tone had become a bit gruff. Now I recognized him! He was the hatted man who had helped the pale one into 221 B Baker Street yesterday.

"We are searching for a man missing since Maiwand."

"Missing since Maiwand! My dear sir, odd that you should mention Maiwand; I had occasion to think of it for the first time in years only recently. How did you decide to approach me on this matter?"

Godfrey, like any perspicacious barrister, leaned forward persuasively in his chair even as he lowered his voice.

"You see, Dr. Watson, we have met one who remembers you ministering to the very man we seek during the battle of Maiwand. In your memories of that time we might discern some clue by which we could trace poor Blodgett."

"Blodgett?"

"Ah, Jasper Blodgett, Miss . . . er, Buxleigh's fiancé, gone missing these nine years."

Dr. Watson looked from one to the other of us. "Blodgett? Buxleigh? Nine years?"

"Exactly. A tragic tale in its simple way. A man called up

to war. A woman waiting at home. The confusion of a battle waged on alien soil. Men wounded, men killed, men gone off their heads and simply . . . lost. Miss Buxleigh has waited faithfully for almost a decade, Doctor, and now has received reports from India indicating that poor Blodgett is yet alive, if not wholly himself."

"This Blodgett has been seen?"

"Indeed. And if we could find some kernel of incident in your memories of the wounded you tended, that might help us find poor Blodgett."

The doctor's face grew distressed. "My dear sir, my dear Miss Buxleigh, my own memories are uncertain. I was wounded myself at Maiwand."

"Oh!" I exclaimed in my disappointment that our long-sought connection was so useless. Dr. Watson took my interjection for sympathy and went on more warmly.

"Jezail bullet in the shoulder," he confided to Godfrey in a bluff man-to-man way that I was not supposed to overhear, though I did. "If it had not been for my orderly Murray slinging me belly-down over a horse and leading me from harm's way, I would not be here." He flung one of his limbs beneath the desk. "Took another in the leg and never knew it, I was so fever-ridden. Most embarrassing for a physician to suffer a phantom wound. I doubt I can help you."

The wounded leg, once mentioned, thrashed again beneath the desk, like a child fidgeting when it hears its name called. I saw a mottled semicircle of snake protruding from under the bottom lip of the mahogany desk.

"Still, Dr. Watson," I put in, "what you may have witnessed before your wounding could help us."

The doctor nodded. "Many men escaped injury that day, but on my knees amid the battle dust it seemed that every man around me was half done-for. Well, Miss Buxleigh, I confess that I admire a woman eager after many years to reunite with the man who has commanded her love and loyalty. Jasper Blodgett is a lucky man."

"Thank you, Doctor," I said modestly, wringing the cords

of my reticule and looking significantly at Godfrey rather than at the slow but steady resurrection of the cobra. Time for Godfrey to play the barrister and begin questioning.

"Perhaps you remember Maclaine—?" he began dutifully.

"Poor devil! He was taken prisoner during the retreat, but I never knew him. Died, of course, at savage hands."

"If he had not died, do you think he would have been blameless?"

A sharp glance from eyes used to making diagnoses appraised us. "That is politics, sir. I fear that war brings out the worst as well as the best in men, as do political skirmishes. I heard talk that Maclaine, being dead, made a good target on which to pin hindsight, though I have no opinion either way on the affair. I was a lowly medical officer in a battle that was no more than a rout for our forces. There is a tale with a different twist to it for every man who was at Maiwand."

"Our man," said Godfrey, "was wounded early in the afternoon, early in the retreat. He had a head wound."

"How do you know if you have not found him?"

The doctor's piercing eyes did not meet mine, for I was looking modestly down—at the carpet. Godfrey answered this challenge, as well he should, since the entire fairy tale was of his spinning.

"Those who have seen him in Peshawar saw the scar."

Dr. Watson nodded. "I remember a man with a blow to the head—odd, for we had not come to hand-to-hand combat. Of course, in the scramble to retreat one of our own might have given him a knock. It was not a pretty sight, miss, almost three thousand men trying to elude bullets and blood in blinding dust and artillery fire. I do not wonder that your Jasper lost his wits afterwards—and the head blow could have done it. The fellow I remember had a desperate air, raved that he needed to see the command. He did not want to retreat, or save his skin, so much as to see someone in authority, if anyone was then. Clawed at my uniform as if he were drowning, would not let me leave. Yes, the head blow could explain much, even the fact that he has not been seen in civilized climes since—"

"Hazel!" I said. "Were his eyes hazel?"

"Eyes, Miss Buxleigh? A field surgeon does not notice such things. Pallor, perhaps, and what is broken or battered."

"J-Jasper had very compelling hazel eyes," I insisted. "If you remember him as being agitated, you must have noticed. He must have looked directly at you, imploring you—"

The doctor leaned back in his creaking chair, his bootheels thumping the floor, his chin resting on his chest. "If I had a bit of something to induce a trance, I might recall," he said with a wry expression I understood more than he suspected. "My mind has fixed on Afghanistan more than usual lately. Perhaps it is this leg acting up." He banged his foot on the floor for emphasis, and his boot shifted the rug as it landed.

More of the cobra coiled into full view at my and Godfrey's feet. Despite the provocation, we both managed to present Dr. Watson with rapt faces.

The physician suddenly clapped his hand to the desktop. "By St. Harry, you are right, miss! Peculiarly light hazel they were, like murky lakes in all that evil ocher dust. I remember thinking that it was a pity another brave young fellow was going to carry Afghanistan in his kit bag for the rest of his life, and that is when—" Dr. Watson's own eyes blinked, as if again in the heat and dust of the battlefield "—that is when something ripped into my left shoulder as cold as ice in that devil's oven. I have never recalled it before, the actual moment of my being wounded."

"What happened to—to Jasper?" I put in before the doctor's memories should fade again.

He shook his head in a daze. "I next remember Murray. 'Can you hang onto the mane for a minute, sir?' he was saying. I was swaying by the side of a horse—a stringy packhorse—and then Murray slung me over and I thankfully remember nothing until I awoke in the makeshift hospital in Kandahar. It was four weeks of fever and short rations until Roberts came to relieve us."

"And that is all you remember of poor Jasper?"

Dr. Watson nodded soberly. "That is more than I remembered yesterday. But, yes, how he clung to me, as if I were more than a mere lifeline! They will do that, you know, in the field, but this man was desperate beyond fear for his life. He would not release my arms, and as I moved to leave, his hands clung even to my medical bag. Then that icy furrow ploughed through my being, quickly followed by the heat of fever. Jezail bullets are manufactured crudely and often bear disease as well as death." Dr. Watson sighed. "Sometimes forgetfulness is a blessing."

We both nodded somberly, there being little else to say. Godfrey rose. "I thank you, Doctor, for your time and recollection. Your story explains at least why Jasper may have lost his head and failed to return to England and Miss Buxleigh."

I rose also, and the doctor saw us to the door. "Certainly," he said, with a gallant glance at myself, "he would never have neglected to return to as charming a lady as Miss Buxleigh of his own will."

I was unable to savor or shrug off this gallantry; my eyes flicked back into the room. From the door, the dead cobra looked like a wrinkle in the rug. I wondered if the Watsons' maid had good, steady nerves like myself. . . .

We started down the passage to the outer door.

"I hope that I have been of help," said the doctor.

"You have indeed," Godfrey said heartily. "I'm sure that Miss Buxleigh's mind is more at rest for our interview."

Godfrey had ever been an optimist.

"I fear," the doctor added, "that my attention has been somewhat distracted by a matter of some moment apart from my practice. If you have gleaned anything useful from me, you are welcome to it."

Godfrey donned his top hat and smiled as he took my arm in a solicitous way. "You have been an invaluable help, sir, and will never know how deeply I and Miss Buxleigh appreciate your assistance. It has been most enlightening in every respect. Thank you again. Good day, Dr. Watson."

"Good day, Miss Buxleigh, Mr. Marshwine."

On such cordial commonplaces we parted company.

Paddington unfolded before us in all its everyday homeliness. I had almost expected to exit into a dusty, throbbing battlefield full of wounded men and dead snakes.

"Godfrey!" I demanded as soon as we had walked a decent distance from the Watson abode. "What of the cobra? We have left it simply lying there, halfway revealed, without warning anyone."

"It is not our cobra," he said with something of Irene's offhanded manner.

"But what shall they do when they find it?"

He smiled as he spied a hansom to take us back to the heart of the town. "It should make a fine puzzle for Dr. Watson's friend, Mr. Holmes."

"The doctor will say that we were there, that we were inquiring about Afghanistan."

"All the better. I would like to see Sherlock Holmes try to track down Mr. Marshwine and Miss Buxleigh."

I settled into the cab in some unease, glancing out the window on the fine day. I clutched Godfrey's arm.

"Look! That street boy. I saw him before—yesterday in Baker Street—the one with the cap that is too large!"

Godfrey leaned to peer out. "Only a lad trying to make a few pence running errands. I would not fret about him, Nell."

"Baker Street is a far way from Paddington for a lad afoot."

"Perhaps he was hired to escort some elderly person home by hansom cab."

"He is signaling another cab—an urchin like that! How can he pay?"

Our vehicle jerked into motion, wresting away my view of the boy.

"Likely his patron gave him the fare back, though I admit that a cab is rather royal for his sort."

"He could be a minion of Sherlock Holmes, set to follow us."

"My dear Miss Buxleigh," Godfrey said, drawing the curtain on the passing scene of the street outside, "did I ever tell you that you are possessed of a most ungoverned imagination?"

## Chapter Twenty-Two

# DIVINELY INSPIRED

**A cable** from Irene awaited us at the hotel: "*Mes amis*, you get on splendidly. I am having abominable luck finding the captain of my heart in Paris. I await your next developments breathlessly." She had signed it with an unmistakable code name, "Sarah."

"How odd. She says nothing personal," I noted to Godfrey. "No word of missing us. You."

"It is only a cablegram, Nell. Brevity is the soul of clarity." Godfrey was pacing my small sitting room, his hands locked behind his back, his long legs scissoring across the thick Turkish carpet. "What Irene has chosen to say is significant. If she can find no trace of Captain Morgan in Paris, with all her resources of intelligence and connection, then he is no longer there. I doubt it is coincidence that cobras have emigrated from Paris of late as well."

"Snakes stick together," I sniffed. "So you suspect Captain Morgan of perpetrating the bad business in Montmartre?"

"Suspect? I am certain of it, and so is Irene."

"Yet you left her behind to his supposed mercies."

"Actually, Nell, I believe that you and I have drawn him here. In that our jaunt is an unqualified success."

"Indeed, if I wish to spend my life entering rooms into

which serpents have preceded me, I have been uncannily successful!"

"Morgan, mysterious as he is, must be the key to Stanhope's difficulties. Obviously, he is also trying to murder Dr. Watson."

"And yet we have not warned the poor man!" I remonstrated. "We have left him defenseless."

"Hardly." Godfrey stopped pacing to eye me with a twinkle. "The dead snake cannot fail to alarm him. He will immediately acquaint his friend with the mystery. So Dr. Watson will have as guardian the formidable Sherlock Holmes."

I remained silent, aching to add "Formidably given to strange drugs," but I dared not. If I did, I would be obliged to confess to my forbidden reading. Nor did I want to mention my knowledge of the intense impression Irene had evidently made on this man who sneered at women and softer emotions, but reverenced hypodermic needles.

"But we must not rest on Mr. Holmes's laurels," Godfrey said. "Tomorrow we will begin hunting the hunter. I will make inquiries at the gentlemen's clubs devoted to sporting pursuits. You can try the hotels."

"You wish me to inquire after a male resident at a series of hotels? That is most improper, Godfrey."

"Would you rather visit such institutions as The Royal Rhinoceros Regiment? Besides, many clubs forbid women the premises."

"And what sensible woman would wish to visit those masculine enclaves? No doubt they are filled with decorative weapons, rank odors, hollow elephant feet, stuffed snakes and such."

"Yes," he said, laughing, "just like Madame Sarah's Paris salon. What woman could possibly relish such an environment?"

"I am glad that Irene is not here, for she would surely grasp any pretext to storm the gentlemen's clubs in false whiskers. I have it! We will make our rounds together. Admittedly we will lose time, but we will have the advantage of two view-points to compare. That is the solution."

"Not so soon!" said he, taking my new determination for instant action. "We must devise a plan of attack. The hotel will have a recent map of London, as well as some suggestions of where a former military man might stay. I suggest that we repair to the dining room. Brown's *table d'hôte* was famous even in my Temple days."

I smiled tentatively. "I have never dined alone in public with a male escort, but I am sure the experience will be bracing."

And so it was. After a tasty dinner in the quite respectable hotel dining room—whitebait and brown bread, followed by summer pudding, all so delectably English, so fresh, so garlic-free!—we retired to my sitting room again to plan the next day's campaign.

"There is just one thing that troubles me, Godfrey."

"Only one?" He seemed pleasantly surprised.

"If Quentin intended to warn Dr. Watson, why has he not done so?"

"We cannot be sure that he has not."

"Dr. Watson seemed a bit weary, but not at all wary. There is a great difference, Godfrey. He was quite willing to sit down and speak of Afghanistan with two virtual strangers. No, I am certain that he knows nothing of this matter. He will be as mystified by the dead cobra in his study as I would be to find an expired toad in my glove box."

An unwilling smile tweaked the corners of Godfrey's lips, much more visible now that he had shaved off the mustache. "When you put it that way, I must confess that the circumstances are comical despite their seriousness."

"Yes, the world finds much that is serious laughable. That is its main trouble."

"You must admit the melodramatic nature of finding these dead serpents, and realizing that whatever sinister purpose they may have had is moot."

"The motive, whatever it was, is not moot," I pointed out.

"Oh, I do wish Irene were here! She has a genius for taking some totally unforeseen course that nevertheless cuts to the heart of the matter. And what will we do about finding Quentin?"

Godfrey sat on a small tapestry-covered chair with a woebegone expression. "That is the purpose of our visit, true, and yet our only routes to the mysterious Mr. Stanhope are indirect. Well—" he rose with a sigh, his hands clapping his trouser legs "—our tasks are set for the morrow. Perhaps we will encounter some piece of luck."

Luck, I was tempted to answer, was not something Irene relied upon in the slightest. After Godfrey had bid me good night, I reread her cablegram. The blithe good humor underlying it ill became an Irene forced to keep a safe distance from anything. Yet Godfrey was almost supernaturally calm in the face of our frustrating search, and remarkably resigned to the absence of his wife. . . .

Of course I smelled what is known in certain, cruder circles as a rat, and it was not Captain Morgan, no matter how well qualified for the role. This would not be the first time that my two friends had conspired to keep me ignorant for my own good. They might even be acting from some misguided impulse to "spare" me the ugly truth about Emerson Quentin Stanhope. I neither welcomed nor wanted such protection. From now on I would keep a weather eye out for well-intentioned subterfuge.

The next morning we set out from Brown's Hotel in fine weather. Flowers bloomed in window boxes above the shopfronts and the ubiquitous pubs. A pure blue sky dipped down between the five-story rooftops of the great city's buildings.

Gentlemen's clubs, I soon discovered, are like vermin: they lurk everywhere, but are seldom seen. Discreet doorways marked only by severe brass plates that would mean nothing to the uninitiated lead to such eccentric environs as "The Oryxians," "The Fox and Hounds Club," and "The Norfolk Jacketeers."

Godfrey was quite right that I would not be admitted, although I was permitted to teeter on the stoop while he inquired within. My presence was helpful, however. I donned a perpetually doleful look so that Godfrey could point out "poor Miss Huxleigh, who has lost her only brother. Yes, quite genuinely lost. In Injah." Would the hearer know a certain Captain Morgan who had served in that quarter, a renowned heavy-game hunter, particularly of tigers—?

His hearers always denied knowledge of renowned tigers or their hunters, although almost every club kept a mounted tiger head about the place. They were most adamant on their ignorance of "Captain Morgan."

As we made our rounds, I became ever more annoyed at having to stand on the stoop like a domestic servant. However, I was not too lost in indignation to fail to notice the ebb and flow of people around us. Mother London's thronging four millions never allow a citizen to feel lonely.

Godfrey, recognizing my irritation, paused at a flower vendor's near Covent Garden to comfort me with a posy.

"Please, no, I do not require such an extravagance," I protested.

The flower girl, a young person with an extremely freckled face liberally powdered by soot, grimaced at me for discouraging a sale. She need not have worried.

"Nonsense." Godfrey presented me with a knot of pansies and fragrant verbena that was all the more charming in contrast to its grimy vendor.

I had bent my face to sniff the posy, when I spied a familiar face in the crowd.

"Godfrey!"

"Yes, Nell?"

"It is that ruffian again!"

"Which ruffian?"

A good question, for the area teemed with ragged folk of all sorts.

I lowered my voice, speaking as I sniffed the posy in the best Irene-approved method of surreptitious communication.

"That boy that I saw outside 221 B Baker Street," I mumbled into the petals, "and then in Paddington near Dr. Watson's. I am convinced that he is following us."

"That may be, Nell," Godfrey said without alarm. "Then let us give him something to do and go along to the next club."

So we did. It was a fine day, and despite my concern over the ragamuffin I savored the sights of Covent Garden. The vicinity attracted people from the opposite poles of London life; though it literally shone as the theatrical district each night, by day it merely twinkled in the sunshine, genial and friendly.

Here the unlovely strains of pure Cockney echoed off the stone buildings, sounding like a convention of Casanovas. Here, too, strolled retired military men wearing old-fashioned muttonchop whiskers, their backs ramrod straight, their shoes mirror-polished. Fashionable ladies in flower-strewn summer bonnets of Neapolitan straw and summer wraps of the lightest lace, silk and wool ambled among them.

Children too wove through the passing parade, young girls in pleated skirts and wide-brimmed shade hats and very young boys in long curls and short skirted frocks, looking like miniature courtiers from another and more gilded age.

These small ladies and gentlemen capered like kittens beneath the benign summer sunlight. I realized that my visit to Grosvenor Square, as well as my warm encounter with the ingratiating Allegra, had led me to attach only the rosiest memories to my governess days. I reminded myself of tantrums and falsehoods and stubborn silences. No burst of nostalgia should lead me to seek such employment again.

"Your pardon," snapped a dowager in mourning dress as she collided with me, the words courteous but the tone outraged.

I flushed, aware that I had been moonstruck. "I am so very sorry." I reached out a hand to steady her. She glared at me from under wild iron-gray brows before crabbing forward again without acknowledging my apology. On she went, navigating these crowded streets like a sable ship with her sails broken-backed, clothed from neck to toe in braided camel's hair, mantled in a crape-banded black and bonneted in gauze and beads. Though stooped as if by a terrible, invisible weight bundled to her shoulders, her person suggested no fragility.

"I must have been sleepwalking, Godfrey, to have collided with that poor creature."

"She seems none the worse for wear," he said to comfort me. Indeed the old dame was scuttering away at a brisk pace. "In truth, the fault was hers. She careened into you. No doubt her sight is failing."

I sighed. "Certainly my foresight is. I seem to be walking in a fog. Perhaps I have been away from London too long."

"Perhaps your distraction began in Paris," he said.

"What do you mean?"

"Only that you have confronted your past. That is always a shock to the equilibrium."

"That is the whole trouble, Godfrey! I have no past, only a history, like a public edifice. Sarah Bernhardt once said that a woman without a past is like a poodle without a pedigree: alive, but who is interested enough to notice?"

"And for how long have you heeded what Sarah Bernhardt says?"

"Never! But I remember. Even Irene seems to have a past."

"Irene 'seems' a great deal of things."

"Have you never wondered, Godfrey, about her life before you two met?"

He shrugged. "She lived with you for several years."

"But before that? She did not burst upon London fully formed at the age of three and twenty. And she will say nothing of her American days."

"Assuredly that makes them more interesting. Irene is never one to neglect sowing subtle seeds of interest."

"As long as no one around her reaps the result! Perhaps that is what Sarah means by 'a past': the assurance that at some time one has been interesting. I have never been 'interesting'; I have been in Shropshire."

"Shropshire is, I am sure, most interesting."

"But you have no desire to go there."

"Not in the immediate future, no."

"Never."

"It is not likely," he admitted at last.

"I even come from a dull place. Irene would never allow herself to come from a dull place."

"Nell, I am certain that New Jersey is a dull place, or else Irene would not be so close-mouthed about it. Has it ever occurred to you that an unmentioned 'past' may simply be unmentionably dull?"

"No, Godfrey, it has not."

"Well, it may. Besides, the present is all that matters, and here is the next sporting club on our agenda, The Frontier Fusiliers."

Another black-painted door with a brass knocker inset discreetly into a row of redbrick Georgian facades confronted us. Godfrey rang the bell, then introduced us and our business. This time the porter suffered me to enter the hall, where I waited on cold marble, not wishing to sit upon the red-velvet upholstered chair formed from animal horns, and glimpsing a warm red-damask room beyond where deer antlers bristled on the walls.

Godfrey soon returned, his face transparently disappointed.

"This club had a directory of the memberships of all the others; no Sylvester Morgan, Captain or not, honors their rolls. The senior member present suggested that Morgan may have been expelled from one of the other clubs years ago."

"Expelled?"

"Hunters' clubs on occasion resemble their game for behavior. The odd member of the pack 'goes rogue' from time to time. He said this Morgan sounded like 'a bad 'un' who may have had less than honorable dealings with both the hunters' fraternity and the public, if he dealt in rare pelts."

"A perceptive gentleman. So what is our next course?"

"Retreat, I suppose." Godfrey escorted me down the few stairs to the street.

"You are remarkably calm in the face of defeat," I commented.

"I am remarkably calm at all times," he retorted with a smile that I found winning. I found the absence of his mustache disconcerting. Much as I deplore facial hair on men, I confess that I had grown used to it in mild amounts. Or at least I had made an exception to my prejudice with Godfrey.

We walked in silence. Irene made her investigative efforts look like larks, but without her we made a plodding pair.

"Something bracing is called for," Godfrey announced suddenly, steering me with a featherweight pressure on my elbow toward an ABC tea shop. He was also guiding me away from a convention of beggars sprawled upon the walkway.

I hesitated. Under normal conditions, I am not swayed by public beggary, no matter how pathetic. Much of it is polished into a vehicle for the greed of the beseecher rather than the generosity of the giver.

Yet only weeks before in Paris one such unappetizing person had proved to be not only truly needful but an acquaintance. Impulsively, I cannot say why, I dug in my reticule for a few pence.

As I was about to drop them into the grimy hand extended, something flashed past with the utmost speed. My reticule was snatched from my hands, the proffered coins clinking to the pavement. The beggar was too stunned to even scramble for the coppers, although his younger fellows hurled themselves atop the bounty.

Godfrey was bounding after the cutpurse, coattails flying, and I hurried after. I had my suspicions. I had nursed them all along, and now I was certain. No one would make off with my reticule twice in the same week, and only one person would remember a similar incident of many years ago. . . .

I shortly came even with Godfrey, who had paused to search the crowd from his not unrespectable height.

"I fear the scamp has escaped, Nell," he told me.

"No," I told him, "I fear that you have *let* 'the scamp' escape."

"Why, what do you mean?"

"Only that I am tired of this charade! I am not the oblivious fool you take me for! Cablegrams from Paris indeed! Such 'foreign' communications may be arranged from London. It has all been a farce: our search for the mythical Captain Morgan; Irene remaining in France. She is here in London, do not bother to deny it, and hot on a more rewarding trail. Do you think that I have failed to notice the suspicious persons along our route? I have seen that miserable boy three times, and I warrant that you were unable to catch him only because you did not want to!"

"Nell, come into the tearoom and sit down until you collect yourself—"

"No!" I shook off his gentlemanly hand. "I will not be made a public fool, and if Irene does not produce herself soon, I cannot say what I will do!"

"Excuse me," came a deep voice.

Godfrey's eyebrows lifted at the new arrival behind me.

I turned. An old soldier stood there, snowy muttonchops frothing at his jaws, thick spectacles with a dark tint shading his weak old eyes. Apparently there was nothing wrong with his weak old legs, or his weak old arms, for he had the very lad in question by the scruff of his tatterdemalion jacket.

"I caught this one running as if the Queen's Guard were behind him. Since street lads seldom dress with such nicety, he plainly was the reason for the furor down the street. Might this be yours, miss?"

The old man extended my reticule, which I took with relief.

"Anything gone?" Godfrey inquired.

"Not a thing," I replied triumphantly, eyeing the writhing youth. He was a strapping lad. Such street urchins looked depressingly similar, but no matter how he hunched and wriggled, it was obvious he had attained the size of a grown woman.

"Really," I said, regarding the lad unpityingly. "You could

not resist the grand gesture, could you? Was it not enough
that you cast yourself in my path at every opportunity? Did
you expect me to remain completely duped?''

"Nell—" Godfrey said urgently at my rear. I turned on him
with great pleasure.

"And you, you . . . henchman! Oh, I have been very thick,
but that is past now.''

"Nell, in all good conscience—"

"Godfrey, do not try to dissuade me. I am certain that it
will be most mortifying, but she needs to be taught a lesson.
Sir, will you keep a good hold on that lad? Thank you.''

I took a handkerchief from my retrieved reticule and
reached out to scrub at the filth smudging the boy's features.
Immediately a lighter cast of skin shone through.

"You see?'' I spared Godfrey a triumphant glance. He had
a most odd expression. I turned back to my victim, who was
cursing in a Cockney screech that was so unintelligible it
fortunately spared my sensibilities.

"Irene, it's no use,'' I advised the captive. "You cannot fool
me, though of course you had to rub my nose in your deception. Now I am rubbing your nose and it looks far better so.
And as for this ridiculous cap—'' I reached for the item of
apparel in question "—anyone could see it was a clumsy
disguise, too large only because it hid a great, feminine quantity of hair—''

At this I lofted the offending headgear. By now my demonstration had drawn a crowd of onlookers: the beggar family,
more used to entertaining than being entertained; several
nicely dressed children; even the old lady in mourning, with
whom we had apparently caught up again.

"You see,'' I said to my mesmerized audience. "The game
is up. This is not a lad,'' I announced. "This is a grown
woman who likes to play silly games!'' I looked back at the
miscreant.

The sunlight shone down on a dull tangle of cropped black
hair, not the shimmering lengths of cinnamon-brown I had

expected to unveil. The captive's squirmings and epithets increased.

Well, I had heard of theatrical wigs before. I grasped the unappealing head of hair and jerked.

"Owwwwwww!" The creature howled as if to wake any dead within earshot and every living soul all the way to Gretna Green.

"I cannot hold him much longer," the old soldier gritted between a set of wooden teeth. "Do you want to call a bobby or continue on your own?"

"Nell," said Godfrey in soft rebuke that only I could hear, "this is not Irene."

My hand tugged again, to no avail. My gloved fingers uncurled, suddenly aware of the thick, oily texture of the hair they grasped. Even a theatrical wig did not have to be so disgustingly . . . dirty.

Every onlooking eye was nailed to me with lively interest.

"I—I thought . . ."

As my own grip collapsed, so the old gentleman's loosened. The lad wrenched free with a blazingly indignant face, now striped from the cleansing offices of my handkerchief. The young thief whirled to leave, then spun back to glare at me before snatching his . . . truly filthy . . . cap from my nerveless fingers.

"Mad as a moonbeam," he spat at me with perfect clarity before dashing away through a crowd that did nothing to prevent him.

I looked around. "He did steal my reticule."

"Quite so." The old gentleman dusted off his palms as if that would remove his contact with so much uncleanliness.

Gradually, but not soon enough, the onlookers ebbed, going about their business. I stood in the street drawing my reticule strings tight and loose in turn.

"Nell—" Godfrey began, more gently than I should have had the circumstances been reversed.

"Do not say it! I was wrong, but I was right as well. Irene

is in London," I said, raising my eyes defiantly to his at last.

He did not deny it. "Would you care for some tea now?"

Godfrey and I did not discuss the matter further, not even at dinner that night. I recognized that by avoiding the topic he avoided having to deliver any falsehoods. Of course Irene was lurking about London.

At least my reticule had been returned.

Alone in my room, I examined it to see if it required mending or cleaning. As I had told Godfrey, my coin purse was still there, along with the handkerchief, which would require laundering, and a vial of smelling salts, an item that no woman should ever be without. I sniffed it delicately in case any lingering miasma remained from my strenuous afternoon.

The reticule's lining appeared unbesmirched, I noted with relief, for the lad's filthy fingers had not escaped my notice. What had escaped my notice until that moment was a cylinder of pale paper that lay upright against the cream silk lining.

I withdrew it gingerly.

Scratched in faint pencil were the words: "*You must come to the Natural History Museum vertebrate rooms at 11 A.M. tomorrow (the 8th). Urgent!*" One letter signed the note: "*Q.*"

My heart began pounding. How had this message gotten into my reticule? When? By whom had it been delivered? I rose, intending to fetch Godfrey. Then I paused.

I would not make an idiot of myself again in anyone's presence, least of all his. No proof existed that the message was from Quentin Stanhope, but who else should it be from? And as for the method of delivery, that I must puzzle out for myself.

I took the note to my dainty Louis XIV desk. Brown's Hotel was liberally equipped with gaslight, but the desk bore as well an oil lamp, which I lit. I held the tiny piece of rolled paper down by the edges of a crystal stamp box and an ink bottle.

The words had been hastily written, but I was no judge of Quentin's handwriting in any case. I desperately wished I was, having seen Irene dissect the character of correspondents with a glance and a blithe pronouncement.

The penmanship was legible; a pencil—none too sharp—had been used, which bespoke a hasty scrawl made on the street without premeditation; and the words were impossible for me to ignore.

When and how had this missive come into my possession? Certainly not at the hotel; I had filled the reticule myself before leaving. The most obvious choice of messenger was the unfortunate thief. Had he actually been adding to the contents of my reticule rather than subtracting from them?

Perhaps that was why he had "let" himself be caught. I had glimpsed this unwholesome figure several times. Obviously he had been commissioned to watch us. Of course, he could simply be a thief who had decided that my reticule was tasty prey and who had followed us for that reason only. But if the young thief had not thrust this note into my bag, who else could have?

I rose to fetch the reticule, a common kind of faille sack with a wide mouth pulled shut by pursing the strings interwoven into the folds. I drew the cords, noticing that while the reticule was throttled shut, so to speak, the moment that I released the cords they loosened slightly. Sufficient room remained among the puckered pleats to thrust a slender pipe of paper into the depths of the bag.

So. Anyone could have done it. The dowager in mourning who had bumped into me . . . the old soldier who had captured the young thief . . . the flower girl who had handed me the posy, for that matter . . . the ragamuffin . . . even Godfrey.

One of these figures—or even another, unnoticed person—could have been Quentin in disguise. Or Irene in disguise. Or even—never underestimate *the* man—Sherlock Holmes in disguise. Or none of them could be anybody at all.

I leaned my head on my hands and shut my eyes. On the blackness before me floated the figures of the day, as if inviting me to choose one. But my choice that afternoon had been horribly wrong. I would not make that mistake again! And I would attend that rendezvous on the morrow. Of course I dared not tell Godfrey. Besides suspecting that he and Irene had left me out of their game, I could not risk letting him see Quentin again. Godfrey's last promise had been to thrash an explanation for his disappearance from Quentin. I had no intention of allowing such an occurrence.

No, I must somehow elude Godfrey without his suspecting anything. But how? And then I sat up straight, divinely inspired.

I would tell Godfrey that I wished to go to church!

## Chapter Twenty-Three

# 'ONEST CITIZENS

❧

''Church?'' **Godfrey** said in startled tones, as if I had proposed visiting a Whitechapel opium den.

"Yes. Church," I reiterated at breakfast. "I have had no opportunity to attend Anglican services since joining you and Irene in France nearly a year ago."

"I have not been in a church since Irene and I were married," he mused.

"Neither has she."

"I suppose," he began with little enthusiasm, mangling his kipper, "I can accompany you."

"You can indeed, and that would be commendable, save that this expedition of mine is a private pilgrimage. I make it once a year upon the anniversary of my dear father's death."

"Oh." Godfrey looked as taken aback as I had ever seen him. Referring to a death in the family is a proven method of ensuring other people's rapid loss of interest in one's personal affairs.

He frowned. "I never noticed such an annual outing during the years that I employed you at the Temple."

I rather oversalted my kidney pie while composing my next venture into falsehood. "Ah . . . such visitations are more spiritually salubrious if not boasted about, Godfrey."

"No doubt, no doubt," he agreed. "You are the parson's daughter and should know."

"Indeed."

"What church do you honor with your pilgrimage?"

Now I trod upon very delicate ground. My difficulty was the fact that Brown's Hotel was located close to the theatrical district called by the silly name of Piccadilly. Unfortunately, but not unexpectedly, no reputable church was within suitable distance. I would have to name one near my true destination.

"Holy Trinity," I said firmly, hoping Godfrey would inquire no further.

He was not a barrister for nothing. "Holy Trinity?" He spoke with some astonishment. "Why on earth would you wish to go there?"

"Why on earth not?"

"I read about it in yesterday's *Telegraph*. It will be a splendid homage to the Arts and Crafts Movement when completed, with its Burne-Jones and Morris stained glass windows, but it cannot be the goal of your pilgrimage. It is still unfinished, Nell."

"Where is this so-called 'Holy Trinity'?"

"Sloane Square," he replied, watching me carefully.

"Heavens, no! That Holy Trinity is quite the wrong one, Godfrey. Goodness. My Holy Trinity is in Knightsbridge, near the Victoria and Albert Museum, an excellent, restrained example of the Gothic style."

He buttered his muffin. "You are certain that I cannot persuade you to allow me to escort you?"

"I prefer going alone, so that I may think about things."

"Things," he echoed in his newly annoying way, so like Casanova.

"Things," I repeated firmly. At least that part was utterly true.

I insisted on taking an omnibus to Kensington, as I had not done for many months. Godfrey argued in favor of a hansom cab, but I resisted. As my association with Irene and her early "cases" had shown me, a cab journey is easier to track than the crowded comings and goings aboard a public omnibus.

My late father, I told Godfrey, would not have approved such extravagance as a hansom cab, even on his own behalf. Since it is virtually impossible to argue with the dead, Godfrey relented, and soon I was on my separate, if not merry, way.

As I jolted out the Brompton Road toward Kensington among an anonymous mob of fellow travelers, all of us advertising "Dr. Morton's Amazing Foot Powder," I brooded on the extremes to which my attempt to help Quentin Stanhope had driven me. I had never willfully deceived anyone to whom I owed so much. Yet I had known Quentin before I had ever met Godfrey, if one may call such a brief acquaintance as ours "knowing." The poor man had quite literally stumbled across me after all these years and had seemed to take some comfort in that. I had no choice but to see him.

I felt obliged to stop at Holy Trinity and offer a prayer for my father, who had died in mid-February rather than July. Still, my visit to Holy Trinity did me good, and steeled my resolve. I set out for the museum.

This entire quarter of London just south of the velvet-green summer quilt of Kensington Park bristled with new constructions. In the near distance I could spy the awesome spires and domes of the Queen's monuments to domestic bliss and connubial bereavement: the Gothic spires of the Prince Albert Memorial bristling beyond the redbrick bulk of Albert Hall, a modern glass-and-iron domed concert arena.

The Museum of Natural History and Modern Curiosities dated only to the early 'Seventies, and faced the strong sunlight as yet unstained by London's smoke-misted autumns and wet, sooty winters. With its twin spires and central nave, the terra-cotta and slate-blue exterior offered a most reassuring, contemplative and churchlike appearance, though it was a bit Byzantine for my taste.

Within, the religious similarity ended. In the vast entry area loomed some monster of the primordial swamps in all its bony glory. Yet, like a church, the Museum of Natural History and Modern Curiosities was ever mindful of death. As I wandered its many exhibit rooms, for I had arrived well in advance of the appointed time, I felt I toured a mausoleum rather than a museum. All of the exhibits, whether insect, reptile, bird or mammal, were dead, whether shown in the bare bones or in the furred and feathered simulacra of life.

Bright glass eyes stared at me without wavering. Creatures posed as patiently as if for a photograph, only these subjects would never move again, and I was the moving camera that recorded their bizarre forms. I almost wished that I could huddle under a black cloth and peer at them in secret. This public display of so much death, of so many creatures killed that so few of us could gawk at them in echoing marble splendor, seemed truly primitive.

I passed the bloated reptiles coiling in their great wooden cases, stopping before a cobra raised up as I had seen one do in life only recently, its famous "spectacle"-marked hood wide as an eighteenth-century lady's calabash. The maw was open so the fangs glimmered bone-white under the electric lights. This serpent looked as regal as any Queen of the Nile; for a moment I saw it not as a thing of loathing or the Form of the Fall, but rather as a bejeweled and magnificent creation wrested from its true setting, the natural world. And then I shuddered, for it was a serpent after all, and deadly.

Yet the true predator was not the venomous serpent, but the one who sought to put the snake's natural weapons to unnatural, human ends, unthinkable crimes in garrets and consulting rooms.

As I looked about, the vastness of the museum oppressed me. I felt as if I had been immured in some gigantic sarcophagus. What a site Quentin had selected for our clandestine meeting!

With relief I entered the vertebrate area, devoutly hoping that fur would mask all the macabre zoology exhibits. Instead, I was again unnerved. Exotic creatures were fastened high on the walls or imprisoned in glassed-in wooden cabinets oddly reminiscent of Mr. Tiffany's well-secured jewelry cases at 79 rue Richelieu. A faint odor of stale fur and formaldehyde reminded me of the Paris Morgue.

Weaving past the room's mounted occupants, I concentrated with some relief on the moving, human exhibit, the visitors. How should I recognize Quentin? Certainly he would not be attired in the fantastic foreign garb that he had worn in Paris. In that City of Lights the lunatic is a patron saint. In London, only mild eccentricity is tolerated.

As I passed a pair of towering ostriches (such glamourous plumes upon a bonnet; such gawky and unpleasing creatures), I heard a rustle like a great bird's quills. I turned to see a familiar figure bearing down on me—an old woman in mourning dress!

She brushed past impatiently to approach a stuffed ostrich. Even her stooped posture could not disguise her once-great height. She lifted a lorgnette on its black silk cord and bobbed her head upon its scrawny neck to scrutinize the exhibit. Her gestures were so like a chicken's in a hen yard that I could not repress a smile, despite my lively suspicions.

Could this be Quentin Stanhope? Certainly that hump-shouldered carriage could disguise a man's height. I had seen enough of Irene's wonder-working with crape hair and veiled bonnets to know that the unruly gray eyebrows could be false and that a black veil could soften a man's harsher features into those of an elderly woman. As women age their feminine features harshen into those of old men, as if all our differences are designed to melt away by life's end.

The dowager turned from the ostrich, keeping her lorgnette raised while she favored me with the same openly bobbing inspection. Then she nodded, once and briskly, and rustled on.

I did not know what to think. Had she recognized me from the street? Or was this inspection a signal to accost her? What if I were wrong and mere coincidence had brought her here?

"Mere coincidence, Nell?" I could almost hear Irene's amused tones. "I do not know if there is such a thing as the

God defined by the self-declared men of God, but I do know that there is no such thing as 'mere coincidence.' "

I looked around. Figures passed, vaguely seen among the stuffed animal life—or death—surrounding me. An overwhelming sense of observation oppressed me. Perhaps it was engendered by the myriad of glass eyes, shining as if every creature came equipped with spectacles.

I drew out my pince-nez, presumably to better inspect the exhibits, but in fact because my naked face felt so vulnerable. I wished for one of Irene's lavish veils. No wonder she affected them; they allowed her to see without being fully seen—not only an advantage for an actress, but a necessity for the inquiry agent.

And here was I, armed with nothing but my determination and a note that—oh! For the first time the dreadful thought struck: a note that might not even be from Quentin Stanhope, that might be a ruse to lure me here for purposes . . . purposes . . . purposes unguessed at but not good!

I looked about with the intent of making my exit—and spied the old soldier who had collared the thieving boy of yesterday. He was leaning down, whisker to whisker with a gigantic, sprawling male seal!

I hastened around the rear of a most impressive giraffe, and tried to hide behind one of its tall but extremely slender spotted legs. Another unwelcome discovery greeted me. Yes, my eyes were not deceiving me; there, not twenty feet away, was the boy who had stolen my purse, strolling among the monkeys with his hands in his pockets and an innocent expression on his still-filthy face!

I fixedly contemplated the giraffe's tail high above my head: a most ridiculous appendage considering the owner's great height, terminating in a broomlike brush of whisker-stiff hairs. The spots before my eyes were as nothing compared to the mad pattern of notions colliding in my brain.

The boy could not be Quentin, but he might be bearing another message for me. Or . . . I looked about. A number of children gamboled through the rooms, as the animals were a drawing card for the younger set. I would have taken my charges here myself, had I been a governess longer. Most instructive and suitable entertainment, given the number of families in attendance.

But lone, purse-snatching street urchins . . .

I had half convinced myself that certainly all of the previous day's population of Covent Garden had now convened to the Museum of Natural History and Modern Curiosities. The retired soldier was looking in my direction. As our eyes intersected, he nodded and bowed slightly, and why should he not? He had assisted in the recovery of my reticule but a day before.

Coincidences bred like monkeys around me, and so did my own speculations. It seemed as if I were center stage at the Grand Guignol, the leading actress in a gruesome play. Was it Irene's fine Machiavellian hand airily pulling a set of invisible strings high in the building's vaulted ceilings? An air of intense expectation hung above the macabre blending of man and beast executing a clandestine pavane in the scene below.

Then from behind an aardvark hobbled the strangest creature yet: a hunchbacked old scholar buttoned into a rusty black coat despite the warm day, a yellowed beard trailing down his concave chest, his eyes vigilant and owlish behind a pair of yellow-tinted spectacles. He might have been the twisted twin of the stooped dowager . . .

I could not resist glancing at her; she had interrupted her close inspection of a mole peering out from a mossy log to glare at the newest arrival.

Suddenly inspired, I realized that both figures could have been men in disguise; men, moreover, who were gifted, or cursed, with telltale eyes—men like Quentin Stanhope, with his clear hazel gaze that a veneer of foreign sun only emphasized, or Captain Sylvester Morgan, whose compelling cold azure stare was that of the professional hunter!

Could hunter and prey have both found their way here? Which could I trust, if both approached me? And what part did the retired soldier play?

I watched them circle in the exhibition room: the young urchin, the old soldier, the elderly scholar, the stooped dowager. It was not lost on me that three of my four suspicious fellow citizens were apparently old. "Age is the best disguise," Irene had remarked long ago. "It is so commonplace, yet so unspokenly dreaded, that we seldom look it in the eye, much less examine its traces in ourselves."

So. Which of these enfeebled browsers was Irene, then? And why was that idle boy present, if he was not Irene? No matter how I counted up my suspicions, I had one candidate for disguise too many. Quentin; Irene; Captain Morgan.

To give myself time to think, I extracted my pince-nez from my reticule and exchanged soulful gazes with a two-toed sloth that depended most artistically from an artificial tree within a glassed-in case. In its faint reflection I could follow the actions of the principal parties.

The scholar had pressed himself to an opposite case as if to obtain the same once-removed view of us all that I had of them. The dowager was rummaging in her reticule. The boy was surreptitiously removing the prettiest of the small rocks arrayed around the corpulent seal. The soldier was honoring the giraffe with a long inspection, and seemed, viewed through the gaudy bars of the beast's legs, confined in a cage. One must be Quentin, one Irene and one Captain Sylvester Morgan.

But who was the fourth? Who?

When the logical answer occurred to me, I plucked a linen handkerchief from my reticule—no easy task, as I had taken to wrapping the cords twice around my wrist since the attempted theft—and buried my face in it.

The fourth in our game of hide and seek must be: Sherlock Holmes! Now I must conceal my identity. No doubt Dr. Watson had alerted him to the cobra in swift enough time for the detective to discover where our cab had taken us and follow me from the hotel this morning.

My face muffled in white linen embroidered with love knots, I sneezed delicately from time to time and shuffled

along to the next cabinet, which featured an array of goggle-
eyed lizards.

Someone bumped into me from behind.

I whirled, one hand clutching my reticule, one clasped to
my mouth and nose.

The retired soldier stood there, ramrod straight, his features florid against the snowy frame of his muttonchops and
mustache, his eyes in the shadow of a jaunty straw boater a
very familiar hazel.

I felt the hand with the handkerchief sinking into a sea of
surprise and confusion. My mouth opened to say the only
possible thing, which was "Quentin . . ."

"Kweh . . . kweh . . . kweh," I began, only catching myself
in time at a sudden warning cramp in the very pith of my
being. I must not betray his true identity! "Kweh-choooo!" I
declared, muffling my face again.

A long, dark tube like the barrel of a rifle thrust through the
fraudulent foliage of the thick, junglelike display in which a
half-dozen jeering monkey faces perched.

Another figure crashed into us. I reeled as the retired soldier moved to catch me. Something sped past my bonnet
ribbons. At the same instant, the glass case behind me exploded and a shower of pebbles pelted my back. I recognized
the phenomena as issuing from a firearm, but the other museum visitors screeched and milled madly, unsure of what
transpired. Amid all this mayhem, someone was again pulling
on my poor reticule cords.

"No!" I shouted. "Stop, thief!"

The old soldier collared the lad again. I had an overwhelming sense of what the French (they have their few uses) call
*déjà vu*. Over the soldier's shoulder the wizened scholar
stared at us and then darted away. The dowager rustled after
him at a startlingly efficient pace. A stranger was striding
toward us, a black-suited figure with a vertical line of small
suns blazing down his coat front and a helmet upon his head.
He swelled until he blocked out all the rest.

" 'Ere now," said he in a great authoritarian grumble, putting a firm hand on the soldier's narrow elbow. "We will all come along quietly. This 'ere's a public institution, you know. No disturbances in a public institution."

"Let him go!" I screeched, thinking of Quentin, if he *was* Quentin.

Unfortunately, two "hims" were in custody. The supposed Quentin, startled, immediately liberated the boy, who thanked him by tightening his grip on my reticule, which he had never released, and turning to run.

Unfortunately, I had bound it to my wrist all too well. I lurched forward, my feet slipping on shards of shattered glass. I found myself falling toward the sparkling, diamond-strewn floor.

I was arrested in my plummet by a strong arm around my waist, even as the bobby leaped to snag the wretched urchin with the law's long arm.

"Thank you." I adjusted my bonnet as the old soldier righted me. "And there is your thief," I told the bobby while I unwound my snarled reticule and glared at the captive boy.

"You'll all 'ave to come along to the magistrate," the bobby returned in the bored tones of a policeman used to all sorts. "We'll need testimony. And someone's got to pay for that spoiled glass. Was it a slingshot done it, lad?"

His captive squirmed and hunched and muttered unintelligibly.

The soldier was eyeing the blasted cabinet with a sober expression, then caught my glance. Quentin he was! I knew it now. He must not, of course, be forced to name himself to any official. His current identity would no doubt melt like a vanilla ice under the hot regard of the law.

"Come then," the bobby urged, his thick black mustache, most ill trimmed, vibrating with emphasis. " 'Onest citizens must do their dooty, or wot kind o' an example is set for lads like this?"

I would have resisted strongly, save that the sullen lad looked up suddenly from under the brim of his tweed cap and said, "Oh, give it up, Nell; you'll ruin everything if you cause a fuss now."

I would have recognized the unadulterated, bell-like tones of Irene Adler anywhere, even in the Museum of Natural History and Modern Curiosities, and even when she was sounding utterly annoyed with me.

## Chapter Twenty-Four

# FORAGING AT FORTNUM'S

**The bobby** rushed all three of us into a four-wheeler outside the museum. I was unsure by whom to be the more amazed—Quentin Stanhope in the guise of a retired soldier, or Irene Adler as the boy in the disreputable cap.

"Irene, is that you?" I demanded the moment I was seated within the dim interior.

"Of course." She flung herself into the vehicle after Quentin and me, then immediately strained halfway out the open window again. "If I had not been so efficiently restrained, I could have followed Tiger—but it is too late now. We must lose no time in being off! Oh, where is Godfrey?"

"I have no idea, Irene, but I do believe that this bewhiskered old gentleman is Quentin."

Irene flung herself into the seat opposite to regard him. The inspection was intensely mutual.

"It had better be Quentin Stanhope," Irene noted at last, "else we have the honor to share a four-wheeler with Sherlock Holmes, which would suit none of us at the moment, I think."

"Who is this impertinent boy?" the perhaps-Quentin demanded, turning to me. "And why do you keep calling him 'Irene'?"

The streetside coach door opened at that awkward instant,

and in bounded the bobby. "Chelsea, and be quick about it," he shouted over his uniformed shoulder to the driver as he sat.

"Chelsea?" I demanded in shock.

"We must mislead pursuers," Irene answered as, ahead, the reins snapped over the horses's hindquarters.

The carriage gave a fearful lurch, and we began to rattle over the cobblestones at a smart pace. The motion jolted the Disreputable Cap askew on the Disreputable Boy's head . . . and down fell the rich lengths of gilt-tinged brown curls I had envisioned revealing the previous day.

"It is Mrs. Norton!" exclaimed the old soldier beside me, thus sealing his identity.

"Only yesterday you were simply a miserable street lad!" I complained bitterly.

Irene smiled through her filthy ragamuffin's face. "Yesterday I was a Covent Garden flower girl," she corrected me. "Since you so thoughtfully demonstrated that the young thief was utterly authentic in front of so many crucial witnesses, it made the perfect, foolproof guise today. Thank you, dear heart."

"I suppose I am the fool against which it was proof," I said.

"Oh, no. I rather hoped it would be Captain Morgan and Mr. Holmes. We shall soon see." She pressed against the window and peered out. "No hansom in apparent pursuit, but smugness is premature." She rapped the roof of the carriage and shouted, "On to Brixton after you reach Chelsea, and drive like the wind incarnate. There's a half-sovereign in it."

She sat back and beamed at the bobby, who had remained a dark, silent presence in our midst. "I hope you do not mind my borrowing a page from your book, my dear."

At this Quentin turned his dignified head to glare at the bobby. I studied the policeman's eyes under the helmet brim, the slightly aquiline nose that bridged helmet and mustache, the chin strap that slashed across his cheek to the tip of the chin, much altering the features. . . .

246 Carole Nelson Douglas

"Godfrey?" I attempted.

He doffed his official headgear with a bow. "For God and country and Sir Robert Peel."

"Well." I sat back feeling very put upon. "It appears that I am the only person in honest guise among you. Would any of you care to explain?"

"It is Mr. Stanhope who has the real explaining to do," Irene said a trifle sternly, "and much of his explanation is owed to you, Nell. But Godfrey and I will unburden our deceptive souls first, because it is such fun to reveal the moves of a game once the object has been won."

"And what is the object of your game, Mrs. Norton?" Quentin inquired stiffly.

"You," Irene replied with an urchinlike grin. Her expression and tone sobered as she continued. "The ensuring of your bodily safety, as well as that of the distinguished Dr. Watson. Also the uncovering of the plot that enmeshes you both in death and deception, so that your futures can be secure. And the disarming of the villainous and implacable nature behind this scheme that has unwound for nearly ten years. And lastly, my object is the well-being and peace of mind of my dear companion, Miss Penelope Huxleigh, who has come to expect from a gentleman a private explanation rather than a hasty departure by night."

I would have thought it impossible for the old soldier's florid complexion to flush further, but it did.

"Miss Huxleigh's safety and that of yourself and your husband were my sole concerns in Paris," he said. "Hence my abrupt departure. You have no idea of the dangerous waters into which you plunge, Madame."

"Do you?" Irene asked with a wicked gleam in her eye. "And I think a liquid analogy does not become a matter which began in arid Afghanistan."

"Yes, this did begin with attempted murder years ago in Afghanistan. Now more of the same erupts in Paris and London. The situation is far too volatile for new and uninformed players in the game, as you call it."

"Oh, fiddlesticks, Quentin. The Great Game between England and Russia has been waged on the steppes of Afghanistan for decades. While you play the noble spy and tell half-truths and melt into the shadows, the real villain is getting away with murder. What do you know of the Indian gentleman who died of cobra venom in your Montmartre lodgings?"

"Dalip is dead?" Quentin performed the impossible again and paled beneath his greasepaint choler. "By cobra bite?"

Godfrey bestirred himself at the sight of a fine point slithering free. "Cobra *venom*. A cobra was on the premises, but was not the source of poison. Irene shot it."

"Good God." Quentin turned to her in wonder.

"Only after Nell had alertly pointed it out to me," Irene admitted modestly.

Quentin turned to me in even greater disbelief.

"The room was quite dim," I explained. "I only saw a . . . swaying silhouette, but Irene had her revolver and so—"

Quentin abandoned his upright military posture and let himself thud back against the tufted leather cushions with a stunned sigh. "Poor Dalip. A sepoy soldier at Maiwand, and my sole friend in the years after. I begin to feel my supposed age. Do you mean to say that you two ladies were alone in my Montmartre quarters with a cobra and a dying man?"

"He was dead by the time we arrived, Quentin," I assured him. "It was perfectly proper."

"What was most improper," Irene said, retrieving something glittering from her urchin's garb, "was leaving this token behind in Neuilly. You cannot outrun your past, Quentin."

He hesitated before taking the small golden object Irene extended. "Medals make a tawdry memorial for the costs of Maiwand."

"Medals are not made to memorialize the dead, my dear man," Irene told him, "but to remind the living of just those costs. If you choose to give it away, I hope you would do it for better reason than that it weighs heavily on your memory."

His closing fingers eclipsed the small glimmer. "Perhaps you are right. Mementos must be tended gladly, not outrun. I will keep it—for now—as a remembrance of my last peaceful days, in Neuilly."

"What is the plan now?" Godfrey asked in the lengthening silence.

Irene rubbed her grimy face with her hands, a sign more of mental fatigue than a desire for cleanliness. "We must return to Brown's and change hotels. Obviously, Nell was followed to and from it. Nell, since you alone are yourself, you must handle the transfer. Once we have found new headquarters we can restore ourselves to normal, and then compare notes."

Godfrey groaned. "Must we change hotels? That is much to ask poor Nell to stage-manage alone."

"Indeed," I seconded him.

"Unless you care to find a sleeping cobra as a foot-warmer, I suggest that we do so immediately."

No one objected after considering this argument, and the confused driver was instructed to make his way to Piccadilly. How I arranged for payment and the packing and transfer of Godfrey's and my things to the waiting carriage does not make for absorbing reading even in a diary. Let me state merely that I managed it.

"Now, where is Irene staying?" I asked when our luggage was finally piled atop the four-wheeler and I had joined the other three within it.

A silence. "Well?"

Godfrey answered. "Irene was staying with me, Nell."

"With you? From the very beginning? Then that is why you insisted that I required a sitting-room suite, and why our conferences were always held in my room! My sitting room, that is," I added with a quick glance at Quentin. "It was utter deception from the first."

"I am afraid so," Irene said with no compunction. "And great fun it was. Hovering about unbeknownst to you was most amusing." Her expression grew misty-eyed. "There is no place like London for surreptitious following. These grim gray buildings and narrow streets and byways, the gaslit evenings when fog becomes one's uninvited accessory. The broad boulevards, sprawling public buildings and all the electricity of Paris cannot hold a candle to it!"

Godfrey cleared his throat, a favorite courtroom signal of his for attention. Irene reluctantly shook herself out of her reverie, sending more locks of hair cascading over the shoulders of her ragged jacket.

"I digress," she admitted. "Well, Mr. Stanhope, shall we repair to your lodgings for the time being?"

"My—?" He glanced at me askance. "They are not suitable for ladies."

"Wonderful! Where else would such a desperate character as yourself go to ground? I do so long to see them!"

"Truly, I cannot allow it," the poor man said. "A fellow who has lived in the squalor of India or in the wilds of Afghanistan may camp out in a metropolitan sinkhole, but ladies . . . see here, Norton, can you not talk her out of it?"

"Not a bit," Godfrey answered. "Besides, I am curious myself."

"But Miss Huxleigh—" Quentin finished with a plea in my direction.

"—lived in Saffron Hill with me in the early 'eighties," Irene pointed out. "We are both adapted to the Bohemian life."

"Saffron Hill was merely a foreign section, not beyond the pale," he argued. "I am mortified enough as it is that you saw the garret I occupied in Paris."

Irene clasped her hands as if about to deliver a most heart-wrenching aria. "It was superb, my dear Quentin. Quite perfect for a setting in *La Bohème.* You underestimate the attractions of the tawdry. The romanticism. The adventure."

"You *are* speaking of that unspeakable garret in Montmartre?"

"Indeed. Where else could a civilized woman go to shoot a cobra?"

"The salon of Sarah Bernhardt," I interjected in acid tones.

Quentin laughed. "She has got you there. Even I have heard of La Bernhardt's menagerie."

Irene refused to be ruffled. "If I am to shoot a cobra, which I really do not wish to do unless it is a matter of self-defense, I certainly would not want to do it in a drawing room. No. A garret in Montmartre provides the proper artistic ambience. When you know me better, Quentin, you will understand that the proper artistic ambience is always a major consideration with me. Now, tell this most impatient driver where to take us. I do hope it will be interesting."

First, however, Quentin and I were ejected at nearby Fortnum & Mason's in Piccadilly near Duke Street, under orders to return with enough comestibles for an impromptu luncheon at our destination. Godfrey showered me with pound notes before we descended from the carriage, and soon we were wandering the impressive aisles in canyons of piled tinned goods from the world over.

"Mrs. Norton is right," Quentin murmured to me once we were inside the famous emporium. "I owe you an explanation, and an apology. But I must ask why we have been delegated to feed our party."

"We are the least likely to attract undue attention, as we are the most respectable-looking of the quartet. I know Irene's methods. An urchin and a bobby would hardly be shopping partners at Fortnum and Mason."

"And you and I?"

I glanced at his most successful disguise. "A retired colonel, widowed, on an outing with his . . . spinster daughter."

"Not a retired colonel, widowed, on an outing with his second wife?"

I could have sworn that there was a teasing gleam in the pale eyes under the bushy white eyebrows.

"Mine is the more likely assumption. Besides, I have never been anyone's first wife, so I should not know how to enact a second one. Oh, really, I do not know what to buy." I gazed at a depressing display of tins with French labeling. "Irene loved this goose-liver mess in Paris, but I cannot abide it. Do choose what you want to eat. I have quite lost my appetite."

"Are you ill?"

"No! Merely . . . feeling a fool."

He laughed and smoothed his full, white and totally false mustache. "How do you think I feel? My clever plan to approach you without attracting notice apparently drew a full house. Now I am compelled to draw you all further into my sordid life—"

"Oh, you must not think of it that way! Irene is right, you know, in her maddening way. Interesting people often lead . . . irregular lives. I suppose I notice that because I am not interesting."

"My dear Penelope, I cannot tell you how interesting you are to me. Norton has his hands full with Mrs. Norton, I see."

"I do not believe that he would have it any other way, Quentin." We had begun walking down the aisles, Quentin taking my arm, or rather leaning upon it in what I chose to consider quite a fatherly way as befitted his semblance. "I suppose we do not want any tinned peas? No."

"Your friend Mrs. Norton does not strike me as one highly enamored of tinned peas."

"You must call her 'Irene,' as I do, and she has asked you to."

"I prefer calling her Mrs. Norton," he said.

"Then you must take the state of matrimony very seriously." I was suddenly aware of what a personal intrusion this comment was.

"Not necessarily," he returned easily, "but calling such an exotic woman as your friend by the utterly commonplace name of 'Mrs. Norton' amuses me."

The warmth in his eyes unnerved me, and I fell back on my best governess behavior. "I am afraid that you are amused by very trivial matters."

52222

5255

5252

52   Carole Nelson Douglas

"All amusement is trivial, Penelope. That is why there is so little of it in learned books."

"Does 'Miss Huxleigh' amuse you?" I made my next, bold offer rather breathlessly. "Otherwise, you may call me 'Nell.' "

"And will you call me 'Stan'?" he asked so gently that I was quite undone and spoke more sharply than I meant, spoke in the most contrary tone to what I felt.

"I think not."

"You see, commonplace names do not suit us; we are too ordinary to begin with. We shall have to go a long way before we do anything so dignified that it would be droll to call us by nicknames. But I would be delighted to call you 'Nell.' "

His logic had become convoluted, or else I was too distracted to follow it. I would have thought that he was mocking me, were it not that a man whose life is in danger, it seems evident, will not stoop to frivolity . . . or flirting. Of course he meant nothing by it, but our chitchat did not settle the matter of what we should eat. I told him so.

"Why then," said he, "we must outfit ourselves." With that he steered me to the picnic hampers—great, wicker contrivances large enough to house a dozen cobras—and told the gentleman in morning coat who attended us that he wished a good supply laid within of game pies, lobster, prawns, smoked salmon, Parma ham, sandwiches, Stilton cheese and (unfortunately) *pâté de foie gras*, as well as champagne and a trifle for dessert.

"We must celebrate our reunion," he said with a grin at the clerk and a wink at me. Old age apparently entitles a gentleman to all manner of liberties.

Godfrey's pound notes vanished as if swallowed by anacondas, but the hamper was soon full and fitted out as well with napery, cutlery, pottery, china and crystal. Two men carried it out behind us to the waiting carriage, and if we had desired discretion, it was a vain wish.

"Oh, I am famished!" Irene exclaimed as the booty was set on the floor amongst us, for there was no room atop.

"I am afraid that my lodgings will be less appetizing," Quentin said, "but I have given the driver the address."

"You have not been followed there so far?" Irene asked. "You are sure?"

"I am alive," he answered wryly. "No, I have been doing the following these latter days, and busy work it is, too."

"You must tell us more." The backs of Irene's graceful fingers tapped Godfrey's breast pocket, a familiar gesture to me, but new to Quentin. He watched Godfrey produce a cigarette case with lucifers stored in the side, then offer Irene an Egyptian cigarette and a lit match.

She soon had swathed herself in an airy scarf of smoke.

"You smoke away from home, Madame?" Quentin, I noticed, always fell back on the French form of address when amazed by Irene. No "Mrs. Norton" then.

"And you do not?"

"Only the occasional cigar."

"I smoke only the occasional cigarette. It helps me to think."

"I would not believe that you require any assistance in that area," Quentin responded.

Godfrey laughed. "There, Irene. You will have to give up all your beloved props, since peerless logic alone makes you fascinating to Quentin here."

"Ne-vair," Irene answered in a perfect imitation of the Bernhardt manner. "Where are we going for our picnic?" she asked Quentin.

"Houndsditch," he said.

"Fascinating," was all Irene said, crossing her arms and lounging in her seat like the rude boy she enacted.

I bestirred myself. "You have said nothing of your own activities."

Her half-shut eyes lifted to me. "No," she said, and let them fall shut again.

I turned to Godfrey, but he was also lost in his own thoughts, looking most uncomfortable in his bobby uniform. Quentin, too, wore an abstracted, exhausted expression. I could not understand how three such energetic people had tired so easily, when I was as fresh as a . . . a nosegay.

The driver required a generous fare when he deposited us at a doorway that resembled something from the more depressing and lengthy fictions of Dickens.

"It is reasonably clean," Quentin said as he stood and looked up at the four dilapidated stories looming above us.

"You are, I presume," Irene said, "on the topmost floor?"

When Quentin nodded, she asked, "Can your landlady be trusted?"

"To a degree."

"Then I propose we leave our baggage in her care on the ground floor. We shall have to find new quarters this evening. In the meantime, we will take the hamper and ourselves upstairs to plot and picnic."

## Chapter Twenty-Five

# A MESSY PICNIC

**The "we"** who took the hamper was Godfrey and
Quentin, once they had transported our baggage into the dim
front parlor of one Mrs. Bracken. This spare, gray-haired,
gray-apron-clad figure made me long for the rosy cheeks and
flyaway white hair of the landlady who presided over 221 B
Baker Street.

The stairs were cramped and dim; I was unhappily reminded of the Montmartre stairway and the creature that met
us at the top.

But the one large room, though roughly finished, was dusty
rather than dirty. Sunlight slanted through a half-moon window and the chamber had the indolent, secret charm of a
lumber room remembered from childhood games of hide-
and-seek.

"Excellent!" Irene declared. She whisked the coverlet from
the large old bed and spread it on the floorboards as on a
close-cropped lawn.

Godfrey was unearthing the treasures of the hamper with
the air of a blissful epicure. "By Jove, lobster! And ham."

"Parma ham," I corrected him.

"By Juvenal, then. Roman ham. And an inordinately assertive bottle of champagne." He eyed Quentin with approval,
even though his money had underwritten this bounty.

"Cleanliness before gluttony," Irene declared. "We must doff our disguises. Where are your theatrical supplies?"

Quentin pointed to a small table surmounted by a basin and a mirror near the little window. She retrieved a damp square of linen from the tabletop, drew a wooden chair into a shaft of sunlight, and stood behind it, a barber welcoming a customer.

"Come, sit, Quentin. I must be utterly certain of the identity of those with whom I dine. A most creditable job of disguise," she noted as he took the seat. "Had your posture not betrayed you, I should never have recognized you."

"But I took great care to mimic a lifetime of military bearing!"

"Exactly. I knew you had been a military man. Your imitation was too excellent. A retired soldier no longer has to take such pains, and that shows the merest bit—a fine point only an actor would notice. Hmm. The false facial hair and florid greasepaint well served to hide your sunburned skin. . . . You know, I often have used this red paint for lip and cheek rouge, but mixed with white it makes a splendid base for a splenetic gentleman—it also covered your difficulty."

Irene had whisked the crape hair and paint away. Godfrey and I stared at the denuded face of Quentin Stanhope, which looked as if he wore a tawny half-mask over the eyes and nose.

He grimaced at our expressions. "I shaved off the beard thinking to disguise myself, but forgot that the pale skin beneath it had seen no sunlight in many a year. And there was no time to grow another beard."

Irene fetched two small jars from the table, the contents of which she blended in her palm. Then her fingers passed quickly over Quentin's upper face. When they came away, the top half had lightened to match the lower portion.

"Goodness, Irene!" I could not help exclaiming, though I'd seen her perform such tricks with her own appearance. "He looks as if he had never left Grosvenor Square."

She smiled. "Not fine enough to fool a mortal enemy, but sufficient among friends. Next I shall 'shave' Godfrey and then wash myself. Nell we can leave alone; as usual she has done nothing to alter her natural appearance, not even so much as apply a bit of color on the tip of a rabbit's foot."

"I should hope not." I colored quite naturally at this attention drawn to my appearance—or lack of one.

Godfrey had happily removed his overbearing bobby's helmet the instant we were secure in Quentin's lodgings. Calling him to the chair, Irene quickly softened the adhesive holding on his dreadful, bristly false mustache, which was the color of a bleached muskrat.

"You too have a wan upper lip, my love," she said when the mustache fell away like a dead rat-tail, rubbing a forefinger over her palm and then passing it under Godfrey's nose. As if by magic his skin color was of a piece all of a sudden.

Irene finished her transformations by rinsing the artistic arrangement of "dirt" from her delicate features. She turned, still clad like an urchin, but angel-faced.

"There. We are a better-looking crew, except for Nell, who was always lovely." Irene collapsed on the coverlet like the street arab she had impostured. "We can discuss our situation while we eat."

Quentin turned to me, gallantly extending his arm. "May I assist you to the floor?"

"You already did that most effectively in Neuilly," Irene pointed out archly.

I blushed like a schoolgirl while Quentin took my hand in his to steady me until I was safely seated on the floor.

"What is 'our situation'?" I asked Irene, bending my knees into a "side-saddle" position to sit more comfortably. "And why on earth did you suggest that Quentin might be Sherlock Holmes in disguise?"

"Because Mr. Holmes was there, or else I have seriously misjudged his interests and his intelligence!"

"Who is this Holmes?" Quentin asked as Godfrey opened the food containers while Irene and I passed out utensils, plates and goblets.

"Ah!" Irene clasped her now-clean hands in mock rapture.

"Do you hear that, Nell? An innocent who is mine to educate. Sherlock Holmes, dear Quentin, is the foremost consulting detective in Europe—"

"England," Godfrey interrupted sternly.

Irene flashed him a melting look. "Thank you, my dear. What is not debatable is that Mr. Holmes is the greatest master of disguise in—"

"England," Godfrey put in again, opening the champagne with a pop that made me jump.

"In England," Irene repeated docilely. "And by the most delicious of coincidences, he is the dear friend, nay, the former chambermate of the same Dr. Watson who aided you in Afghanistan."

Quentin frowned even as he accepted a large slice of cold game pie from Irene. "You mean that you have found my Watson and that he has a protector?"

"I mean that we have found your Watson and that now he has a barrier against both the assassin and ourselves. So far as I could determine during my own investigations, Mr. Holmes has been engaged on a matter of extreme delicacy. It involves an unfortunate young man who was well placed in the Foreign Office until a violent illness overtook him more than two months ago. I followed Mr. Holmes and Dr. Watson to Woking the day before yesterday and the matter appears to be settled, although after Dr. Watson returned home to Paddington yesterday, Mr. Holmes paid a visit to an extremely discreet and odd establishment called the Diogenes Club. My instincts tell me that the case is not as settled as Sherlock Holmes wishes his old friend to think."

"And this Holmes fellow was at the museum today?"

"Mmm." With great relish Irene was doing something disgusting involving the *pâté de foie gras* and soda crackers. "That means that he was following one of the principals in the case. He was either Queen Victoria's grandmother or the Quasimodo-like scholar."

"And you cannot be sure which one you libel with your suspicion?" Quentin asked.

"I libel neither of them. The other was decidedly the man who has been pursuing you so lethally, and who tried to murder Dr. Watson through the intervention of an Asian cobra."

"Good God!" Quentin would have started up, except that Godfrey had filled his hand with a brimming flute of champagne, which he quickly downed as if it were pale ale. "*He* was there? You cannot know what you say, Madame."

"Indeed I can. I have met the gentleman."

"What gentleman?"

"The man you fear more than death itself, whom you call 'Tiger.' The man who once called you 'Cobra,' and who reminds you of that fact by using cobras as assassins. Did you ever know his true name?"

Godfrey refilled Quentin's glass, but he sat regarding Irene as if she had suddenly turned into the many-armed goddess Kali.

"You are a sorceress." Quentin watched Irene sip her champagne with a regal air, cross-legged on the coverlet. "No," he answered at last. "I doubt that anyone knows his genuine name. He used many identities, for he was a spy, as I was. How then have you 'met' him?"

"We were introduced at the Paris salon of a friend. Does the name Captain Sylvester Morgan mean anything to you?"

"He could call himself Peter Piper and it would mean nothing to me. How can you be sure we allude to the same person?"

"Because this man is a killer—oh, I speak not in any moral sense. I refer only to his nature. It is as brutally and honestly devouring as that of a shark. I am convinced that he is as adept at that specialty as Mr. Holmes is at problem-solving, as Dr. Watson is at healing, or as I am at singing. Or Nell at blushing, for that matter."

"Irene!" I objected.

"I am hurt," Godfrey put in, perhaps to distract her from teasing me so unmercifully. "You have left out my specialty."

Irene was not contrite. "I am ever aware that Nell records

our doings in her diary; I do not wish to force her into censorship," she said primly, "but you are certainly most agile at the law, too."

Quentin paid not the slightest mind to this banter, but was staring into the single shaft of sunlight as if the dust motes that drifted lazily through it were golden. "How are you so sure that you have met my nemesis?" he asked Irene again.

"For one thing, our meeting with this Captain Morgan occurred after your stay with us at Neuilly. For another, it was arranged by the Empress of Russia, who broke custom to ensure that I would meet her—and especially him, I think. For the last and most damning reason, it was after I slew the snake in your Montmartre garret. This Captain Morgan showed a most persistent interest in my reptilian victim. He wanted the skin. He said that he collects cobras and wanted mine."

Quentin shuddered suddenly. "He wants my skin. He said as much nine years ago, before any of this transpired, that the man who crossed him was . . . tiger bait."

"Not yet," Godfrey noted.

"I presume," said I in a small voice, "that threat applies to women as well."

"Nonsense," Irene said. "Women and doctors are only *cobra* bait, from the evidence so far. And some cobras are very nice indeed." Mortified, I blushed. Again. "One of them saved Dr. Watson's life."

I glanced wildly at Quentin, who was looking startled.

"We have a mystery," Irene announced with suppressed amusement. "Perhaps you can solve this one small matter, Quentin, being an old India hand. Your friend Dalip died of cobra venom, but the cobra that confronted me in that garret was not the snake who bit him. And now Godfrey tells me that the dead snake he found in Dr. Watson's consulting room had not been shot or stabbed, but appeared to have had its neck broken. I believe that you had been keeping watch on Dr. Watson's establishment, that you found the cobra in the consulting room, or saw it introduced there—and disarmed it, shall we say?—before it could harm the good doctor."

"You credit me with too much. I cannot crush snakes with my bare hands," Quentin said evasively.

"But you did have an accomplice, one who has traveled with you since Paris, and before. One brought with you from India, who escaped that fatal Montmartre garret along with you."

"Irene! He has admitted to the company of the dead Indian, but no other. Are you accusing Quentin of lying?"

"Not yet, Nell. He has not yet answered me."

Quentin's hazel eyes narrowed, which only increased his distinguished appearance, in my opinion. "It is impossible to conceal anything from Mrs. Norton. How did you guess—?"

"I never guess, my dear man! I merely put myself in your place, quite literally. I asked myself who and what I might take with me from India for protection from a madman who would use any means to harm me. How, I wondered, would a 'Cobra' protect himself against one of similar cunning and subtlety? Of course the empty milk dish was a clue, though I was misled by the fact that Nell's little green snake, Oscar, drank milk. On reflection I realized that Oscar was an aberration and only warm-blooded animals drink milk, so the resident of the vacant cage was unlikely to be reptilian."

Quentin made a resigned gesture, then rose and approached the dilapidated trunk at the foot of the bed. He threw off a torn scarf and opened it, bending to withdraw something—a boa of sorts, a dark fur-piece perhaps two feet long . . . that wriggled!

"Poor little beast." Quentin stroked the object he held. "The trunk admits air enough to keep her alive, but it is not home. I had to leave her cage behind in Montmartre. She had killed the first cobra, but I never dreamed that a second was still loose to slay Dalip when he came in after I'd left. Out the window and over the rooftops we fled together with a sack of my belongings and money. I did not want my absence to cause a stir, so I took the cobra's corpse with me."

Irene's eyebrows raised. "And—?"

Quentin looked sheepish. "I . . . deposited it in a handy drainpipe. This one"—he stroked the dense, coarse fur—"rode inside my tunic front, which she likes to do. I've had her for many years."

He placed his pet on the floor, a long, low, weasel-like creature with clever clawed paws. It pattered swiftly to our picnic, thrusting its ratlike snout among the remains of the game pie.

"Oh, the darling!" Irene laughed and applauded. "I've never seen one. Does she bite?"

"Only to eat," Quentin replied wickedly.

"How would she kill a cobra?" Godfrey asked.

"With speed, daring and skill. She darts in and out at a great rate, teasing the snake until its guard is down. Then a quick twist and a pounce, and she is behind it, the snake's head caught in her tenacious teeth. A proper shake, and the cobra's skull is cracked, with one bite."

"Ah!" Irene sat back and nodded. "Rather like a rat terrier. I thought so. You see, Nell and Godfrey, that explains the deceased cobra in Dr. Watson's consulting room. One must set a thief to catch a thief. In this case it took a Cobra to forestall a cobra's killing: a human Cobra and his pet mongoose."

"Is that what this is?" I inquired carefully. I dared not move, as the creature was nuzzling my lace-edged sleeve.

"Her name," Quentin said, "is Messalina. I call her 'Messy' for short."

"That is undoubtedly true," I noted, watching the animal overturn a tin of Irene's beloved *pâté* and lick it clean. "And Irene guessed its existence from an empty milk dish?"

"And from the empty cage, which we first assumed had been used to contain the snake," she said, handing Godfrey a fresh tin of *pâté* to open. "But if the cobra had been imported to the premises in order to kill someone, why leave the evidence of the cage behind? Therefore, the cage must have belonged to another—and now missing—animal. Besides, I could not envision Quentin traveling with a cobra, a rather large and infamous snake to conceal, whereas a mongoose might be mistaken for a weasel or a monkey, and accepted as a pet in the poorer quarters he haunted. Still, having the creature forced him to seek even tawdrier lodgings than his finances or inclinations required."

"She is a remarkable creature," Quentin said fondly, offering Messalina a bit of boned chicken. "To see her dance with a cobra is to watch an ultimate exercise of beauty and terror. I often feel pity for the cobra."

"A misplaced emotion," Irene declared, waving about a *pâté*-smeared cracker, "in a world where cobras abound and mongooses are far too rare. Now that you have finally introduced your accomplice, you must tell me everything you know or guess about this Tiger. Hold nothing back. You do realize that the mysteries of the Montmartre garret reveal him to be a formidable opponent who will stop at nothing?"

"How so?" Quentin asked.

"Surely you have reconstructed the sequence of events that produced the dead cobra you found, and later left your friend Dalip dead of venom not administered by a snake, as well as a second cobra hidden to attack Nell and me when we arrived after you and Messy had fled."

Quentin was most sober, almost stunned. "No, Madame, I have not."

"Ah." Irene wriggled happily into a more comfortable and therefore less ladylike position on the coverlet. "Allow me. Tiger, seeking your death and unaware of your association with poor Dalip and the mongoose, entered your garret while you were out and left two cobras to ensure your demise. Before he could release them, he was surprised by the return of Dalip, overpowered him, and resorted to a more sinister method of administering venom: via human snake."

"Tiger is poisonous?" I exclaimed, for I would put nothing past this abhorrent man.

"Not quite literally, but almost. Twice he has used an air rifle to attack Quentin: once in Neuilly and now again in the

Museum of Natural History and Modern Curiosities. A famed heavy-game hunter would have a mastery of weapons, would even invent his own. I posit that Tiger has applied the spring-loaded mechanism of the air rifle to a smaller and more subtle form, one that can be silently and discreetly used at close quarters—"

"By Jove!" said Godfrey, sitting up. "Quentin's poisoning near Notre Dame—a spring-loaded syringe of sorts!"

Irene nodded sagely. "And the same weapon was used on Dalip, to preserve two full measures of cobra venom for Quentin. Of course Tiger could not know of Messalina."

Quentin nodded. "I kept her cage in the trunk, but I found it open when I returned. When I saw the dead cobra, I knew she had escaped in her frenzy to confront the creature; she is clever. But I never saw Dalip dead. . . ."

"My dear Quentin, Nell and I barely noticed him in that dusky garret. I assume the second cobra could have been dormant for some reason, and hidden."

"Or hiding," Quentin added. "It had seen its fellow killed by a mongoose and would not wish to repeat the ritual."

"This Tiger must be the very devil," I finally put in, "to so cold-bloodedly kill poor Mr. Dalip!"

Irene for once agreed with my estimation of someone's character, and looked severely at Quentin. "That is why you must be absolutely frank with me now, my friend. Tiger has already marked me and mine for his loathsome interest. I cannot afford to tangle with the likes of Sherlock Holmes while only possessed of a smattering of the truth."

"What I know is only half-truths and suspicions," Quentin said.

"They were enough to have stirred you out of Afghanistan," Godfrey pointed out. "We are all endangered now. And the first explanation you owe is to Nell."

"Not at all!" I objected in confusion. I would never aspire to claim that Quentin Stanhope "owed" me any attention whatsoever, nor could I bear to have him think that I so presumed.

"Godfrey is right," he said with a level look at me. "I fell upon your hospitality, upon your friendship, like a starving wolf, and then absconded at the first opportunity. You must understand my state of mind. I was ill when I met you, and half poisoned, if Mrs. Norton's theory is credible. Further—" he regarded me with a troubled gaze "—I had encountered unexpected forces from my past. It was as if I was awakening from a dream that had lasted for almost a decade.

"First my life was attempted in Afghanistan, after years of safe obscurity. Suspicious that the attempt stemmed from the sad events of the past, I attempted to trace this Dr. Watson through the military and medical records, and found that another had been there before me, and had abstracted those very documents." Quentin glanced sharply at Irene. "You are not the only person to become addicted to a mystery. I became uneasy in my soul to think that this Watson's life might be sacrificed because I was moldering in obscurity in Kandahar. I came west, but apparently did not come unnoted. That is why I left Neuilly, Penelope; my self-exile, once voluntary, was fast becoming necessary, enforced by a lethal threat that could destroy all that I knew and loved should I attempt to see England again. The shot from the garden was a reminder that there is no rest for an outcast."

"But why?" Irene was adamant. "You admit that the events that cause these attacks today are almost a decade old. What does this Captain Morgan stand to lose that he would resort to such desperate ploys—and to attempt to slay by the means of a cobra an associate of the foremost detective in—" she caught Godfrey's implacable eye "—er, England?"

"If Morgan is the man I knew as Tiger, he has been abroad. He may know nothing of your Sherlock Holmes."

"I am sure that by now the reverse is not true. Pity the man or woman who attracts the concentrated attention of Sherlock Holmes. Holmes will not rest until he knows everything, once he is convinced that serious matters are involved. Morgan's bizarre attempt on Dr. Watson's life, as well as your equally exotic counter to it, have truly stirred a sleeping cobra.''

"He is an enemy of yours, this man?"

"Call him rather a competitor," Godfrey suggested. "Still, Irene treads a fine line. To the European public she is dead. Her presence in London compromises her privacy, and perhaps her safety."

"You have not said why Mrs. Norton must conceal herself."

"Nor have you said why someone would wish to kill Dr. Watson and yourself," Irene pounced.

Quentin had the grace to look abashed.

"I have crossed swords with a king," Irene said. "Oh, not literally, but in a matter of will. He is not a very important king as kings go, but in his little corner of the world his will is law, and he is not used to having it scoffed. He is not likely to forget it. Sherlock Holmes was his agent in England, where our . . . duel ended. Neither the king nor Mr. Holmes got what he expected—or wanted. Therefore, it behooves me to avoid drawing the attention of either, that is all."

Quentin stroked the mongoose, which had settled near him, its glossy sides panting with the excesses of freedom, which included devouring all the remaining smoked salmon, the last bits of lobster, and the Parma ham, as well as the first tin of *pâté*. "Turnabout is fair play. I tell you my suspicions only because you have encountered risks on my behalf. It was to spare you all that I left Neuilly so rudely. Since you have not allowed me the privilege of disappearing, I agree that you are too involved to remain ignorant. Yet I am not sure where the significance may be found in my tale."

I shifted my position for what promised to be a long recital. My knees and ankles were aching and one foot had gone completely numb. However Bohemian it may be to lounge on garret floors drinking champagne and gobbling lobster in the company of a mongoose, it is exceedingly hard on the lower extremities.

Quentin Stanhope rubbed the back of his neck with his

hand, but his hazel eyes seemed fixed on a distant place and time despite whatever discomfort he felt in the present. Irene leaned forward to offer me a half glass of champagne. I took it, hoping it might have a medicinal effect on my sorely tried joints. I did not want to miss a word of Quentin's testimony.

Godfrey leaned forward in his turn to offer Quentin a cigarette from his case, and of course then Irene must have one, and there must be an intricate ceremony of lucifer lighting and cigarette lighting and lucifer snuffing and cigarette inhaling, and I must end up smothering in clouds of smoke like an explorer in a camp of Wild West Indians. . . .

"Please," I suggested, coughing discreetly, "may we get on with it? I am eager to hear Quentin's story."

"Spoken like a true adventurer," he said with a smile. And then he sighed. "You have heard me confess that I had a facility for native languages and that this skill drew me deeper into the landscape than my superiors approved. Yet they were eager to employ me as a spy, and I confess that I preferred that work, despised as it was, to my ordinary camp duties."

"You must harbor a streak of the actor in you," Irene said, "and acting under the threat of discovery and death must add an excitement that even the most adoring audience cannot provide."

He nodded. "I took a perverse pride in going among the natives, be they Indian or Afghan, as one of them. This man Tiger was a British officer in India who also had a taste for dangerous assignments. He would don native dress, as I did, but his aim was to slip through their lines, not to mingle with them. He ranged Afghanistan from the barbaric Russian cities on the northern border to the eastern skirts of China and south to the cool hill country of India. He had a wicked reputation as a hunter of dangerous game. He was older than I and my senior as a spy. The command trusted him implicitly."

"You did not." Irene blew a soft plume of smoke into our midst.

"No."

"Why were spies needed?" I asked. "Surely the Afghanistan troops were not so sophisticated."

"Afghanistan is the greatest sinkhole of skulduggery on the globe. It has been considered a 'land' for barely a century, being little more than a loose alliance of squabbling tribes and lawless brigands. Its ruling families are fraught with brother slaying brother, father betraying son, and vice versa," Quentin added. "Oriental politics are intricate and utterly vicious. The loser may sacrifice not only his life, but first his eyes, his ears, nose, hands, feet, even—most brutal torture of all—his beard, which is holy to Allah."

"Even," Irene added, "more delicate appendages, I imagine."

"*I* cannot imagine. What appendages?" I put in.

"We are speaking of savagery beyond imagining, Nell," Godfrey said quickly. "I believe that we have a sufficient picture of the scale."

"I do not! They would cut off his ears and his nose, put out his eyes, cut off his hands and feet . . . what else is there to truncate but his beard?"

"His . . . pride," Irene put in. "We were speaking metaphorically, Nell."

"Oh." I still did not see, but did not wish to interrupt the tale for a fine point.

"We did not need to spy only on the Afghans," Quentin went on.

"The Russians," Godfrey suggested. "They have spent several decades dancing all over that region trying to get their bearclaws into India."

"Yes, exactly. And while the Russians are not quite as savage as the Afghans, they are far more consistent, being a bit less casual about killing off their leaders. So any mischief against our troops was as liable to be plotted with a Russian accent as a Pushto or an Uzbek one."

"Do you speak Russian?" Irene asked suddenly.

"A smattering, but my specialty was the difficult dialects of Afghanistan. As engagement became more inevitable, I was expected to go amongst the enemy and report his numbers and weapons."

"Which you did at Maiwand."

"Yes." Quentin crushed his cigarette in a well-licked *pâté* tin. "Except that the command did not take my report of the Ayub Khan's intimidating number of artillery pieces seriously. We were British, you know, and bound to beat the turbans off these savages who so outnumbered us." He laughed bitterly. "And then I became suspicious of Tiger, who had not been where he had claimed to be, as I knew from my own native contacts."

"Where *had* he been?" Irene wondered with raised eyebrows.

"Tashkent, near the Russian border."

"Just before Maiwand?" Godfrey asked.

Quentin nodded soberly. "I did not like it either, especially since a formidable Russian spy known as 'Sable' was also in Tashkent, and Tiger was the senior spy on the battleground. Then, the day before the battle, Tiger laid a pretty obvious tidbit on my plate, expecting me to run howling back to the command with it."

"Maclaine's supposed betrayal."

Quentin nodded again. "Mac was a friend of mine, unbeknownst to Tiger. Suspicious, I searched Tiger's kit bag and found an odd bit of paper, not really a map but similar to one, with some backwards Russian alphabet markings on it. I took it, meaning to slip it back into his kit later if it proved innocuous.

"Then I went on an errand before returning to camp to confront Mac, who acted as innocent as a Paschal Lamb, as I expected. That was the night of twenty-six July. I had already scouted the immediate area and discovered a secondary, unreported ravine near the one our troops would defend, one at right angles to it. I slipped out of camp to explore further, but when I was digging up my native clothes I was knocked unconscious."

"Oh!" I winced in sympathy.

"A wicked blow," Quentin recalled, lifting his hand to the old wound, "meant to kill. I next awoke to find the ground thrumming beneath me, the sky veiled by yellow dust, and gunpowder perfuming the evil air. Men and horses screamed in tandem. Smoky figures milled in the murk. I viewed a scene from a Renaissance hell. I was frightfully dizzy, and could hardly focus my eyes, but managed to stagger up and head for what English voices I heard. To make a sad story short, I found myself in the ignoble retreat from Maiwand to Kandahar some sixty miles south. We left good guns behind, and horses and camels. And men. I staggered along unnoticed until I finally collapsed. Luckily, I'd gotten far enough from the front lines that some plucky medical officer sprinted to my side through the dust. The Sixty-sixth Berkshires had valiantly stood their ground so that the rest of us could retreat, and this surgeon must have been attached to them.

" 'Water,' I croaked, and he had a canteen of warm spit that helped some. 'Thank you, Doctor—' I knew enough to say.

" 'Dr. Watson,' said he, as if we were meeting in Pall Mall. 'Take it easy, lad, I'll find your wound.'

"Well, I'd bled all down my back, so he naturally thought I'd been shot and spent some time turning me over and finding me whole where I should not have been. The fighting was not hand-to-hand, and my head wound puzzled him when he found it. He seemed more a stickler for the how and why of my wound rather than just the tending of it. I was not coherent then, but I knew the battle had been a disaster. I did not expect to live to tell the true tale of it, so I worked the paper I'd taken from Tiger into the doctor's kit bag. My fingers found a nice little tear in the bottom, the answer to a spy's prayer, though one gets clever in moments of desperation, even when off one's head. I was about to drift into sleep or death or whatever would come when a piece of thunder exploded in my ear and the doctor's fingers slip and he falls down in a faint beside me. Now it is my turn to probe for a wound, and I see that a jezail bullet has sliced into his shoulder. His uniform is slowly soaking as red as my bloody back.

Right shoulder it is, but the heart seems safe. So I use the bandages in his bag to poke over the wound when some young fellow stops beside us.

" 'Tis Dr. Watson!' says he, 'can you help me wi' him, soldier? I have a horse.'

"So it is patient tending doctor, and we two get him belly-down over the poor beast's back. The orderly snatches up the bag and straps it to the saddle, leading horse and doctor off.

"I realize that I must look fairly hale from the front at least, and start walking again for the rear, knowing my paper will stand a better chance of getting to Kandahar and being found than if it was with me. That orderly was a goer, and a horse is better than gold in an out-and-out rout. I truly expected to die," Quentin said, and was quiet.

"Why didn't you?" Irene asked shrewdly.

"Irene!" I remonstrated, shocked that she would speak so. She ignored me. "The most important part of the story is yet to come, Nell." She leaned forward, the better to fix Quentin with her magnetic eyes. She reminded me of a queen cobra at the moment, bewitching a victim. "Why didn't you die as Tiger intended?"

He stared at her, equally shocked, then he laughed. "Perhaps because I almost wanted to, and Maiwand was not an occasion when I got what I wanted."

Irene, startled, settled back on her coverlet for further interrogations. Like a mongoose, she relished a foe—even a friendly one in a duel of words—capable of surprising her. And like a mongoose, she intended to ensure that she surprised him last.


If Godfrey Norton had one facility that proved invaluable on innumerable occasions, it was his ability to arrange things. Such talents are seldom hailed as they deserve.

Leaving our oddly companionable picnic under the dusty gables, Godfrey vanished into the great maelstrom of London life. He returned two hours later with a fresh carriage and assorted outer garments for our more oddly attired members, namely Irene in her street urchin's rags. In the interim he had also obtained rooms for our party of four. Quentin, Irene and Godfrey said, must reside with them for safety's sake until the threat to his well-being was resolved.

We were whisked to a private hotel in the Strand with as much discreet ceremony as if we had been Cinderellas in search of coronation balls rather than errant cobras and double-dealing spies.

In the company of Irene and Godfrey I often found myself being snatched from the most humble, even disreputable of circumstances to the most glorified. Certainly I never learned more of the world than when I accompanied them, and if I did not always like the nature of my lessons, I could not quarrel with their necessity.

At the new hotel once again I was provided with a sitting room. Irene and Godfrey took a two-bedroom suite that would accommodate Quentin and his trunk as well. I, for one, was relieved that the clever but lethal mongoose remained on the other side of my door.

We met again that evening, all properly attired, in Irene and Godfrey's sitting room. This was a grandiose salon with gilt cornices crowning scarlet brocade draperies and an inordinate number of small tufted settees upholstered in shades of lavender. I finally brought myself to sit upon one of these dollhouse sofas. Quentin joined me, looking utterly urbane in one of Godfrey's city suits, which fit him surprisingly well.

"You have transformed yourself completely," I said in some surprise. "You could walk up to the door of number forty-four Grosvenor Square and enter without a challenge."

He frowned at the familiar address. "You have visited in Grosvenor Square?"

"We had to learn," Irene put in quickly, "whether you had informed your relations of your return."

His face grew remote. "I have made a point of keeping them clear of my miserable affairs for almost a decade. If you have betrayed my existence, my condition—"

"We have not," Irene said in firm tones. "Or rather, I

should say, Nell and Godfrey have not, for they were my emissaries to Grosvenor Square. However, they did learn a useful piece of information."

"Which is?" Quentin was not mollified, and I could not blame him.

"Which is that a certain commanding blue-eyed gentleman called upon them two months ago, seeking news of yourself."

"Two months ago!" Quentin had risen abruptly. "That is before I was attacked, before I even left India. Why did Tiger wait to renew his persecution of me until this time?"

"Because," Irene said thoughtfully, "something of his is at stake at this particular moment. Some . . . scheme which that paper you took from him years ago could harm."

"But that scrap likely does not exist anymore. Tiger is pursuing a phantom. The piece of paper must have been lost in Afghanistan or at Peshawar years ago."

Godfrey nodded. "Dr. Watson lay delirious with fever for many weeks, even months. He does not even recall how a second wound to his leg occurred. Certainly his medical bag was taken from him during this illness, or more likely was destroyed during the month-long siege of Kandahar."

"Still, it may survive," Irene said. "We have little else to pursue. In fact, unless we wish to wait for Captain Morgan to find us and subject us to more reptilian chambermates, we shall have to resort to desperate measures at once."

"How desperate?" I asked dubiously.

She sighed and shifted upon the overupholstered love seat she occupied alone, like Sarah Bernhardt reclining on her polar-bear-pelt-strewn divan.

"Some of us," Irene answered, "will have to return to Paddington and search Dr. Watson's residence."

"Some?" I pursued with foreboding.

"I have not decided who will execute this delicate task," Irene said airily.

"I will go," Quentin said manfully. "I can identify the bag."

"No," Irene answered, "you will not."

"And why not?" I asked indignantly on his behalf. Irene

was entirely too high-handed with virtual strangers. Godfrey and I were used to serving as milady's equerries, but Quentin had never enlisted in her army.

Her warm golden-brown eyes, all innocent inevitability, regarded me. "Because anyone who ventures near Dr. Watson risks seeing Sherlock Holmes, or worse, being seen by him. And that would be ruinous, since in the near future Quentin Stanhope will be in Baker Street consulting with Mr. Sherlock Holmes on precisely the problem that faces us."

## Chapter Twenty-Six

# A BRACE OF BURGLARS

"**The matter** involves Afghanistan, I presume," my friend Sherlock Holmes pronounced as he viewed the dead cobra beneath my desk. "You have not moved it?"

"Not a bit. I know your methods."

"Hmm. Someone has, and rather rudely." Holmes wriggled farther under my desk, lost in that utter concentration that any sort of mystery evoked in him. "There also has been someone sitting at your desk, Watson."

"Someone sitting at my desk?"

"A woman with a small foot attired in a boot, not new, with the heel worn evenly. Most unusual, one might even say irregular. A preternaturally well-balanced lady. A Turkish rug is better than fresh-mown grass for absorbing slight imprints. I see that your leg has been bothering you again, for the shoe that leaves the lighter impression has been most active . . . Were it not for the interesting marks behind the head, I'd say that you yourself had kicked the snake to death. A pity that you did not apprise me of this situation sooner."

This was unjust. "It was not discovered until the girl came to clean this morning, and after all, you were not in until evening yesterday."

Holmes emerged carefully from under my desk, his thin cheeks flushed from his efforts and the compelling oddity of the mottled souvenir. "I had some tidying up to do in the naval-treaty affair. How is Mrs. Watson taking this intriguing discovery?"

"She, of course, had a thrilling introduction to the world of mystery and crime in 'The Sign of the Four,' and—"

" 'The Sign of the Four,' Watson? That is an abstruse figure of speech."

I found myself at a loss, for Holmes had no notion about the extent of my literary recreations of his cases, even to the liberty of titles. "That is to say, the matter of the Agra treasure, in which her late father was involved. Mary, I can report, is absolutely unruffled, although she has no wish to inspect my late . . . visitor."

"Hah!" barked Holmes in an outburst that passed for laughter. "Quite wise on the lady's part. This fine fellow has grown a tad fragrant and had best be removed soon. Now I must inspect the windows."

He went to the casement, magnifying glass in a white-knuckled grip, his sharp features bent to the lens with the intensity of a hound's nose to the spoor.

"Keeping a ground-floor office has its drawbacks. You have had a brace of burglars in the last two days, Watson, although I doubt either of them were London cracksmen in search of remnants of the Agra treasure. Yet each bore something with him—a middling-size box. See where the wood has been rubbed raw? When a man swings one leg and then the next over a windowsill, anything that he is carrying is likely to scrape the frame."

"But what is the point of bringing a poisonous snake into my office, Holmes?"

"The point is all too obvious. The motive is less so." Holmes dropped to his knees before the window and undulated across the Turkey carpet to my desk. "Our number-one man is powerful. Stealthy strides taken far apart. Boots of foreign manufacture—I should say German. Cologne. I see the impress of a most assertive nail in the right front sole. This was our cobra importer. See the line in the carpet where the container rested while our snake charmer prodded it under the desk? The man had no fear of his lethal partner, that is certain."

"I see a small line in the carpet, Holmes, that is all. It could be the tracery of a design element."

"Nonsense, Watson. It is the right front impression of a box two feet in length and, from the depth of the impression, roughly eighteen inches in height. The corner is marked because that is where the man leaned his not inconsiderable weight as he rose again once he had loosed the snake."

"How could he be sure that it would stay hidden beneath my desk?"

"That is elementary." Holmes rose to stalk to the window again. "He simply had to feed it beforehand. Snakes are torpid after eating, but if roused from slumber will strike at the interruption."

"That is what Mary claims that I do following Sunday dinner," I remarked.

"You make light of your uninvited guest, Watson, but its purpose was anything but to amuse," Holmes said sharply. "And what is this in the flower bed outside the window? Traces of a lighter man, one still showing the effects of a recent illness. Note the uncertain footprints. This chap did not advance beyond the window frame. Ah—here is where he set down his casket."

"These men sound more like the suitors in *The Merchant of Venice* than housebreakers, Holmes."

"Their business was deadly serious, Watson. This second fellow does not set toe to carpet, so he suspects the nature of his vile precursor into the room. I refer to the serpent rather than to the human reptile who brought it. And examine the sill, where the new man's fingernails have scored the wood . . . he was well aware of the cobra lying in wait. He must have watched for a while, then left—why?"

"I am sure that I cannot guess, Holmes."

"No, I doubt that you can."

Holmes returned to my desk and began to pull the carpet

from beneath it until the snake's long mottled form lay exposed. He then pored over the corpse, the magnifying glass to his eye.

"You can see where the scales are rubbed against the grain; the tender mercies of your unheeding foot. Do you remember doing this?"

"I remember the carpet being rumpled, that is all."

"Fortunate for you that the reptile was already dead. The bite of an Asian cobra is deadly within minutes."

"Do you mean to say that the first man deposited a dead cobra on my premises?"

"Absolutely not. The creature was alive, and ready to take lethal exception to your habit of rug-kicking, when the first man left it."

"Then the second man killed it."

"From the window, Watson? I have heard of snake charmers, but I doubt even they can induce death at a distance. Think how the annals of crime would swell were such a dread skill added to the murderer's arsenal."

"Then the second man left me to my fate."

"I think not. He managed to disarm the snake somehow. Hmm. Those are tooth marks behind the head."

"Human teeth?" I asked in horror.

Holmes rose from his inspection, his thin lips pursed. "No." He walked to the back of my desk and gazed down at the surface and the empty chair before it. "Nothing was taken?"

"Er, no."

"You sound uncertain."

"Some . . . papers were disturbed."

"What papers?"

"Simply . . . notes I had jotted to myself."

"On your cases?"

"On . . . cases in which I was involved, yes."

"Watson, you are hiding something from me. Out with it, dear fellow. This matter is too serious to allow for anything but total candor."

"I merely noticed that some papers I had lying atop my desk were disturbed, but that was after I had returned to find the couple waiting in my rooms."

"They could have riffled the papers at least, or killed the cobra, though I think that highly unlikely. Who did they say they were?"

"The man introduced himself as a solicitor, Feverall Marshwine. The woman was a Miss Buxleigh, who sought news of her missing suitor, who was lost at the battle of Maiwand."

"Ahhh." Holmes cast himself into my chair. "I knew it involved perfidy abroad."

"Maiwand was a terrible battle, but I doubt that there was much perfidy in it."

"The perfidy is evidencing itself here. Consider the cobra." Holmes pointed eloquently with his magnifying glass to the front of the desk. "And these visitors are most suspicious."

"They seemed quite credible."

"Feverall Marshwine? My dear Watson, that is a childishly obvious pseudonym."

"Why do you say so?"

Holmes smiled thinly. "You often chide me for my patch-work education, but even I know that Feverall Marshwine was a notorious eighteenth-century highwayman."

"I have never heard of him!"

"We each have our areas of expertise. Mine is crime. Rely upon it, Watson. So what did these fictional personages Marshwine and Buxleigh want?"

"Tales of my experiences at the battle of Maiwand."

"Did you oblige?"

"As much as I could. My memory of the disaster is clouded."

"Much like poor Phelps's memory of more recent events. Odd. His dilemma involved a treaty between nations; your puzzle seems to revolve around an old war between nations."

"There can hardly be a relationship, Holmes."

"The more unlikely the possibility of connection, the more

likely the probability. Did this pair of visitors say why they specifically required your recollections of Maiwand?"

"Only that I may have tended the lady's lost fiancé there."

"Nine years is a long time to mourn."

"That is just it. The fellow went off his head and vanished. One Jasper Blodgett."

Holmes raised a dubious eyebrow. "Blodgett. That name is ridiculous enough to be true. Perhaps your callers were innocent, though I am by no means convinced. Certainly the snake was not."

"But nothing came of it, Holmes."

"That does not mean that something cannot come of it. Quite the contrary. Do you have any paper—? Ah, here is some, under the Gray's *Anatomy*."

"Here is fresh paper." I leapt for the drawer and seized my poor scribblings from the desktop. I put several clean sheets of writing paper before Holmes, while he shook my pen until it drizzled ink.

"Excellent, Watson. That is what is so utterly valuable about you, old fellow. You are prepared for anything. Now pray do not worry about that cobra. I fancy that there is more dangerous human game about, and I vouchsafe I will catch it."

## Chapter Twenty-Seven

# DR. WATSON'S BAG

**On the** morrow we had our marching orders.

Godfrey and Quentin set off first thing, bound for the Military Archives to seek records of the military careers of John H. Watson, M.D., Emerson Quentin Stanhope and one Sylvester Morgan.

"What of . . . Grosvenor Square?" Quentin asked before he left.

Irene turned from adjusting her bonnet in the mirror. "I suggest that you not venture there yet, Quentin, unless you wish the residents to come under the closer scrutiny of Tiger."

Quentin nodded, added a plush beaver top hat and cane to his attire, courtesy of Godfrey's well-stocked trunk, and left with a last quizzical look at me. I was swathed once again in the feature-blurring veiling that I had found the simplest and most effective disguise for someone of my theatrical ignorance.

"Do I look suitably demure?" Irene asked me. She did not often request the loan of my clothes. I was astounded to see her in them; the effect was much like confronting a distorted image of myself.

"You will never look demure," I told her.

"Tsk, Nell, I am an actress. I can look like anything I wish."

"Here," said I, going over to assist her. "For one thing, you have tied the bonnet ribbons too successfully. There. Uneven tails and a loop turned inside-out looks much more ordinary. And your handbag straps are not twisted . . . that's better. I do presume you wish to resemble a parson's daughter with no deep abiding concern for the frivolities of fashion?"

"You do presume, Nell," she chided me. "You are not nearly so dowdy as you imply."

"Nearly?" said I.

Irene had swept away from the mirror. "Well?" she demanded.

She had donned my spring gown of Empire-green serge, with cream border stripes that edged her high neck, the mid-forearm-length sleeves, the bodice reveres and the pleated flounce on the hem. All in all a neat and quiet toilette that did nothing for her coloring. The skirt was a trifle too short, revealing two-tone brown spectator shoes tied with dull orange tassels.

"Irene, the shoes are dreadful with that gown!"

She grinned. "I thought so too. And now, for the *pièce de résistance.*" She whipped something from her thoroughly utilitarian leather handbag, which I had not seen since it had transported the photograph the King of Bohemia sought to Godfrey's Temple chambers more than a year before. On her nose perched my pince-nez, now accompanied by a brown cord that was affixed to her bodice with a brooch bearing a cheap, foil-backed glass stone the color of tobacco spit.

The indignity done to my spectacles was as nothing compared to the transformation that now occurred. Somehow Irene's posture altered: her shoulders rounded, her bosom sank, her toes pointed ever so slightly inward. A more gawky, unfortunate creature I had not spied since first catching sight of myself next to a full-blown Irene in Wilson's Tea Room windows eight years before.

"How shall I see?" I wailed, that being the only issue I dared address.

"It will not be necessary. Besides, a squint will add a 'character' touch to your portrayal." Irene eyed me critically over the gold-wire frames of my purloined pince-nez. "You will have to be the Lady Bountiful of our pair, while I play the shortsighted church mouse. But you must take care not to put on too grand airs, or the whole effect will be ruined."

"I? Put on airs? Irene, what can you be thinking of?"

She paused near the door to snatch up my umbrella, which was plain and black. "Ours is the more delicate mission, Nell. It may even be the more dangerous."

"What could be more dangerous than consulting Sherlock Holmes?" I thought of poor Quentin soon to be sent to beguile the foremost detective in . . . England in the service of some master plan Irene would not disclose.

She lifted the umbrella like a standard and swept open the door into the hotel's dim-lit hall. "Broaching the second-most dangerous woman in London: Mrs. John H. Watson."

"Who is the first, pray?" I inquired.

Irene simpered modestly over the pince-nez. "Myself."

We took the Metropolitan Railway to Paddington. A carriage, Irene said, would attract attention, and we were humble seekers after pence for the poor, unable to afford such grand transportation.

I cannot say I much cared for the ultramodern urban railway. Most of the line ran underground in great steam-choked tunnels, which magnified the racket of the carriage wheels over the tracks to ear-jarring proportions.

What a noisy, dirty method of transport! Yet many respectably attired women milled among the crowds thronging to board these metal monsters.

"Really, Nell," Irene urged cheerfully as an unattractive area of the city sped past during one of our infrequent aboveground transits, "you needn't look so sour until we arrive in Paddington. It is true we are on an ostensible mission of good works, but we do not have to look like it quite yet."

"Nothing good has ever come of a rail journey in my life," I retorted.

She paused to consider. "That is true. First to and from Bohemia under great duress. Then to Monaco, in the company of the Lascar and Jerseyman—" She did not, I am glad to say, mention the incident of the yet-unnamed Oscar and the gasolier. "But the return trip from France was without incident!" she reported triumphantly.

"You did not share my unfortunate encounter with the traveling corset salesman."

Irene looked instantly chastened. "No, that is true. I did not." And she said no more in praise of trains.

Once above ground in Paddington, Irene pulled a small sketch from her large handbag and squinted at it through her—that is, my—pince-nez. "Can you read this, Nell dear? I am not used to spectacles. Godfrey has drawn directions to the Watson residence."

I sighed and took the paper, bringing it to eyelash distance. "It is only a short walk," I determined. "But what is this phrase in French here in the corner? I do not recognize those words. . . ."

"Nothing!" Irene snatched the map back. "Godfrey has a habit of leaving unanticipated messages. I will, er, interpret it later."

Luckily, I had seen the map long enough to commit its simple directions to memory. We set out, attracting little attention. Apparently Irene's transformation was dazzlingly successful.

"I still do not see," I fussed as we neared the Watson domicile, "why you think that the medical bag Dr. Watson carried in Afghanistan is still in his possession, or how you expect to wrest it from him without revealing yourself."

"I do not plan to wrest it from Dr. Watson, but from Mrs. Watson. There is nothing so reliable as a wife's innate instinct to dispose of any articles of her husband's that she believes he has kept for no good purpose for far too long."

"Dr. Watson keeps his office on the premises. He will not permit you past him."

"I will not have to 'pass' him. Now, where is this establishment that is so attractive to cobras?"

I told her that we were about to turn into the proper street; Dr. Watson's house was only three doors around this corner, on the opposite side. She pulled us both to a halt before a chemist's window. While we stared at bunion remedies she doffed the pince-nez and surveyed the quiet thoroughfare.

"I need an idle boy, Nell. Do you see one?"

"Usually the London streets teem with them."

"This is bucolic Paddington, with fewer enterprising urchins."

"Will an idle girl do?" I asked.

Irene turned to regard a young miss attired in a navy-blue sailor dress sitting atop the steps leading to a dressmaker's establishment across the street.

"Even better!" Irene smiled and waved the child over.

The little girl gave one cautious over-the-shoulder glance, then decided that her mother would be occupied for some time and that we, despite our painstaking dowdiness, looked much more interesting. Over to us she skipped, poor lamb.

"Oh, my dear," Irene began, bending down and declaiming in a voice that would wring pity from an oyster. "My uncle is so very ill. I have just stopped at the chemist for a remedy, but he desperately needs a doctor."

The child started to look in the desired direction. "There is Dr. Watson—"

"Wonderful! Now." Irene was scribbling frantically on a scrap of paper, using her handbag for a writing desk. "You must give him this note. It will tell him where to find my uncle . . . Frost. Jonathan Frost. He must hurry! Uncle is having a terrible chill. White as a sheet. And for your trouble—" Irene produced a five-pence piece.

"No, miss," the child trilled. "I'm not allowed to take pay for a good deed."

Off she trotted, all officious, Irene's note clutched in her hand. Irene grasped my arm and bustled me into the chemist's, which smelled of wintergreen and mothballs.

Through the murky window glass facing Dr. Watson's domicile we watched the plain and simple pantomime: child reaching up to ring the bell. Maid answering. Child vanishing within. Child reappearing, sans note. A few moments later, the door opening to disgorge Dr. Watson.

"Hastily, Nell," Irene hissed. "We must both get a good look at the bag. If we have sent him off with the one we want, a different scheme will be necessary." She thrust my appropriated pince-nez at me. I was able to position it in time to see the doctor's bag swinging beside him as he trotted past us toward the underground station.

"Brass!" I gasped.

"What?"

"I saw the glimmer of bright brass fittings. Surely a new bag."

Irene nodded. "I thought so, too. Then we wait until our little miss leaves."

This looked to take some doing. The child had returned to her step across the way. I scouted the chemist's and found some French pastilles—the only thing of French manufacture for which I had developed a taste—but Irene hailed me to the window again.

"Gone inside to watch Mama's fitting at last, thank God."

We scuttled around the corner like thieves, Irene donning my pince-nez again despite my warnings. There are none so blind as those that will not see. Soon we were poised before the door that Godfrey and I had broached but three days before.

I rang the bell. When the maid's broad pale face appeared behind an opening door I recalled that this poor unsuspecting soul must have been the one to "discover" the dead cobra. For a moment I was tongue-tied with shame.

Into the breach leaped the golden tongue of my shameless companion. "Is the master or mistress of the house in? We are seeking donations to St.-Aldwyn-the-Bald's-on-the-Moor. A most worthy cause."

The maid's lips folded in undecided reluctance.

"What is it, Prudence?" came a kindly voice. "The doctor is out on a case," the speaker continued, drawing the door wider to see us and thus revealing herself to be Mrs. Watson.

"That ith quite all righth," I found myself saying, "you would do nithely." Irene had decided that pretending to a catarrh would allow me to press a handkerchief to my lower face, and the concurrent lisp would serve to disguise my voice. All I need do was breathe through my mouth, as I had on one key occasion in France. . . .

"Do?" The poor lady looked utterly puzzled.

Irene made a great business of glancing at the brass plate proclaiming the resident's name and business. "Mrs. Watson, is it? We would most appreciate speaking with you in your husband's absence. We are parishioners of St.-Aldwyn-the-Bald's-on-the-Moor, a church in nearby Notting Hill, which has suffered from a fire."

"Oh, dear." Mrs. Watson frowned at the notion of the mythical fire. "I have not heard of your congregation . . . or your conflagration—"

"Of course not," Irene said sadly. "The fire has grievously reduced our numbers and resources. That is why we must go door-to-door seeking what charity we can."

"I suppose I could—" the good woman began. "But, how rude I am. Come in, ladies."

Thus we entered the Watson house, I for a second occasion. We were led into a charming little parlor, with a lace-covered table in the street-facing window. A stereopticon upon it caught a stray beam of sunlight.

"Now," Mrs. Watson said, once we were seated. She was a tiny, fine-boned woman; it would be unforgivable to lie to her transparent blue eyes. I cringed on both our behalves. "I can spare a few coins—"

"Oh, no!" Irene raised a forbidding hand. "Please. We do not seek money."

"Then how can I help you?"

"If you have some unused item about, something that

could prove useful to our congregation . . . old books, for instance, that you would rid yourself of anyway."

"Books? I do not think John would care to donate those. Nor would I . . . I could never part with my Mrs. Gaskells, or the Waverlys, or Miss Austen . . ."

"Since your husband is a doctor," Irene said briskly to stop what promised to be a complete catalogue, "perhaps you could spare some older medical books, even a medical bag he no longer uses."

Mrs. Watson shook her head. "There is nothing of that sort that I could give away in his absence. You must admit that a husband's possessions are sacred."

"I am sure of it," Irene said.

Mrs. Watson looked politely to me.

"I would nod know." I sniffled sadly into my lacy bit of Irish linen. "I am not married."

"Oh," she said sympathetically. "And you?" she asked Irene.

"Oh, yes. That is why I asked if there were something lying about that you could spare. My own husband is so determined to cling to every old pair of hunting boots or souvenir of his youth, things he would not possibly use in a hundred years! But there it is. Men must have their clutter."

Mrs. Watson smiled. "The doctor is remarkably neat about his possessions. It comes from his sharing lodgings with a bachelor friend in the days before we married. Excellent training."

Irene joined her in a wifely laugh at the expense of the absent spouses. "Your good fortune is our misfortune," she said lightly, rising and blinking pitifully behind my pince-nez. "We must look elsewhere. A cast-off medical bag would be just the thing for parish sick calls, but if you are wed to a wonder of organization we will have to seek elsewhere."

"Wait!" Mrs. Watson cried as we neared the doorway to the passage. "There is some musty old thing at the bottom of the wardrobe. I believe John had it with him in Afghanistan. He has had no earthly use for it since . . . would not even miss it after all this time, I am sure. I will fetch it. If it is in any proper condition—"

"Oh, bless you, Mrs. Watson," Irene murmured fervently (and most sincerely), clasping her gloved hands. "You are an angel of mercy."

The poor woman flew up the stairs, returning shortly with a battered brown leather satchel.

"It is not new looking," she said, turning it over in her hands. "It survived a war, after all. If you think that it would serve—?"

"It will serve magnificently." Irene clutched the flattened old bag to her bosom. "You have no idea how delighted we are to see this. How . . . useful it will be. I vouchsafe to say that you and your husband will walk safer these next few days because of this good deed. Heaven has a way of helping those who help others."

Mrs. Watson's faced showed sudden anxiety. "How odd that you should say that. I have been worried, actually. We had an . . . incident at the house recently. But I'm delighted to help St.-Ethelwed-the-Bold's-on-the-Mire. Are you certain that a monetary donation—?"

"No, no," I said firmly. "To take mere money is begging."

"To take cash is to take trash," Irene paraphrased *Othello* shamelessly, and somewhat disjointedly, on our exit, "but he—or she—who offers hard goods will always have a sterling reputation."

We stood again on the stoop. Mrs. Watson, shadowed in her doorway, still looked puzzled, and even slightly worried. Perhaps the recent incident with the cobra troubled her.

"There is a sign in the Bible," Irene said, abruptly employing a serious tone. "To find a dead snake upon one's doorstep signifies that a powerful protector is watching over you and yours."

"Truly?" Shock paled Mrs. Watson's complexion even more. "How odd you should say that." A sudden smile made that poignant face radiant. "Certainly my husband does have such a benefactor—the most mentally powerful man in London."

"Doubtless the Good Book had other, unseen allies in mind, Mrs. Watson," Irene said, "but an honest soul can never have enough angels on its side."

## Chapter Twenty-Eight

# SHERLOCK HOLMES'S LAST CASE

**Irene spent** the next evening brooding.

This she managed with the panache of Sarah Bernhardt on the stage. First she attired herself after dinner in a close-fitting crimson velvet gown of the princess cut. A heliotrope taffeta caftan over her shoulders swept to a wide train in the back and was edged in snowy ermine along the front floor-length reveres.

This garb was ideal for pacing, which she proceeded to do, the hotel's rococo decoration fading to a dull backdrop indeed for her formidable foreground presence. Mind you, I do not claim that this performance was planned; merely that Irene's nature required the properly dramatic setting before her mind could explore its most creative and instinctive territories.

Naturally, she smoked during this exercise, but fitfully, letting the cigarette in its gold-entwined mother-of-pearl holder smolder unheeded in a dish, until a pale length of ash crowned it like an eighteenth-century French lady's powdered wig.

Or she would suddenly seize the holder and her pace would quicken, even as her eyebrows plunged together in a concentrated frown. She would sip swiftly from the delicate holder until her cigarette end burned a constant ember-red. And always wreaths of smoke drifted around her like the fine-net veiling they call "illusion."

She finally stopped, turning at the same time, so her heliotrope train crackled before swirling to rest in a graceful spiral around her lower limbs.

"No doubt you all have wondered what I did today."

We waited attentively, the gentlemen nursing after-dinner cigars whose odor reminded me of burnt burlap. I suffered much in their rank company, but confined myself to embroidering a handkerchief. The one with which I had attempted to clean the actual urchin's face not four days earlier had been sullied beyond redemption.

"Dare we suppose that you have done as Quentin and I, and visited the London shops?" Godfrey said.

I glanced at Quentin, dashing in evening dress like Godfrey, as all good hotel dining rooms required. I had not inquired into the funds for Quentin's outfitting, suspecting one of my friends' quiet but spectacular acts of charity, from which I also had benefited in the past.

Irene sighed. "Not yet, I fear. I wish I had done something as interesting as that; I do not often have the opportunity to shop in London. No, my activities were far more commonplace. I was in Woking."

"Woking again? Whatever for?" I burst out. "That is an excessively idyllic locale for one with your proclivities for mayhem."

Irene smiled at me. "Mayhem is not snobbish about address; it may reside as well behind the moss-grown facade of the manse as the Whitechapel pub. Perhaps you have heard of the Poisoning Parson of Tunbridge Wells."

"No, I have not. I think that you have made that up."

"I? Make something up? Heaven forbid, Nell."

"It often does, but you never listen."

"Do go on, Irene," Quentin said. "I am most anxious to learn what you found so fascinating in Woking, though any place that you would honor with your presence would perforce become irresistible."

Irene laughed heartily. "Clothes do make the man! Put a desperate exile into white tie and tails and he spouts drawing-room hyperbole."

Quentin bit at his infant mustache and smiled shyly. He seemed a stranger in civilized clothes. I found that I actually missed his air of wild incongruity.

Irene laid her cigarette holder in a tray, from which supple ribbons of smoke wafted up like visible incense. She crossed her arms and eyed us with that suppressed excitement that betokens revelations.

"I went to Woking because that is where resides the young gentleman upon whose behalf Sherlock Holmes's most recent efforts have been made. Briarbrae is a most impressive house with extensive grounds, and in it dwell Mr. Percy Phelps and his fiancée, Miss Annie Harrison. Mr. Phelps has been ill and under a great strain, but I had a most pleasant tea with Miss Harrison."

"I do not know how you do it," Godfrey said. "How you persuade strangers to give you not only tea but confidences."

"That is because you were trained as a barrister, Godfrey, and expect people to resist telling you things. I, on the other hand, tell them everything about me. They are so overcome that they reciprocate in kind."

"It is more than that," I put in. "You make it seem that only by telling you everything will they have any possible chance of doing the right thing. It is a pity that women cannot take holy orders; you would make a most effective clergyman."

"It is all a matter of convincing others of an Unreality," Godfrey added. "Clergymen and actors are not so different."

"Be that as it may," Irene said, bringing our attention upon herself once again; indeed, in her flowing, royal-hued gown she did resemble a pagan priestess. "That simple tea in Woking answered an entire menu of questions."

"The first one is why are you concerned about Sherlock Holmes's last case?" Godfrey put in.

She smiled at him in sweet patience, faultlessly acted. "Be-

294 Carole Nelson Douglas

cause it is linked to the matter that Quentin presented to us."

"I?" the man cited objected. "Surely not."

"Surely so," she replied, absently stroking the soft ermine of one revere. "I first sniffed the matter when I followed Mr. Holmes to the Diogenes Club—an extremely intriguing establishment! The membership is gentlemen only, but of course that was no barrier to me."

I sighed pointedly. Quentin, who had seen Irene only as a street boy, not in the full and impressive range of her talents as a male impersonator, looked puzzled.

"I entered the premises," Irene explained, "as a waiter in hopes of a position. I regret to say that I failed to achieve one. It must have been my Italian accent." She shrugged soulfully. "However, I did learn two or three interesting points about the place. The Diogenes Club is one of the oddest, if not the oldest, in London. Members retreat there for utter isolation and silence, not fellowship. Among them is a certain Mycroft Holmes. According to my hasty but thorough reading of the visitor's ledger, this Mycroft Holmes is indeed sought after by the most highly placed men in London, including his relation—a brother, I'd think—Sherlock."

"So after penetrating the Diogenes Club, you next go gadding off to Woking?" I asked.

"Yes. How nicely put. I gadded off to Woking. But first I made a few other trifling inquiries. At the Foreign Office, for instance, I had a long chat with the commissionaire's wife, a rather surly woman. However, once I professed myself a friend of 'poor Percy'—remember, he worked there—she kindly revealed that he had been under suspicion over a 'missing paper.' She also indicated that 'even a decent God-fearin' woman' was suspect in the case, namely herself. She was not treated gently by Scotland Yard, I gather, when she was subjected to a search, always a mistake with the humbler classes. They take offense and are exactly the type to fume and fuss about the matter to all comers."

"That paper sounds like a sensitive document." Godfrey thoughtfully knocked the ash from his cigar into a low dish.

She answered his comment with a question. "How sensitive would you consider a secret naval treaty between England and Italy?"

Quentin looked puzzled. "I have long been ignorant of current foreign affairs, thanks to my sojourn in Afghanistan."

Godfrey pondered the question. "The only interested parties would be those who would lose by the alliance. Perhaps . . . France," he suggested. "Both Italy and France have Mediterranean ports."

"Bravo!" Irene said. "That is exactly it."

"And how did you know this?" I asked her.

She donned a modest expression. "Rumors of this event reached the press last spring. I looked up back copies of the *Telegram* and the *Times*."

"Anyone could do that!" said I indignantly.

"Of course. But would anyone? And would anyone know what to make of this fact as regards our end of the tangle?"

" 'Our' end?" I repeated.

"Ah, you do miss Casanova, Nell, but I do not require an echo at the moment. There is another nation, as well, that would squirm at news of any such English alliance abroad, and that is her ancient enemy in another quarter of the world."

"By Jove—that I do know!" Quentin was sitting up, his precious cigar abandoned in the dish beside him. "Russia! Russia has no European ports. She would be most uneasy with such a treaty, especially since Czar Alexander spurns European connections, except for those few French ones he tolerates for his Empress's sake."

Irene's smile grew radiant. "There speaks the soul of a spy. There stands the link to the two puzzles: the Afghanistan Events of 'Eighty and the recent hushed scandal of the missing English-Italian naval treaty. I propose that solving one muddle will resolve the other."

"It is preposterous," Quentin said, sadly. "Ingenious . . . Ireneous, even, but erroneous," he added with a flash of humor I had not yet seen in him. "If you can posit a connection between the disaster at Maiwand, Maclaine's death, my and Dr. Watson's recent brushes with death and this obscure treaty, my hat—nay, my head—is off to you, Madame Mystery-solver."

Irene positively glittered at the challenge. "You think it is impossible? Then listen to what Miss Harrison told me at tea."

"Irene, how did you persuade the young woman to tell you anything at all about such a secret matter?"

"I told her the truth," Irene answered.

"Shocking," Godfrey muttered. "You must have been desperate."

"We did not have much time together," she said tersely. "I had already learned that her fiancé, Mr. Phelps, had spent several weeks abed with brain fever and that recently, to gather from the behavior of Lord Holdhurst, his uncle, and others in the Foreign Office, all pressure had lifted from him. A significant figure present in this matter was Sherlock Holmes, I might add. So when I called upon Miss Harrison I told her of my concern for a noble-spirited Englishman who was a virtual exile from his homeland because of a false disgrace in war. I also told her that I had heard rumors of her recent trouble and that a Mr. Sherlock Holmes was said to have assisted in the matter. Did she think Mr. Holmes could do anything for me?"

"Who did you tell her you were?" I asked suspiciously.

"You," she answered promptly. "The poor wronged gentleman's fiancée."

"Irene!" I could not look at Quentin—an agonizing surge of pleasure made my cheeks burn at Irene's blithe endorsement of our mock engagement as an actuality to be appropriated for her own purposes—though I was well aware that he looked at me. "And what did you learn as a result of this outrage?"

"Much." Irene rubbed her palms together in the approved Del Sartian acting method for conveying intense satisfaction.

She resembled a glamorous Lady Macbeth immediately after the Gruesome Deed.

"You see," she went on, "a woman will confide almost anything to another woman if it involves a matter of the heart. And the treaty has been safely returned—yes, thanks to Mr. Sherlock Holmes. Her Percy is now blameless. She could not praise Mr. Holmes more highly. The only trace of sadness was when she confessed that her brother, Joseph, who had recently lost heavily in the stock market and knew that the Russians or the French would pay heavily to see the document, was the culprit who had taken the treaty, it was thought impulsively."

" 'It was thought,' " Godfrey repeated.

"Yes, Casanova?"

"*You* do not think it was a spur-of-the-moment theft?"

"No, I most certainly do not, and there is where Mr. Sherlock Holmes has made a fatal mistake. By the way, Joseph was punished for his act by an awful irony. He hid the treaty in his bedroom at Briarbrae—but that was the very room where Percy Phelps was confined when he collapsed at once of brain fever and where he stayed for almost two months. And there the treaty sat, unreachable to either man.

"According to Miss Harrison, Mr. Holmes lured Joseph into attempting to recover the document, then took it by force when Joseph attacked him and fled. Mr. Holmes presented it to Percy over breakfast in Baker Street, after first pretending that the document was unrecoverable. Poor Percy fainted, but luckily Dr. Watson was present to revive him. I told you years ago, Nell—" she glanced my way "—that a detective like Mr. Holmes would find association with a physician handy. Suffice it to say that this 'surprise' has redeemed Phelps and the Foreign Office. Joseph fled, and no one is minded to apprehend him now that the treaty is recovered. In a matter of weeks the alliance will be public knowledge, anyway."

"So the treaty matter is closed," Quentin said. "That has

nothing to do with cobras appearing in my Montmartre garret or Dr. Watson's Paddington consulting room."

"One would think not," Irene said demurely.

"One would," I parroted. "What would Irene think?"

"Ah, Nell, you do anticipate my methods. First there is this puzzling paper we have retrieved from Dr. Watson's Afghanistan bag. I wonder if he will ever miss it?" She shrugged. "Quentin, you have had time to study it, as you did not nine years ago."

He lifted it from the marble-topped side table with a shake of his head. "I have played with it until my eyes ache. It is written in Cyrillic Russian, and combines elements of a map and a communication. Frankly, I believe it is a fragment and I cannot make head or tail of it. Certainly it was not worth my pains to preserve it," he added ruefully.

"It is worth great pains to someone. If it is not for the contents, could it be for the mere fact of its existence?"

Quentin dubiously regarded the heavy, soft paper that wilted in his grasp like a leaf of yellowed cabbage. "Only one person might wish to destroy this, and I know you suspect him of the evildoings. Tiger."

"Tiger." She articulated the word with relish. "Whom we suspect to be Captain Sylvester Morgan, whom in turn we now know to be one Colonel Sebastian Moran, late of Her Majesty's Indian Army. Thank you, Godfrey, for your investigations among the military records."

He bowed his head slightly and smiled.

I could not help commenting. "This fabled Tiger certainly showed little imagination when it came to false identities."

"This man secretly wishes credit even for his misdeeds," Irene answered. "And the long, lashing tail of his arrogance will be the thing that will trip him up. Quentin, does the word 'Tiger' appear anywhere on that paper?"

"Why, yes. The salutation. That is why we had code names."

"Then if that paper came into hands that could trace the

identity of Tiger then and now, it would link him to the Russians?"

"I suppose so," he answered doubtfully. "Certainly there were rumors that he had been seen in their territories, which is why I suspected him of betraying us at Maiwand. But I cannot prove any of it! No one cares at this late date. The villains have been designated for the history books. The issue is moot."

"Perhaps not to Tiger," she replied. "Perhaps not to Tiger's current activities. Consider that he may protect not the past, but the present and the future. Perhaps he cannot afford the slightest trace of suspicion about him. To prevent it, he would stoop to murder."

"That would mean," Quentin said slowly, lifting his abandoned cigar to his lips, "that he had *monitored* me in Afghanistan and India; that he only sought my life when my existence endangered his current activities and I began my return to Europe, and to England."

Irene nodded soberly. "Perhaps he did not observe you in person. He was in London in May inquiring about you from your family. He was a spy. He must have had henchmen. Or henchwomen."

"So it was Tiger—Moran—or his minions who looked up Dr. Watson's name in the military files in India, and purloined the documents of his service!"

"Yes. Do you see what that means?"

"It means that . . . that I was safe only so long as I remained abroad; that my journey has brought these attacks on myself, perhaps even on Dr. Watson."

"My dear Quentin, you are too swift to blame yourself in everything," Irene rebuked him. "Do you see what it means for the battle at Maiwand? How it colors every incident, from Maclaine's killing to Dr. Watson's wounding even as he tended you?"

"My God—" Quentin's voice was hardly audible. "Even then . . . even then."

"What does he mean?" I asked Irene, whose attention was utterly bent on Quentin's bowed head. "Godfrey?"

Irene swiftly turned to me. "If Tiger/Moran was spying for the Russians in Afghanistan, he not only misled thousands of men into a battle they could only lose, he is responsible for Lieutenant Maclaine's posthumous slandering."

"And *he* hit me over the head after I'd talked to Mac, meaning to kill me!" Quentin exclaimed. "Except—"

"Except that you not only survived," Irene interjected, "but Tiger later discovered you had taken a paper that was extremely dangerous to him. He suspected you the moment he found the paper missing, of course. He could not risk letting anyone survive to reveal his role in neglecting to report the secondary ravine. Obviously you had told Maclaine about it, or your friend Mac would not have dashed beyond the ordered lines to fire upon the Afghanistan forces."

Quentin's head shook dully. He seemed as dazed as when we had found him—or he had found me—in Paris. "Then Tiger saw that I had survived the retreat. You believe that the bullet that wounded Dr. Watson in the shoulder was meant for me?!"

She nodded slowly, watching him. "Most likely. You mentioned dust and confusion. I suspect that Tiger was not among the confused at that time. I doubt he knew you had put the paper in Watson's medical bag, but now that events have come to a head in London, he knew that he could not take the risk that you had told Watson anything. Some happening here in London in the past year made him see ghosts of the conscience from the past and move to make them ghosts indeed; first you in India and en route to London; then hapless Dr. Watson in Paddington."

"What about Maclaine's death?"

Irene reversed direction and paced toward the draperies, resting her chin on her tented fingers. She seemed to change the subject. "Were not the Russians and the British both aching to claim Afghanistan? Would they not attempt to do so by subterfuge if force couldn't prevail?"

"Of course. The game has gone on for decades. We British had 'our' candidate for Khan who would favor our interests; the Russians had theirs. Spies were everywhere, and the Afghans, being long used to treachery in their own ruling families, played both ends against the middle. Who can blame them?"

"In this case, I think the Ayub Khan behaved honorably. He did leave orders for his six British prisoners—Lieutenant Maclaine and the five sepoys—to survive. Instead, Tiger intervened. Dressed as an Afghan and disguised by his desert robes—he hardly needed your command of their language for this work—he swirled into the prisoners' midst even as the rescuing troops were riding in, and slit Maclaine's throat."

Irene stopped and turned, her hands dropping to her sides. "Maclaine's death was murder, Quentin. Cold-blooded murder in the guise of a casualty of war. With one ferocious stroke Colonel Sebastian Moran virtually beheaded the one credible witness to your suspicions. Maclaine could never testify to the unreported second ravine, testimony that would lead to more damaging investigations."

"Maclaine murdered. I had not considered that." Quentin looked up with eyes whose luster had been dulled by shock. "A fiendish use of a fiendish weapon: war itself. Then why did I survive so long?"

"What did you do after the battle?" Irene asked with a terse smile.

He frowned. "I . . . arrived at Kandahar in one piece, which was a significant achievement. They needed a scout to try for headquarters in India, so I volunteered. My suspicions about Tiger were only that, and no one but Maclaine could confirm them. I knew Mac had been taken prisoner—there were witnesses—but his death would not come for another month. They gave me a horse, and I made my way to the new railway at Sinjini and then on to Peshawar in India, where I collapsed."

"Hence the medal," Irene interrupted him, "not for the collapse but for the deeds before it."

Her words scarcely touched him. "I had recovered by the time of the relief of Kandahar at the end of August and was gone long before the wounded from Maiwand were transported to Peshawar."

"So you and Dr. Watson never crossed paths again?" Godfrey asked.

"No. News of Maclaine's dreadful death came to Peshawar before the wounded, of course. I thought only that a witness to the treachery was dead by an ironic stroke, not by . . . murder. Yet, spying was still needed, and the waste of lives at Maiwand had sickened me. I went out, as commanded, into the godforsaken wasteland, which was still sweeter to me than the waste we had made of ourselves and our enemies at Maiwand. Out of sight, out of mind. Everyone seemed to forget about me. Eventually, I was honorably discharged." Quentin laughed bitterly. "What a phrase for an honorless place and time! I took my bit of brass and lived where I wished, among those I liked."

"And your life was never threatened?"

He eyed Irene with a sudden glint. "Many, many times, but not by anyone European, and most often by nothing human. Why did Tiger spare me then?"

"He had better things to do, and he found you no threat as long as you remained in the wilds. He probably supposed that you would never return to civilization as he knew it."

Quentin nodded. "I would have struck some as a broken man. Life was simpler with those complicated people of the steppes. Goat cheese and salty tea and hospitality with a vengeance, if they were not trying to kill you for your boots or a bit of brass." He shook his head.

Godfrey—at last—extinguished his cigar, rather thoughtfully. "What events here have compelled Moran to reach back into the past?"

Irene strode to the marble-topped table to pick up her cigarette holder and fit it with an Egyptian cigarette. Quentin leaped up to light a lucifer for her, a useless gallantry that made Godfrey smile like a complacent cat. A woman who had shot a cobra needed no help striking a match.

As soon as Irene had drawn a veil of smoke around her, she spoke again. "Recall my most extraordinary invitation *chez* Sarah."

"There was nothing at all extraordinary about it," I said promptly. "You are invited to that address all too frequently, in my opinion."

"Perhaps." Irene shrugged. "Yet never at the behest of the Empress of All the Russias. Why? Surely not because she wished to meet an obscure English barrister's wife who was known to sing a little."

"I hope," Godfrey put in, "that you mean that the wife is obscure, not the barrister."

"Of course I do," Irene said with a bow. "You are gaining quite a reputation in Paris."

"Irene," I interrupted, my eyes on Quentin's distracted visage, "we did not come all this way to sharpen fine points between ourselves. Can you not simply come out with it?"

"But it is so much more amusing to edge up to the obvious, rather than pouncing outright upon it!"

"I see nothing so obvious that it merits pouncing upon," I returned.

"My command performance before the Empress was an excuse. She no more wished to meet or hear me than she wished to sail a balloon over Lombardy! Obviously her influence was used so that 'Captain Morgan' could inspect us. He knew that we had sheltered Quentin Stanhope; he wanted to know why, and he wanted to gauge our mettle. Like any good hunter, he studied the lay of the land and the disposition of his prey."

"Why should so dreadful a man have influence over an Empress?" I demanded.

Quentin came to life. "If you mean, Irene, that Tiger is still spying for St. Petersburg, and I am now certain that he is, it would be no great thing for the Russian embassy to convey his wishes to the traveling monarch. Royal figures often smooth the path for clandestine subterfuge. They are told nothing of the true reason for such requests, only that they are necessary to the state, and think nothing more of them."

Irene nodded. "Then, I ask, why has this Moran now made his headquarters in London? He has indeed, for once Godfrey found out his real name he immediately returned to The Frontier Fusiliers and discovered the hunting club to which Moran belongs, the Anglo-Indian. His membership dates to more than a year ago."

"He has business here." Quentin leaped up to join Irene in pacing. "Why had I not thought of it? He is English by birth. He could do the Russians inestimable service—he could do England irreparable harm—in London. With his hunting credentials and his military title, no one would suspect him. He is the perfect Russian agent because he is not Russian!"

"Honestly, Irene," I put in, "you have asked an excessive number of questions but you have been remarkably stingy with answers. I believe you do not know precisely why this Colonel Moran is here."

"But I do," she retorted. "He has been the key agent in the case which Sherlock Holmes thinks that he has just solved: the stolen naval treaty. Moran may even be a double agent representing Russia and France; both nations yearn to glimpse that interesting document. More likely, I think that he represents only himself, planning to award the treaty to the highest bidder."

"But Joseph Harrison took it!" I objected. "You said his own sister admitted that."

"Joseph Harrison took it, and for the reason that she gave: he was in debt because of bad investments. Yet Joseph Harrison never had the sophistication to deal with the embassies of foreign nations. He was recruited for the task by Colonel Moran, who may even have arranged for his investment disaster. Moran has used agents before: remember the striking but nameless blonde woman at Sarah's soirée? Was she not possibly among the strollers near Notre Dame when Quentin was injected with poison? I never forget a stunning ensemble."

I nodded vigorously with sudden, shocked recall, aching to go and consult my diaries on the matter, but Irene returned to the immediate question.

"Yes, Joseph was ideally positioned to take the treaty, and did. As for Joseph's eluding the infallible Sherlock Holmes, I am not convinced that Mr. Holmes failed to prevent Joseph's escape as much as permitted it."

"Why?" I asked.

"For one thing, the awkwardness. Poor Percy Phelps might be cleared of losing the treaty once he returned it with Mr. Holmes's help, but having his own brother-in-law-to-be arrested for the theft would hardly enhance Phelps's reputation or his personal life."

"You think that Sherlock Holmes let Joseph go out of the goodness of his heart? That is hardly likely, Irene."

She smiled, started to say something, then smiled again. "Even the foremost consulting detective in—" she glanced at Godfrey "—England . . . may have a trickle of mercy in his veins. And I am not certain that Mr. Holmes has actually ended his investigation."

"Yet," said Godfrey, still sitting comfortably as Irene and Quentin paced and I fumed, "Moran has been balked. The treaty is safe. I doubt even he would try to steal it again."

Irene sighed. "Nothing is so ferocious as a wounded tiger. He may blame the old Afghanistan business for his failure here, seeing its survivors as a continuing threat to his future enterprises in London. Surely he must know by now that Dr. Watson, whose life he has threatened on two widely different occasions at two opposite ends of the globe, is a close and valued associate of the one person most dangerous to his future freedom."

"The one person who resides in London most dangerous to his future freedom," Godfrey corrected.

"No," she added, pacing again in opposite rhythm to Quentin so that as he came, she went. "Quentin still is not safe, nor is Dr. Watson. Nor are we three, for that matter."

306    Carole Nelson Douglas

She paused before Godfrey and extended both her hands, which he took.

"Forgive me, dear and glorious barrister, but there is only one person in London who can pull the teeth of this Tiger; who can expose him to the secret community of diplomacy and subterfuge; who can reveal his perfidy then and now. And to him we must go. Set a thief to catch a thief. Moran is not only a Tiger, but as treacherously toxic as a cobra. And to stop a cobra, we need a clever mongoose domesticated to our defense. We need Mr. Sherlock Holmes."

## Chapter Twenty-Nine

# HOLMESWARD BOUND

"Nell!" **Irene** sounded utterly exasperated, like a nanny at odds with an obstreperous child. "You are being completely unreasonable!"

We were in my hotel bedchamber the following morning, each tugging at opposite ends of the same paisley silk shawl.

"I am not being unreasonable! Even you must admit that I am impeccably reasonable. You cannot go. I will go."

"It is too dangerous."

"Dangerous! Irene, if Sherlock Holmes recognizes you, the entire scheme will be ruined and who knows what measures against you he may take? Besides, Dr. Watson may be present, and he has already seen me."

Irene drew breath but let go of the shawl not one whit. "When I have finished dressing in character, you and I will look like twins. Besides, I am sure that Dr. Watson did not engrave your features upon his memory during the brief visit you and Godfrey paid to Paddington."

"You always tell me not to underestimate Mr. Holmes, but you underestimate Dr. Watson. Merely because he associates with *the* man does not mean that he is equally as indifferent to women."

She tugged on the shawl, but I held fast. "Quentin's riveting story will mesmerize them both, Holmes and Watson," Irene insisted. "Do you think two such Englishmen, already addicted to domestic malfeasance to an alarming degree, will be able to resist an international stew reeking of blood and thunder and battle and infamy—not to mention venomous serpents? The woman's role in this scheme merely reveals the unity of the two incidents. Now stop being such a ninny and do give me that shawl!"

"No! It is mine. If you wish to impersonate me impersonating someone else, you will have to find your own costume!"

"Nell—!" Irene sighed gustily and released the remarkably tenacious material so abruptly that I tumbled back onto the bed. "This is ludicrous."

"I only wish to protect you from yourself. You are far too tempted to flit near this awful man on Baker Street. Godfrey does not like it, either."

That gave even Irene a moment's pause. "Godfrey does not—? What are you saying, Nell?"

I was sorry I had brought it up. "He thinks you overly fascinated by this fellow."

"Godfrey is jealous?"

"Perhaps. A little."

She collapsed beside me, as only Irene could, in her most gracefully unladylike manner. "Well then, it is decided. I *must* go!" she said in Sarah Bernhardt tones. "As the French say, nothing is bettair for the average 'usband than a little jealousy, no?"

I could not help smiling. "Godfrey is not the average husband. Truly, Irene, you should not risk going near that man. He warned you in Monte Carlo to stay out of his affairs."

"I should not breathe then, in this London smog," she erupted, ready to explode temperament as Mount Etna spews hot lava. Then she eyed me narrowly. "Nell, are you certain that your true objection is not to the fact that I wish to go to Baker Street, but to the role I will be playing?"

"What do you mean?" I edged myself and the shawl out of her easy reach.

"You know what I mean! I will be posing as Quentin's fiancée. *You* are jealous!"

"I am not! I am not," I repeated in a lower, more restrained tone. "I merely point out what is logical: I have already approached the doctor in the guise of someone's fiancée, that of Jasper Blodgett, late of Godfrey's imagination. Dreadful name."

"Blodgett, you mean," Irene said, nodding.

"No, Jasper."

"Blodgett will be harder to make credible," she muttered, "but I expect Quentin to carry it off. A successful spy is an actor first and foremost. What poetic justice to leave both you and Godfrey behind on this venture—Godfrey especially, for creating Jasper Blodgett. Besides, you are both jealous and there is something of the Feydeau farce in all this."

"I am not jealous! But if you persist in this madness, you may not have a stitch of my wardrobe for it." I clasped the shawl to my bosom.

Irene lunged forward and shook the fringe. "Oh, keep it, Nell. Wear it in good health, Miss Buxleigh. At least we were fortunate that Mrs. Watson misheard your surname. You shall go with Quentin, and mind you that you do not miss a detail of the conversation. I expect you to report every word and every nuance."

"Oh, thank you, Irene!" I leaped up, still embracing my shawl.

Irene stood as well.

"Where are you going?" I asked.

"To my chamber, to cross-examine Godfrey on certain behavior unbecoming a barrister, such as jealousy."

"You cannot," I wailed.

"Whyever not?"

"You have to help me choose what to wear."

"But you are going as yourself."

"But I am pretending to be someone else."

"Nell, that is still the same thing."

I regarded her with silent rebuke until she clapped her

hands to her sides. "Very well. What to wear: your 'surprise dress'—the housedress that closes into a plain, side-buttoning coat for street wear. A fiancée of Jasper Blodgett would be practical to a fault, I think. Boots, of course, no dainty slippers for her. Pale kid gloves and a most subdued bonnet, perhaps the ecru straw with the ghastly spotted ribbon."

I paled. "I never knew you thought the spotted ribbon ghastly."

"I am usually diplomatic, despite those who think me brazen," she said pointedly.

I had begun assembling the items in question as she spoke and draped them over the bed, except for the boots. "You don't think that this ensemble will be too . . . dowdy?"

"For the fiancée of Jasper Blodgett? Any woman engaged to a man whose Christian name is Jasper cannot be too dowdy."

I dared not mention that the first man to engage my romantic interest was a Jaspar, but I determined to remove and destroy the spotted ribbon as soon as my mission to Baker Street ended.

"Besides . . ." Irene bent over the severe, black silk surprise dress that was trimmed only by a five-inch hem of ruching. When she flipped open the front, the pale old-rose lining embroidered in black bloomed like a flash of color on a blackbird's wing. She leaned conspiratorially near to whisper, "When your task is done, you can return to the hotel, swiftly fold back the gown's reveres to reveal its sumptuous undergown, and 'surprise' Mr. Jasper Blodgett at dinner."

She left the room before I could answer that I had no such ambition, a typical example of how aggravating Irene could be on occasion.

Early that morning, we had sent a note to Baker Street requesting an interview with Mr. Holmes. Irene had composed it with an eye to making it impossibly irresistible.

"Mr. Holmes would detect any discrepancy between the penwomanship and the purported fiancée," she insisted, so I copied it in my own hand:

Dear Mr. Holmes,

   Your help is desperately required in a most mystifying matter upon which may hang the fortunes of several nations, as well as our own lives.

   The problem involves my poor fiancé, Jasper Blodgett, missing in India these nine years and now miraculously returned to me with his life in grave danger. We have no notion what to make of these awful events.

   We have made what inquiries we can on the matter ourselves, and now find our lives in danger in a most repellent manner, which I cannot even commit to paper without a shudder.

   Please do us the honor of hearing our tale. We should be forever grateful for any assistance you may be able to render us.

Yours very truly,

Irene paused in dictating this breathless missive. "What name shall we give you, Nell?"

"Mrs. Watson has already renamed me 'Buxleigh.' Surely that is disguise enough?"

"I mean for a first name. It is best not to offer such a quick man as Mr. Holmes too many genuine clues. Have you never longed for another Christian name?"

I shook my head.

"Never yearned to be called 'Chloe,' say, or 'Aurelia'?"

"Never."

"Not even 'Melisande' or 'Cressida' or—"

"Irene, please! Penelope is classical enough for my tastes. If I must choose a pseudonym, I have always been partial to 'May.' "

" 'May'! That is all? 'May'?" My plain choice appeared to plunge Irene into a minor melancholy. "The entire world unrolls before you and you are content with 'May'?"

"Yes," I answered. "I am, after all, from Shropshire." And

I had already signed the missive "May Buxleigh," so that was that.

Within three hours, a note penned in a brash but legible hand was returned to us by our messenger. This was a street youth who had been instructed to wait for Holmes's reply, but to indicate another hotel as his destination, if pressed.

"*You intrigue me,*" it read. "*Three o'clock today. S.H.*"

"A man of few words," Irene observed, smiling tightly, then tying the paisley shawl over my plain-Jane coat-dress.

Quentin and I set out by hansom cab taken from a neighboring hotel at two-thirty.

Returning to Baker Street filled me with anxiety, despite my having seen it previously. Irene had draped my bonnet with the spotted veiling, but other than making me dizzy, it likely had little effect on muting my appearance, should Mr. Holmes choose to remember that he had met me twice before: in my servile role at Briony Lodge and as myself in Godfrey's Temple chambers. Quentin looked most proper but ordinary in a suit he and Godfrey had bought earlier in the day at a department store, quite nice broadcloth but not personally tailored. It perfectly fit his part of returned prodigal son.

We said little in the hansom, both aware of the roles we must soon assume before a man reputed to see through criminal subterfuge.

"That is the key," Irene had prompted us before we left. "You are there to speak the truth, after all. You must only omit certain inconvenient facts."

"Such as you and me," Godfrey added wryly.

So Quentin and I rehearsed the truth in our minds as we left the cab poised before 221 B Baker Street.

This time Quentin, not Godfrey, pulled the bell. My tongue suddenly cleaved to the roof of my mouth. Why had I fought Irene for this dreadful privilege? I remembered *the* man's piercing iron-gray gaze, fixed on me for a few, unnerving minutes when I had undertaken the role of housekeeper at Briony Lodge. This interview could last an entire hour. Or more.

"Yes?" The cheery white-haired woman opened the door with a welcoming smile. "Mr. Holmes said he was expecting visitors. Go right up."

So I climbed another momentous flight of stairs, this one with only a figurative cobra awaiting us at the top.

"Come in, come in!" A cordial, though slightly high voice greeted us as we entered the room above. "Miss Buxleigh, Mr., er . . . Blodgett."

I recognized the Holmesian manner. He was tall, thin and quick in motion and speech. We were shown to a sofa while our host cast himself with a kind of caged energy into a basket chair that should be cool seating indeed at midsummer.

"Now," said he, "you must tell the tale that your—that Miss Buxleigh's—uncommonly intriguing letter began. I have requested a colleague of mine who is peculiarly suited to throw some light upon the matter to join us later. For now, however, I must hear the facts." He laid an elbow upon the chair arm and leaned his head upon his hand, a position of rapt attention belied by the sleepy droop of his eyelids.

I immediately recalled Dr. Watson's reference to cocaine use. Had Mr. Holmes been indulging this outré habit before our arrival?

"Begin," he suggested with the brisk command of a maestro to an orchestra, "at the beginning, if you please, Mr. Blodgett."

Quentin and I exchanged an uneasy glance.

"We cannot, Mr. Holmes," I said, "however much we may wish to oblige you. The fact is that a mere three days ago I was in search of—" I glanced at Quentin in a melting manner that Irene would have applauded "—dear Jasper. That we have found each other after so long is a wonder; that our reunion has been shadowed by the most bizarre incidents and danger is a cruel twist of fate."

"Tell me, then, of this most amazing recent reunion. How did it occur?"

I glanced again at Quentin, not having thought to invent this supposed occurrence. He plunged into the dangerous waters of this topic like a trout into a pool.

"On Angel Street," he said promptly. "Quite the most amazing coincidence. I had returned to England only after a long and not totally willing sojourn in India and Afghanistan, sir."

"You are, of course, a veteran of the battle of Maiwand," Mr. Holmes interjected with a kind of weary smile.

"Why—yes! Indeed. That is extraordinary, Mr. Holmes. I can see why your reputation shines so brightly."

Mr. Holmes leaned forward with the speed of a hawk diving on a dove. "How *did* you learn of me, then?"

"Why—" Quentin glanced at me to gain time for his fabricating faculties to grind into gear.

I was inspired. "From my solicitor, Mr. Marshwine."

"I have not heard of him," Holmes said in a way that struck me as deliberately challenging.

"That was not necessary," I replied tartly, "since he had heard of you. He has connections in France—a Monsieur Le Villon of the Paris police, I believe, speaks highly of your amazing deductive abilities." In a bit of inspired deception, I slightly changed the surname, so my story should not be too neat.

"Monsieur Le Villard," Mr. Holmes corrected me.

I bridled a bit, then feigned confusion. "I beg your pardon?"

"Is the French connection you speak of Monsieur Le Villard, not Le Villon?"

"Yes, you are right! These French names are so similar."

Mr. Holmes nodded and leaned back in the basket chair, his eyes on the gasolier. "Continue."

Quentin accepted his invitation. "As I said, I was strolling down Angel Street when I spied Miss Buxleigh in the window of a . . . I suppose it was a draper's shop. I was so startled that I paid little attention to the surroundings. You see, my fiancée and I have been separated for nine years. Imagine meeting one another purely by chance!"

"Yes, it is unlikely to the point of incredulity," Mr. Holmes noted dryly. "Why had you not returned from that rough quarter of the world for so long, Mr. Blodgett?"

Quentin and I kept our innocent visages bland.

"Severe fever following the battle of Maiwand," Quentin answered. "I lost my senses and ultimately my memory. It was only in March when I was set upon by thieves in the bazaar at Peshawar and hit upon the head that I woke up whole again."

"I have heard of such miraculous returns to the senses," Mr. Holmes said. "It appears your path of late has been salted with happy mishaps."

"Indeed." Then Quentin drew a long face and took my hand. I was wearing kid gloves, naturally, but still could not quell a thrill of excitement utterly unrelated to the terrors of our impersonation. "Poor May has had restored to her a fiancé who is dogged by some malign god. An attempt was made on my life when I embarked from Bombay. Another occurred in Belgium; the latest and most exotic transpired in my hotel room on Oxford Street."

"What was this latest assault?" Mr. Holmes inquired.

I gave a mock shudder, quite without guile.

"An . . . object was left in my room while I was out. A poisonous snake."

"An Asian cobra, in fact," Mr. Holmes interjected.

"Exactly!" Quentin regarded me with innocent joy. "Utterly amazing. You see, my dear, this is just the man to aid us."

"How did you," the detective inquired next, "live to tell the tale?"

Here Quentin looked modestly down. "I have lived in India for nearly a third of my life, sir, and have picked up some exotic habits, perhaps. One of my acquisitions is a devoted pet. I go nowhere without it."

Holmes leaped out of the chair. "Of course! A mongoose."

Quentin regarded me with another wondrous look. "Is not this wonderful, my dear! Mr. Holmes is quick to the point of prescience. Surely he can help us. As you evidently know, Mr. Holmes, there is nothing a mongoose likes better than a dance-to-the-death with a cobra. My Messalina was out of her cage in a wink—clever with her feet, she is. All I found when I returned was a dead cobra . . . sorry, my dear . . . and a bit of damage to the draperies. Messalina can be quite a climber on occasion."

Mr. Holmes drew a pocket watch and studied it in silence while its gold chain swung hypnotically. From the links swung a small yellow sun—a gold sovereign set into a bezel; an odd souvenir. I was pleased to have spotted a detail about Sherlock Holmes that I could legitimately report to Irene, as ordered. (Certainly I could never tell Irene the dreadful words Dr. Watson had penned about *the* man's obsession with her!)

Mr. Holmes lifted his head intently like an animal. "Ah, I hear my associate's step upon the stair. How convenient that your tale has reached a point where it should prove most interesting to him."

He rose and opened the door to a man who was no surprise to me; the same Dr. Watson among whose writings I had shamelessly read and from under whose desk I had quite unintentionally kicked a dead snake.

I experienced some nervousness during the introductions, while Miss Buxleigh professed great amazement that Mr. Holmes knew Dr. Watson, but the doctor merely nodded politely at me and Quentin. All of Dr. Watson's attention was on his friend.

"I am happy to see, Miss Buxleigh," he said bluffly, "that you have managed to retrieve your missing fiancé, uh, Blodgett, is it?" He turned to the much taller, thinner man beside him. "Holmes, what has this to do with the Paddington mystery? Your note promised revelations."

"And we shall have them, Watson," Mr. Holmes said with great good humor, gesturing his friend to a velvet-lined armchair that must have been hot for the day. "Pray continue, Mr. Blodgett."

"Not much more to say. I discreetly disposed of the snake—"

"Therein lies a tale," Mr. Holmes commented sotto voce.

"—but I fear that an old tangle I have remembered from the war underlies this perfidy."

"War?" Dr. Watson asked. "Perfidy?"

"Mr. Blodgett will explain directly." Mr. Holmes fixed his disconcerting attention on Quentin.

That was Quentin's cue to unravel the true tale within the false construct of our fiction as he told the detective and his companion what he had revealed to Godfrey, Irene and myself.

Quentin spoke thrillingly of his spy-work in Afghanistan and of his suspicions toward another British espionage agent called Tiger when the man libeled his friend, Lieutenant Maclaine. He dramatically described the blow to the head after his talk with Maclaine, and his awakening the next day in the midst of a harrowing British retreat.

Dr. Watson listened intently at first, then began to fidget subtly, tapping his fingers on the velvet pile of his armchair, shifting to find a more comfortable position for his leg.

"Yes," Dr. Watson interrupted when Quentin paused for breath, "Miss Buxleigh thought I might have treated you. I remember encountering only one case of a blow to the head at Maiwand. I received a wound from a jezail bullet to my shoulder shortly after. The man I treated could have been you, but I cannot swear to it, Blodgett. I am sorry."

Quentin sat forward on the sofa. "I am not, Dr. Watson, for I am sure of it! I was indeed he whom you tended moments before being shot in the shoulder yourself. Heavens, man, how amazing that we should meet again nearly a decade after Maiwand. Remember the dust?"

Dr. Watson laughed shortly. "Dust and Ghazi fanatics by the yard—who could forget? And the infernal heat. But I confess, Blodgett, that I did not even recall the exact instant of my wounding until Miss Buxleigh brought it back by inquiring after you a few days ago.''

"How did you find Dr. Watson?" Sherlock Holmes inquired suddenly.

Quentin was ready for him. "The last name. He mentioned it at Maiwand, one of the first things I remembered once my memory was resurrected from the past." Quentin turned to the doctor with genuine emotion. "You will never know how relieved I am to see you again, Doctor! I feel in some way that my mislaid past has been redeemed.''

"I have recaptured some lost memories myself," the doctor admitted.

"These mysteries unravel at a fearsome pace without my aid," Mr. Holmes noted wryly. "You two gentlemen would seem to have more in common than a battlefield meeting and bad memories. You both have been recent recipients of Asian cobras.''

"Blodgett, too?" Dr. Watson demanded. "What is going on, Holmes? Is London infected by some sort of imported-serpent ring?"

"For that answer we will have to apply to Mr. Jasper Blodgett. He can begin by explaining how he managed to find you in time to set his trained mongoose on the cobra in your consulting room.''

"No!" Dr. Watson appeared sincerely shocked. "A mongoose. Why, I never thought of that, Holmes.''

"It is fortunate that I did, then, although I had not yet tracked the owner of the mongoose. Remember the nail marks on your windowsill? Obviously an animal's. Well, Mr. Blodgett?"

"Utter simplicity, Mr. Holmes. Having finally remembered Watson's name, I had determined to find any physicians named Watson in England, for by last month I had realized that Tiger was tracking me. In fact, when I attempted to look up Dr. Watson in the records at Peshawar, I discovered that a previous party had recently found—and removed—them. That is when I knew your life to be in danger, Doctor, and why I came to London. That you were the proper Dr. Watson came clear shortly after I found your residence and set watch upon it, planning to introduce myself to you if I thought you a likely candidate. That very night I saw a housebreaker import a box into your study. I may not be a detective—" here Quentin nodded at Mr. Holmes with some pride in his voice "—but I know the average cracksman doesn't convey goods, beyond a few tools, into a house he's planning to rob. I looked in from the windowsill after he had gone—a good clean job he made of it, too—and soon heard the rasp of a creature that chills the blood of any man who has spent time in India, the cobra."

"You happened to have the mongoose with you, no doubt," Holmes suggested with a trace of disdain.

"After the cobra I found in my hotel bedchamber, I went nowhere without it," Quentin said with such feeling that it took me a moment to realize that this was a complete untruth.

In the ensuing silence, Quentin and Mr. Holmes regarded each other with narrowed eyes. Quentin radiated conviction. I was quite perversely proud of him, even though he was lying through his teeth. Mr. Holmes exuded another attitude, one I could not quite name. Perhaps it was skepticism.

"Go on," the detective urged my supposed fiancé.

Quentin only said, "So I nipped onto the sill, set the cage down, and let Messalina loose to do her work—"

"Oh, Jasper," I found myself simpering like any genuine fiancée (and for a brief second, in a strange way, felt that I was), "weren't you frightened that your adorable little pet would succumb to the awful snake, especially in the dark?"

"There, there, May," he said, startling me, for I had forgotten my recent rechristening. "I had not a thing to worry about. No mongoose can choose when to confront a cobra, and Messalina has never lost yet. Cobras can be a sluggish, slow-swaying sort of snake as well as deadly."

"Yes, Miss Buxleigh," *the* man said in obviously insincere consolation, "we humans may learn quite a lesson from the interaction of mongoose and cobra. Its results are applicable to London affairs daily."

I had the dreadful sense that the detective was playing with us all, including his friend, as a mongoose may taunt the slower-moving snake. In this he reminded me of Irene at her most sphinxlike. I shuddered slightly at the insight. Mr. Holmes seemed as cold-blooded as his friend had described him in the pages I had read in Paddington. "... *his cold, precise but admirably balanced mind.*" Now I suddenly saw that Irene shared some of that same clinical distance.

"Messy nipped back to her cage when the job was done," Quentin said, describing, I am sure, exactly what had occurred. "I shut her up and slipped away, knowing Dr. Watson's maid might have a bit of noxious tidying up to do on the morrow, but the doctor's life was safe."

"Indeed." This time Dr. Watson shuddered. "The serpent was discovered under my desk, quite dead, but well positioned to bite me in the leg."

"So Mr. Blodgett's imported mongoose averted a tragedy and a second leg wound, Watson," drawled the detective in an odiously knowing manner.

"There is no first leg wound, Holmes!" Dr. Watson insisted with some irritation. "I merely get a bit stiff in the joints as a lingering symptom of enteric fever. This London weather is dank to one who has broiled in the kiln of Afghanistan and India."

"Utterly true," Quentin put in fervently.

Mr. Holmes turned to him with an air of having toyed enough with too-tame prey. "So is there an explanation for this villainy, Mr. Blodgett, or is that what I am being consulted to detect?"

Quentin paused as if perplexed. "There you have me, Mr. Holmes. I have my suspicions, and we have the two dead cobras to show that something is up."

"Not to mention the irregularities at the battle of Maiwand," I prompted.

Quentin nodded soberly. "They are more than mere irregularities, my dear. If my suspicions are correct that the spy I knew as Tiger was secretly working for the Russians, it could mean that our troops lost that day only by treachery. Many more lives hang on that than poor Maclaine's."

"What are you saying, Blodgett?" Dr. Watson asked. "That an Englishman betrayed his own kind? Maiwand saw much carnage. I witnessed that before I myself was wounded. The Sixty-sixth Berkshires standing to cover the retreat took dreadful losses. I would be most angry to learn that all of this waste could have been avoided."

"If I am right, Dr. Watson," Quentin returned, "your own wounding could have been avoided. I now believe that the bullet that shattered your shoulder was intended for me. Tiger knew that I was suspicious. I am certain that he struck me on the head the night before battle, intending to kill me and have me taken for a casualty. During the retreat, he saw me still alive under your care, and used the dust and confusion as a cover to try again to kill me. That is why I have come all this way after all this time: to warn you and preserve you. To my mind, you saved my life that day by taking a bullet meant for me."

Nothing could belie the sincerity of Quentin's words, the concern that had driven his return to an England that was not only personally dangerous, but dreaded. The two veterans sat silent, affected by the emotion of his voice as much as by what he had said.

"My dear fellow," Mr. Holmes told Quentin with more warmth than he had yet used, "there is no doubt in my mind that you saved Watson's life by introducing your animal ally into his consulting room, and for that I am most grateful. On that score rest easy. That does not mean that the puzzle is solved, or the wrongdoers brought to justice. Do you have any proof that this Tiger is the traitorous spy that you claim he is?"

"Only this, Mr. Holmes." Quentin reached into the breast pocket of his department-store suit and withdrew the paper

Irene and I had prized from Dr. Watson's Afghanistan bag only a day before.

I quite loathed to see Quentin hand it over to the detective, who bounded up and swooped it away to the light of the bow window. Irene had insisted that a copy of this nine-year-old document would not deceive the eminent detective, that Quentin had to surrender this precious paper, his only proof of Tiger's betrayal, if indeed the cryptic scrawls could prove that. Still, I hated seeing Quentin surrender another piece of the past in which he had submerged so much of his life.

"Now we have something to grasp," Mr. Holmes exclaimed. "Watson, my glass!"

He hunched over the document as if to consume it with his eyes. When his associate brought a magnifying glass, Mr. Holmes swept it across as well as up and down both sides.

"Hah! St. Petersburg deckle with a rag content that is no less than forty percent—and cut so that the watermark is conveniently missing." His thin fingers rubbed the paper as appreciatively as Irene's sensitive fingertips judged the weight of Chinese silk.

"This paper is so fine, so sturdy, it has virtually aged like cloth. First it was kept in arid circumstances—some of the fibers are desiccated."

"That is not so mystifying," Quentin said, "I obtained it in the Afghanistan steppes in the horrid heat of July."

Mr. Holmes barely glanced his way. "Since then, I mean . . . most odd. I would judge it to be on the brink of rotting, having spent most of its span in a cool, damp climate. Where has this been kept all these years, Mr. Blodgett?"

I kept my glance from straying accusingly to Dr. Watson, who had allowed this invaluable document to languish in a London wardrobe, all unknowingly, of course, but ignorance is no excuse.

"Ah," Quentin was saying as he flailed for an explanation that would not betray our latter-day acquisition of the paper. "With me. In India. I lived in the cooler hill country most of the time," he lied with such conviction that I listened admiringly. "During the rainy season the climate there can indeed be hideously humid."

"Hmm." Mr. Holmes did not sound convinced. "Certainly little care has been taken with it."

"I had forgotten much that occurred before the blow upon my head," Quentin said. "It is a piece of luck that I kept it at all."

"Yes," Holmes mused, "luck and coincidence have a great deal to do with this case. As to the characters upon the paper, a language expert could translate them better, but they are written in Cyrillic Russian and list geographical locations. I recognize the Russian word for tiger." The detective smiled briefly. "I have been invited to contribute to a matter or two in Russia, including the Trepoff murder in 'Eighty-eight. You may have heard of it. These Russians are a most . . . er, assertive people."

Mr. Holmes suddenly lowered the magnifying glass and strode to the sofa. "I am afraid that I cannot help you. This scrap contains nothing incriminating. There remains only your word that you took it from the belongings of this 'Tiger,' whose actual name you do not even know."

I cannot convey the idly dismissive tone that the detective used, as if all of his interest in the matter had vanished.

"Mr. Holmes!" I said sharply. "For a famous detective you have omitted to ask the obvious. We *do* know the name of Tiger, for my solicitor has discovered his military records. We even know the name of his London club. Since he is the individual responsible for throwing live cobras into everyone's path—it is not his fault that they die before they can do damage, thus far—I should think that a person deeply interested in crime in our metropolis could show a little less ennui and a bit more . . . energy."

Dr. Watson spoke hastily. "You must overlook the lady's distress, Holmes. She is remarkably devoted to Mr. Blodgett, as you can see."

At this the detective leaned forward to sear me with his

disconcerting gaze. I bit my lip, unsure whether I should suddenly confess all under that merciless inspection.

"Yes, Watson, a woman's loyalty is commendable, if often misdirected, as may be her anger." He turned to Quentin. "Do you have any notion why this Tiger would wait nine years to stalk you and Dr. Watson?"

"He thought me harmless," Quentin answered promptly. "My memory was gone, and I was marooned in India and Afghanistan. Yet he still might fear that I had raved about the paper, about his treachery, to the good doctor. It was only as I ventured from the East that these attempts on my life began."

Mr. Holmes softly rapped the paper against his open palm. "The entire affair reeks of the operetta stage. Were Watson not involved I would not waste my time on it, but I will look into your terrifying Tiger, though I suspect that London has tamed him. What is his name?"

"Colonel Sebastian Moran. His club is the Anglo-Indian."

"To your knowledge, Mr. Blodgett, you have not seen him since you arrived in London?"

We shook our heads in unison.

"Watson, does my *Index* list the gentleman?"

The doctor once again rose to do the great man's bidding, picking a massive volume off the bookshelf above the desk, which was cluttered with much domestic effluvia, such as pipes, vials and other oddities, no doubt including whatever appliances are necessary to the consumption of cocaine.

"There is indeed a reference, Holmes! Colonel Sebastian Moran, here between 'Morais, Sabato, born 1823 in Leghorn, Italy, expert on Italian straw fabrication; emigrated to the United States in 1851' and the Countess of Morcar."

"We need no specifics on Her Ladyship," Mr. Holmes said. "What are the particulars on Colonel Moran?"

" 'Moran, Sebastian, born 1840. Unemployed. Formerly First Bangalore Pioneers. Educated at Eton and Oxford. Heavy-game hunter in India. Served in Jowaki Campaign, Afghan Campaign at Charasiab, Sherpur and Kabul. Clubs:

The Anglo-Indian, the Tankerville, The Bagatelle Card Club.' ''

Mr. Holmes fixed Quentin with a stern eye. "No mention of Maiwand, then?"

"Tiger was a spy," Quentin returned. "He did not always say where he was, and neither did the military reports."

"Hmm. Anything more, Watson?"

"He is the author of two monographs: *Heavy Game of the Western Himalayas* published in 'Eighty-one, and *Three Months in the Jungle*, in 'Eighty-four."

"To a hunter used to such prey, one would think a domestic Paddington doctor would be something of a comedown," Mr. Holmes said with a sudden twinkle in his formidable gaze. "Any threat, however unlikely, to my associate is one I take very seriously," he added, his eyes again cold and speculative as they fastened on us. "I will look into the affairs of this Moran. Call on me tomorrow at four o'clock."

"That is wonderful—" I began.

"Four o'clock tomorrow?" Quentin echoed. "Surely that is not time enough to unravel such a mystery."

"It is time enough for me," Mr. Holmes said sharply. "I have, in fact, one or two notions about the case that may bear rapid fruit." He turned his back on us to rummage among the objects atop the rather crowded mantel. I saw him lift a Persian slipper, the most decorative of the objects to my view, and prod the toe.

Quentin and I had risen in a daze, recognizing our sudden dismissal. Then, to my horror, my wandering eyes found a familiar object among the odious and untidy assortment—the cabinet photograph of Irene in evening dress! It stood near a mass of papers skewered to the wooden manteltop by a large knife.

I may have whimpered during my sudden intake of breath. For whatever reason, Dr. Watson rushed anxiously to my side. "Now do not worry," the good physician counseled me. "Holmes can be brisk about his work once he sets his mind upon it, but he has rarely failed to help those in far more desperate circumstances than yours."

"Oh, I do hope so, Dr. Watson," I said in perfect honesty. It was time for Quentin to lead a free life without Tiger's ominous shadow at hand, and certainly Mr. Holmes should do something to earn the trophy he flaunted from the Briony Lodge Affair. Irene had intended it as a consolation prize for the king; instead this detective, this . . . commoner . . . had claimed it. I had seen the claiming at the time, yet I had not known then of Sherlock Holmes's cold and cocaine-consuming nature, nor of his apparent obsession with my dearest friend. How fortunate that I had insisted she not come in my stead! No good could come of these two individuals' further association.

"Be cautious yourself," Quentin advised the doctor during their parting handshake, as I nodded vigorously. "My tale may sound extravagant, but it is true. You have seen the proof of it on your consulting-room rug."

"If there is any way to pull the fangs of this human pit-viper whom you suspect of being responsible for the deaths of so many good men at Maiwand, you may be sure that Sherlock Holmes, however reluctant, is the man for the job."

"Thank you for your assurances," I told the doctor in farewell, wondering if he would ever discover that his Afghanistan bag was missing, poor man.

"Good day, Miss Buxleigh, Mr. Blodgett. Many happinesses to you both," he added warmly.

I blushed like a bride at his remark, however well intended, yet it pleased me enormously in an odd way.

Quentin took my arm in a most proprietary manner, all in his role of Jasper Blodgett, of course.

"We will see what the morrow brings," he said vaguely.

"Thank you," I added to our good-hearted physician. I longed to tell him that he would find far more satisfaction keeping to his own hearth than in accompanying his unconventional friend on wild adventures of a criminal sort. Nothing good could come of such an association; certainly his pathetic scribblings would never amount to more than kindling, from what I had glimpsed of them.

But discretion sealed my lips. Instead of endowing Dr. Watson with my honesty, I simply mumbled a cowardly "Good day" and left.

"Oh, it is too delicious! Better than a Punch and Judy show. Are you saying that by four o'clock tomorrow the unenthusiastic Mr. Holmes expects to have done with Colonel Sebastian Moran? That is a contest I should like to witness. You must tell me everything!"

Irene stopped pacing in the salon of her suite and flounced down onto an embroidered ottoman, sitting raptly as a child, staring at Quentin and myself.

We told her what we could, but none of our efforts satisfied her hunger.

"What sort of 'odd things' were 'lying about' and where, Nell? Do you realize how maddeningly vague such a description is? You should memorize an environment as an actor commits a stage setting to the senses. No detail is unimportant. A man with so little patience for triviality as Sherlock Holmes would tolerate nothing unessential about him."

"I did notice a gold coin upon his watch chain," I put in hesitantly.

"Excellent!" Irene's exuberantly clasped hands showed thanks for any small crumb of intelligence that escaped me. "A gold coin. Not a terribly original watch-charm, but still . . . an observation."

"What kind of gold coin?" Godfrey put in with a frown.

"A sovereign."

Now Irene frowned. "A sovereign? But that is the—" She suddenly stopped speaking.

"Is what—?" Godfrey asked.

"Is the oddest thing," she finished with a light laugh. "Who would expect Sherlock Holmes to adorn himself with such a commonplace token?" And she sank into silence even as I stuttered my way through a few more vague and uninteresting details, such as the Persian slipper and the basket chair.

"The most important fact," Quentin said, "is that this Holmes is willing to pursue the matter despite himself. I sensed that he has other objectives than the obvious."

"Ah!" Irene revived again, like a puppet whose strings have been pulled. "He always has his own objectives, I fancy. Such a man never fails to be working on a master puzzle. Why else do you two babes-in-the-woods think I sent you to him?"

"Out of perversity," I answered a bit crossly.

I was not pleased to be found wanting for not having made a mental inventory of the clutter at 221 B Baker Street. Naturally I said nothing of the prominent place accorded to Irene's photograph. It would encourage an elevated opinion of herself, and Godfrey would fret to hear it.

Irene shrugged blithely. "I really must see this fountainhead of crime-solving for myself. I am determined to go as Miss Buxleigh tomorrow."

"Irene! You cannot."

"I most certainly can. You wore a concealing veil, Nell, and I will, too. My acting and camouflaging techniques are sufficient to overcome any discrepancy in our height or hair color. Oh, I am longing to see this den of detection for myself. Who knows when we may be in England again?"

"Irene, I have sacrificed myself and committed several untruths to masquerade as a fictional person's fiancée. It shall not be for naught. I absolutely will not hear of you interjecting yourself into a plan that is working well only so that you may satisfy your abominable curiosity."

"I agree," Godfrey said suddenly. "No matter how well you do it, Irene, you risk the greater venture. Besides, to substitute yourself for Nell treads far too close to exposure. It is one thing to hide behind the unlikely facade of a street urchin or a grande dame; aping Nell would allow for very little disguise and too much risk."

"Thank you, Constable," she grumbled in return, for Godfrey was right. The more out-of-character the guise, the more likelihood of deception. It was the very fact of my never expecting to see Godfrey in the role of a bobby that allowed him to sweep us all into a carriage without Quentin's or my recognizing him, though he wore virtually no disguise other than the helmet and a false mustache.

"I do not suppose I could wear a false mustache as Nell," Irene admitted glumly. "Oh, well. Another time."

We dined that night at Simpson's in the Strand, a restaurant famed for its rare roast beef, which Quentin savored with the intensity of an exile. That entire evening was a pleasant, almost tranquil time. Our foursome chatted like old friends, as Quentin and I recalled new details of our outing to Baker Street that amused our companions. I truly felt that Quentin and I had been fellow adventurers in a sense, even as I considered with a pang that the necessity should soon be over and our paths would part.

The evening ended with the usual smoking session in the Norton sitting room—I was thankful that my draperies were not subjected to such a cloud of ill-smelling smoke. But how could I deny my friends their small vices, especially in the face of looming triumph?

"Sherlock Holmes is the key," Irene said expansively, lounging rather casually on the sofa in her pale peach-colored *mousseline de soie* gown. "The problem that has enmeshed Quentin also echoes in far-off corridors of power. I am convinced that Mr. Holmes can disarm Colonel Moran for us, or I never would have sent you to him."

"A pity," Quentin noted, "that we will have to wait until tomorrow to know anything."

"Yes, it is." Irene offered a sympathetic smile. "How you must long to see your family again."

"Actually . . . I rather dread it. I do not know how they will accept me after my foreign sojourn."

"With open arms!" she insisted. "I propose that after your second interview with Mr. Holmes, and if his results assure you that your life is not in such danger that your family must be avoided, you and Nell pay a visit to Grosvenor Square."

"Oh, Irene, I could not intrude at such a time!" I objected.

"Whyever not? You were associated with the family years ago. They have met you again recently. Your presence will cushion any awkwardness. You are the perfect go-between in this instance."

"That is true," Quentin said with pathetic eagerness. "Will you go with me, Nell? After all, had I not found you in Paris, I would not be contemplating a return to my family."

"I do not see the necessity—"

"This would not be necessity, Nell," Irene told me. "It would be nicety."

"Of course I cannot object to nicety . . ."

"Then it is decided," Irene said, with an air of having settled a vital matter.

She was the most definite of persons, and never more so than immediately after her will had been thwarted.

## Chapter Thirty

# A LUKEWARM SOLUTION

**A message** from Holmes summoned me from Paddington to Baker Street at noon the day following his interview with Jasper Blodgett and his fiancée. Our maid Prudence had refused to cross my carpet since the incident with the cobra, so I was forced to take the note at the consulting-room door, then went to the window to read it.

"Watson," it read. "Come at once. All is solved."

In this case, I had a more than casual interest in Holmes's effort to stop a man determined to kill me as well as Jasper Blodgett. No patients had appeared all morning, so I had been writing my memoir titled "The Adventure of the Devious Diva." As much as Holmes might pooh-pooh my literary ambitions and my taste for "sensation," as he called it, I was loath to leave my desk, being in the midst of a stirring account of *the* woman's trickery at Briony Lodge.

Once I had informed my wife of my destination and taken a brisk walk to Paddington Station, my enthusiasm for real life as opposed to fiction had revived. I was, after all, fairly twitching to know what Holmes had learned of the bounder who had introduced a venomous serpent into my home.

I found the windows of 221 B open and Holmes sitting in the basket chair, his feet upon an ottoman and the familiar pipe perfuming the balmy air.

"Ah, Watson, as prompt as the tax collector, as usual. Si[t] down. Mrs. Hudson left some lemon curd tartlets from ele[e]venses."

"Oh, excellent, Holmes. I thought, though, that I was t[o] return at four o'clock."

Holmes set his black clay pipe in an empty gravy tureen "No. I am afraid that you have seen the last of Mr. Jaspe[r] Blodgett and his most definite fiancée, Miss Buxleigh."

"Surely they have not been attacked again—and success[-] fully?"

Holmes's smile was weary. "Of course not, my dear fellow They are as safe as houses, or as safe as anyone can be i[n] modern-day London, and so are you."

"Then you've performed the miracle of permanently cut[-] ting the Tiger's claws?"

"Not I, Watson. My brother Mycroft."

As I frowned in puzzlement, he rose and went to lea[n] against the mantel, his eyes idly resting on the photograph o[f] the very woman whose actions occupied the current exercise of my pen.

"The matter is far more complicated—and dangerous— than assassin cobras and spoiled spy-work long ago at Mai[-] wand. It involves the most eminent figures in the government of three nations, Watson. Colonel Moran has influence wit[h] two of them, so it was a tricky bit of work, but he will troubl[e] you and Mr. Blodgett no longer. He now has worse worrie[s] that render his past concerns moot."

"What wonderful news, Holmes! Mary is the most under standing of women, but the matter of my reptilian visitor wa[s] most unsettling."

"I do not doubt it. That is why I am informing you a[s] quickly as possible of how things stand. Certain facts in th[e] matter must not be made public, not even to the pair wh[o] commissioned me to investigate. Too much would be risked This Colonel Moran is a vicious piece of work, Watson. Hi[s] reptilian emissaries are creatures of great integrity compared to their keeper.''

''You have seen this man?''

''More than that. I was very nearly required to horsewhip him from the Anglo-Indian Club.''

''Indeed!''

''You see, Watson, I was not entirely unaware of his existence even before the unfortunate Blodgett called. Yet matters were of such delicacy that I was forced to appear more ignorant than I was.'' Holmes's dark eyebrows clashed above his aquiline nose. ''A most unpleasant necessity, Watson; I trust I shall not be compelled to do so again.''

''But what more evil has this man Moran done beyond our suspicions of skulduggery at Maiwand, wounding me and harassing poor Blodgett?''

Holmes sighed. ''I must ask you to keep this in strictest secrecy, old fellow. You cannot even begin to dream of so much as committing it to paper.''

I nodded and assumed a sober expression as proof of my worthiness.

''Pray do not look so gloomy! The worst is over, and the odd thing is that this new case is linked to the old one.''

''Old one? Which old one?''

''The matter I have just dealt with involving your old school friend Percy Phelps.''

''But that was solved, Holmes. I sat here in Baker Street not a week ago as you passed Percy his missing papers under cover of Mrs. Hudson's breakfast dishes. I will never forget his expression as he lifted the cover and found the cylinder of paper in place of the likely kippers.''

''I will never forget his faint,'' Holmes added with a smile. ''The poor chap was exhausted by his ordeal, or the surprise solution to his dilemma would not have had such a severe effect on him. At least a doctor was present to tend him.''

''I have never seen a more grateful man.''

''Or a luckier one, Watson. His precious paper was safe.

You know, of course, that the culprit, Joseph Harrison, escaped after surrendering the treaty to me, and taking something of a beating at my hands."

"Yes," said I. "You felt that both the young couple and Percy's uncle the Cabinet Minister would prefer discretion over justice in this matter."

"And so it is with the case of Jasper Blodgett." Holmes suddenly rose and went to the open bow window to gaze down on Baker Street in all its hustle. "Have you ever noticed how crime follows a certain natural law, Watson? Where a flower will put forth petals that mirror one another, so too the unhappy works of the criminal mind often produce a parallel symmetry?"

"No, Holmes, I cannot say that I have."

"Consider the engaged couples in the two cases: both faithful and devoted women; both men whose reputation and future have been sullied by events beyond their control. Granted that Blodgett's unhappy circumstances began nine years ago, but otherwise these two men's situations are not that different.

"Now, Watson, consider the fact that the same evil influence has governed both men's lives: Colonel Sebastian Moran, late of India and Her Majesty's forces, and now all too thoroughly of London."

"Then Blodgett was right!"

"Oh, Blodgett was right enough, but he can never know how much so. Had it struck you that the naval-treaty affair had a rather lukewarm ending, Watson?"

I pondered his question. "I must say that if I had any desire to turn it to fiction, I would find the ending rather inconclusive and unsatisfactory. Happy enough for poor Percy, of course."

"And that is how we must leave poor Blodgett as well, Watson: reunited with his fiancée, safe but in the dark. You see, however in debt Joseph Harrison was, and however well placed to seize the document from his future brother-in-law in the Foreign Office, and however vicious his temperament, he is not the sort of mastermind who could begin to handle the delicate business of hawking this stolen treaty to either France or Russia, or most likely to the higher bidder of the two. Joseph was the thief, but he was a mere hireling."

"Then this Colonel Moran—?"

"Watson, once again you leap on the train of my logic with your usual promptitude. Colonel Moran commissioned Joseph to take the treaty and planned to force France and Russia to pay a pretty penny to see it. He has had a Russian connection since his Afghanistan days, from Blodgett's rather damning testimony. I don't doubt that his nefarious career has taken him to France. In fact, I have sent cables to both Inspector Dubuque and Le Villard on the matter."

"How fortunate, then, that Blodgett found me. Without him, you would never have been able to link the two cases."

"Yes." Holmes went to the mantle to delve in the Persian slipper that contained his shag tobacco, but paused to lift the photograph of Irene Adler. "How . . . amazingly fortunate." He abruptly set the frame down and returned to burrowing for more tobacco.

"How have you disarmed this renowned game hunter, Holmes? He does not strike me as one easy to discourage."

"He is not," Holmes said grimly. "First I spoke to Mycroft, who had already been making inquiries among his diplomatic sources. There is no man in London better placed than Mycroft to stir the subtle threads of international relations. Mycroft has discredited Moran with his supporters in both camps by revealing his double-dealing nature. Every nation needs spies but none need counterspies. I predict that the colonel will be much occupied with finding work, now that his important supporters in foreign capitals have melted from him like snow leopards in winter. He has no reason to kill to protect his past since it is no longer worth protecting, nor is his present. Besides, he now has sworn to kill me instead, and that should serve to divert him from lesser prey."

"Good God, Holmes! Is he serious?"

"Absolutely. I had a most unpleasant interview with him at the Anglo-Indian. It seems that my call interrupted a crucial card game. A powerful and intelligent man, Watson, gone over totally to evildoing. All life to him is a game, a tiger hunt, and he is the supreme predator. I fancy I can teach him a thing or two about that game. Certainly he knows that if he lays a hand upon a hair of your head he will have more to answer for than even he would care to."

"Did you really horsewhip him out of his club, Holmes?"

My friend's often melancholy face took on a rare radiance of joy. "The club walls were accoutred with every exotic weapon known to man and many of the exotic animal victims of those weapons. In fact, an Argentinean bullwhip was at hand—actually at shoulder level. Moran tried to surprise me with a revolver."

Holmes flexed his knuckles, which still bore the marks of Joseph's knife attack of a few days before. "See how crime blossoms in parallels, Watson? Moran's hand bears a slash much like mine, only from a bullwhip, not a knife. There is a certain justice, do you not think, in a man who has used snakes to do his dirty work being disarmed with the long, leathery length of a bullwhip?"

"Perhaps . . ." said I, even then envisioning a parallel literary construction: two tales told in matching tracks like a train's that met and entwined into complementary denouements. . . .

"But you must not write a word of this, Watson. I know your habits. Even though your scribblings are unlikely to ever see the light of public print, it would be too dangerous to commit them to paper. See how an old piece of paper, miraculously preserved, helped undo Moran? You must say nothing of this to anyone."

"Someday perhaps, Holmes, it will all come out." *The Puzzle of the Naval Treaty*, my mind formulated. And *The Adventure of the Catatonic Cobras.*

"Someday, Watson, but not while you and I yet live."

"Let us hope that day is long after the demise of the unpleasant Colonel Moran."

"Let us hope, Watson," he answered as he relit his pipe with a series of cheek-hollowing puffs. "And let us ensure that it is so."

## Chapter Thirty-One

# A MOTHER NOSE

**The day** following our first interview with Sherlock Holmes brimmed with errands. Immediately after breakfast, we again repaired to the Norton sitting room, where Irene declared herself bound for Liberty's of Regent Street and a fitting for the flowing gowns in the oriental mode for which the establishment was famed.

"I will go, too," I suggested.

"Nell, you know you loathe the fashion for aesthetic dress," Irene said quickly. "I plan to order a gift for Sarah as well as a few things for myself."

Godfrey rolled his eyes at this announcement; Irene's "a few things" invariably filled trunks.

"I might reconsider," I said, glancing at Quentin. It occurred to me that a gown *à la* Saracen might find favor in his Eastward-oriented eyes.

Irene was stuffing a formidable roll of pound notes into her reticule. "Nonsense," said she even more abruptly. "We are not suited as shopping partners. You always reject my suggestions and I yours. Besides, we shall all be returning to France soon and I wish to accomplish a great deal in one swoop. I should return before your appointment with Mr. Holmes."

With that she swept out, the empty carpetbag she carried certain proof that she intended to collect items for immediate consumption as well as ordering gowns to be sent along later.

At her exit, Quentin, too, bestirred himself. He had seemed distracted this morning. I fear the afternoon's meeting with Mr. Holmes and the proposed reunion with his family were occasions for anxiety as well of hope. He also had errands to accomplish, he announced, among them a pressing need to "find fresh food for Messalina." I did not offer to accompany him, nor did I inquire into the specifics of this process, being hopeful that it involved the butcher's rather than the domestic pet vendor's. He left soon after Irene.

Godfrey smiled over the *Times* at me. "Time will hang heavy today, Nell. Perhaps we should arrange an outing of our own."

"I have nowhere I wish to go."

"Not even 'church'?" he jibed me wickedly.

"Godfrey, you know that fiction was necessary to deceive you. Quentin's life was at risk."

"Not among that crowd at the British Museum."

"It was a charade, was it not?"

"Still . . ." Godfrey lowered the paper as if beset by an unpleasant thought. "If Colonel Moran was among those odd folk milling around that exhibition room—and he must have been, given the air gun fired into the exhibit case—he is fully as duplicitous as the incomparable Irene, or even Mr. Sherlock Holmes, or—lately—Miss Penelope Huxleigh."

"Godfrey, you do me an injustice to place me in such professionally duplicitous company," I answered with a mock pout, for I knew that he enjoyed teasing me. "But you are truly worried?"

He nodded, running a forefinger over his bare upper lip, no doubt missing his mustache. "I fear that Irene underestimates the rapacious nature of Moran. Such men do not lose easily, and never give up if once they develop a grudge. I only hope that we do not become the object of it. She also overestimates the esteemed investigator of Baker Street."

"Then you think that Quentin's difficulties may not be solved?"

He sighed and folded the newspaper. "I will not know what I think until the events of this afternoon, but meanwhile I have thought of the perfect diversion for you and me to make the hours fly until you can return here and depart for Baker Street again."

"Oh, really, Godfrey? What is this treat?"

"The zoo," he said, with an expression of immense self-satisfaction. "You and I are going to the Regent's Park zoo."

I could hardly tell him that my distaste for dead animals, as displayed in the Museum of Natural History and Modern Curiosities, was only exceeded by my abhorrence for live animals, especially eccentric ones.

We returned at three o'clock, my vision spotted from gazing upon so many beasts of conflicting patterned hides. Sarah Bernhardt would have been ecstatic.

The Norton suite was not unoccupied, but Irene had not yet returned. Instead, a strangely subdued Quentin greeted us. With him was a lady of such age and frailty that she barely seemed able to sit upright despite the ebony cane around whose golden top her blue-veined hands were curled.

"Godfrey. Nell." Quentin paused as if to gather his thoughts. "I should like to present my mother, Mrs. Fotheringay Stanhope."

Godfrey and I nodded dazedly at this fragile figure in rich shades of half-mourning: heliotrope, lavender and gray. The white-haired head inclined in greeting.

Quentin spoke on quickly, as if embarrassed or unusually nervous. "I must apologize for surprising you in this way, but I had given some thought to Irene's advice of yesterday that it was high time I overcame my shame and approached my family. I decided to visit Grosvenor Square, in suitable disguise to protect the family. Only Mama was at home, but when I gave the name 'Quentin,' she saw me at once. Her health has been fragile and she has mostly kept to her rooms upstairs, but when she heard my story, and that you and I, Nell, were to hear the end of it today in Baker Street, she

sisted on accompanying me there to personally thank Mr.
olmes for safeguarding my return to England and to her."

We stood in shocked silence, Godfrey and myself, as
Quentin must have done only hours before in the upper
rooms of number forty-four Grosvenor Square.

For how could anyone deny the request of this lovely little
old lady whose hazel eyes—so like her son's—had faded to
the color of old gold?

"I—I am most pleased to meet you, Mrs. Stanhope," I said,
falling into a sort of schoolgirl curtsy. I glanced quickly at
Quentin. "I imagine it will not be necessary for me to accompany you to Grosvenor Square from Baker Street now."

"Quite the contrary, Nell!" he replied as if cut to the quick.
"Mama must be taken home, and I cannot think of revealing
myself to my dear sisters without having at my side the
woman who first convinced me to return."

"You said that Irene—"

"Irene suggested that I no longer put off the time of the
reunion, but you were the one who made me see that such a
thing was possible when we first spoke at Neuilly. I hope I
have not angered you."

"No. I seldom anger."

"And only in defense of her friends," Godfrey put in. He
went to the old lady and bowed. "Good afternoon, Mrs.
Stanhope. It is a pleasure to meet you." The grande dame
carefully lifted one slightly trembling hand from the head of
her cane, which Godfrey saluted with a very Continental kiss.
Then he turned to me. "You will wish to refresh yourself
before leaving for Baker Street, Nell. As soon as you are
ready, I will see you all down to a carriage."

"Yes," I said pointedly before I left. "The zoo was hot and
crowded. And . . . pungent." I was not angry but I was a bit
annoyed.

One could not blame Quentin for an impulse to visit a
mother who thought him long lost, I told myself as I retreated
to my rooms to don my Miss Buxleigh garb. Still, I was
utterly disappointed, and could not say why. Perhaps I saw

that once Quentin had been reclaimed by his family, his regard for me would pale. I was, after all, only a means, not an
end.

The journey to Baker Street required a four-wheeler rather
than a hansom cab, and was quieter than the trip Quentin and
I had made the previous day. The lavender ostrich plumes on
Mrs. Stanhope's hat nodded dolefully at me as we jolted
along. She and Quentin occupied the opposite seat. Already
the "fiancée" was being usurped by the mother, even in our
fictional relationship. I no longer looked forward to my return to the Stanhopes, although I wore the "surprise" dress
Irene had suggested I wear yesterday, so I could smarten my
ensemble in the carriage with a few discreet adjustments on
the way to Grosvenor Square.

Again the elderly woman admitted us to 221 B Baker Street.
Again we climbed the stairs. Again Mr. Holmes invited us in
and assigned us seats. This time Quentin and his mother
occupied the sofa. I took the velvet armchair claimed yesterday by Dr. Watson, who was absent today.

"Delighted to meet you, Mrs. . . . er, Blodgett," the detective said. "I believe I have excellent news for your son."
(Despite her advanced age, Mrs. Stanhope had understood
the need to muddy her son's identity and readily accom-
modated the charade.)

She nodded graciously, if a bit vacantly, and withdrew a
lorgnette from her ruched violet satin reticule. She gravely
unfolded it, then brought the device to her eyes and honored
Mr. Holmes with the kind of up-and-down inspection only
the very elderly—or the very young—are permitted in polite
society.

"Thank you . . . Mr. Holmes, is it?" Her voice, which I had
not yet heard, was one of those that ages like apricots: dry,
fruity and shriveled. Her tones wavered in the midst of words,
producing an unfortunate tremolo. Quite frankly, it would
grate on anyone with any ear for music. Mr. Holmes's features became pained of a sudden, and he took a sharp intake
of breath.

'Holmes it is, Madam, as Blodgett is your name."

This statement, and that unlovely, fraudulent name, he left hanging in the air. I was quite unsure what this imperious lady would say in answer. She was perfectly capable of forgetting her pose and telling the truth.

"Fine, upstanding English names, both," she finally asserted in her voice so like an ill-sawed violin. "I am relieved to hear that you have released my long-lost Jasper from impending danger. How was it done, young man?"

Mr. Holmes turned to Quentin and myself with an apologetic look and a conspiratorial smile. "I am sorry to say that the particulars must remain veiled. Certainly you realize that the matter of Maiwand involved persons who are now highly placed in the government. Yet I can assure you that some of these same public and private figures are also in a position to see that this Colonel Moran troubles you no more."

Quentin frowned. "Then poor Maclaine's reputation must remain compromised?"

"I fear so." Mr. Holmes strode to the mantle from where he could fix us all with his compelling gaze. "Past injustices must on occasion not only go unpunished but celebrated in monuments. Such is the history of war since the Trojans. Maiwand was a minor battle in a far quadrant of the globe in which our nation no longer invests any real interest. I vouchsafe to say that Russia's ambitions there are also fading and by the new century will be nonexistent. Colonel Moran only resurrected the past because his current activities were endangered by those who might know of it."

"You still do not say how it was done, sir," Mrs. "Blodgett's" commanding quaver piped up like a creaky old organ. "I was given to understand that you are some latter-day wonder-worker. A Daniel come to judgment."

"Even a Daniel may not necessarily name his lions," Mr. Holmes returned. He turned to include us in his remarks. "Suffice it to say that I have taken the teeth and claws from the man. No one he was accustomed to dealing with in his spy-work will associate with him. There is no reason for him to protect his past when his future ground has been cut out from under him."

"Will not such a beast be dangerous, rather like a wounded tiger?" Quentin's mother asked.

Holmes smiled condescendingly, although his tone remained ever courteous. "A terrifyingly apt expression, Madam. No. Colonel Moran will be too busy hunting for his own survival to harass others in theirs."

"Humph." The old lady leaned slowly forward, putting all her weight on those two frail hands folded over her cane top. Then she pushed herself slowly upright, inch by inch. We all stood, feeling we should assist her, yet fearing to topple her with the very offer of our aid.

Straightening gingerly, she began to hobble about the room, the lorgnette at her face, as she inspected the furnishings.

"That basket chair needs a bit of reweaving, Mr. Holmes," she said. "I hope that my son has recompensed you sufficiently for your services that you can afford a bit of repair to your belongings."

"Not yet," Quentin put in hastily, "but I will before we depart."

"Speaking of which, we should—" I began, watching Mrs. Stanhope scuttle along the opposite wall toward the cluttered desk.

She stopped suddenly and pointed with her cane to an object in a dark corner of the chamber. "Ah, a fiddle. Play, do you?"

"It is a Stradivarius, Madam," was all Mr. Holmes said, in an icily polite tone.

She bent over it, viewing the instrument through her lorgnette. "Needs oiling, young man." Then she was skittering along the well-worn red carpet to pause before the sofa Quentin and I occupied. Her neck craned to study, not us, but the wall above us.

"Most patriotic, sir," she trilled approvingly and traveled

on around the chamber to a cluttered corner where hand-labeled bottles and vials glimmered in the low lamplight.

I turned to inspect the dusky damask-pattern wallpaper behind us: what I had taken for some unevenness in the pattern now stood revealed as bullet holes in the graceful script of V.R., complete with a small crown above them.

Mrs. Stanhope had paused before the hearth. Her cane tapped the head of a brown bear that lay prostrate before the fender. "You are more partial to bears than tigers, it appears, Mr. Holmes. A pity this Colonel Moran who has caused my dear boy such grief cannot be trapped and turned into an object of use, if not beauty."

She eyed the jackknife stuck into the middle of the wooden mantel to pin down a fan of papers and cocked her head in a most uncouth manner to try to read some of the text thereon. I glanced at Quentin, feeling wretched for his mother's appalling behavior. And he was worried that his family would find his life abroad irregular and spurn *him!* So much for a house on Grosvenor Square, apparently no guarantee of gentility.

"Now," Mrs. Stanhope croaked in a tone all too reminiscent of Casanova, "there is a lively-looking lass. A mother could not ask better than that for her son to marry. Your sister, sir, no doubt? Perhaps you will introduce my boy when he gets his feet on the ground."

I gasped, for the old woman had stopped before the photograph of Irene. The very idea of proposing Irene for Quentin as a fiancée in my presence was too appalling to entertain for even one moment. Did this dreadful old busybody have no limits?

Mr. Holmes's expression hinted that he, too, had been goaded beyond his endurance. He went to the mantel and lifted the frame from the elderly woman's rapt gaze. "A lady of my acquaintance," he said coldly, "a rather private person." He paused. "Of my 'late' acquaintance," he added finally.

Mr. Holmes had also discovered how admirably mention of death deters impertinent inquiries. Mrs. Stanhope recoiled at this implied rebuke, but a moment later lifted a hand from her cane to jab a crooked finger at Mr. Holmes's midsection.

"Now that is a lovely charm, sir. No doubt a memento from a grateful client, eh? Jasper, son, you must find Mr. Holmes something suitable, too. A sovereign would hardly do, as he has one already. Why, sir," she jibed him slyly, "if you are as successful in the detection business as they claim and receive a small token from every satisfied client, you will hardly be able to walk, your watch chain will be so laden with booty."

He drew his jacket over the chain with great dignity, like a man closing a curtain, or perhaps veiling a wound unsuitable for public viewing.

"Please be seated, Mrs. Blodgett. I fear you will trip upon a wrinkle in the rug; though your eyes seem remarkably sharp, you are somewhat unsteady on your feet."

With that he took her elbow and guided her back to the central table and into a chair beside it, bending his remarkably penetrating, almost fierce, gaze upon her.

"Now," said he, "our business is concluded. Ah, thank you, Mr. Blodgett, an entirely satisfactory commission."

"I hope," Quentin said, "that pound notes will not inconvenience you, Mr. Holmes. Being newly arrived in the country, I have not yet had time to establish credit."

"Not at all, not at all. I have accepted gold coin as happily," he added, with a sharp look to the elderly lady.

Mrs. Stanhope looked a bit taken aback and began her pained rising once again, the cane wobbling between her clasped hands until every eye was fixed upon her in the same breathless way one watches rope dancers at a circus.

Her trembling hand paused on Mr. Holmes's forearm. "Sir," she said, "I hope you will accept a mother's full measure of joy at witnessing the restoration of her son's safety and freedom."

"Indeed I will, Madam," he said swiftly, guiding her once again with such courteous skill toward the door that for a moment he almost seemed a courtier escorting a great lady to a moment of mutually lamented farewell.

Quentin and I followed, mortified; at least I was. And then it was over—the charade. We stood on the threshold. I could glimpse beyond Mr. Holmes a room that had become, after two visits, familiar in an odd way. What bizarre experiments unfolded under the bright glow of those gaslights high on the walls! What high- and low-born clients passed over this very threshold, bearing problems of every description like gifts to the strange man who lived there!

I saw the chamber for an instant as an exotic private railroad car hurtling through time with its cargo of crime and punishment. I felt I would never be able to return to Baker Street with quite the innocence with which I had first viewed it, just as I would never be able to return to Saffron Hill or Shropshire. And then I realized that *I* was the train, and that my life was the tracks that were hurtling me away from my past into an uncertain, an ever-mysterious future. I began to understand Irene's fascination with the curious and the criminal; these things were the velocity that made the journey fast and frightening and . . . interesting.

Mr. Sherlock Holmes rode such a track as well. I could tell by studying his quick, nervous and yet admirably controlled features that he would never forsake it, and never could forsake it.

"Thank you," I found myself saying quite sincerely, not as Miss Buxleigh or even as Miss Huxleigh but as my Real Self. He was Irene's last resort. He had served to complete the rescue of Quentin Stanhope from his past, and—unfortunately, I feared—from my future.

Quentin helped his mother down the stairs and to the street while I slowly followed, wrapped in uncustomary emotions. I was once again the odd one out, but had anything other been destined for me?

Baker Street was dim. A fleecy black sheep of cloud had rolled over the town like an endless, billowing coverlet of smoke. The air had grown still, just as time seemed to have stopped.

Quentin drew out a whistle and blew twice. A four-wheeler veered across the thoroughfare at a reckless pace to fetch us. Even the horse sensed the storm sulfur in the air; its hooves churned the pavement and its eyes rolled nervously despite the driver's hard hands on the lines.

After Quentin seated his mother, he took my arm to assist me within, where it was even darker than the drab day. None of the gaslights had been lit yet, but they ought to have been.

We clicked away from the curb, Mrs. Stanhope covering her face with a fall of lace handkerchief. Her entire fragile frame quivered at the mercy of a coughing spell.

"Your mother must have overdone," I said, trying to sound properly sympathetic.

"I fear so," he answered, bending nearer the old woman to inspect her. "It should pass in a moment."

I stared politely, for Mrs. Stanhope was shaking now as with an ague and was burying her face in the folds of handkerchief in paroxysms of breathlessness.

"Quentin, perhaps we should stop—"

"We will," the old lady croaked, "just as soon as I remove my nose."

## Chapter Thirty-Two

# THE DREADFUL TIFFANY
# SQUID

"Irene, this is your most appalling mischief yet! It was unspeakable—and most unwise."

"You are quite right as usual, Nell," she admitted cheerily, peeling away theatrical putty wrinkles like some giddy reanimated corpse on Judgment Day. In fact, this was the first thing I could picture Irene doing on Judgment Day. "I will be out of your way in a twinkle, once I have restored some semblance of myself."

She reached under her crackling taffeta petticoats to draw out the carpetbag, into which went the literal pieces of her face as well as a snow-white flock of various "rats" and hairpieces. Only a bit of white remained at her hairline, and that she was vigorously shaking out, until the powder clogged the carriage like smoke.

"How did you manage to turn your eyes yellow?"

Irene flourished a small vial. "The opposite of belladonna, which enlarges the pupil and makes the eyes appear darker. This handy potion reduces the pupil for the opposite effect. Of course, it makes it a bit troubling to see. Mrs. Stanhope's bumbles through the chamber were not fakery." Still, she glanced at me sharply enough. "You need not fear, Nell. I will not intrude on your pilgrimage to Grosvenor Square. *Two* Mrs. Stanhopes might cause confusion, and Quentin's triumphant return is excitement enough."

"Quentin." I turned to him, shaken from the strange reverie that leaving Baker Street had caused. "You must have known about this ruse even before we left the Strand."

"Guilty," said he with no more contriteness than a boy who had eaten all the teatime scones. He smiled at my rising indignation. "My dear Nell, after all Irene has done to insure my safety, even my sanity, during this troubled time, I could hardly deny her an opportunity to play my mother."

"And I was mad to get inside Baker Street!" Irene pled her own case even as she resumed her own face with quick, skilled movements. "What a glorious hodgepodge in which to find such a supremely logical man living! It is quite endearing."

" 'Endearing' is not a word I would apply to Sherlock Holmes or his environment," I retorted.

"No, I am sure that you would not," Irene said, leaning over to jerk at my hem.

I recoiled, both from startlement and from a sense that she had wronged me. I would not accept additional liberties from her at the moment.

"Now, Nell, I am only hitching up the side on your overskirt. We both have transformations to accomplish in this miserable little carriage and not long to do them. You do not wish to look . . . dowdy at Quentin's homecoming, do you?"

The word "dowdy" instantly drove all other considerations from my mind. Irene began unbuttoning the diagonal closing of my bodice as if I were a recalcitrant child who had to be guided through even the most elementary process.

"Irene!" was all I could say in objection to the notion of being undressed with a gentleman present.

"Hush!" she ordered. "I am merely folding back the reveres. Old rose," she told Quentin. "Quite the thing on Grosvenor Square, I assure you."

He laughed, a carefree sound I had not heard from him in a very long time, not since Berkeley Square days. "Do not apply to me for approval. I am ten years behind the times."

"Then you will have to take my word on it." Irene fluffed the folds of rose chiffon at my bodice. "As will Nell. There.

And see what I brought!" She plucked something from her carpetbag and then her fingers lunged at my throat. "Oh, do be still, Nell! I'm not trying to garrote you, merely affix this brooch."

"Oh!" My fingers went to my collar. "It's not the dreadful Tiffany squid, is it?" My fingertips traced a cool, irregular shape.

"Nell, you wound me." She shook her hair into a lavishly ungoverned mane, then twisted it up with a few flicks of her wrists and transfixed it with long pins she had grasped in her teeth. No doubt she would argue that her cigarette smoking was the ideal preparation for dressing her hair in a moving carriage. "Lish-en," she articulated fairly well through her diminishing mouthful of tortoiseshell quills as her fingers swiftly drove them one by one into place. "You must not tell Godfrey about this. He will be cross."

"I cannot abet a woman who intends to deceive her husband!"

"Goodness, Nell, most of the wives in Mayfair and Belgravia make a religion of it. I am merely following Fashion. Besides, you know how obsessed he can be on the subject of Sherlock Holmes."

"Godfrey? *Godfrey* is obsessed?"

"It was my plan," she said. "I had a right to see it accomplished, though Mr. Holmes was annoyingly coy about the exact means. Never mind, I can guess it, and if we are lucky there may be some cryptic reference in the newspapers. Now—" she opened the carpetbag, drew out a bonnet and donned it "—I am ready to leave you to your next interview. For some reason I do not have the same curiosity about the goings-on in Grosvenor Square as I do about the doings in Baker Street."

Irene leaned to the window. "Quentin, signal the coachman to stop at the next corner. I will take an omnibus back to the hotel."

I could only shake my head, my nerveless fingers still massaging the brooch at my throat.

The carriage jerked to a slower pace as soon as Quentin rapped on the ceiling. He leaned across to release the door when the vehicle stopped, and Irene darted out with the zest of a street urchin. I leaned after her.

"Wait! Irene . . ." She was grinning back at me, and then she blew me a kiss. "Irene—this brooch. Tell me that it is not the ruby star given you by the King of Bohemia—?"

"It should look very well in Grosvenor Square," she caroled back, even as she hurried away.

"But rubies . . . and old rose don't go together—"

"Rubies go with everything, like blood," came her fading answer as the carriage jerked us past all sight of her.

I shuddered as my fingers fell away from the gemstones.

"Are you cold?" Quentin inquired with a certain solicitude that would have been warming had I really been chilled.

"No. Merely outmaneuvered."

He laughed again. "Pray do not be angry with her. She must have her masquerades or she does not feel quite alive."

"Is that what spying was like?"

"I suppose so. The times of greatest danger are also those of the greatest exhilaration."

"You will miss it," I said.

He shrugged, but his eyes had a faraway look. "I will have to find something other to do, that is all. I am not sure what."

"What did you do when you were abroad after the war for so long?"

"I traveled among strange peoples, learned odd languages and odder customs." His eyes fell to the jewel at my throat. "Rumors abounded of a lost ruby mine in far northeast Afghanistan among a blue-eyed, yellow-haired people. I convinced myself that I was looking for it, that this intriguing treasure was why I stayed."

"Was it?"

He shrugged. "It was a convenient reason to stay. Going home has become frightening. There is too much to explain."

"Then do not do it all at once," I advised.

He nodded and fell silent until the carriage stopped again.

By now dusk had crept like smoky ground fog over the square, between the great houses, and curled like a sleeping black panther around the statuary in the square's central gardens.

Quentin helped me down from the carriage. The wheels rattled away behind us, drowning out the patter of my heart as we approached the ranks of windows glowing with the evening's first-lit lamps.

"Perhaps we should have warned them," I suggested.

"No." He took my arm, and I had the oddest sense that this gesture was for his support, not mine.

The black-painted double door bowed away from us at Quentin's knock, revealing the austere butler. I paused, wondering if he would recognize Quentin, but apparently he had not been in service until after Quentin's departure.

"Whom shall I announce?" this personage asked in disapproving tones, his eyes pausing respectfully on my borrowed brooch.

"Quentin Stanhope of Afghanistan and Miss Penelope Huxleigh of Paris," Quentin said, a twinge of humor in his voice.

I found my fingers curling into his coat sleeve. His hand briefly covered mine. Even through kid leather I could feel its warmth. We followed the butler across the marble-floored hall as vast as a ballroom, past a dining room where linen lay like melting snow and candles gleamed like stars. Our footsteps reverberated with the same soft patter the rain makes in autumn on fallen leaves.

We were announced at the open double doors of a drawing room, in which the family had gathered before dinner. After passing through the spreading dusk outside and the inner shadows of the hall, we crossed that threshold into a room that exploded with blinding light.

The family sat as frozen as in the Sargent portrait I had imagined, dressed for dinner, the men in regulation black and white, the women a blurred watercolor swirl of gowns and skin tones and startled blue-gray eyes.

"Uncle Quentin!" cried one vague pastel pool. Then Allegra Turnpenny was tripping across the Aubusson carpet and over the marble floors like a child on Christmas Eve. She flew at him, throwing her arms around his neck while he repeated, "Allegra? Allegra—is it you, really?"

And those calm, composed Stanhope women deserted their places in the portrait and came flowing over in clouds of silk and satin, followed at a more sedate pace by the puzzled men in evening dress.

Introductions were made, of myself, of course, of the two married sisters' husbands. Even Quentin required a formal greeting from each member of his family, as if to place them once again in his current landscape.

I watched Quentin sink into his family as one might ease onto a down-upholstered sofa, talking with first one, then another, pausing to embrace a sister who only now had overcome the strangeness of this reunion. The men, the brothers-in-law, kept circling back to him with hand pumpings and astounded looks.

Then came a pilgrimage to the upstairs domain of his elderly mother. If I had any tendency to smile after the travesty of Irene's impersonation, old Mrs. Stanhope's condition crushed it in an instant. She was a frail, silent lady in a wheeled chair attended by a capped nurse. Her memory was a gray hummock of ashes from which no phoenix would arise. While she smiled her tremulous pathetically polite pleasure at the hubbub, she clearly had no recall of her son whatsoever, and virtually none of the older siblings who cooed around him.

Sobered, we went downstairs again, the family keeping up a gay repartee as if to drown out the old woman's utter silence of voice and mind.

Dinner, needless to say, was delayed. By the time we all migrated into the long dining chamber, the butler's expression had hardened into an icily polite, harried fury.

At table Allegra quite literally took me in hand and plied

me with questions, all the while admiring her favorite uncle from afar.

"He doesn't look a bit different. Not really," she added. "Not even older."

"That is because as a child you considered every adult as ancient as Egypt."

Her giggle implied guilt, but she denied my charge with newly adult dignity. "That is not true; I have never considered you at all Egyptian, Miss Huxleigh. Or may I call you 'Nell,' as Quentin does?" she added mischievously.

"It remains to be seen whether we two will associate enough in future that such issues will require settling."

"You are not leaving London?"

"My home is in France now, near Paris."

"Near Paris, how divine!" Allegra's eyes sparkled like star sapphires, soft and fugitive with youthful illusion. "Oh, the couturiers, the courtiers, the utterly romantic French gentlemen—!"

"I see that you have not seen much of Paris."

"Oh, but I may come and visit you! Do say I may! I have never known anyone who lived in Paris."

"Near Paris," I corrected, "and you must ask Mr. and Mrs. Norton, at whose cottage I reside."

"A cottage. How picturesque. What else have you there?"

"A rather fiendish black cat named Lucifer. He is of the breed called Persian, but Quentin informs me that the animals are actually Afghan in origin. We also are endowed with a parrot I inherited from one of Godfrey's—Mr. Norton's—clients, a nasty gaudy prattlewit named, er, Casanova."

"It all sounds such fun," Allegra said wistfully with the optimism of the very young. "Not dull and stuffy and dark like London. And I think your friend Godfrey must be as charming and handsome as real Frenchmen."

I omitted pointing out that her experience of Frenchmen vied only with her experience of Paris. "Godfrey is also married."

"Oh, yes, you said so." She was young enough to sound disappointed.

"His wife is my friend Irene, who used to be my chambermate in Saffron Hill years ago."

"Saffron Hill? You really lived there? How Bohemian."

"Yes, Irene and I are devout Bohemians," I said. "We always seem to be poking around the more colorful quarters of great cities."

"You know, Miss Buxleigh," Allegra said as she leaned back in her chair to accept a bowl of exceedingly thin soup in which floated several unidentifiable objects sliced unbearably fine, "I am sure that Uncle Quentin's war stories will be quite interesting, as well as his life in the East, but I am also convinced that your adventures since we last saw you in Berkeley Square are much more enthralling."

"Such delusions apparently run in the family," I muttered as the serving man presented me with my own pallid pool of soup. The lusty bouillabaisse of Provence began to look edible in comparison. "I doubt that your uncle will speak of his war days. His work was secret and he has suffered much since then."

"Secret?" She looked down the glittering tabletop to Quentin, who was speaking with her mother. "He is always so amusing and I adored him, but I can't imagine Uncle Quentin doing anything actually important, can you?"

So much for the adoration of nieces. It required biting my tongue, which fortunately rendered sampling the soup impossible, but I refrained from telling her in detail just how exciting and vital a life her uncle had led of late.

The tall-case hall clock had rung half-past ten before we took our leave of Grosvenor Square. After dinner the gentlemen had slipped away to the study for cognac and cigars. I did not much miss the miasma of smoke such masculine pursuits engendered, but found my time in the drawing room with the ladies almost as stifling. Save for Allegra, they had little to say to a governess turned acquaintance of the family Lost Sheep. I had even less to say to them. The London scandals and sensations that struck them as cataclysmic seemed trivial matters indeed compared to the international plots and attempted assassinations of the past few days. As I listened, I realized that Quentin had been right. However low-born and obscure, I led a more adventuresome life than most women.

Once again Allegra escorted me and a gentleman out, but on this occasion she hung upon her uncle and myself a trifle desperately.

"Please do come again to call, Miss Huxleigh," she begged, "or at least invite me to Paris. And Uncle Quentin, say that I shall be seeing more of you. I have missed you dreadfully!"

He sighed and gently untangled her arm from his. "It seems like yesterday, dear Allegra. I was the youngest of my family. Miss Huxleigh can tell you how deeply I was impressed by you and your schoolroom friends when I was . . . mislaid in Afghanistan. It was for you I fought, the new and vibrant generation. I am delighted to see what a charming and lively young lady you have become. Whatever you do, never surrender your spirit."

She clung to his arm as if afraid of losing him to another decade-long exile. He patted her hand and kissed her cheek and finally extricated himself.

Mrs. Turnpenny had offered the Stanhope family carriage for our return to the hotel in the Strand, but Quentin had expressed a polite wish to stroll into the square before seeking a hansom.

"I hope you do not mind, Nell," he commented after we had traversed the walkway to the square.

I had indeed been anticipating a ride in the family's undoubtedly first-rate carriage after a lifetime spent on public transportation, but I said only, "It has been a busy day."

"Busy indeed," he answered. "My head is spinning."

"No doubt that is the cognac."

He laughed and led me down one of the diagonal walks crisscrossing the square's central garden. It was quite dark, yet the gaslights circling the square, if such a contradiction is possible, glowed like multiple moons in the misty distance.

"Ah, smell that cool, London summer air, Nell. It was growing close inside."

"Was it?"

He paused to take my gloved hand. "I wonder if you know what you have escaped, what you would have been like after ten years more in a household like that."

There seemed no answer to such a question, to such a mood. Certainly I recognized that this reunion had been a crucial one for Quentin and that his emotions must be at a high pitch. Yet I had been privileged to witness him encompassed by his own kind, and to see how separate I stood from that kind, as did my friends, Irene and Godfrey, however gloriously they improvised their lives.

## Chapter Thirty-Three

# FALLEN ANGELS

"**Will we** find a hansom?" I asked timidly after we had been walking for some few minutes. While I applauded Quentin's optimism, I was certain that no cabs could be had at this late hour.

He laughed again. "Hansoms hover about the squares looking for fares. They like such fares even better when they are tipsy, for the tips will match the condition of the riders."

"We are not tipsy."

"No." He sounded sorry.

Yet once we had crossed the square we heard the crisp clop of a single horse's hooves. They seemed to be pacing us.

"It could be a resident carriage," I suggested.

"Resident carriages invariably sport at least two steeds. That is a hansom."

"You are right."

Yet there was something ominous about that invisible equipage gaining on us in the cool mist of a midsummer evening, about the tick-tock rhythm of the unseen horse's hooves. It seemed ordinary life was bearing down upon us both after a sojourn in fairyland. It seemed the past was winding closer on its steady orbit toward the future. It seemed a time had ended, and with it an understanding between ourselves that was unsaid and would ever be so.

"You see!" Quentin announced as the vehicle came into view. "A cab. Soon we will be regaling Irene with the details of our outing."

"You believe that she will wait up for us?"

"Can you doubt it?" Quentin nodded to the cabman at the back of the shiny black vehicle that loomed from the darkness, its twin lamps shining like beast eyes at midnight.

"The Strand," he called up to the driver, who in his top hat and muffler seemed a Christmas pantomime figure rather than a humble London cabbie.

Quentin helped me inside, his hand resting for a moment on my waist. How intimate a hansom cab is at night! One sits side by side with another, bound for a common destination. The way was unexpectedly deserted, so alone we seemed to be journeying. I reflected that Irene and Godfrey and I would leave Quentin behind, as he and I should leave this vehicle behind once our goal was reached. Quentin had come home at last.

"You do not have any family," he said of a sudden.

"No." I was surprised. I had not thought of it that way, but it was true. "Father was a widower who died more than a decade ago. I had no siblings, no known cousins. Except for—"

"Irene and Godfrey. They do not have much family either."

"No, you are right. Godfrey's mother died long ago, and he is estranged from his brothers. He despised his late father, rightfully so. As for Irene, who knows?"

"It is apt that Irene sprang unaccoutred, like Athena, the goddess of wisdom, from her father Zeus's forehead. She invents herself and does not require antecedents."

"I am sure," I said, "that Irene would have given any father a gruesome headache. She has done sufficiently well with me, and I am not even related. You are fortunate to have found your kin again."

"Am I? Forgive me, but I feel crowded among them. I have lived among . . . clans, tribes, in which there were more individuals and more individual freedom. They all expect something of me."

"I thought you would . . . rejoin them, live with them. What else does one do with a family?"

"Fight them, escape them." Amusement salted his voice. "Explain to them."

"If civilization wears upon you, you are welcome to visit us in Neuilly again. And bring Allegra as well. She seems in need of a change. I am certain that Irene can provide something provocative in that area."

"I do not doubt it!" He was silent, the dreary beat of the horse's hooves marking time to his discontent, to the exhausted evening.

"Is something wrong?" I asked finally. I am ever blunt.

"Only that I expected my returning home to answer questions instead of pose them."

"Do you mean that you will not . . . rejoin your family, and resume your place in society?"

"What is that 'place'?" he asked, his voice bitter. "What is 'society'? I do not 'fit' any longer. I do not recognize my own, and they do not recognize me."

"You must allow some time."

"Perhaps I will return to France."

My heart leaped up, as if a poor dray horse had leaped ahead when its only lot was to plod.

"France?"

"And then—"

He said no more, for the horse suddenly did hasten under the quick flick of a whip. Our hansom was spinning faster along the dark thoroughfare. Quentin was leaning against his window, his face brushed with the yellow rays of the sidelight and his hair riffled by the increased wind. We lurched to our left.

"We must have been traveling South Audley Street," Quentin murmured. "Why would we go left, then? Ah, I remember now. We must make a jog and go down Hamilton

Place before we arrive at Hyde Park corner and proceed east up Piccadilly."

"Oh, then that is the park." It unfolded rapidly on my side of the street, a blot of darkness lit by such distant gaslights that they winked like tiny stars.

"We are at Stanhope Gate," Quentin pointed out with amusement, his features catching the glimmer of a passing gaslight.

A whip snapped in the darkness and our cab veered abruptly right.

"Quentin!" I exclaimed as the sudden turn tossed me against his side.

Moments later we were rattling under that so aptly named keystone into Hyde Park itself, into the deep velvet darkness.

He had caught me firmly and did not let go, and well it was, for the poor horse had been whipped to a frightful pace. Its hooves tattooed a rapid clickety-click like a railroad car as we shot straight ahead at the heart of darkness, the wind raking into our faces.

My heart played a staccato tune, not helped at all by Quentin's unflagging grip upon my person; totally necessary, of course, given the wild progress of our vehicle.

Suddenly we veered right again, the cruel snap of the whip answered by the hooves' frantic speed. I was struck with a flare of fury at our driver for abusing the poor beast so. Quentin's gloved hand tightened on my shoulder.

"He is taking us along the Serpentine!" he said. "This is not the way to the Strand, but its opposite."

Our speed had pressed me against Quentin, and his window was now my window. I saw the water, glimmering like buoyant diamonds in the vague light. We lurched left again. I was slammed against my own side of the hansom, Quentin pressing me close to the tufted upholstery.

"This is mad," said he, rising in his seat to rap frantically on the ceiling. "Stop it, man! Stop this race at once! You are going in the wrong direction."

The water on our left flickered like dying embers as we

careened past, then winked out. For a moment we rode in total darkness, silent and bewildered. Then the hansom tilted violently left again. Quentin and I were again tossed like dice in a box against my side of the hansom.

I glimpsed an ironic address in the fleeting light of a corner gaslight: Stanhope Terrace.

"Bayswater Road," Quentin gasped, straining to see. "We are bound west from London. What deviltry is this—?"

Gaslights sped by, precious smudges of light in an onrushing blackness. The hansom's sidelights illuminated only our own worried faces washed in a harsh yellow glare resembling a Paris painter's impression of a bistro.

I had no doubt been bruised by the jostling, but felt nothing but a sense of wild, untrammeled danger. Quentin was wrenching the mechanism that opened our half-door.

"It is damned difficult—or stuck somehow," he said.

His language did not shock me, only the bouncing of the well-tried springs, the pounding of the runaway horse.

"The driver must be mad," he said again.

"Or stricken," said I, thinking of Jefferson Hope.

"Dead," Quentin speculated with a grim look at me. "Stay here," he ordered.

Where did he think I would go?

He leaned back in his seat and kicked both feet at the half-door. It remained shut.

"I'm going atop," he shouted, turning to face me, then sitting on the half-door while gripping the top of the hansom, thus riding backwards in the streaming wind.

I nodded then, assurance being all I could offer, and clung to the seat with one hand.

Slowly, Quentin vanished above as if being devoured by a rather dilatory dragon. It was awful to watch: first his head and shoulders rising out of sight, then his trunk and finally his legs.

I cast an anxious glance out the window. Our speed made observation nearly impossible, but I saw warm tavern lights wink by and the occasional wagon. We rattled through terra

incognita now. My poor mind could not even conjure what
lay beyond this outskirt of London besides utter dark and
empty wilderness.

We climbed a hill. We passed under another, more ancient
gateway than the one named Stanhope near the corner of
Hyde Park. We were far from such civilized venues now,
hurtling into nothingness.

Thumps above indicated Quentin's presence. Still our
horse's wild race continued. I was tossed from window to
window and saw nothing I recognized, saw nothing, in fact.

Ahead unwound a tunnel of darkness, and then within it,
an arrow of tiny lights, gaslights beaming through heavy mist
under a boiling charcoal sky lit by a suddenly revealed full
moon. I saw towers. Soaring, churchlike towers. And flying
buttresses. A bit Romanish for my taste, but any port in a
storm of this proportion.

The thumping aloft doubled, and redoubled. I could hear
reins slapping, and the horse screamed like a woman. Then
the hansom veered and jolted over some obstacle, creaked,
swayed, stopped. . . .

I swayed with it, clutching at anything and finding only the
fastened half-door, which never gave.

Rudely tossed and turned, beaten and bruised, I finally sat
still in my seat. My bonnet had fallen onto one ear. I could
hear the horse gasping like a giant bellows.

For I moment I did not move; then I struggled upright.
There was no other course but to climb over the half-door as
Quentin had done. I did so, my skirts catching on the impediment. I tugged and they would not loosen, so I tugged again
until I heard the rip of cloth. Then I clambered over until I
was snagged again, and further ripped my dressmaking.

At last I desisted. I was hopelessly snagged, but at least I
could see ahead. Then I regretted even that. My place of
sanctuary, my "church," was no refuge. The twin towers that
drew me repeated into the distance, mere architectural decoration on the supports of a bridge. The flying buttresses were
the bridge's spans, upheld by wrought-iron bars.

Gaslights lit the way across, reflecting on the night-damp paving stones. On either side a body of water, so broad that it must be the Thames, shimmered like Irene's most lavishly bejeweled black velvet evening gown, reflecting the sad, drowned face of the moon.

Quentin stood beside the stalled vehicle, his top hat fallen away. The driver had dismounted, too: a bulky silhouette blocking the river's glitter, he still wore his battered top hat. The long pointed line of his whip seemed to pierce the churning gray clouds.

Quentin glanced back to assure himself of my survival. Then he spoke to the driver. "You are quite, quite mad."

A voice spoke that I thrilled to recognize. "No, only damned inconvenient to those who thwart me."

"You are a long way from the jungles of India, Tiger," Quentin said in a tight, careful voice.

"And you are far from the forbidding steppes of Afghanistan, Cobra," Colonel Sebastian Moran answered with a guttural laugh quite awful to hear. "They are hunting old Tiger because of you. You took that damned paper nigh ten years ago, and now they have hung me with it. I told you then and I tell you again that it is not profitable to meddle with a tiger."

"Let the lady go."

"You let her go, if you survive to do so."

They spoke of me, but I was miles removed from their calculations. I was a distant pawn upon a board that had broadened to encompass two continents and ten years. I could do nothing but watch.

"What will revenge gain you?" Quentin asked, moving carefully away from the hansom.

"Satisfaction," Tiger articulated so precisely that he hissed like a great cat, or a snake.

"Small meat for one used to triumph."

"It was that meddling detective! Did the fool think that I would not see his hand in this—and yours?"

"And mine," Quentin agreed calmly, "no thanks to your efforts."

"I sent a snake to catch a snake. Pity it didn't work."

"Your emissary killed on one occasion, but not me."

"A greater pity."

"Will you shoot me?" Quentin asked coolly.

"I would not waste a bullet on such poor game," Tiger snarled.

Those words acted as a signal, for then Quentin knew that a pistol was not pointed at him. He leaped—one shadow pouncing on another. Tiger and Cobra, snake and mongoose, Moran and Stanhope. These words were symbols of the elemental battle unfolding; even I knew that, even as I knew I was powerless to prevent or alter one bit of it. Oh, for Irene's wicked little revolver! Oh, for Irene, or Godfrey!

Tiger's long agile whip lofted against the boiling sky like black lightning. It cracked and then struck Quentin. I recoiled, but he did not. He advanced on Tiger, shadow stalking shadow until the spitting whip was too close to snarl, a scuffle, and then it rose . . . in Quentin's hand.

He advanced like a madman himself, cracking the whip until the poor stalled horse trembled in its traces, wielding the lash with a demonic energy that drove the figure of Tiger back against one looming gatepost of the bridge.

Tiger leaped onto the stone dais some four feet up and crouched at the foot of a leafy stone scroll as high as a man. The whip danced in the air beside him until he scrambled up the carved scrolls to the next level.

"This is the way to train a cat," Quentin announced, himself a shadow that leaped lithely atop the first level.

And so they progressed, ever upward on that strange manmade mountain. Perhaps the gatepost was not so very high. It seemed Mount Everest to me, and both men like quarreling fallen angels contending against a murky, ill-lit sky.

The gatepost ended in a three-pronged bloom of ironwork across the way, etched against the cauldron of the sky. I watched them labor upward in their common enterprise of individual destruction.

My heart had long since left my body for my throat. I was

aware of nothing but the contention so near and yet so far. Around them the thin sinuous line of the whip wove like a script. Quentin wielded it, for emphasis rather than defense. It was as if he would drive Tiger back to Afghanistan, back to the past to undo the waste of Maiwand, undo the deaths of countless men. He seemed to me at that moment an avenging angel, a Michael to a Lucifer. One must fall, I knew that. Yet, for all my worry, it was a thrilling scene.

And then one figure leaped suddenly down a notch on the face of the gatepost. The whip lashed out one final time— upon the tried horse's haunches—as Quentin cast it away.

"Go!" Quentin shouted.

Whether he addressed me or the horse did not matter. The poor beast sprung forward as if released from the gates of hell.

"Go, dearest Nell!" I heard these extraordinary words end as if choked off. Still standing at the half-door like a chari- oteer, I looked back to see the figure of Tiger leap down on Quentin's silhouette. They struggled just beneath the gate- post's crest. For a moment both men teetered under the im- pact of their clash and then . . . and then they fell. Against the ghastly, moonlit clouds above the silver river, their sil- houettes hung larger than life, the fleeting moments of their plunge stretched into a dreadful, false eternity.

I saw them both: together yet separate, falling . . . oh, falling. By some divine blessing, in those horrific seconds the lovely lines of Lucifer's fall from Milton's *Paradise Lost* flared into my brain like a burning brand even as I watched:

> From morn to noon he fell, from noon to dewy eve,
> A summer's day; and with the setting sun
> Dropp'd from the zenith like a falling star.

I had memorized those lines at my father's school table, as well as the sad plaint from Isaiah: "How art thou fallen from heaven, o Lucifer, son of the morning?"

Two men fell, my becalmed heart accompanying only one. Then I recalled that "Lucifer" meant light, despite the name's dark associations, and thought it bitter irony that one man's light must die in order to snuff out another's darkness.

At the last, I briefly saw them diminished, as birds or bats against the lowering clouds at the horizon. Then they plunged together into the glittering moonlit maw of the Thames and the black waters below.

My driverless hansom cab bolted on, its impetus pushing me back into the seat. I do not believe that I screamed; the situation was beyond such trivial measures. The hansom rattled across the empty bridge, spans and bars and proud towers flashing past me. . . . I heard nothing and saw very little.

I returned to the hotel in the Strand at two the following morning. A kindly fruit vendor bound for Covent Garden had come upon my vehicle and taken charge of both the winded horse and myself. Godfrey was in the lobby waiting. I managed to stammer out some version of the events before he whisked me to the Norton suite and plied me with brandy. They both had been mad with worry at our long absence and Irene, he said, was out interrogating cab drivers. I never asked in what guise she undertook this assignment. I barely remember her coming in, though someone bundled me into bed, for that is where I awoke the next day.

When we three met again in the morning, I related the circumstances more coherently. My friends instantly realized that any action was useless, that both men had plunged together into the swift current, and perished.

That afternoon we traced the route in a four-wheeler until we came to what proved to be the Hammersmith Bridge. By day the impressive architecture seemed puny. I seemed to observe it from a distant point, like the invisible moon. A drive along the river revealed nothing but gray water. Irene and Godfrey were indefatigable for the next few days, but their inquiries uncovered nothing. New Scotland Yard reclaimed no bodies from the Thames that day or in the next five. The visit we three made later to Grosvenor Square drains through my mind like muddy tea to this day. I remember that

Allegra wore black and did not ask to visit Paris. I seemed to have contracted the amnesia that follows brain fever.

We prepared to return to Paris. Irene packed. I do not know what she did with Quentin's new clothing.

Shortly before we left, Godfrey came out of the bedchamber that had been Quentin's.

"I have been seeing to it," he told me, "but I don't know what to do with it now."

"I beg your pardon?"

"The mongoose."

"Oh." I had forgotten about it.

"Should I . . . dispose of it here?"

"How exactly do you propose to . . . dispose of it?"

"Perhaps there are rare-pet dealers."

"It is a bit late to think of that," I reminded him.

"We could take it on the boat-train to Calais."

"Would they allow it?"

"Would they dare *not* allow it if Irene insisted?"

"Messalina is as untidy as Casanova and as predatory as Lucifer."

"Undoubtedly."

"Most inconvenient."

"I cannot argue with you."

"We will take it."

And so we went.

On the Channel passage, I was standing by the rail watching the white cliffs of Dover pale to vague clouds on the horizon, when someone came to stand beside me.

It was Irene, the wind blowing her veiling back. Her face was as sober as I have ever seen it.

"We have miscalculated dreadfully, Nell," she said. We had not spoken privately since the morning after the awful night on the Hammersmith Bridge Road.

"How have we miscalculated?"

"Not you and I. He and I."

"He?"

"Sherlock Holmes and I."

"I did not know that you were in partnership."

"We were, unknowingly, and we both failed horribly. Neither of us guessed that Colonel Sebastian Moran would be so ferocious when cornered. Neither of us anticipated that he would strike out at the one who first foiled him in Afghanistan. We were . . . too prideful. We each pictured ourselves contending with the Tiger. We did not see that his oldest enemy was most likely to be his target once we had frustrated him."

"Is Mr. Holmes as remorseful as you?"

She smiled wanly. "He is unaware of this tragic outcome. He did not even know Quentin's true name."

"Quentin is dead," I said, as I had not before.

"It seems so."

"And Tiger as well."

"Likely."

I looked at her directly for the first time in days. "Do you truly believe it so?"

She paused, then brushed the veiling back from her face as if it were hair. "I will not if you do not."

I lifted my chin to the sea breeze. It was salty and raw and I did not care for it. "Then I have not decided yet."

## Chapter Thirty-Four

# THE CARDBOARD BOX

**One thing** can be said for French skies: they are more frequently blue than English ones.

Unfortunately, an abundant animal life wishes to share in this natural bounty, so the garden at Neuilly that August hummed with cricket song while birds darted down for seeds among the beds of fading roses.

I had persuaded André to move Casanova's cage outside for the afternoon, and sat in the shade of a plane tree, where I could keep an eye on both the bird and the mongoose. Lucifer was no difficulty; since I was doing some stitchery, he was at my feet alternately unraveling a ball of crochet string and snagging my petticoats.

Messalina had adapted well to country life. At least she waxed fat and sleek and had proved a tireless guardian of the garden, retreating to her cage near the kitchen door only now and again.

A mongoose, I had decided, fell between a cat and a parrot as a pet: Messy was far cleverer than Lucifer, less lazy, yet even more independent than Casanova. If she mourned her master, I was not expert enough in mongoose manners to detect any sign.

That August was quiet to the point of stagnation. Most Parisians fled the city during the last blast of summer heat.

The country hummed and chirped in tuneless monotony, and nothing disturbed the sunlight or the breeze or the endless days and long, light-bathed evenings in which the setting sun seemed reluctant to depart.

"And, Nell, what are you doing today?" Godfrey asked as he strolled up the flagstones toward me.

"What I did yesterday: fancy work."

"That seems fancier than usual."

I glanced at my project. "It is a pillow cover for Messy, composed of a new stitch—French knots. Being French, they are needlessly intricate and time-consuming, but the result is bright and flamboyant."

"So I see. I am sure that the mongoose will appreciate it."

I let my handiwork rest in my lap. "Truly, Godfrey, we cannot know whether a mongoose even appreciates a mouse for lunch. I am merely occupying time."

He sat beside me on the stone bench. "I never told you what Irene and I discovered during the days before we left London." I regarded him with a blank gaze. He added, "After the . . . bridge incident."

"Was there anything to do beyond comb the riverbanks?"

Godfrey laced his hands and kept his eyes on them. He seemed ill at ease, as everyone had seemed with me since what Godfrey called 'the incident' at Hammersmith Bridge—everyone except the animals, who were as obnoxious as usual and quite a relief.

"I—I kept an eye on Moran's club, in case he had survived and should return, secretly or otherwise."

"Did you really? I had no idea, Godfrey."

He looked rather sheepish. "Irene insisted on it. She will never give up."

"I know." My sigh drifted into the lazy air. "She is too hopeful for her own good."

"At any rate," he said with forced enthusiasm, "Moran never came back, so I finally represented myself as an interested barrister and gained admittance to the chamber he kept there. I also learned of a fearsome dustup at the club the day before Moran left, never to return. It seems a tall, thin gentlemen came to see Moran on some private matter and nearly bullwhipped the colonel from the premises. You can guess, of course, who the high-tempered visitor was," Godfrey added archly.

"No, Godfrey, I cannot." He regarded me with disbelief. "I have not much had my mind on past events. It seems . . . better."

"Well, that gentleman certainly was Sherlock Holmes himself. I had no idea he was such a Tartar."

"I am not surprised," I said, thinking of the glimpses that Dr. Watson's clumsy scribblings had offered of Mr. Sherlock Holmes's temperament and habits. A cold and precise personality was exactly the sort to explode with self-indulgent emotion, especially if he had been drugging himself with cocaine.

Godfrey sat back, then began again. "Perhaps you would be more fascinated by what I found in Moran's abandoned chamber, which even Mr. Holmes has not likely penetrated."

"Perhaps." I finished a knot and broke it from the skein with my teeth, a technique that disconcerted Godfrey, but I am a practical woman, and I had not invited spectators to my homely pastimes.

"Dr. Watson's service and medical records," Godfrey said with a pride that reminded me of Lucifer presenting me with a dead field mouse.

I paused. "Then Quentin was correct in guessing that Tiger had taken them in India."

"Yes, but the contents were most . . . puzzling. The papers record all that we know—Watson's wounding at Maiwand and the fever that followed, his orderly Murray rescuing him, his stay in Kandahar, his transportation by pack train to the railway at Sinjini and hence to Peshawar—"

"Godfrey, at the moment I am not up to a geographical tour of Indian frontier settlements." I still could not bring myself to more than glance at my sole remembrance of Quentin: the disreputable Montmartre portrait Irene had bought.

"I am sorry, Nell," he said so meekly that I immediately regretted my petulance. "Yet I found an astounding fact among the papers: an account of a cobra that had gotten into a patient's cot at Peshawar. The snake was found before it could strike, but an overzealous guard drew his sword to kill the creature—and accidentally stabbed the patient in the leg."

I did pause in my French knotting at that juncture. "Dr. Watson? Wounded again?"

Godfrey nodded. "Is that not odd? He was still incoherent with fever at the time, and likely did not even recall it, but I should say that our old friend Tiger was having another lethal go at the much-tried doctor. It certainly proves that Colonel Moran had resorted to cobras before."

"Imagine being stabbed in the leg by a clumsy defender!" I shuddered despite the warm day. "At least we have managed to protect Dr. Watson."

"Assuredly," he told me quickly.

"So Quentin achieved what he wished," I mused, setting down my work and staring into the distant poplars shivering silver in the breeze.

"Yes, he did. He saved another man's life—perhaps many more—by ridding the world of a predator like Moran."

I regarded Godfrey. "No doubt that thought is supposed to be comforting, but I do not find it so."

"My dear Nell," Godfrey began, reaching for my hand at a moment that was edging perilously close to treacle. . . .

The wooden kitchen door banged shut, a sound that turned us both like vigilant watchdogs. Only Irene was impetuous enough to leave the cottage in such a loudly advertised manner.

She came quickly toward us, walking on the flagstones only when their artfully meandering path crossed her direct one. "Look at what has come! The post."

I understood her excitement. As exiles from our own land and strangers in France, we seldom received mail, except the overscented invitations of that Bernhardt woman. Irene in the presence of an unopened missive was like a child handed a surprise present: curious, excited and greedy all at once.

"Look." She sat between us, her buoyant mood altering our more somber one by mere proximity. "From Grosvenor Square for you, Nell! If it is from that delightful child Allegra, tell her, yes, of course, she must visit. It would do us all good."

"You mean me," I said, struggling to slit the heavy parchment paper with my only implement at hand, a crochet hook. Naturally Irene had not thought to bring a letter opener with her.

"I mean us all," she iterated. "Nell, we too are devastated by the loss of . . . of one who meant a great deal to us all. Well, is it from Allegra? Does she want to come?"

"No." My eyes could hardly read the script, despite my pince-nez. I removed the spectacles the better to see through a glaze of sudden tears. "It is from Mrs. Turnpenny. Mrs. Stanhope has died."

Silence held for a few moments, while Casanova juggled consonants and vowels in his cage, mingling phrases and producing a model for Mr. Carroll's jabberwocky.

Irene's hand closed around mine. "I am so dreadfully sorry, Nell. I had hoped for better news." She patted my hand as her voice reached a more cheerful, albeit forced, tone. "But see, this package is for you as well. You must open it."

I held it on my lap as if it contained a cobra. "There is no law that I must."

"If you will not, I will!" She reached for it.

"It is addressed to me."

"Then open it!"

"I do not recognize the hand," I said, "and even without my spectacles, I can tell that the paper and string employed are quite coarse and common, even cheap."

Irene sighed dramatically. "Heavens to Hecuba! You are not Sherlock Holmes, Nell. It is a simple package. You will not know what it contains, or who sent it, until you open it.

Perhaps it is a present from Allegra. She seemed quite taken with you."

I finally found my curved little embroidery scissors. Irene watched stormily while I methodically cut the string and carefully unfolded the brown paper wrapping back from what appeared to be . . . "a cardboard box," I said in disappointment. I had spent enough time in Irene's vicinity to know that nothing very valuable ever came in a hard-paper box.

Even the ever-optimistic Irene drew back. Godfrey was frowning behind her, wearing a look that said that Cruel Circumstance must not deal me another blow or he would know the reason why. . . . Dear Godfrey and Irene, they were so helpless in the face of real adversity.

Then I opened the box. A trinket shone there, a small gold brooch.

"Nell." Irene's voice sounded very strange. "I believe that you had better don your pince-nez to examine this very . . . rare . . . gift."

I put my fingers to the hollows impressed on the bridge of my nose; one notices the price of modern aids only when one ceases using them. Then I snapped the spectacles onto my face again and lifted up the box and its contents.

I would have dropped it had Irene's hands not been fanned beneath mine, ready for just such an event.

"Irene! Godfrey! It is Quentin's medal."

"Yessss," Irene hissed under her breath, her glowing eyes resting on it with a nameless emotion. "Is there a message?"

I turned over the medal, and moved the cotton fabric upon which it rested. "Nothing. Who has sent it?"

Irene was already scrambling for the wrapping paper, which had slipped off my lap in the excitement. "How provident that you were so agonizingly cautious about opening the parcel, Nell. Ah! As I feared. It has been posted from Marseilles."

"What is wrong with being posted from Marseilles?" Godfrey inquired.

"Only that it is a port city," she retorted. "The person who sent this could be on his way . . . anywhere."

"The person?" I asked.

"Oh, Nell, do you not see? It must have been Quentin!"

I stared again at the humble package in my lap, at the bright bit of brass, as he had named it, and shook my head. "There must be another explanation. You found no trace of him in London. Perhaps this was recovered at his lodgings and—"

"And the landlady immediately knew to mail it to you at Neuilly. Besides, I believe that he kept it upon his person after I returned it to him. There was no medal among his effects. Nell, do not be such a dedicated dolt! Of course Quentin sent it. Who else knew where we lived?"

"Irene," Godfrey began in a warning tone, putting his hands on her shoulders.

"Of course it is Quentin," she repeated to me, her beautiful face even lovelier, abrim with the hope she meant to give me. "There is no other answer."

"Irene," Godfrey said, turning her to face him. "There is another."

She stared at him for a confused moment, she who so delighted in outthinking everyone, who was so adept at it unless concern for another clouded her judgement. "Who else would care to send Nell—us—a message that he still lived?" she demanded.

I looked gratefully at Godfrey for sparing me unfounded hope. "Colonel Sebastian Moran might, Irene," I said. "He might wish to tell us that *he* still lived and that Quentin did not."

Irene twisted back to face me. "Oh, no . . . Nell. No." She sighed as Godfrey released her, and cruel inescapable reason returned. "Yes, Colonel Moran, if he survived, could have. He could have wrested the medal from Quentin's . . . form. He did know we lived at Neuilly since he shot at Quentin here, but he is not the kind of man to tease his game in such a way. His message would come on a bullet, or the fang of a serpent."

"Perhaps it already did—" I nodded to Messy's lean brown form; the mongoose was pattering along the flagstones making for her cage "—and was stopped."

Godfrey spoke suddenly. "I congratulate you, Nell, on your gruesome turn of mind. You outdo Irene. But in this case I think Mrs. Norton is right, however overhasty she may have been. Moran would go for Holmes, not us. We are incidental to his downfall, at least as far as he knows."

"Perhaps," I said.

Irene lifted the box. "Quentin left the medal here before, only I returned it. I thought then that he sought to elude his past, and the glory due him. I was wrong. Quentin left the medal for you even then. Now he has survived this duel with Moran and sends the medal to announce his triumph, and to acknowledge yours."

"Which is?" I demanded incredulously.

"You are an admirably adventuresome woman, Miss Huxleigh." Irene pinned the token to my shirtwaist below my left shoulder. "If not for you, Quentin Stanhope would have never gone home and Dr. Watson would be dead."

"Then why has he not come himself?" I had not meant the words to blunder out in such a childishly distraught way.

Godfrey lent the matter its final fillip. "Perhaps Colonel Moran survived the contest, too. Perhaps Quentin dares not show himself, not with a man of Moran's mettle on his trail."

"Then he is an exile again, after all that has happened! Why must everyone I know be presumed dead? Except that . . . that miserable Sherlock Holmes?!"

Irene's expression grew bittersweet. "But Quentin is alive, my dear! Surely that is better than the alternative."

"And we shall never know for certain what transpired?" I asked.

They were silent. Finally Irene spoke. "At least you know that he is alive."

I remembered what I had said to Godfrey on our way to England. I caught his concerned gray eyes and smiled ever so wanly. "I have concluded before that knowing is better than not knowing."

Irene leaned back against Godfrey's shoulder, her half-shut eyes sharpening in sudden speculation. "And even better is knowing of ways to find out. . . . Another tantalizing question arises: Do you think that in future Mr. Sherlock Holmes should be on the watch for cobras?"

# A BRIEF AFTERWORD

**The foregoing** selections from the Penelope Huxleigh diaries and newfound Watsonian fragments in my possession shed welcome new light on two areas dear to minutiae hunters in the so-called Holmes canon: Dr. Watson's vacillating wound and the hitherto unknown history of the man Holmes would later call "the second most dangerous man in London," Colonel Sebastian Moran.

Sherlockians have long debated the whys and wherefores of Watson's injuries at Maiwand. The author of these tales (i.e., John H. Watson himself) first mentions a shoulder wound and later refers to a leg wound, with no explanation of how the second occurred, if it actually did.

We can now see plainly in these additional Watsonian fragments and the new Huxleigh material that the good doctor was wounded unawares in the second instance, and was naturally sensitive to admitting to his loss of memory in Afghanistan, especially in the presence of his prescient detective friend. No wonder his accounts are inconsistent; he never made peace with this situation, or fully understood that both wounds were attempts on his life, made not in the heat of battle but through the cold-blooded designs of a murderous spy.

As for the revelations of the history of Watson's attacker,

the spy "Tiger" who is revealed to be Colonel Sebastian Moran, anyone acquainted with the Sherlockian canon must heave a sigh of comprehension. Diplomatic considerations compelled Watson to delay recounting what he called *The Adventure of the Naval Treaty*; the same reasons forced him to suppress all mention of the first encounter between Holmes and Moran, that was to bear such bitter, better-known fruits in latter escapades of Holmes that Watson was free to relate. These newly narrated events clearly show how Moran lost his credibility as a spy, thanks to the efforts of Sherlock Holmes and Irene Adler acting in unknowing (on Holmes's part) concert. His livelihood cut out from under him, Moran was forced to enlist his nefarious but formidable talents in the service of Sherlock Holmes's archenemy, Professor James Moriarty. Of that association came only grave ill, with which every dedicated reader of the Watsonian canon will be familiar.

As for the Nortons and their chronicler, further probes of the Huxleigh diaries will indicate whether the events in this narrative had equally severe repercussions on their lives.

Fiona Witherspoon, Ph.D., F.I.A.*
November 25, 1991

*Friends of Irene Adler

If you enjoy the Irene Adler series
then you should meet—

# *Midnight Louie*

in Carole Nelson Douglas's

# *Catnap*

(0-812-51682-6)

the first book
in the

---

## *Midnight Louie mystery*

---

series, available from Forge Books
February 2007.

## Prologue

# Midnight Louie, P.I.

I have a nose for news and pause at nothing. That is why I always find the body.

This time it is one dead dude tucked at the back of one among three thousand booths cramming the half-million-square-foot East Exhibition Hall of the Las Vegas Convention Center.

As usual, my presence on the scene—not to mention my proximity to the corpse—puts me in a delicate position. For one thing, my unappetizing discovery is made in the wee hours of morning. Security with a capital *s* is blissfully unaware of my presence among the aisles of merchandise on display, which is the way I like it.

Now Las Vegas is a twenty-four-hour town and I am a twenty-four-hour kind of guy. That is why they call me Midnight Louie.

It is in my veins, Vegas. I know every back alley and

every gawdy-awful overelectrified Strip sign. Vegas is people on the take, people on the make, people just out to have a good time—to win a little, maybe lose a lot. There are times I might be wiser to skip town (I am no angel), but I stay and even try to go straight.

But it does not pay to know too much in this town, not that the tourists ever suspect half the stuff that goes on. Naw, to them Las Vegas is just a three-day round-trip junket of blackjack, singing slot machines and free drinks with more paper umbrellas than booze in 'em.

Some say that Las Vegas is no longer the hotsy-totsy town that it was back when Bugsy Siegel hung out the first resort hotel-casino sign in the forties. Some even say that a certain Family has loosed its hairy-knuckled grasp on the profits from gambling, girls, and anything that gives the folks any illicit fun, including substances of a pharmaceutical nature. (Drugs are not my vice of choice, let me make clear, though I do take a wee nip now and then.)

Still, it does not behoove a retiring soul like myself to admit to knowing too much. My habits are quiet, my profile low and, while I have a certain rep in this town, it is among a choice acquaintanceship, most of whom are like-minded about discretion always being the better part of discovering dead bodies.

Death broadcasts an unmistakable whiff. No lurid pools of blood need apply to advertise the fact. All five senses recoil from lifelessness, whether in the remains of a mouse or a man. I never met a corpse I liked, but the feeling would be mutual, I suspect. In a philosophical moment, I muse on how the late, possibly lamented (nothing is a sure thing in this town), would view being discovered by the likes of myself, for the fact is that among some circles I am known as something of a rambler, if not a gambler.

So I stand over the *corpus delicti* in *flagrante delicto* and consider the fragile nature of life and death in Las Vegas and my propensity for scenting the scene of the crime. It is dark except for the fluorescent glow of distant security lights, but I see well enough to observe no visible signs of violence on the body—no guarantee of natural causes, not even in this town, which can cause fatal shocks to the pocketbook, if not the system.

I picture explaining my presence to the local constabulary, a ludicrous scene for the simple reason that I always keep my lips buttoned tighter than a flasher's London Fog when he finds himself in custody. Midnight Louie does not talk—ever. I have my ways of getting the word out, however, and I review options. I am not one to pussyfoot around a problem.

First and most important, the Las Vegas Convention Center is far from my normal purview. How I got here is like this: I am undercover house detective at the Crystal Phoenix, the classiest little hotel and casino to flash its name in neon on the Strip. This is a tasteful, if not tasty, sign with a mythical beast of an avian nature exploding its pinfeathers in blue-and-magenta neon with a dash of emerald green; in other words, a first cousin to the NBC peacock, another mythical beast of more recent manufacture.

Some around town find it unusual that a dude with my, shall we say, pinstriped, if not actually checkered, past would snag a responsible job like unofficial house detective. I owe it to the Crystal Phoenix's founder, Nicky Fontana, a sweetheart of a guy and the only one in his large Family to go as straight as the Las Vegas Strip itself.

Nicky inherited eight million in legitimate dough from his grandma's pasta factory in Venice (California, that is). So he throws this considerable yeast into remodeling an abandoned hotel into a showpiece of what Vegas could be if the whole town had the taste to employ a marzipan little doll like Van von Rhine to manage the joint.

This pint-size doll also managed to marry Nicky, and therein lies the source of my present disenchantment. The union, while profitable to the hotel, has produced an offspring. The Crystal Phoenix, an around-the-clock palace of high-stakes poker tables, glitter, glitz and free food, now knows the Patter of Little Feet.

Time was when *my* little feet were the only ones welcome in the establishment, from the chorus girls' dressing room to the owners' penthouse. However, the newcomer—who has no obvious attractions other than the dubious ability to scream like a harem of Siamese in heat at odd hours of the night—is the center of an epidemic of cooing that leaves myself cold.

I express my distaste by strolling far from my now-unpleasant turf to the Las Vegas Convention Center, which I see by the local rags is hosting the ABA, aka the American Booksellers Association.

I figure on perusing a booth or two, since I always was a bookish sort, having nodded off over many great tomes—including the collected works of Dickins. I like nothing better than curling up on a good book. And I personally know a literary figure or two, the most famous of which—besides Boss Banana, whose memoirs sold quite a few guys upriver—is my hard-shelled pal, archy, whose nightly tap dance on the typewriter keys (he is an old-fashioned kind of guy) brought much fun and profit.

So I decide to broaden my horizons, no easy thing to do in Vegas, which is all horizon, and hotfoot over to the convention center.

I plan to scout the rear service areas, normally deserted at my namesake hour, except for the presence of a few local cats in search of tidbits among the refuse. Even Vegas has its homeless these days, in addition to the usual shirtless.

There are a thousand ways to get into a locked building, especially if you are a stealthy but wiry little guy, and Midnight Louie knows every one. Soon I am ambling through a maze of booths, gazing at piles of books, posters and plastic bags bannered with pictures of every description.

I am vaguely in search of the Baker & Taylor concession, where I am given to understand that a pair of famous felines are on display. Apparently any live acts at a book convention are newsworthy. This duo made all the papers, being official library cats at a little town in the West.

From their mug shots, Baker is a white, gray and what-have-you feline of no distinguished ancestry, and Taylor is likewise. Neither has much to speak of in the way of ears, which gives them a constantly frowning expression. As for tail, I cannot say as I am always the gentleman. Still, a celebrity cat—much less two—is something to see, there being few around since Rhubarb, the long-gone marmalade tom of motion-picture fame. Of course someone has scrammed with both Baker and Taylor for the night; the booth offers nothing but empty director's chairs and slick catalogs. I sniff out the area and am in the process of withdrawing—perhaps the sole individual in history to leave the ABA without a free book—when my nose for news fastens on the dreadful truth that the stale atmosphere is not the only thing dead about this place.

I poke my puss through a curtain, clamber over an Everest of disheveled cartons, dodge several empty Big Gulp–size paper cups and a Big Mac wrapper that has been sucked clean—and find myself nose to nose with a white male sixty-some years of age with specs as thick as the lens at Mount Palomar and no more earthly use for them.

He is supine among the effluvia and deader than a stripper's Monday afternoon audience at the Lace 'n' Lust downtown. I trot around front to catch the booth number. The booth itself is fairly unmistakable, being blazoned with illustrations of assorted bodies in a similar if more spectacular condition of permanent paralysis than the current corpse. There are also depictions of such sinister implements as hypodermic needles dripping blood and embossed silver scalpels lethal-looking enough for Lizzie Borden to be alive and well and using them to practice medicine without a license.

I commit the name bannering the booth to memory—Pennyroyal Press—and retreat to more pleasant ven-

## Chapter 1

# Chester's Last Chapter

"Some cat's cutting loose on the convention floor," the guard grumbled, heading for the office coffeepot. "Thought we were supposed to be on the lookout for international terrorists."

"A cat!" Temple's head whipped to attention, abandoning her computer screen. "Where?"

The guard shook his own head, which was decorated by a wilted lei of hair, and donned his cap. Caffeine piddled from the spigot until foam lapped the rim of his Styrofoam cup. "Kitty Kong. Some terrorist."

"Listen, Lloyd, a very valuable cat happens to be missing from an exhibit this morning—two, in fact. We need to corral them before we open the floor to the exhibitors. Where was it seen?"

Lloyd scratched his scalp, almost dethroning his cap. "You office girls are all cat crazy."

Temple made her full five feet one as she stood, slamming the oversize glasses atop her head to the bridge of her nose.

"I'm not an 'office girl.' I'm liaison for local PR for this convention, and I don't give a flying fandango about pussycats on the job unless they're relevant to public relations, so you can bet that corporate mascots like Baker and Taylor are bloody vital to the American Booksellers Convention. Baker & Taylor happens to be one of the country's top book wholesalers."

Temple paused, breathlessly, to dive under her desk and withdraw a formidable canvas bag emblazoned with the words "*Temporus Vitae Libri.*" A freebie from Time-Life Books.

She edged around the desk, frowning. "Now where is this rogue feline? If he's beneath your notice, I'll bag him personally."

Lloyd examined her three-inch heels, her elephant-bladder-size bag and her implacably determined face. She didn't look a day over twenty-one—despite being in imminent danger of thirty; July was her natal month and this was the cusp of May and June—and regretted it bitterly.

Lloyd's head jerked over his shoulder. "Somewhere near the sequined zebra on the stick."

"Zebra on a stick? Oh, you mean the Zebra Books carousel. Damnation"—Temple eyed the silver-dollar-size watchface that obscured her wrist—"the doors open at nine. Good thing book people sleep late. Probably up reading all night."

She clicked out of the office, bag flapping, while Lloyd muttered something uncouth about "modern women" into his scalding coffee.

Lights glared on the mammoth exhibition area, making the booths' glossy posters and book-cover blowups into vertical reflecting pools. Temple threaded the maze of aisles. A few early-bird exhibitors were already at work, unpacking book cartons and readying their wares for opening day.

# CATNAP

She bustled past arrays of next year's calendars, juicy dust jackets promising sex and violence in lavish doses, past lush photographic covers on massive art books, past ranks of reading lights and tasseled bookmarks.

She heard Lloyd faintly calling "Miss Barr" and minced on. Few would believe how fast Temple could travel on her upscale footwear; in her favorite Stuart Weitzmans she was even a match for a footloose feline.

"Here, kitty-kitty-kitty," she crooned as she neared the Zebra booths, slipping the Time-Life book bag from her arm in preparation for a genteel snatch.

Nothing stirred but a dedicated exhibitor who was fanning book catalogs on display cubes.

"Hee-eere kitty. Nice kitty."

Zebra Books's life-size papier-mâché namesake glittered, seeming to move in stately splendor amid the eerie quiet.

"Here kit-eee, damn it to—!"

A scream of outrage deleted the rest of Temple's expletive as she tripped on what felt like thick electric cable. She stumbled forward, looking down to see an abused feline tail streaking from the needle-sharp exclamation point of a single Weitzman stiletto.

Lloyd ambled up to announce the obvious. "There it goes."

Temple went after, darting down aisles, careening around corners, caroming off unwary pedestrians.

"The cat, catch it!" she yelled.

Bemused exhibitors merely paused to watch her sprint past. A bald man with a wart on his nose pointed ahead without comment. Temple hurtled on.

A black tail waved from behind a stack of paperback Bibles. Temple followed. The Tower of Babel fell again.

"Baker! Taylor! Candlestick-maker," she implored inventively. "Come back, little Sheba—"

The flirtatious extremity bobbed and wafted and whisked through exhibit after exhibit. Flatter feet pounded behind Temple's—Lloyd and a train of diverted spectators on the move at last. Temple sighted the cat's tail vanishing under a booth's back curtain and dove after.

"Trapped!" she announced, her insteps grinding down heaped cardboard boxes, her elbows dueling the odd umbrella—very odd; who would bring an umbrella to Las Vegas?—and boxing aside rolls of tumbling posters as if they were origami bones.

Her quarry was at last within grasp. Temple tackled a fat black shadow, throwing herself full-length, such as it was, indifferent to impediments, as she handled most situations.

The cat, cornered in the dimness, sat regarding her prone body. Someone yanked back a curtain, admitting a swath of light.

"Don't let him get away," Temple murmured, feeling for her glasses, which had decamped during her flying tackle.

"Oh-my-God," someone said.

Temple patted the assorted lumps upon which she reclined until she found her frames. She assumed the glasses to glare triumphantly at the cat.

"Holy cow," Lloyd murmured behind her.

"Someone help me up," Temple ordered, "and don't let that cat get away."

She had noticed by now that the escapee was solid black; from their publicity pics, Baker and Taylor were particolored. And this animal's large, fully perked ears were nothing like the missing cats' stingy "Scottish fold" earmarks.

The heels of Temple's hands pushed down for purchase. Then she realized that they pressed a man's suit jacket, that her recumbent length was, in fact, badly wrinkling cold-cocoa-colored worsted.

"So sorry, sir. I'll just—" She thrust herself halfway up, palms digging into a hard irregular surface. "Ohmigod." Temple gazed down into a man's eyes. He was in no condition to protest her presence—or that of additional suit wrinkles.

Someone grabbed her elbows and yanked. Upright, Temple stared at what had already mesmerized the crowd, and even, apparently, the cat: a man lay face up amid the booth's backstage litter, a hand-lettered sign reading "STET" askew on his immobile chest.

"Well." Temple turned as the crowd began buzzing behind her. "Lloyd, secure the area until the authorities arrive. And put that cat"—she pointed, if there were any question—"in this bag. Please clear the area, folks. There's been an accident; we need to let the proper people attend to it."

Anyone minded to argue didn't. Temple had pumped her tone with equal amounts of brisk authority and hushed respect for the dead. The crowd edged back. Moments later a dead weight hung from the Time-Life book bag Lloyd slung over Temple's forearm. Bored green eyes blinked from the bag's midnight-blue depths.

Temple went to the front of the booth, the cradled cat swinging from her arm. It weighed a ton. A copper and black Pennyroyal Press sign glinted in the exhibition lights. So did the graphic image of a skull and crossbones rampant over an Rx prescription symbol.

Temple studied the booth's macabre illustrations before glancing nervously at the cat in her bag. Its yawn revealed a ribbed pink upper palate soft as a baby sweater, but its mouth was equipped with rows of sharp, white teeth.